His Wicked Smile

Also by Heather Hiestand

The Marquess of Cake

One Taste of Scandal

His Kidnapped Bride
(coming soon)

His Wicked Smile

HEATHER HIESTAND

KENSINGTON BOOKS
KENSINGTON PUBLISHING CORP.
www.kensingtonbooks.com

KENSINGTON BOOKS are published by

Kensington Publishing Corp.
119 West 40th Street
New York, NY 10018

All Kensington titles, imprints, and distributed lines are available at special quantity discounts for bulk purchases for sales promotion, premiums, fund-raising, educational, or institutional use.

Special book excerpts or customized printings can also be created to fit specific needs. For details, write or phone the office of the Kensington Special Sales Manager: Kensington Publishing Corp., 119 West 40th Street, New York, NY 10018. Attn. Special Sales Department. Phone: 1-800-221-2647.

Kensington and the K logo Reg. U.S. Pat. & TM Off.

First Electronic Edition: May 2014
eISBN-13: 978-1-60183-113-2
eISBN-10: 1-60183-113-7

First Print Edition: May 2014
ISBN-13: 978-1-60183-229-0
ISBN-10: 1-60183-229-X

Printed in the United States of America

For Madeline and Tommy

Acknowledgments

My critique partners and beta readers are always so helpful! Thank you to Eilis Flynn, Delle Jacobs, Judy Laik, and Jacquie Rogers for your support. Thank you to my friends who long ago awakened my interest in natural medicine when they gave me an enormous gift basket of remedies. Uzma Khan, Rupa Guha, Marlene Kilpatrick, Cheryl Schy, and Ester Abenojar were behind the basket, as I recall, but it was the late 1990s and my memory is fuzzy! At any rate, it's never wrong to take the time to thank old friends for being part of my life. Also, I'd like to thank my editor, Peter Senftleben, and the Kensington team, and Pam van Hylckama Vlieg and the Foreward Literary team, for their continued support of the Redcakes series.

Chapter One

March 16, 1888

When a man's best friend marries, it is time for his own thoughts to turn to matrimony. The tables at Redcake's Tea Shop and Emporium were filled with wedding breakfast guests, the families of shop manager Lord Judah Shield and Magdalene Cross. Gawain Redcake wanted to add to the splendid moment with a marriage-minded request of his own. His friend might have just married the niece of an earl, but Gawain had even higher hopes for himself.

"Might I have a word, Hatbrook?" Gawain leaned over from his seat to the main table.

The Marquess of Hatbrook, his brother-in-law, glanced at Gawain, then spared an anxious glance for his wife, due to give birth to his heir in a month. Gawain held his ground. Alys was fine and would likely approve of his offer, for all that their father was a recently knighted tradesman, rather than a blue-blooded aristocrat.

"Yes, of course. The private dining room should be available." Hatbrook led him out of the main tearoom and down the hall.

The intimate room had been recently converted to electricity and seated four. Gawain was finding it difficult to adjust to the increasingly common bright lights in interior spaces. He was nearly blind in his right eye, thanks to the bloodthirsty Pathan tribesmen of India, who had cost him his military career some four years ago.

Hatbrook cast himself into one of the ornate dining chairs and stared up at him. "What is on your mind?"

Gawain leaned against the carved wooden mantelpiece. "My personal importing revenues were so great last quarter that I was able to give my father notice of my resignation from the Redcake factories. It is time to consider my future."

"Ah," Hatbrook smiled. "Whom do you have under consideration?"

"Your sister, Lady Elizabeth." Gawain rubbed his palms together, feeling the tingle of nerves and sweat there. His future was ripe for the taking, independence and a place in the fashionable world. He had the funds. Now all he needed was the right wife.

"My sister?" Hatbrook frowned and ran his hand over the back of his neck.

Gawain could see the calluses from farm labor on the marquess's palms. For a high-ranking aristocrat, he knew the benefit of hard work. "Yes. I would like to ask for your permission to court her formally, with the idea of proposing marriage in the near future."

"She's a decade younger than you are," Hatbrook commented.

"Having lost her parents and weathered all the dramas of Lord Judah's life, in addition to tending my sisters through illnesses and expectations, she has proven herself ready to manage an establishment of her own," he countered.

"You have a mistress." Hatbrook's tone was flat. Gawain remembered Hatbrook had not kept a demirep of his own before his marriage. But that was because he hadn't been able to afford it at the time, or so Gawain thought, not because he had a constitutional dislike of the practice.

"I will sever the connection instantly."

"Comtesse Valery will not like that. Even an old married man like me knows her reputation for rages and revenge."

The famed actress was descended from poverty-stricken survivors of the French Revolution. The most famous courtesan of the last decade, Gawain had won her away from a duke only a few months before, which had catapulted him to the cream of London bachelor society.

"She knows I must marry."

"Why?" Hatbrook asked, with a quizzical tilt of his head. "You do not have a title to secure."

Gawain felt the stab acutely. "I wish for one, however, and the Queen is not likely to grant knighthood or other offices to a young bachelor."

Hatbrook chuckled. "What do you plan to be knighted for?"

"Medicine, most likely, or my tea business, in the same way my father was knighted for his famous desserts. If I have to, I'll go into politics in the end."

"Medicine? You are not a doctor."

"No, but I import medicines from India. Only real, proven remedies with explanatory pamphlets written in native tongues and translated by former soldiers here at home. I could even be knighted for the employment I have created."

"You are working every angle, I see," Hatbrook said, rubbing at his neck as if the subject pained him. "But no, I am afraid I must decline your request to court my sister. The family has been aware you admire her, but famous bachelors do not make good husbands for young girls. You are not for my Beth, Gawain."

Gawain stiffened. His pulse beat so loudly in his ears that for a moment he felt quite deaf. How could Hatbrook not see things his way? "I have only been connected to the comtesse for a few short months. I hardly think that is a problem."

"You are not the one making the decision," Hatbrook said smoothly. "I have to think of my sister. She is simply too young, too countrified, and too untried for a tested man of the world like yourself."

That tone reminded Gawain so well of his father's. How he hated having to ask for anything. He'd joined the army at sixteen to escape his family's dictates, never expecting he would become the heir when his older brother died. Even then, he stayed in the army until he was cast out because of his injuries. Now that he'd finally escaped from under his father's thumb, he had no expectation of any man ever telling him what to do again.

"What can I do to change your mind? I will write to the comtesse tonight. Give me a week or two to weather her anger and find her a new protector. I will cease going out in Town. Everyone will forget me inside a month."

"No, Gawain," Hatbrook said. "I am sorry." The marquess stood.

Gawain clenched his hands into fists. Farm labor or no, this aristocrat had never been a soldier, probably never fought in his life. If only Lord Judah had been the head of the Shield family. He knew Gawain's worth. But the next step in his plan occurred easily to him. After cutting ties with his mistress, he could apply to his friend to soften Hatbrook.

This was a much better solution than punching his pregnant sister's husband in the nose. "I will make you regret your decision, my lord."

"Now, Gawain, no need to be so formal. You must see you are unsuitable for Beth."

"I do not."

Hatbrook smiled. "Stubborn, stubborn, just like your twin. Come now, can we be friends again?" He held out his hand.

Gawain shook it reluctantly, knowing he had no choice. He could not make family drama at the end of Alys's pregnancy when his sister Matilda had nearly died during hers. Alys needed calm. "We are always friends, Hatbrook."

"Good. Now let us get back to staring at that magnificent cake. I wonder if my brother realizes he married a woman so like my wife? Yet another Shield bride who insisted on decorating her own wedding cake."

"If they have the skills, they might as well show them off," Gawain said, leading the way out of the room. He gritted his teeth at the thought of making merry for the next couple of hours, but Lord Judah was now the best weapon in his arsenal, and Hatbrook couldn't stop him from chatting with his sister at a wedding breakfast. He might as well take what time with her he could. She would be returning to Hatbrook Farm tomorrow until after Easter, when the Season would be in full swing. This was her first year on the marriage market, and he resolved that it would be her last.

Lady Elizabeth Shield might not be an erotic seductress like the comtesse, but he knew passion lurked underneath those virginal debutante gowns. Her enthusiastic manner and tempestuous piano playing told him there was much the right man could flare to life, given the opportunity.

* * *

Gawain and his inventor cousin, Lewis Noble, were enjoying a cigar on Easter Sunday evening at their club, the Euphonious Commerce Society, when a door slammed against the wall behind them. Gawain looked up to see Lord Judah all but galloping in his direction.

He hadn't seen his friend so fired up since he'd led his men against the Pathans the day the bloodthirsty mountain villagers sent a bullet into Gawain's hip and ripped open a quarter of his face with a dirty dagger. Lord Judah had not sustained a scratch, even though, unlike many officers, he had actually fought in battles. Gawain had been an enlisted man, not an officer, but since he'd been in charge of the Officer's Mess stores, he hadn't expected to be wounded in a battle either. But on that unlucky day, the Pathans had brought the battle right into the village where Gawain was stationed.

Gawain fingered the long scar running down his cheek and wondered what today's fuss was about. His friend was of measured temperament.

"She's gone," Lord Judah cried.

Gawain could see the anguish in his friend's face. "Who, your wife?" He held back any gibes about it being only two weeks since the wedding.

"No, my sister."

Gawain stood, galvanized into action. "Beth? Has she been kidnapped? I saw her just this morning at the Easter service."

"And at Hatbrook House after," Lewis said, standing as well. "Who saw her last? What was she wearing?"

"It isn't like that. Well, not exactly," Lord Judah said, wiping street dust from the corners of his eyes.

"Explain," Gawain demanded.

"She left a note."

"What did it say?" Lewis asked.

"That she was eloping to Scotland."

The bottle of port that Gawain had just finished stirred menacingly in his stomach. His innocent debutante had eloped? Who had stirred her hidden fires to life?

"With whom? Some fortune-hunter?" Lewis asked.

"Not exactly." Lord Judah's stance shifted uneasily. He folded his arms over his chest.

"Explain," Gawain said again.

Lord Judah huffed. "She is eloping with Manfred, my brother-in-law."

"He is poor, correct?" Lewis said.

"He is nephew to Earl Gerrick," Gawain added. His family had an uneasy relationship with that connection, given that Gerrick's daughter had been blamed for a family disaster.

"Your wife must be beside herself, unless she colluded," Lewis said to Lord Judah.

"Magdalene is as shocked as anyone. We thought Manfred to be in thrall to Lady Mews. I scarcely realized Beth and Manfred noticed each other's existence."

"She is quite a dissembler," Gawain said, his vision of purity destroyed in an instant. "Will you allow the connection?"

"I'm going after her. It is not as if they can elope to Gretna Green as in the early part of the century. They have to establish residency in Scotland first."

"Why not simply hide in London?" Lewis asked. "Call the banns at some small church?"

"They are less likely to be recognized in Scotland."

"They are young," Gawain said. "I'm sure this seems the height of romance to them."

Lord Judah looked at him, his gaze full of sympathy. Gawain sneered back, furious that he'd shared his own hopes with his friend. He hated pity.

"I'm going after them," said the dutiful brother. "I feel responsible, given that I am the conduit between Beth and Manfred. He's only twenty. They are both too young for this elopement."

"What about Redcake's? You cannot abandon your position. And Alys . . ." Lewis trailed off.

Lewis had offered for Alys once, and still bore the scars of unrequited love. Gawain hoped his wounds from Beth's betrayal healed better.

"Hatbrook has refused utterly to have her help, given she is so close to confinement," Lord Judah confirmed. "But Alys has deputized Magdalene to work with my secretary, and it should be enough for a few days. At least she knows part of the business, having worked in the Fancy."

"Since Alys is staying in London, I'm sure she can take questions by mail."

"Or telephone," Lord Judah said. "Hatbrook had one installed since the doctor has one at his office now. They will manage."

"I'll come with you," Gawain said. "Are we going to take the train straight to Scotland? If we check the timetable, we might only be a few hours behind them."

"It is too late in the day," Lord Judah said. "I do not know how to get ahead of them."

"My steam buggy is at your disposal," Lewis said. "I will even act as boiler man. It can go up to thirty miles an hour on good road."

"You've made improvements," Gawain said.

Lewis grinned. "Always. I've sold seven of them this year already, which allows me money to continue upgrading."

"That could get us to Scotland by morning," Lord Judah said, rubbing his hands together.

Gawain rubbed his bad hip instinctively. He didn't travel well, and Lewis's contraption was not the most comfortable. Still, he was not quite ready to give up on his dreams of marrying a marquess's sister. "A word?" he called to a footman standing at the door.

The man walked toward them and bowed. "Yes, sir?"

"We need a hamper, plus rugs and cushions for the three of us. As quickly as you can, please." Gawain fished for a guinea and flipped it at the man.

He nodded.

"And coal," Lewis called, rushing after the footman. "I need to fill the stores."

"We should be able to leave in half an hour," Gawain said, seeing the worry lines on Lord Judah's face. At twenty-six, he was too young for such marks. They had never appeared during those stressful years in India. But Gawain knew the man had been through a lot with his mother's death and a busy employment he had not been trained for. Gawain had helped when he could, but managing his father's factories and his own businesses had taken a great deal of time. "You know, it is amazing I ever have time to be in London at all."

"Redcake's is one of your biggest customers, plus you test your blends at the tea shop," Lord Judah pointed out.

"True."

"And the best women reside in London." Lord Judah's strangely striated brown and amber eyes glinted with momentary humor.

"Not anymore, with your sister flown," he said. "*Gor blimey.* How can Beth prefer Manfred Cross to me?"

"Did she know you wanted her?" Judah asked.

"A woman should sense these things, but your brother wouldn't hear of me telling her how I felt. I never directly approached her, except to converse at family gatherings."

"Obviously Manfred used a more direct approach."

"He does not care for the proprieties." Gawain wondered if it was his own self-consciousness about his social position that had hampered him. He was as good as the earl's nephew, and certainly wealthier, but didn't have the free time the lad did to woo.

"The curtain has not yet come down on this particular drama. Are you prepared to marry her if she's been abandoned?" his friend asked.

Gawain's spirits perked. "Will Hatbrook acquiesce?"

"I have no intention of leaving Scotland until the matter is resolved," Lord Judah stated.

"I'm not going to raise a Scandalous Cross bastard as my own," Gawain declared. "If Beth has been compromised, she will have to settle in and wait for the result before I agree to marry her."

Lord Judah frowned. "You'll stay in Scotland until we know?"

"I will, with Manfred chained to a wall if necessary. But you need to return to London. I won't see Redcake's run into trouble because of the Cross boy."

"I understand."

"I do wonder," said Gawain, "if your brother would have agreed to Manfred Cross's suit if he'd presented it as I had."

"Not a chance," Lord Judah said promptly. "He was against me marrying Magdalene. From his perspective, Manfred is nothing but a fortune-hunter."

Gawain was happy to hear this. "What does Beth see in him?"

Lord Judah shook his head in sad wonderment as the footman returned.

"The hamper and other items are being loaded into your conveyance, gentlemen," he said. "Mr. Noble said you should be able to depart in ten minutes."

Gawain whistled a ballad popular a decade before in the Royal Sussex Regiment. He had marched to it many a time as a recruit.

Lord Judah smiled wanly and clapped him on the shoulder. "Who would have thought we'd ever go on campaign again?"

"Not me," Gawain said, pointing to his eye patch.

"You should stop wearing it," Lord Judah pronounced. "You have some small amount of vision in the eye. I cannot help believing it would improve if you would not keep it covered."

"It gives me headaches as it is, and people stare less at the eye patch than they do at the scar." Gawain whistled again and strode through the room.

Outside, the night air felt more like February than April, though it wasn't quite as coal-soaked as it had been. Gaslight winked against the gravel, catching bits of glass or mica. He heard a motor roar as Lewis cranked his steam buggy to life. Steam and smoke filled the sky, tainting the night.

"Gretna Green, gentlemen?" Lewis called.

A footman jumped down from the front seat. "Everything is aboard, Mr. Noble."

"Who is going to steer?" Lord Judah asked.

"I will. I've done it before," Gawain said.

"I can take over for periods of time," Lewis shouted over the motor's roar. "But we'll get the best speed if I sit in the back and monitor the engine."

"Then monitor you shall," Gawain said, climbing onto the step and swinging his bad leg into the seat. "How do I turn on the lamps? I've never driven this bloody thing at night."

After instructions from Lewis and a general settling of cushions and rugs, Gawain drove into the night. It quickly became obvious that it would be unsafe to drive at full speed in the dark.

Still, they made good time even while battling the occasional badger and rabbit crossing the road, and had ventured far into the north, when factory smells set the two men in front to coughing mightily.

The sky had scarcely begun to lighten. "What time is it?" Gawain asked, pulling his scarf over his nose.

Lord Judah pulled out his pocket watch and squinted at it. "About five, I believe."

Gawain estimated their rate of travel versus their location. "I expect we're coming onto Leeds."

"That's not bad. I was afraid we hadn't made it to Sheffield yet."

"No. Leeds is notorious for its smells and slums. I'm sure that's where we are."

"I can't see the sky anymore."

"That would be the smoke. Of course we've created our own miasma tonight."

Lewis protested. "We are well on our way. At this rate, even though it is slower than expected, we might make it to Scotland by noon."

"What about food?" They had demolished the contents of the hamper several hours before.

"We can stop at Harrogate," Lord Judah said. "I know Lady Bricker is not your favorite person, Gawain, but we'll get reprovisioned beautifully at her house. She loves her food."

"And we are only about an hour away," Lewis said. "I wouldn't mind tucking into a solid breakfast."

"I'll brave the lady for breakfast," Gawain allowed. "But we don't want to waste time with idle gossip."

They had passed hours during the night speculating about when Manfred and Beth might have reached the border. Late at night? What funds did they have? Where might they have stayed—somewhere respectable or shady? How compromised was the lady by now? Certainly she'd have to marry someone before her adventure ended.

At least she couldn't be married by their arrival at noon, or, more likely, late in the afternoon, if they were going to stop in Harrogate.

"Your cousin will fill up our coal stores, right?" Lewis asked.

"She's Magdalene's cousin," Lord Judah corrected. "I'm sure she will. As generous with her possessions as she is with her advice. She nearly married Magdalene off to a baronet up this way. If Manfred hadn't taken ill with a serious fever, I'd have lost my bride to Yorkshire."

"So you want to salvage Manfred's reputation as well?" Gawain joked.

"Oh, he's a rotter," Lord Judah said, but not without affection. "The Crosses are just one scandal after another, the lot of them.

Earl Gerrick had hoped I would become friends with his sons, but I much prefer the more serious pursuits of you lot."

"We are superior," Gawain said. He had just heard the sound of Lewis's voice, most likely in agreement, when a loud pop came from the rear of their chariot, and the entire structure shook. Though they continued to roll on, Lewis swore creatively and began to search through their baggage for tools. Gawain smelled oil and very hot metal.

From the sounds Gawain heard momentarily, Lewis was banging on a pipe with a wrench. Within a couple of minutes, the carriage swaying as Lewis moved this way and that on the rear seat, he found the steering very hard going. Another minute after that, on a street full of tiny back-to-back houses, the steam carriage rattled to a stop, braking against a barely visible pile of foul refuse.

Chapter Two

"Not here," Lewis groaned.

Around them stretched a vast row of mean, two-story houses, with no lamps to be seen in any of the windows. The only reason Gawain could see anything was because of the lamps at the front of the carriage.

"Not now," Lord Judah said, seeing the activity on the street was quite limited.

"Factory hours start at five," Gawain commented. "Few people will be home."

"No one here would have anything we need to assist us," Lewis said. "We must have a blacksmith's shop."

Gawain pushed open the side door that had protected him from the worst of the elements, and kicked down the step. He got his good leg onto the metal plank and then swung his bad leg to the cobbles. "Should I turn off the headlamps?"

"We need to knock on doors until we can find someone to point us to a blacksmith's shop," Lewis said.

"You have that great bag of tools," Gawain growled. "Don't you have what you need?"

"A pipe exploded," Lewis said, pointing to the offending metal as Gawain limped to him. "I need a new one."

"That will take time," Lord Judah said, as he joined them and stared at the engine.

"I'm sorry, old man. At least you'll be able to catch a morning train from here."

"That's true." Even as Lord Judah spoke, they could hear a train's whistle off in the distance.

"I'm not going to bang on any doors in this street," Gawain said. "It's obviously deserted. Let's push the carriage for a bit, until we find some sign of occupation."

The other two agreed, though Lewis wanted to steer around the refuse pile, rather than power through it.

"No point in being fastidious in a slum," Gawain said. "It won't be the only mess we have to get through."

It took them quite some time to push the heavy carriage through the bumpy street. They found nothing at the first turning and kept on to the next. An hour later, they found themselves on a street with some light industry. They walked along, puffing misty breath into the air, hunting for a blacksmith.

"Let's stop there," Lewis said, pointing to an inn.

"That isn't a blacksmith's," Lord Judah wheezed.

"They'll know where one is, and we can eat," Lewis said.

"I'm in," Gawain called from his position on the far side. "Do I need to turn the wheel?"

"To the left," Lewis said.

They pushed, pulled, tugged and swore until the carriage was parked next to a stable that ran alongside the courtyard. The inn itself was a stained, three-story brick structure called The Old Hart, judging from a wind-beaten wood sign dangling over the door.

Gawain straightened when he noticed all three of them were pressing palms into their backs. "Are we all not hearty young men still in our twenties?"

"No," Lewis said. "I turned thirty last October."

"I had forgotten you were older than I," Gawain said.

"And I'd forgotten you could limp that badly," his cousin observed. "You walked like that when you first came home. I suspect you won't be able to walk upon rising tomorrow."

"That presumes I will have to stay up all day?" Gawain asked. "I can sleep on the train."

Lewis shook his head. "Do not, Gawain. You'll be crippled for a month. Let Lord Judah continue the hunt, and we'll drive up as soon as I get my pipe. We'll be just a day or so behind."

Lord Judah's mouth tightened at the mention of their mission, but he pushed the door of the inn open and they walked into the front hall together. Gawain could hear tableware clinking against dishes and the sound of voices from the paneled breakfast room off to the left. A wide staircase led upstairs. No one manned the table to the right, where a ledger rested.

"Food first," Lewis said. "Then we'll get Lord Judah on a train."

The room was largely full and no one gave them a second glance as they seated themselves at a free table near the kitchen. Gawain looked longingly at the enormous medieval stone fireplace, but no tables were available near it. At least every time the kitchen door opened, warmth drifted over him like smoke. The smells were deliciously spicy.

A young girl, just budding into womanhood, approached them. A lock of mousy hair fell into her face as she placed a tray with a sturdy teapot and three cups onto their table. Then she held up a slate board, which asked the question, "English or Indian breakfast?"

"Let's all have the Indian breakfast," Lewis said. "I'm curious."

"What's your name?" Lord Judah asked.

She pointed to the upper right corner of the slate board. The word "Fern" was written there.

"Fern, can you direct me to the train station?" Lord Judah asked.

The girl smiled but shook her head.

"I think she's mute," Gawain said. "Or she wouldn't have the slate. We do have a couple of questions. Could you send someone to us after breakfast?"

She nodded and went into the kitchen. Lewis drummed his fingers on the table, then pulled out a scrap of paper and began to scratch down the specifics of the pipe he needed.

"I hope they took enough money," Lord Judah muttered.

"Surely Beth would have money."

"Why? Hatbrook has accounts at all the stores."

"If they had planned this, they'd both have been saving for it. They knew they needed to survive for weeks, right?"

Lord Judah shook his head. "I don't know. They might think it is still possible to dash over the border and jump over an anvil, or something equally old-fashioned."

Gawain rubbed at his hip. The hard chairs were making his pain worse. He hoped he'd be able to rise again. With a sigh, he stroked his scar. "If they are serving an Indian breakfast, do you think they'd have Indian remedies?"

"Let's take a look at the breakfast and see what they serve. If it is just kedgeree, probably not," Lord Judah said.

"The breakfast will give us some hint as to the region of the cook," Gawain mused. "That will help me ask for more specific medicine."

Clearly losing patience, Lewis stood up. "Can anyone here direct me to a blacksmith? I have a commission for him."

A few of the men around the room glanced up, while simultaneously the closest woman pulled her young daughter closer to her on the bench.

"What you be needin', sir?" asked a man in broad Yorkshire tones.

"This." Lewis flourished his paper. "A metal cylinder."

In less than a minute, three men were standing over Lewis, poking fingers at his paper and muttering. After a moment, one of them rubbed his nose and spoke. "I'm Thomas Hammer, and my shop is just down the way."

"That is an excellent name for a blacksmith," Lord Judah commented.

"My father and his father before him, for I don't know how long, have been farriers."

Lewis smiled for the first time since they heard his pipe explode. "Then you are an excellent man for the job. Can you do it?"

Hammer rubbed his nose again. "It can be done, sir, but I've an herd to shoe today. Be midweek 'afore I can fashion it."

"I can pay," Lewis said. "Come now, name your price."

The blacksmith named a figure that sounded outrageous to Gawain's ears. Lewis snorted. "What is your price for having it done today?"

"It's not worth my shop," Hammer said. "But I can do it early tomorrow morning." He named another price.

Lewis nodded and they shook hands on the deal, then he handed the blacksmith his paper.

"What is the purpose?" Hammer asked.

"It is for my steam buggy. Would you like to see it?"

The man smiled for the first time, exposing yellowed teeth. "Oh aye, I would."

Lewis grinned and patted Gawain on the shoulder, then led the trio out of the room. Lord Judah rubbed at his forehead.

"I hope you didn't think retrieving your sister would be easy," Gawain said, draining his teacup.

His friend chuckled. "Only if they'd already found a way to wed. I like Manfred, to tell the truth. He's a good lad in his way and did his best for my wife during their elder brother's worst excesses. But he is too young for Beth."

"I agree."

Lord Judah dropped his hand to the table. "And you are too old, Gawain. Not just in years, though you have a decade on her. Pain and hard work put time on a man."

"That's why I didn't discourage you from marrying," Gawain said. "I knew you understood your own mind. And I want your sister, old man."

"Oh, you lust after her and she fascinates you. I don't deny it. But she's not complicated enough for you."

His speech was interrupted by the kitchen door swinging open. Gawain's eyes went first to the tray, which surely held their breakfast. He saw chickpea curry, flat bread, eggs and a potato dish. A North Indian breakfast, he thought, redolent of ginger, onions and chilis, among other spices. Then, he gazed higher and saw *her*.

Regal, was his first thought. Her thick mass of wavy black hair was pinned into a knot, but heat had created a dark nimbus of individual midnight strands around her ivory brown skin. She had large, dark eyes and unusually sharp-arched eyebrows. Her lips stunned him with their kissable plumpness. Now this was lust. He forgot his hip pain as blood surged to his groin. Pale and pretty Lady Elizabeth Shield vanished from his mind's eye, to be replaced by this, this—kitchen maid?

She smiled at Lord Judah, a seductive uptilt of those siren lips, and began to remove items from the tray. Why hadn't she smiled at him? Was he too fierce? He tried a few words of thanks in Hindi as she set his plate before him, but she looked at him, confused.

"I don't speak Hindi," she said in the local accent, smoothed by her naturally husky voice.

"You are obviously Indian."

"My mother came from Caliata. I admit I was born in India, but we came to England when I was five."

"Your father was English?" asked Lord Judah.

"Yes. A soldier. You must have been soldiers, too. No other Englishmen order the Indian breakfast."

"Royal Sussex Regiment," Lord Judah said.

She nodded. A man called from a cozy table by the fireplace. She smiled at them and tucked her tray under her arm, then walked to the other table. Gawain watched her hips sway, mesmerized. She had a tiny waist, created by stays, no doubt, but the generous curves flaring below were nature's gift. He had hardened so fast that it hurt to be dressed. Shifting in his seat only made his hip surge with white-hot pain.

He thought he would be sick if he tried to eat anything. His hand shook as he reached for his teacup.

"I'm sure I can find some laudanum if it is that bad," Lord Judah said.

"No, I won't take the stuff," Gawain snapped. "I'll get a room after you eat and order a few bottles of port. Getting blind drunk will do the trick. I don't think Lewis will need me today."

"Is this a solution you use often?"

He forced a smile. "God no, man. I couldn't function. But it will force me to relax and remain in bed. That's what I need."

Lord Judah sighed and began to fork up his food.

The stunning woman walked back their way and frowned when she saw Gawain wasn't eating. "It is not to your liking?"

He spoke slowly, fighting the nausea. Tea on an empty stomach combined with pain was a dangerous combination. "No, it looks delicious. I wonder, are you familiar with Kaishore Guggulu?"

" 'Tis a pitta balancing powder," she said promptly. "Yes, I know it."

He nearly sagged with relief. "Do you have any?"

"Yes, I made up some tablets last winter."

He wished she had his own formulation, but still, this news was miracle quality. "Who trained you?"

"My mother. She had the best teachers."

He preferred to deal with the teacher rather than the student. "Is she here? Could I consult with her?"

"No, she died ten years ago, now."

He hoped this goddess of serving wenches wouldn't poison him. "Very well. Could you bring me a dose, please, and a bottle of port? Also, we will need two rooms for the night, stocked with a half dozen bottles, and a hansom to take Lord Judah to the train station as soon as he is finished with his breakfast."

She nodded with each request. "I'll send Harry Haldene to you. He is the innkeeper."

Gawain felt so relieved to know he had these things on the way that he took a small bite of egg. When that went down, he broke off a piece of flatbread and dipped it into the curry.

"Freshly made," Judah said. "Not quite authentic, but no doubt the best she can do with what is available locally."

Gawain was surprised to see an evil-looking fellow approaching them from the kitchen door when they were half done with their meal. He wore baggy, stained trousers, and his coat was of some foul, checked cloth. With a strong smell of the stable emanating from him, he was glad this man wasn't the cook.

"You be wantin' rooms then?" he said, in a voice altogether less cultured than his cook's.

"Two of them. For myself and my friend in the courtyard."

"I saw them outside," said the man, pushing coal-black hair out of his eyes. " 'E's showing off some fancy buggy to the blacksmith and 'is cronies."

"Exactly. Do you have the rooms?"

The man tipped forward and back on his water-stained boots. "I 'ave one room free. You can share it, or one of you can put up down the street. It only has one bed."

Gawain knew he couldn't tolerate another body moving around the bed. "I'll take the one you have and send my cousin down the road. Is it closer to Mr. Hammer's establishment?"

"Indeed it is, Mr.—"

"Redcake," Gawain said.

"And you're the one wantin' them bottles of port?"

"I do. All of them, please."

Haldene shook his head and called out to a younger version of himself, except for straw-colored hair instead of black, skulking in a corner, where he was slowly piling dirty plates onto a tray. "Jeremy! Tell Fern to fetch up some bottles to the first floor! Then secure a room at the Rose and Crown under the name . . ."

"Noble." Gawain was glad to hear he would not have to climb to the top floor of the inn. One flight of stairs was probably more than he could manage.

Lord Judah was just finishing his hasty meal when the regal cook reappeared, a small dish with tablets in one hand and a bottle of port in the other. "Your hansom is waiting, sir. I have the timetable memorized if you need information."

"I'll take anything going north, but Scotland is my destination," Lord Judah said.

"Edinburgh?"

"Gretna Green for now."

Gawain opened his bottle and poured port into his teacup, then swallowed one tablet. He'd take one every ten minutes, wanting to get the medicine into his system, but not desiring to become ill. He drank steadily while they discussed timetables, then pushed back from the table when his friend realized he might be able to catch a direct train in half an hour. Limping heavily, he followed Lord Judah to the courtyard and spoke to the cab driver while his friend gathered his possessions from the steam carriage.

Lewis followed him back into the breakfast room upon being reminded that his food was getting cold. "I have great confidence in Mr. Hammer. He seems a competent fellow. We should be on our way by tomorrow night."

"Might be best to wait until the next morning. Less risky to travel in daylight when things are going wrong."

"You make a good point." Lewis sighed. "I feel terrible about slowing down the search for Lady Elizabeth."

"Do not trouble yourself, there's a direct train coming through. Our friend should be on his way with scarcely a delay." Gawain winced as he put too much weight on his bad hip. They both sat.

Lewis picked up his fork. "Do you think he'll find her?"

Gawain guzzled another cup of port. "That all depends. If they are not expecting pursuit, then yes, I expect he can. But if they are deliberately hiding, one man, or even three, looking for them, unfamiliar with Scotland, will not have much hope."

"I cannot stay to aid in the search," Lewis said. "Eddy, you know."

"Oh yes, Eddy." They shared a smile. Lord Judah had persuaded the former newsboy to leave the streets and the brutal man who housed him in return for all his earnings. He had hoped to educate him with a live-in tutor, but in the end Eddy had been happier living and working in Lewis's machine shop. One of the most inquisitive lads Gawain had ever met, he frequently blew things up. "You may not have a workshop after a couple of days away."

Lewis shuddered.

"Why don't I take the train north once I know your carriage is working again? That way you can return immediately. I will hire a horse to give me mobility once I'm in Scotland."

"I should finish what we started."

"Not at all. Frankly, I'm in no shape to travel today even if you talked your friend into getting the pipe done."

"You should take to your bed for the day."

"That is my intention." Gawain poured another glass.

"I'll take one of those," Lewis said, passing over his teacup. "I've always heard that men join the army for drink. It does soothe travel."

"We hardly drank at all on the drive up."

"Three flasks of whisky, all empty? And that bottle of champagne? You'd think we were on campaign."

Gawain laughed. "We'll never make a soldier out of you. You don't have a thick enough skull."

Gawain finished off the second and third bottles in his room, along with all the tablets. By then he realized he no longer had a soldier's capacity for alcohol. Blearily, he let his head drop to the mattress and soon fell asleep.

When he woke and checked the window, the sky seemed to be leaning toward twilight. Not surprising that he had slept the day through, between staying up all night and drinking so much. He adjusted his hips, making sure the pressure was off his bad bits, and pushed himself slowly into a seated position. His head didn't ache so he must still be a bit drunk.

He heard a rustling and forced his eyes open. A girl was seated in front of him. Was she a ghost? Her face was pale enough, and he conjured up a servant girl, strangled by some rotten innkeeper of years past, doomed to haunt the room. No doubt some ancestor of Harry Haldene, who looked evil enough to kill, with his long, unshaven face, shadowed eyes and lank hair. The air was chilled. Had the phantom brought the damp, decayed air of the grave with her? He shivered a little in drunken fantasy.

She leaned forward and he recognized Fern Haldene. He put his head in his hands and groaned. No tolerance for drinking at all, anymore. Never had he felt less of a military man.

When she saw him move, she got up from the chair and dashed out of the room. He put his feet to the floor and stood wearily. His leg did hold his weight, but it took a great deal of effort to make his way downstairs to the water closet, then upstairs again. But, when he reentered, it was to more comfort than he'd left. A fire had been lit and the empty bottles cleared away. A pot of fragrant tea and a covered plate of what smelled like samosas waited on a tray beside the bed. The blankets had been pulled back, to air the sheet-covered mattress. He sat on the one chair in the room, a sagging, flat-backed affair, and ate his tea. The flavors took him back in time. Even the taste of the tablets had their effect in whisking him in memory from his current life.

He had met Lord Judah Shield, called merely Lieutenant Shield then, when he'd been promoted out of the ranks to sergeant and been put in charge of the officer's mess. With his background as a Redcake, his superiors had assumed he'd know how to manage stores. And learn he did, though as a lad he'd done nothing but work in his father's factory, while his brother Arthur learned the business. By the time he'd come home injured, Arthur was dead and his father had insisted he learn the money side of the business.

He'd resented all of it, and it wasn't until his father was knighted that he realized he wanted anything his father had. A title, that was the thing. He had a goal greater than survival from one day into the next.

Sir Bartley Redcake was a changed man overnight. No longer a work-obsessed, child-browbeating bore, but a country gentleman, accepted in the local community. A daughter married into the aristocracy. If Gawain had been knighted too, Hatbrook would not have refused him Lady Elizabeth. He pulled out the notebook he always kept in his jacket and began to make some more notes of ways he might come to the Queen's attention. Didn't Hatbrook lose a man of business to knighthood because he saved the life of a prince? Hatbrook's cousin had been knighted as well.

He needed to learn why. Gawain had studied the lists. The most likely path would be becoming a Member of Parliament. He wondered where best to focus his interest. In Bristol or London? He preferred London, but there were more men of ambition there. Of course, his family was down in the south now, in Sussex, but his father would not help him into local politics. He wanted Gawain focused on Redcake's, would get him back if he could. The man did not like daughters in his business. He'd all but destroyed Alys before she'd found her way to Hatbrook. Sir Bartley had a very traditional view of women, for all that women comprised a large part of his work force. And now, he was forced to bring in his daughter Matilda.

The door opened and he glanced up, expecting to see Fern again. However, the alluring cook stood in the doorway, rubbing a glass jar between graceful, dark palms.

"Do you want my tray?" Gawain asked. "I am finished."

With a nod, she put down her jar and picked up the tray, then walked out of the room. He blinked when he realized he'd watched her swaying hips all the way to the door. Her movements were mesmerizing to a man in his condition. He picked up the jar and pulled the stopper. Sesame oil infused with lavender filled his nostrils. The astringency of the herb cleared his head a bit.

"I saw you downstairs. You were limping right badly," the cook said, returning.

"I don't think I heard your name before," he said.

"Mrs. Haldene. Ann Mai Haldene."

"You are married?" Surely she wasn't married to that appalling innkeeper.

"Widowed. I was married to Harry's brother."

"You aren't in mourning."

"No, he died two years ago. He was the older brother, and survived more than a decade in the army, only to die here in Leeds."

"Were you married long?" He handed her the bottle and she began to roll it along her palms again.

"Four years. He was in the army most of that time, but stationed in Ireland, thankfully, so I did see him sometimes. He inherited this inn from his uncle the year before he died and we came to work here. Me, Harry, Jeremy and Fern."

"My family is business-minded as well."

"It's nice to work with family. Not everyone has that luxury anymore, but I think it's best."

The motion of her hands along the bottle was making him harden. How could any man not think of those long fingers and flexible palms doing the same with his manhood?

His voice came out gruff. "Were you bringing that oil for me?"

She smiled, her lips parting to expose perfect white teeth. "You need a massage and I am trained to do it properly."

"By your mother?"

"Aye. Her cousin was a famous Indian physician and she taught my mother well. In her first marriage our cousin had no children. She was often in the *zenana*, the women's apartments, caring for the women of the household, and taught my mother a great deal."

"How interesting."

"Aye, missionaries sent our cousin to school. She was from a very good family, but her parents died and the missionary school saved her from an early marriage. After she finished school, she studied traditional Indian medicine as well, which was more acceptable to her patients."

"All that leads to me benefitting here in Leeds."

"Strange, the paths that life takes us on," she said. "I come from a line of strong, adventurous women. But you, you cannot be comfortable in that chair. The seat is sagging."

He was afraid to stand, since the bulge beneath his jacket might be revealed. Turning his head away from her always-moving hands, he thought of factory ledgers, rows and rows of numbers all needing to be re-tallied. His Grandmother Noble, complaining. Hatbrook telling him he wasn't good enough for Lady Elizabeth.

That did it. He stood and moved to the bed, then sat down on the edge.

"You'll have to disrobe." She handed him a towel. "Place this beneath you so the sheets are not stained."

"Disrobe?" He felt stupid. Also, aroused again.

Her lips tilted up again. "I'm a widow and a healer. Don't concern yourself with propriety."

His gaze was pulled inexorably toward her fingers rolling the bottle but he forced himself to untie his shoes. She turned away, allowing him to disrobe, place the towel on the bed.

"I am ready," he said, keeping thoughts of ledgers in mind. Also, the thought of how she might react to his scars. They were not for the faint of heart.

"I'm going to drape this towel over your waist for now. Then, I'll do a general application of oil over your body. It's good for health."

"Do you massage your relatives?" he asked, unable to imagine her hands on any of the Haldenes.

"No. In truth, I rarely have male patients, but I'm not afraid of them. Some of the men from my husband's regiment still come to me." She placed her hands on his shoulders, then he heard the stopper of the jar being pulled. He smelled the astringency of the oil again. The first drops hitting his back were warm and soothing.

He floated in a pleasant reverie while her hands worked. Her touch seemed disinterested somehow, but he could feel his muscles relax. She clucked her tongue when she saw the scars on his hip and leg.

"You must be in a great deal of pain."

She hadn't pulled away. "I can forget them most of the time."

"Except when you walk or sit for long periods?"

"I cannot stay in the same position for very long," he admitted.

Her skillful hands worked into the muscles of his hip and leg, bringing pain, but also relief. He gritted his teeth and tensed instinctively, then forced himself to relax so she could help him. After a long while, she sat back in the chair with a sigh.

"You must be thirsty after all that hard work." He hastened to sit up, then felt the room spin.

"We should both drink something."

He gestured to the three port bottles still unopened. "This is what I have in the room."

She yawned and opened one, then poured the liquid into glasses. They must have thought he'd be drinking with Lewis since they had supplied two originally.

"Do you know what happened with my cousin?" Gawain asked. "Mr. Noble?"

"Oh, I forgot to give you this." She reached into her apron and handed him a note.

He opened the brief missive. "No relief until tomorrow. Mr. Hammer really can't make the pipe today."

"That's best for you. You shouldn't travel tonight."

"Is that a medical opinion or a request?" He grinned at her.

She took a sip from her glass. "You, sir, have the most wicked smile."

He realized he wore only the towel, draped across his lap, and the linen was starting to tent. "You have me at your mercy."

"I'm a healer," she protested.

"You said that before. But you have discharged your duty to me, and yet here you are, still in my room, with no thought of leaving." He put a hand on his good thigh, increasing the sight of the bulge.

Chapter Three

Despite her dark skin, he could see her cheeks flush. "Fern's preparing the evening meal, with the kitchen maids. We don't have very many diners, what with all the rain."

He listened and was rewarded with the sound of raindrops hitting the pavement outside. "I didn't realize it was raining. It is quite an oasis in here, with the wine and candlelight."

"Massage can put a body into a stupor," she observed. "It's very relaxing."

He watched her gaze dart to his groin, then move away quickly. She bit her lip. He smiled again, noting that she seemed to have no urge to go. Was the lady as intrigued by him as he was by her?

"As does wine." He put down his glass and took one of her hands in his. "Your hands must be tired." He rubbed his thumbs into her palm.

She curled her hand around him. "I'm used to it. This was nothing compared to what I perform when I act as midwife."

"But it is still tiring," he murmured. He scooted to the edge of the mattress, shifting his towel up his thighs, and took her other hand away from her wine glass so he could massage the palm.

She let out a breath somewhere between an exhalation and a moan.

"It feels good?"

She let her head drop to her chest, then stretched it from side to side. "I touch other people. No one ever touches me."

"Aren't you training Fern?"

"She doesn't like to be touched."

"Poor wounded soul," Gawain said. His fingers moved to her wrists, then up her arms. Her cuffs were unbuttoned and turned up. When he found a particularly tender spot, her eyes closed and her head tilted to the side. He switched to the other arm, curious to see if the same tender spot would be found on both, but in doing so he leaned in until he could smell her, not just the lavender oil, but sandalwood too, and cooking, and the scent of her hair.

He wanted to kiss her. Her mouth, her slender neck, her full breasts. He wanted to see the color of their tips, find out how tiny her waist was, how voluptuous her hips. His fingers moved to the buttons at the neck of her dress. Her eyes widened but she, astoundingly, didn't stop him as he unbuttoned, just drank steadily from her wine glass.

Eventually, her glass was empty. He took it from her and placed it on the bedside table while she finished taking off her dress. Then, as he watched, his manhood throbbing with need for her, she disrobed fully, until she was as naked as he.

He could see her swallowing and he didn't want her nervous. Standing himself, he limped toward her. She parted her lips and watched. When he pulled her body against his, he could feel his oil-slick skin sliding against her flesh.

"You have the most beautiful body I've ever seen," he said, quite honestly, moving his fingers to her hair.

"Don't unpin it," she said, pulling back.

"Why not?"

"You'll get oil on it."

"Ah." He spread his fingers down her back instead, and nibbled at an earlobe. She shuddered against him.

"Like that, do you, Ann?" he said, and did it again while his hands measured her waist, then the flare of her hips. Her curves were firm with youth and good health. She had a body made to fulfill his every desire. Her mouth was moist, hot and eager when he put his lips to hers. She didn't hesitate when his tongue stroked her skin. She opened to him eagerly and explored his mouth in turn.

Knowing their time might be short, he stroked between her legs with his fingers. A widow knew what she wanted when she undressed in front of a man. She gasped and bucked her hips. He could feel her readiness. Their pleasure moved much too quickly, but he was a little drunk, a little dizzy from the massage, and too aroused for finesse.

He massaged the pearl just inside its protective hood until she cried out and crushed her lips to his. His leg gave out and he half-fell to the bed. The pounding rain dampened the sound of the frame creaking. Ann's weight came down over him, his hand still between her legs. Her hands covered his ears and she kissed him, artless yet not entirely untutored, her tongue tracing his lips and darting into his mouth. He rolled them over on the bed and she wrapped her legs around his waist in the most blatant of invitations. In no position to deny her, and with less will, he did what he was compelled to and found her slick channel, thrusting deeply. She cried out against his mouth and only then he realized how tight she was despite her obvious arousal. He stopped moving instantly.

"I am sorry for being so little a gentleman."

"You are not so little," she protested, then wriggled her hips. "Oh, sir, you are quite large."

"Gawain," he said, laughing. "My name is Gawain Redcake."

"Gawain Redcake, nothing will come of this if you do not move." She wriggled again.

"I take it you are ready?"

She poked one of his bottom cheeks with a finger. He laughed again and began a long, slow, drugging plunge, more intoxicating than the wine by far. Her scent was the oddest combination of India and England. The sandalwood and oil, smells of deep, earthy spices, and English wine. Lemon in her hair. And those musky scents of sex they created together.

He was beyond the pain in his hip, the pleasure more than overcoming the strain. Or maybe the massage had done its job along with the pills. Ann eagerly took her share of their intimate efforts, her hips meeting his with every stroke. This was a woman who liked sex and clearly wasn't having much of it. She made delighted sounds every time he thrust home. Her nails dug into the small of his back, then she danced her fingers up his back before clutching his bottom, pulling him against her.

"Faster," she panted.

"You like a furious pace, madam?"

"I can feel it coming. Please, more."

"I'll oblige." He gave her his best high-speed performance, though he wanted to savor her fragrant scent.

"Don't ever stop," she whispered.

He wanted to comply, but the drugging heat gloving him was too much. "I don't want to. But we'll do it again."

"Yes, tomorrow."

"Of course," he promised, not knowing what he said. She gloved him with silky warmth, maddening pressure. He would be unmanned soon. Anything she might ask, he would promise to grant.

"Oh, I'm coming," she gasped, her head falling back.

He licked her upthrust chin and sank even deeper inside her. She clutched at him, the pulsing on his manhood more than he could resist. He followed her down, everything focused on the tight pull of her body, her animal scent, her soft cries.

His groan of satisfaction was that of a wild beast. She laughed softly. He opened his eyes and saw tiny beads of sweat on her temples. The sheet tangled around them, locking them into one satisfied mass of flesh.

"Am I crushing you?" he asked.

Her arms tightened around his back. "I like it. I haven't felt this weight since my husband died."

He felt a tug of irritation at that. While he'd known she could not be his mistress as he never came to Leeds, he did not like to think of himself as a despoiler of proper widows. "You must have been very lonely." Though he wondered at the truth of her words. She did work in an inn, and what inn didn't have a willing barmaid to provide comfort for the night? Fern was the only other female in residence and he hoped to God the young girl wasn't forced to provide her body to the customers.

"Very lonely," she said. "But this was Wells's dream, and I haven't any family of my own."

"You could marry again. You are in position to meet men."

"Someday." She stirred restlessly underneath him, and his manhood perked up with interest. "When I fall in love again."

"I don't think your body wants to wait for love," he murmured, nuzzling her neck.

Her head tilted to give him access. "Again so soon?"

He wrapped himself around her and flipped until she was on top. "Like this."

"You want me to ride you?" She laughed, and he grabbed fistfuls of her fragrant hair, pulling her mouth to his. Despite her wishes to keep it free of oil, it had loosed from the pins, and proved irresistible to him. When they kissed, his erection surged, making her gasp and wriggle her hips. They began again, without ever having separated.

April 22, 1888

Gawain saw the Marquess of Hatbrook standing by a trap outside the Heathfield train station. The day was fine and he must have wanted to escape the house, given over as it was to females and babies. Hatbrook had sent a telegram to Scotland announcing the birth of his daughter, Lady Mary Ellen Shield, a week earlier and Gawain looked forward to seeing his first niece.

"Looking a bit haggard, Hatbrook," he said by way of greeting.

"All the house arrangements are in a muddle because of the baby," Hatbrook said, stifling a yawn. "You look none the worse for three weeks of travel."

Gawain lifted his traveling case into the box at the back of the trap, then carefully maneuvered himself onto the seat. Hatbrook jumped up with considerably more grace.

"Leg troubling you?"

"Travel does not agree with me. I had to stay over in Leeds while your brother went north. Once I could walk again, I followed."

Hatbrook lifted the reins. "Judah sent me a telegram every few days."

"We tracked Lady Elizabeth and Manfred Cross to Edinburgh but then lost the trail," Gawain admitted. "Lord Judah is in the process of hiring a private inquiry agent who is a Scot. We were hampered by being strangers in the north."

"Neither of you would have social acquaintances there."

Gawain ignored the commentary and grabbed the seat to steady himself as the trap jolted forward. "Neither would your sister or the Cross lad."

"I am most disappointed at your lack of success."

"As am I, since I did hope to make the lady my wife." He had to admit Lady Elizabeth's charms had faded very quickly in his mind's eye. His female fantasies were entirely taken over these days by thoughts of the alluring Ann Haldene. If it hadn't been for an eagerness to see the baby he might have stopped in Leeds again.

"Too late for that, I suppose." Hatbrook didn't turn his head.

"They should have been able to marry by now, or at least by sometime this week, given the laws in Scotland."

"I wonder what they will live on," Hatbrook mused.

"Have you discovered any source of income?"

Hatbrook's mouth worked. "My mother's jewelry box was raided. Beth's was stripped as well. Nothing too fine, as the best jewels were in the bank, but such things that had been left in Mother's room at her death. I expect Beth could have pawned enough to live on comfortably for six months or so."

Or more, if she did not try to live like someone of her station, Gawain suspected. If she had, she'd have been far easier to find.

They spent the remainder of the journey going over the investigation in minute detail. "I suppose my brother will have to return soon."

"He does have a new wife waiting," Gawain said.

"It is cruel to keep them apart," Hatbrook agreed. "And Redcake's is sorely missing its usual guidance. Sir Bartley has taken to reading the reports and offering Lady Judah advice, since Alys has been focused on the baby."

Gawain wondered if Beth knew what havoc her departure had wreaked. She had chosen the exact wrong moment to run off, or the exact right moment, in terms of having the fewest people able to search for her. For his part, he consigned her to the Fates, as he was done with her. Three weeks of discomfort and inattention to his business was quite enough trouble. He rubbed at his hip and again thought of Ann. In Scotland he'd been unable to find his Ayurvedic medicine, and once he'd finished Ann's stores, which she'd offered to him upon departure, the pain had rapidly reappeared.

"Do you think illicit behavior runs in families?" Hatbrook mused. "My mother—"

"Lord Judah told me the story," he said. "I'm sure your mother was a very unhappy woman, but your sister had no reason to be."

"Which is why I wonder. Some weakness of the blood?"

Gawain knew that what Hatbrook was really worrying about was his child. A new baby had a way of focusing concern on inheritable family flaws. He had heard similar rumblings from his sister Matilda in terms of her illegitimate child's wayward father, Theodore Bliven. "By the time you discover her nature, you will be too careworn and gray-bearded to care."

"Good God, man," Hatbrook said, laughing. "She will likely be married off before I am fifty."

"That will be after the turn of the century. Have you thought of it? Our children will marry in the twentieth century."

"Do you have a new bride in mind? Now that my sister is lost to you," Hatbrook said, an edge in his voice.

"No," Gawain said. "I shall not marry where there is not some social benefit. I will have to attend society events next spring when I can get back to London. Unfortunately, my attentions cannot be focused there this year. I am needed in Bristol and I may go back to Scotland to pursue some possible customers I met while up there."

"You did not spend so much time searching for my sister then."

"Of course I did," Gawain snapped. "But one does offer one's card and discuss business."

"I apologize," Hatbrook said instantly. "Of course, you are right."

Gawain was pleased to see Hatbrook Farm coming into view. He rarely had a long conversation with his sister's husband and he could see now that Beth's specter would hang between them, creating ill thoughts. "You should be pleased that I am returning north, as it will give me the opportunity to supervise the inquiry agent."

"I am all for it," Hatbrook said with false heartiness as a groom ran up to take charge of the horses. He jumped to the gravel driveway and Gawain followed more cautiously. A parlor maid opened the front door and Hatbrook took only the time to throw off his coat, hat and gloves before leading him to a warm family parlor on the first floor where Alys and Matilda were comfortable with their babies on their laps, a nursemaid hovering protectively in the background.

"Shouldn't you be abed?" Gawain asked, when he saw Alys, looking considerably slimmer than when he'd seen her last.

"Not at all," she said, tilting her head for a cheek kiss. "It was an easy birth and I am not delicate."

He compared one baby to the other, a tiny, unformed child with a scrunched-up face to the great boy of some four and a half months, grinning toothlessly at him. "It is amazing to think that in not too much longer these two will be indistinguishable, age-wise." What he didn't say was how utterly different their lives would be, a girl with an assured title and position in the highest society, and a bastard born to an unmarried tradesman's daughter. But for now, they were equally comfortable and self-satisfied.

When he had children, he wanted them to have the security of Alys's child, rather than the hard road of Matilda's. He still wished he could have forced Theodore Bliven to marry his younger sister, but when he had given the man funds to go to India and source new tea plantations for him, he'd had no idea Bliven had seduced Matilda. Now, he had failed Beth too, though, like his sister, she'd had a part in her seduction. He hoped Beth at least had a wedding out of the mess.

"You look exhausted," Alys said. "More than I do."

"Are you telling me I look older, twin?"

"You are older," she grinned. "By seven minutes."

"Father will never let me forget it," he said. "Are he and Mother here at the Farm or at home?"

"Mother is here but Father is in London keeping an eye on Redcake's. Do you think Judah will come home soon?"

"It depends somewhat on your husband and how insistent he is on keeping a relative in Scotland."

"I shall ensure Judah is allowed to leave," Alys said firmly.

"What of you, Matilda? Moving to Bristol soon?"

"Once you have staffed your house properly. I cannot learn the business from you if you do not have a nursery and appropriate staff."

"Isn't that your duty?"

"Where do you expect little Jacob to sleep? A drawer?"

Gawain dropped stiffly into a chair. "It is not so bad as that. We all lived in that house until eighteen eighty-four. You know it has a nursery."

"We didn't move into it until about five years before then. Even Rose was thirteen by then," Alys said.

Gawain frowned. "It does have a nursery on the second floor. I'm sure of it." He never climbed stairs he didn't have to. Going up one staircase to his bedchamber at night was quite enough. He'd insisted on installing a full bathroom in his suite as well, once he'd taken possession of the house.

"I'll send a note to your housekeeper," Alys said, "with the necessary instructions. I'm sure she can have proper furnishings ordered and staff hired by June."

"Very well. I will wait to go to Scotland until August then."

"Redcake's business?"

"No, my own."

"I've been waiting for you to speak of Beth," she said gently.

He shrugged. "Nothing to say. She has vanished into the highland mist."

"She's such a bright, eager girl," Alys mused. "So enthusiastic."

"She's a fool," Matilda said with a sour expression. "I wish she had spoken to me. You would think my example alone—"

Alys glared at her. "How do you think Jacob would feel to know you speak so? Given his beginnings he could not have a better life."

"Beth should have known better, chasing after such a young man like that."

Gawain's sharp mind picked up the fresh detail. "Wait. Are you saying they did not run off together?"

Matilda pressed her lips together. "She had threatened to do it, but I did not think she was serious."

"You didn't tell anyone?"

"I was here and she was in London, for the Season! Who would I have told? It was just a young girl's fancy, written in a letter."

"Then Manfred Cross didn't want her?" Hope flared for a moment, then extinguished again. No matter how things had begun, it had been weeks.

"No, he did. But with no prospects, he was concerned. He told Beth he didn't want to be a fortune hunter."

"We never thought to look for them separately," Gawain mused. "Manfred Cross might not be hiding. I must write a letter to Lord Judah immediately."

"Yes," Alys agreed. The babe in her arms let out a tiny cry and the nursemaid rushed forward. "I need to take my little one to her room."

Gawain nodded absently. Alys pointed out the writing desk on her way out, and he went to it and opened the drawer, looking for paper.

"Your limp is worse than ever," Matilda said.

"It's from the travelling. Worst thing I can do for it."

"I am sorry you've gone to all this trouble. Beth thinks of you as a brother, you know. She wouldn't have wanted you to suffer for her."

Gawain turned with a snarl. "She's a thoughtless, silly girl, just like you, with no thought of consequences to herself or her family."

Instead of yelling back, Matilda straightened in her chair. "I have made my apologies and I have paid in blood besides. At any rate, I do not know what difference it makes to you."

He sat. Matilda may have matured, but she did not seem to realize how each member of her extended family suffered for her mistake. All of them, Hatbrook, Alys, himself, and their youngest sister Rose, had found themselves a part to play in the disaster that led up to Matilda's unwed pregnancy. The guilt had kept them all together in a sense, as Gawain knew for a certainty that Hatbrook detested Rose for her gossipy sins, yet housed her because both she and Matilda had been so ill, Rose with her asthma and Matilda with the pregnancy.

As he sat there with a pen, looking out over the rose garden behind the house, he realized that even Beth's drama had a start in Matilda's history. For Lady Bricker had been a catalyst in it as well, and she was Lady Judah's and Manfred Cross's first cousin. Since Hatbrook's opinion of the Cross family was as low as his opinion of Rose, had he created a Montague-Capulet fantasy in Beth's mind? She had proved herself as lovely, innocent, and wayward as any Juliet. But it sounded as if Manfred had no desire to be Romeo.

Gawain didn't want to get back on any swaying carriage the next day, but he did need some exercise, so he took a horse into the village. Of course, this did not agree with his bad hip, so he tied up the horse outside of the first pub he saw in Heathfield and went in for a glass of ale.

He limped up to the wood plank bar and seated himself on a stool, hoping the alcohol would ease the burn in his hip. Unfortunately, he would need to stay at the Farm another day or two until the pain lessened sufficiently for him to be able to tolerate the train. His mother was pleased to see him, and he'd had fun bouncing Jacob on his good knee, while telling Alys about his Scottish adventures. He'd even mentioned Mrs. Haldene in a roundabout way, telling her that he'd met a genuine Indian healer.

"Sergeant Redcake, that you?"

Gawain turned on his stool to find the homely face of Sergeant Bowler Martin grinning incautiously at him. He hadn't seen the man since he arrived in England. "Is this where you retired to, you old bastard?"

"Best weather in the country," the retired soldier said. "I grew up not too far from here. I never understood how you ended up in the Royal Sussex."

"I wanted to go to India," Gawain shrugged.

"She didn't like you much," Martin said, pointing to his eye. "Ever get your vision back?"

"Not enough of it."

Martin had been in the same battle, and had lost a couple of fingers. They had been shipped home together and spent months playing cards as they headed toward England. "Come down to see your sister? I've heard she married well."

"That she did and yes, she just presented her husband with a daughter."

"Ah, a little one. Everything went well?"

"Yes. Alys is up and about already. Seems determined to keep the nursemaid as idle as possible."

"She's from sturdy stock. Look at you, a great businessman now, I hear, despite the licking you took from the Pathans."

"One thing about running the officer's mess is I made good contacts among the traders."

"Doesn't hurt that you had the capital from your family either." Martin pulled out his pipe.

"No, that never hurts," Gawain agreed. He had taken his share of abuse from his comrades when they discovered his family had money.

"I remember you telling me you did not want to return home because you thought Indian medicine would fix you up better than the home doctors."

"I'm still searching. Actually, I met an Indian healer up north recently. Ann Haldene." He took sharp pleasure in saying her name aloud.

"Ann Haldene," Martin mused, lighting his tobacco. "Any relation to Wells Haldene?"

"That was her husband, I believe. Dead a couple of years now."

"Too bad," Martin said slowly. "She is half-Indian, right? Sounds English to the bone, but very dark."

"Yes. Why ever would you have heard of her? Never thought you were into the Hindoo mumbo-jumbo."

"She's famous. At least her mother was."

"Why is that?"

Martin puffed out a perfect smoke ring and squinted. "My lad, her mother was an Indian queen. Some maharajah's daughter."

Chapter Four

Gawain frowned. "Pardon me?"

"Yes, and a maharajah's wife as well. Husband, that's the maharajah, died in eighteen fifty-nine. They were going to burn the maharani on the pyre with him."

Gawain drank deeply from his ale glass. "Obviously they didn't."

"No. A subaltern, one of ours, obviously, swooped in and stole her from under the noses of the maharajah's men. She was a famous beauty, known for her healing powers. He married her. Of course, the subaltern's career was ruined after that. They had to be sent off to some remote station."

"And made their way back to England eventually."

"Yes. A great love story. No brilliant ending. The subaltern's family had scarcely enough money to scrape together the funds to buy his commission and he never advanced. Lived very quietly with the lady, who was much loved for her work among the sick in that remote station."

"Just the one daughter?"

"Yes, also a great beauty, they say. She married Wells Haldene, a young soldier. I don't know why her family didn't try to do more for her, but perhaps there wasn't anyone left."

"You might be right. She said her mother died a decade ago, and she lives with her husband's family now. But she may own the inn they run, now that I think of it. Her husband inherited it."

"So the Haldenes were prosperous business folk, at least."

He thought of the ragged appearance of Harry Haldene. It might be mere eccentricity. The inn itself seemed to have plenty of customers. "I saw no signs of imminent disaster."

Martin shook his head. "One hates to think of a princess running an inn."

"Come, man, she's not really a princess."

Martin shrugged. "Why not? Her mother was the daughter of one of their kings. Her father might not have had a title, but the marriage was real enough. If she'd been raised in India, she might be sitting with Queen Victoria now, having tea, if she visited here. You know they fawn over foreign titles at court, no matter the color of the royal skin."

Tea with the Queen instead of breaking her celibate widowhood with a romp in the sheets, courtesy of a half-drunk tea merchant. What had possessed her? He was no legendary beauty himself. Yes, he dressed a few steps above the average customer of the inn, appeared to be a prosperous sort, though he had not the speech of a true gentleman, but she'd asked him for nothing. In fact, all the favors had been offered on her side. The Haldenes hadn't even charged him for her medicine when he'd left, just the food and room.

Women. She must have been out of her mind with loneliness. The worst of it was he liked her. But it would never do to get involved. An Indian wife, even of half-royal birth, would not get him where he wanted to go in life. No, it was best to stay away from Leeds. Martin's history changed nothing.

December 27, 1888

Gawain sat in the first-class compartment of a Leeds-bound train. His hip pained him so badly that he'd been using a stick for support these past three weeks or more. His temper had flared repeatedly during his attempts to enjoy the holidays with his sister's family.

Mother had declared him overworked and blamed his bad mood on incessant traveling. He'd been to Scotland three times, and France twice, since Lady Elizabeth had vanished. Then there was the commute from Bristol to London to Sussex. What he needed was a massage. And sex. No one could perform either so well as Ann Haldene. Despite his spring promise to leave her be, he decided to go north and see if she could work her special magic on him again. For a week, at least. Or the remainder of the Twelve Days of Christmas. Or until he felt ready to travel again. After that, he'd promised to return to Edinburgh to receive the inquiry agent reports on Lady Elizabeth. At least stopping at Leeds broke up the train journey.

At the station, he hired a hansom to take him to The Old Hart. Less than twenty minutes later, they were pulling into the stable yard. Dirty snow piled up against the buildings, though a clear path had been shoveled from the street to the inn's door. The windows showed yellow from lights glowing within. He'd expected some sign of the holidays, but none was evident.

After he paid the driver, he hoisted his valise and limped into the entryway, leaning heavily on his cane. A sudden realization that this was madness descended upon him. How could he have thought Ann could help him when no one else could? It seemed he'd made no progress of any kind since he first met her. Not on the hunt for Lady Elizabeth, not in finding an herb to cure his eyesight, not in helping his damaged hip. It had all been work, work, work. He was richer, but ever more miserable, more set in his angry ways. His youngest sister Rose had even called him a Scrooge when she only received tea for Christmas, even though it was a rare tea blended with roses only grown by certain mute French nuns.

He took a breath in the deserted hallway and knew at once something was different in the inn's atmosphere. What had changed? He glanced around, then turned into the dining room. Too late for luncheon, too early for tea, it was all but deserted. A couple of old men played chess in a corner by the fireplace he had so coveted last April. Now, the blaze was low and the room dim.

He smelled the coal fire and tobacco smoke, then realized the difference he'd sensed. Before, the spicy scent of curry had hung on the air. The Indians used spices with an unsparing hand and you always knew when they'd been cooking. But he suspected no curry had been cooked here for a week or more. Were the Haldenes on holiday?

The door to the kitchen pushed outward, and he saw a woman in a dirty white apron peer into the room, as if she expected a customer. When she caught sight of him she stepped out of the door-way and moved toward him, a smile of welcome creasing her middle-aged face.

"Come for a meal, sir? I've a fine pot of stew bubblin' away, and I just made bread this morning."

"Excellent," Gawain said, dropping his valise to his feet. "But I expected a curry."

"Oh, you must have come before, when Mrs. Haldene was cookin'. She makes a fine curry."

"Is she out of town?"

"Yes, sir, she is. Left a fortnight ago."

"Where did she go?" Rude of him to ask, but he couldn't help himself.

The woman put her hand to her mouth. "Oh, I couldn't say, sir. I'm sure I don't know."

Gawain frowned. "Bring me a meal, would you? I'm fresh from the train. Are you in charge of the inn while Mrs. Haldene is away?"

"I'm just the cook, sir. Mr. Haldene is manager 'ere."

"Harry Haldene?"

"Yes, sir."

"Send for him, would you?"

"You would like a room?"

"I would, yes."

She nodded. "You shall 'ave both the meal and the manager presently."

He sat, gritting his teeth as pain laced through his lower half. Reluctantly, he pulled a couple of tablets of Antifebrin from his waistcoat pocket and swallowed them dry. They would help but gave him a terrible stomachache. Still, they did better for immediate pain and inflammation than any of his Indian remedies, like turmeric. Not that he liked to admit this. At least he remained fully convinced that he would have no vision in his bad eye at all without his remedies. In the warm months, he never needed more than these either. It was only when the damp set in, or long periods of travel, when he had to resort to the stomach-churning Western medicines.

He had already finished his bowl of stew when Haldene arrived at his table, looking even more dissolute than in April. His shirt gaped where a button was missing and his jacket sleeve was ripped. Ann must have been his seamstress.

"Seen you before, haven't I?" Haldene said, with a ferocious smile.

Gawain offered the man a cool stare. "Yes, I spent a night here in the spring. I'd like a room for the night."

Haldene pulled a handkerchief from his pocket and wiped his forehead. "Very well. Traveling salesman, are you?"

"Not exactly. I was looking forward to a good curry. What has happened to your cook?"

"Took herself off to London. She and me sister, a fortnight back."

"Visiting relatives for the holidays? Returning soon?"

Haldene shrugged. "Got a girl who'll get your room ready. Up the stairs, front of the buildin'. Sign the ledger in the front passage on your way up."

"Thank you," Gawain said, figuring nothing more would come from this laconic fellow.

Haldene turned away, then looked back at him. "Say, weren't you the chap with the interest in all that Indian business? Ann's pills and such?"

"Very much so. I'm an importer of Indian remedies, spices and tea."

Haldene scratched his unshaven chin. "Right. See, we have a Indian community here. Can you supply me what they need? The curries and pills and powders and such? I'm already out of some of the favorites and it does bring in the ready."

Gawain dug in his valise and pulled out a brochure. "This is a list of my wares. If you see what you need we can make arrangements."

"Excellent." Haldene's tongue curled in the corner of his mouth as he perused the brochure. His fingers left dirt marks on the cream pages. "Do you have samples with you?"

"I do not. But I can cable my office and have what you need sent tomorrow on the train."

Haldene frowned. "I'll just compare this to the list I was makin', then. I expect the spellin's are all different."

"Do you have an address for Mrs. Haldene in London? We could have her compare the lists."

"No," the man said absently. "Haven't heard from her yet."

"Doesn't she own the inn?" Gawain asked.

"Mmmm," said Haldene noncommittally.

"I'll just go and find my room then." The pills had yet to take effect. He debated asking for a couple of bottles of port, but he'd found the pills, which he'd only discovered a couple of months before, would work, given time. Still, he'd rather have had another of those massages. And sex.

He signed the ledger and made his slow way upstairs, grateful he had only brought the one bag. The maid, an undersized girl about the same age as Fern Haldene, was making up the bed as he walked in.

"Just the one night, sir?" she asked as he set his valise on the table.

"I think so, unless Haldene wants to discuss business with me tomorrow."

"You buyin' a share of the inn too?" she asked.

"Who has been buying shares of this property?" he responded. "Mrs. Haldene is selling it?"

"She gave some of it to Mr. Haldene," the girl said. "For travelin' money, and for the baby, of course. I think she should've stayed, a woman in her condition, but no one asked me. Expect she wanted to go before the customers knew what she was about."

Gawain reached unsteadily for the chair. When his hands found the back, he pulled it close and sat down, not taking his gaze from the maid. "She's having a child? Remarried?"

"No, sir," the maid blushed.

"When is the child coming?"

The girl righted her cap, which had slid over her ear when she pulled up the blanket on the bed. "Early in the year, she said. Gone off to London to find the father afore it's too late."

Early in the year? He mentally ticked off the months in his head. Was the child his? He could not think of what to ask next, so he blurted, "The father is in London then? She knows that?"

"Said his name was Redcake, and there's a famous tea shop in London by that name. Thought she could find him there."

His eggs and rashers shifted greasily in his already irritated stomach. "Why didn't she just send him a letter?"

The girl shrugged. "Dunno. You wantin' anythin' else?"

"Her address," he said hoarsely. "Have you heard anything? Has Fern?"

"Fern went with her. I've got her position," the girl said proudly.

"The address," Gawain repeated.

"No, you ought to ask Mr. Haldene."

"You can go," Gawain said, feeling like he would retch.

The girl scrambled for the chamber pot under the bed and held it out to him, then trotted out of the room. He leaned his head against the lip of the clean pot, willing his stomach to settle. Damn pills. He needed to get on the next train for London, but he was a prisoner of his own body.

How could he find Ann in such an enormous city as London? When his stomach finally calmed, he collapsed onto the bed and fell into an uneasy doze, tormented by images of her round with his child. Had she waited for him to return all this time, only leaving to search for him when the birth was imminent? How could he have done to a woman what Theodore Bliven had done to his sister Matilda?

Ann Haldene might be a woman with property, but she had nothing like a Redcake's family connections and money. An illegitimate child would drag her down into infamy. Her best hope might be to start over, claiming the babe was her dead husband's.

Except the timing was wrong. Ann Haldene was famous in her way. She'd have to change her name and try to blend into the East End, where her dark skin would not be unusual.

His head tossed on the pillow. Images of babies with dark skin and his hawk nose mixed into some strange vision involving Harry Haldene and an Indian funeral. When he woke the next morning, he couldn't even blame an overindulgence of port, just his own troubled thoughts.

He packed up his bag, grateful that he could move that morning, and collected an order form from Haldene. After Gawain promised to send the requested goods as soon as possible, Haldene himself drove Gawain to the station, talking artlessly of the local Indian community he served. Gawain suspected Ann had never mentioned the father of her child to her brother-in-law. Otherwise, he'd have expected one of those filthy mitts to leave the reins and land on his nose. Instead, he received the gratitude of one businessman to another, when their minds have met on a point of commerce.

They shook hands in front of the station and then Gawain limped inside, bemused by the entire experience. As the train sped southward, he resolved to keep his story private from his family. He had a few days to make inquiries before he'd have to go to Scotland. It would have been far more pleasant to stay here in Leeds, in bed with Ann, as he had planned, but now that he knew she'd flown he could not stay still. He must find her. Until he ascertained if the coming child was truly his, this adventure was none of his family's business, though. Ann might have left word for him at Redcake's, since she'd expressed her intention of going to the tea shop.

January 25, 1889

Noel Redcake was one month old today. Ann Haldene tucked the sleeping baby into his cradle, curled his one lock of red-gold hair around her finger for a moment, and nodded to Fern. They both crept out of the bedsit of their two-room flat and returned to the kitchen.

"I have to leave for work in a minute," Ann said. "Do you have everything you need?"

Fern nodded.

"Make sure you dress Noel warmly when you bring him to me," Ann instructed. "And take him to Mrs. Cook down the hall in two hours for a feeding."

Fern nodded again. This would be the first day of their new ritual because she was starting a position as a specialty cake baker at Redcake's Tea Shop and Emporium. She had planned to go there and ask about Gawain Redcake when they had first arrived in London. Unfortunately, the train trip had given her a feverish cold, and led to a nightmare time where she'd been all but bedridden, culminating in the unexpectedly early birth of Noel. Gawain had been completely absent from her mind for a time. A week ago, she'd felt ready to leave Noel for the first time. She'd gone to Redcake's and it seemed that Bertha Short, the tearoom manager, had misinterpreted every word out of her mouth, as if it weren't quite English. She'd been passed on to Alfred Melville, the manager of the basement baking rooms. He'd said Gawain Redcake wasn't employed there, nor did he own the place, but he'd offered her a position when he realized she was experienced in the professional kitchen. They needed someone to make cakes for the Fancy, the part of the baking rooms where the wedding and other specialty cakes were decorated.

How could she refuse? Once inside, it wouldn't take long to figure out how Noel's father might be connected to the place, and meanwhile, she could use the money. Doctors and midwives had nearly wiped out what she'd thought was quite sensible funding from selling ten percent of The Old Hart to Harry. She had never paid rent before, since her husband had taken care of those things, and in any case they lived at the inn. The prices in London were beyond her wildest fears.

She had a two-week trial at Redcake's. Hopefully she could find Gawain by then, and go back to Leeds with no hard feelings from Alfred Melville.

February 8, 1889

Gawain admired the Redcake's window display as he passed through the front courtyard. Winter still held London in its mighty grip, so he didn't linger in front of the charming display of Redcake's Plantation Tea tins, topped by platters of scones decorated in Valentine's Day themes. He tapped his cane forward, checking for ice, but the area was dry. A nasty fall in Edinburgh on the first of the month had made him cautious.

He had stopped in Leeds on the way back and spent another night at The Old Hart. Harry Haldene had been an effusive host, grateful for the Indian herbs and spices that Redcake's Indian Imports had sent, but Harry had still had no word from Ann. Gawain had been blunt, telling him this seemed hard to believe when the lady still owned most of the inn. Harry had shrugged this off, saying he was sure to hear from her in April, when she was due to be paid her share of the first quarter profits.

Gawain didn't want to wait until then. The baby must have been born by now if it was really his. But the infant, Ann and Fern were all beyond reach, beyond any ability to find even by the London-based private inquiry agent Gawain had hired.

Gawain pushed open the front door, reflecting that he ought to have hired an Indian detective, rather than a white one. Ann might be living in an immigrant community. He hadn't thought of the possibility at first, since she had Fern with her, but now he wondered. Why hadn't she left word for him here? Had some calamity befallen them? His dreams exhausted him with lurid possibilities. First Lady Elizabeth vanished, now Ann and Fern.

The lobby welcomed him with its lush decorations of fern and dangling, pink cupid cutouts. He barely glanced at them as he turned in to the bakery. One of the cakies, as Redcake's waitresses were called, recognized him and let him through into the back, looking a bit startled when she saw his cane. He hadn't needed one back when he'd worked here two years ago.

"Were you in an accident, Mr. Redcake?" she asked.

He thought her name was Meredith. "Too much traveling."

"I'm covered with bruises each time I go to see my mum," she agreed. "Beastly things, trains."

"No name badge there, eh, Meredith?"

She smiled hugely. He'd remembered correctly. "There has been a bit of bother with followers. Lord Judah decided it was best if we were more anonymous-like."

He frowned. "I see. Anyone hurt?"

"Just scared, I think."

"I'll have to ask him about that." He tipped his hat. "On my way upstairs."

"Lovely to see you again, Mr. Redcake," she said with a blush.

He could feel her gaze following him as he moved past the trays containing extra baked goods. If she hadn't been watching he might have cadged a gateau but he remained strong against the temptation. Then he was in the back hallway where the stairs were. Unfortunately, the lift only made the trip from the ground floor to the basement. He made his slow way up two flights of steps, grimacing with pain. Why hadn't he told Lord Judah to meet him in the tearoom? He took his hand off the bannister to check his pocket for pills, knowing he would need them soon.

Ewan Hales, Lord Judah's secretary, wasn't in his customary place at his desk in the anteroom. The ambitious employee had left a stack of ledgers on his desk, so he couldn't be far. Gawain heard voices coming from the slightly open door of the inner office and recognized Hales's pomaded hair just inside.

"Congratulations on passing your probation," Lord Judah was saying as Gawain peered in. "That's astounding. Not a single burned cake in your first two weeks."

"The ovens here are much less primitive than I'm used to," said a sultry voice.

Something in Gawain's chest tightened at the sound of that low-pitched female speech. He pushed the door open and stepped into the room. Hales turned, frowning, then his expression flattened into neutrality when he saw Gawain.

"We are happy to clear your probationary status," Lord Judah said. "Betsy Popham has pronounced herself satisfied with your cakes."

"As am I," Alfred Melville, the baking room manager, interjected.

The female baker turned her head to acknowledge Melville. When Gawain saw her profile, his vision blackened for an instant. He blinked, and then focused on her as if she were the only person in the room.

Black hair, frizzy from the heat. Full lips, caramel skin. Strong nose and chin. No wonder the voice had sounded familiar.

"Ann?" he croaked, the sound of his voice barely audible over Melville's laudatory boom. Was he dreaming?

Lord Judah's head appeared over Ann's uniformed shoulder. "Gawain?"

His brain couldn't take it all in. The Ayurvedic healer and inn owner, the lover who had stuck in his brain and ruined him for other woman, the mother of his putative child, was working at Redcake's Tea Shop and Emporium as a baker?

He limped to one of the armchairs by the fire and collapsed into it. He'd wanted to find her, of course, and she'd been under his family's very nose all along. The thought was unbelievable. What was she doing at Redcake's?

Ann turned when Melville finished speaking. He saw her figure was fuller than he remembered. At first she looked confused, staring at the space on the carpet where he'd stood and spoke. Then she saw him in the armchair and gasped, covering her mouth with her hand. Her eyes were wide and he could see a burn on the side of her hand.

"I've been looking for you," he rasped. "Ann Haldene of The Old Hart in Leeds."

"I've been looking for you," she repeated, the words muffled behind her hand. He thought she'd gone a bit pink. "I thought you didn't work here. I asked everyone."

"I stopped working here in eighty-seven," he explained, gripping the silver handle of his cane. "My father sold the place and I went to work in Bristol. But someone should have given you my direction."

She removed her hand from her mouth, and folded her hands under her chin. "I was afraid to ask too many questions. There has been much talk of inappropriate followers here, and I didn't want to seem a dangerous woman." Her eyebrows lifted comically.

He laughed. It gave him a moment to consider her. Was she calm or a bundle of nerves? While she didn't look as slim as she had when they had met, she was not with child either. Her newly rounded body could belong to a woman who'd given birth a month before, but where was the child? He pressed his lips together, not willing to ask questions in front of Melville.

Lord Judah cleared his throat. "Gentlemen, I believe we have a reunion pending. Ann, when does your shift end?"

"At four, m' lord."

"Gawain can collect you at the back and you can have your chat then."

Melville took Ann's arm. "Thank you, m' lord," said Melville. "Mr. Redcake, Mr. Hales." With that, he towed her out of the room.

Hales closed the door behind him. Gawain continued to stare in the direction of the exit.

"You couldn't take your eyes off her," Lord Judah commented.

"She's the one. My Indian doctor from Leeds."

Lord Judah grinned. "You don't say. What a funny coincidence."

"It isn't a coincidence," he snapped. "She was looking for me. You have no idea . . ." he paused, not wanting to reveal his deep secret.

"I instituted a policy of performing the probationary review myself, so that I would get to know each of the staff. But she's an unlikely employee, I'll give you that."

"She must have come here to look for me. But she owns property. I can't imagine why she'd need to work as a baker."

"It's good money," Judah said. "Baking the specialty cakes. Maybe she wanted a change from serving meals to inn customers. She's no stranger to hard work."

"No. But she wouldn't have left her patients for the sake of an adventure. No, she wanted something from me." The truth was, he wanted something from her, too. If that child was his, she would get what she wanted, presumably marriage. Certainly money. She'd never have to work a day in her life as the mother of Gawain Redcake's child. But she would marry him. He was no seducer of innocents, no Theodore Bliven.

"You have a strange, determined look in your eye," Lord Judah observed.

"I often have a determined look in my eye," Gawain snapped. "It isn't strange."

Lord Judah grinned. "You were much more subservient back in our army days."

"*Gor blimey*," Gawain swore. "Our army days were years ago. I'm a different man now, my own man."

"I never said you weren't," Lord Judah said. "Are you sure you want to go down this path? It doesn't fit what I know of you."

"What path is that?"

"Ann Haldene," he said. "I saw the determination in your face, but she isn't the sort of lady you want."

"Why not?" asked Gawain, wanting to hear the words.

"You need a title, someone like my sister, to go where you want in life. Someone with connections, who knows how to be a hostess at the highest level. Not that we know where my sister is. What is so special about this woman?"

This was his closest friend asking. He decided to tell the truth. "I believe she bore me a child."

Lord Judah stepped forward until they were nearly nose-to-nose. "So?"

"I won't knowingly make a bastard," Gawain said, gritting his teeth.

Lord Judah's forehead creased. "But a common soldier's widow?"

"I was a common soldier. And her mother was a maharini. Her grandfather was a maharajah."

His friend's eyes widened. "I wonder how much that would matter to society. I shall have to ask my wife."

"Who wasn't considered good enough for you in the marquess's eyes," Gawain pointed out.

"Because of her family's reputation, not because of her birth. She's the niece of an earl, you know."

"The niece of an earl," Gawain mocked. "Good God, man, you sound like everything you used to loathe."

Lord Judah crossed his arms over his broad chest and widened his stance. "As long as you are still my dearest friend, we shall be certain that my standards are low."

"I should punch you in the nose," Gawain threatened without malice.

Lord Judah winked. "What do you want for luncheon? I usually eat the soup. We have oyster soup today."

"I want to go after Ann."

"Did she really have your baby?"

Gawain kicked his cane. "I will find out at four. Please order some soup."

Chapter Five

Gawain stood next to the loading dock at four PM, concerned that he wouldn't see Ann because of the heavy yellow fog. February was not the best month for outdoor assignations. A procession of cakies, dressed in their black dresses, and bakers, in inexpensive trousers and jackets, streamed out the back and into the cobbled alley. He tapped his cane impatiently, craning his neck forward to get a better view.

The tap on his shoulder came from above. Startled, he dropped his cane as he swung around and stared up. Ann Haldene stood above him on the loading dock, little more than a shadow in the gloom.

She crouched down. "I didn't know if I could see you through the fog so I came out up here."

He held out his hand. She took it, her black gloves hiding her skin, and jumped to the stones. A stray pebble cost her balance, and his attempt to keep her upright wrenched his hip. He swore as a hot flash of pain ripped through his tortured flesh.

She pulled her hand away and bent down, picking up his cane. "Hip is still a problem, I see."

He took his cane. "I went to Leeds to see you in December. I was at my wit's end with the pain. But you were gone."

"Did you talk to Harry?" she asked, matter-of-factly.

"I did. We're now doing business, in fact. I wonder where you purchased your herbs and spices, since he seems to have no idea. He's stocking my brand now." He laughed, the sound round and harsh in the fog.

"He never cared about any of that before."

"You must have become the center of the local Indian community without realizing it, as many have asked for you since you left."

She made a dismissive noise. "That is all you wanted of me? To know my supplier?"

"No, Ann." He swallowed hard, his throat gritty with the nasty London air. "You know what they told me there. About a baby coming."

"I see." She half turned away, giving him a hazy view of her profile.

"Why aren't you home with your infant? Home in Leeds, that is. What about Fern? I barely met the girl, but she's what, twelve?"

"Thirteen now. And Noel was born on Christmas Day."

Gawain thought hard. His chest seemed to take on the properties of ice, cold and unyielding. Was all his worry, his desperation for nothing? "Then he isn't mine?" Had she said Noel or Noelle? Noel, he thought. A boy. Some man's son.

He heard her chuckle echo through the fog. "Oh, he's yours. You'll see."

"Christmas is too soon," he said.

"He came early. I was ill and I think my body knew I needed to birth the child to recover."

That he had a son was confirmed that simply, perhaps. His stomach churned uneasily at her words. "Is he well?"

"Yes, perfectly fine. Ten little fingers and ten little toes."

"I want to see him," Gawain said, the fire inside him beginning to kindle again. "Right away."

"What if I don't want that?"

He took her arm. "No games, Ann. You came all the way to London for this. Here I am. Take me to the child."

"You did not seem so hard before. The pain is changing you, I think."

"Then fix me," he said. "Until I found out about the baby, that was all I wanted from you."

"That is not how you felt in the spring."

"I was drunk. I am sorry I treated you that way. I had no idea who you were, what you were."

Her voice had not been warm, but he could sense a new level of chill. "What is that?"

"A respectable widow? An Ayurvedic healer? A woman of property? A Hindoo princess?"

He heard her sharp inhale, the cough when the yellow fog hit the back of her throat.

"You have made some discoveries."

"You are better known than I might have imagined. I wonder why I never heard the stories before."

"My father was an officer. You were an enlisted man, correct? It might have been a tale only officers told."

He felt the subtle insult as if it were a physical blow. "Your husband was enlisted."

"Who told you that? No, he was an officer. Just a lieutenant and he only served here, not far away. No honors, no glory and an early death."

"I was misinformed," he said, dragging his bearing into an erect position. He thrust his cane in between the cobblestones. "Now, would you take me to this child before we suffocate?"

"And I thought the air in Leeds was bad," she sighed, but she took the arm he offered.

"It should get better next month." He lifted his head, trying to see through the fog. "For now, one step at a time. Where are we going?"

"Catherine Street, near Covent Garden Market. I can walk to Redcake's from there, though you should rest that leg."

"I'm an old soldier, ma'am. We can push through."

He felt the movement of her body as her head shook. "That is not the perspective that a doctor would take."

"You will fix me up soon enough. I have faith."

"It will take a long time, if it is even possible. But there is much we can do. Have you been ignoring it all this time?"

He followed the stragglers from the Redcake's shift change out of the alley, with Ann at his side, then headed east on Oxford Street. "I was hurt in a battle in India. After treatment there I was sent home, months on a ship. Then I immediately went to work in the Accounting Department at Redcake's. I hated it so I began to consider what I might do for myself."

"How was your hip during that time?"

"Less of a concern than my eye, which made it hard to stare at figures for many hours. It is only all the cursed traveling that I've been doing that has made it so bad now."

"Why all the traveling?"

"We've a runaway in the family. An eighteen-, no, now nineteen-year-old girl. Between searching for her and business I'm on the road a great deal." He followed her lead as she crossed a street and headed south.

"Perhaps you aren't the best choice for this search."

"I had thought to marry the girl."

"You were engaged?"

"No, but at the time I met you I had gained the family's agreement to marry her if she was free. To salvage her reputation."

"They would not have agreed otherwise?"

"Paying attention, aren't you? No, she has a title, you understand. The family didn't want her marrying down."

"At least you didn't love her."

"Why do you say that?"

"You wouldn't have been with me in Leeds if you did, with hopes of soon being reunited with her. What's her name?"

"Elizabeth. I find your understanding of gentlemen to be fascinating. You do not think that, being drunk, I would not have been with a beautiful, willing woman, given the opportunity, in almost any circumstance?"

"Love is everything," she said, keeping her pace matched to his.

"To women perhaps, but not to most men."

"I would not have shared such passion with you if I did not feel a kindred spirit."

He laughed. "I feel so misjudged. I am not a saint."

"Have you been with anyone since we met?"

He frowned. They were passing the buildings of the market now, the roofs barely above the fog. "I travelled a great deal. I had just given up my mistress in the hopes of making a marriage with Beth. I've had no time to make any such arrangements since."

"You mean to tell me a wealthy, attractive man in the prime of his life has not had a passionate encounter in ten months because he's had no free time? Come, sir, I do not believe you. If nothing else, you might have found another pretty girl at an inn."

Feeling foolish, he said, "I found a better treatment than port for my immediate pain a few months ago. A sober man is a more sensible one."

She sniffed as he told her about the Antifebrin. "I do not like the side effects, but it has done wonders."

"I'm not sure that it's better than port from what you describe. I don't trust chemical medicine."

"Very often it is adulterated and unsafe. You do not have to persuade me, a seller of Ayurvedic remedies."

"I suppose not. But we shall see what we can do with massage and rest." They came to the top of Catherine Street. "It is not very nice here at night. Too many women working the street. But to live here is respectable enough. Many artisans, the kind of people who appreciate my medicine."

"So you are still pursuing that as well as baking?"

"I don't know. I'm not used to making a living like this, or to having a child. I shall have to see how much time I have compared to how much money I need."

He noted that she did not seem to consider him in her calculations as he followed her into a building that housed a carpentry shop on the ground floor, then up a narrow flight of steps. She unlocked a door and stepped into a small apartment.

He had never lived so meanly. The Redcakes had been gaining in prosperity for at least three generations. Still, the room was clean and warm, though the furniture was scant. He recognized Fern in an armchair by the fire, pushing a cradle with her foot.

"Is he asleep?" Ann asked, shedding her coat, gloves and hat.

Fern glanced up and shook her head to the negative.

"I need to feed him," Ann said, glancing back at him.

"Has he gone all day without eating?"

"No, Fern takes him across the hall during the day. There is a woman who just weaned her own child in the flat. She provides for him." Ann leaned over the cradle and came up with a small bundle wrapped in a blanket. "Do you want to see him first?"

Gawain walked forward slowly, hearing a rushing sound in his ears. This was not how he'd imagined meeting his first-born son, the next step in the Redcake dynasty. First, he saw a white blanket edged with handmade lace. Next, a blue knit cap.

Ann removed the cap, exposing a naked head with just a bit of copper fluff. Gawain had become rather familiar with babies recently thanks to his sisters, and though the infant seemed tiny, his face matched the age Ann had described, about six weeks old. The baby opened his eyes and looked directly at him. Its tiny mouth opened and it let out a little cry.

"This is your son," she announced, with an air of defiance mixed with pride.

"Hello, Noel," Gawain whispered, forgetting Ann for a moment. He had not a shadow of a doubt that this was his child. While his nose would be a long time developing, he recognized the wide-spaced eyes, the shape of the head. Noel was a Redcake. Noel was his son.

He leaned over Ann's arm and unwrapped the baby just enough to find one minute hand, which rose into the air in protest. Gawain placed his index finger on the open palm. It closed immediately around him.

The world was at peace for the space of a moment, as he and Noel shared a look. Then the infant stuck out his tongue and began to bleat.

"He's hungry," Ann said, rebundling her baby.

Gawain moved back reluctantly. Fern stood and Ann sat in the armchair, the only comfortable seat in the room. The girl gestured, and Gawain went with her to sit in one of the two cane chairs pushed against the kitchen table. From that vantage point, he could not see what was going on.

After a moment, Fern stood and began to prepare tea. Gawain remembered he had a box tucked inside his coat and pulled out a tin of his brand of Darjeeling tea and some cheese scones. Fern looked over his offerings and nodded approval. She opened a cupboard, poked around, then handed him a plate. He arranged the scones while she placed two sausages in a pan on the stove.

By the time the sausages were done, Ann had Noel tucked back into the cradle. When she came to the table, Gawain said, "May I hold him while you eat? I'm not hungry."

"Of course," said Ann.

He followed her back to the fireplace and watched as she unfolded the outermost blanket and picked Noel up. "Have you held a baby before?"

"Yes. Two of my three sisters have babies."

"Then you'll know what you're doing. Mind his head."

He held out his arms and she placed the precious bundle on top of them. Noel had fallen asleep and he gave a little snort as he snuggled into Gawain, turning his head against his father's arm. "Eat," Gawain said. "I'll sit here."

As he backed into the still-warm armchair and sat down, the baby never stirred. She watched, then went to the table.

"Did you make those?" Ann said softly. After a pause, she continued, "Oh, he must have brought them from the bakery."

Gawain smiled at the baby, glad he had surprised her. As soon as she was done eating he would surprise her again. Meanwhile, he stared at his child, memorizing every tiny feature. He didn't look much like his cousins, Jacob and Mary Ellen. Jacob had thick brown hair and Mary Ellen had blond curls. Her eyes were already the strange shape of her Uncle Judah's. Jacob had a winning grin that had reminded Hatbrook of Theodore Bliven.

Gawain refused to think of any of that unpleasantness, with a warm, powder-scented bundle dozing in his arms. While he had missed the first six weeks of this baby's life, he would miss no more. The situation needed resolution. Ann didn't particularly like London, he suspected. He could give up his rooms in the St. James's Square mansion his father owned and buy a house in a suburb, a little closer to Leeds, so Ann could keep an eye on her inn. Maybe she would want to sell it all to Harry and focus on her family. She could continue to dabble in her native medicines. There were plenty of Indians in London. Really, they couldn't be more compatible.

Marrying her caused some risk to his permanent goals, but didn't the Queen herself find Indians fascinating? She had Indian servants and the papers said she was learning Hindustani. Maybe marriage to a maharajah's granddaughter would actually be beneficial.

He heard the clatter of dinnerware and a chair being pushed back. The fireplace scents were overwhelmed by the odor of fruitcake as Ann set the kitchen chair next to the armchair.

"What do you think?"

"We'll have to be married by special license," he said, curling Noel's single lock of hair around his finger. "It's Friday, so it will be a few days before I can manage it, but we can be married next week. You and Fern can move into my family home until I can purchase us an acceptable house. I am thinking outside of central London to the north."

"Married," she said.

He did not understand her tone. Glancing up, he saw none of the happiness or relief he'd expected. Instead, the squint of her eyes looked more like derision. "Of course, what did you expect?"

"I wanted you to know you had a son."

"You didn't uproot yourself and sell part of your inn simply to have a conversation with me. In fact, if you'd sent a letter to Redcake's instead of coming yourself the news might have reached me faster."

"I didn't really know if you were connected to the place."

"It doesn't matter now. What does matter is that I can give Noel my name and security. We can give him brothers and sisters. He has two cousins, not much older than he, playmates. They won't judge him for being born before our wedding. In fact, none of the little ones will even need to know."

Her lips curled into a tiny smile. "I'm not going to marry you, Gawain."

"Of course you are," he said. "It is the only way."

"There is never just one way. I've been married before."

"Was it bad? Did he hurt you?" Gawain growled, already feeling out his *pater familias* role.

"No. He loved me. I loved him. Love is everything and I won't spoil that memory with convenience."

"What about all of that nonsense about you and me and the connection we've had since we met. No one but you and all that?"

"Only time will tell if it is a spiritual connection or just a sensual attachment," she said calmly.

He wanted to stand and shout but the bundle in his arms was too precious to wake. "You need security and so does Noel."

"I have a position. I have the inn. I have Wells's family."

"You'll like my family. And I've learned from my sister's experience that I don't want a bastard child. I need to marry you so you and Noel don't have to have my sister Matilda's circumstances. There is no reason for it."

"I do not need you," she said in clear tones. "I will not keep you from seeing Noel, of course, whenever you are in London."

60 • *Heather Hiestand*

"I won't leave again without the two of you."

"Don't be silly. Of course you will continue your business dealings, but I do hope you will stay here long enough for me to treat your hip."

"This is madness," he said, staring down at Noel. "You must be the sort of person who has to think things through very carefully. As I said, I cannot get the license for a few days. I will come back tomorrow. But if you pack, we can move you to the mansion then. I am the only person in residence now so there will be no trouble with rooms and a full complement of servants is available to meet your every need."

"No," she said. "We have everything we need right here."

"You need time to think."

She didn't respond. He had a sudden rush of fear. Did she think she was too good for him? With her dead officer husband and royal mother?

"You gave birth to my child," he said stiffly. "You will become my wife. I will not suffer him to become a bastard." He leaned forward, holding Noel out like an offering, because he knew he might not be able to stand from the low chair without using his arms for leverage.

Ann took the baby, who was transferred without waking. "I need to massage your hip."

"You have already worked a full day and need to care for Noel. I will return tomorrow." Keeping his chin high, he limped to the door where he'd left his things. Once he had his cane in his fist he felt more in control of himself. He nodded to Fern, leaning against the kitchen table, and let himself out.

When he reached the steps he found his hands were shaking. Cold, it must be the cold. He found his gloves in his pocket and pulled them on. Men didn't cry at the sight of babies but for once he wanted to. She could not think to keep his child from him, not when he wanted the child. He was offering her everything a woman might want.

Gawain went to Ann's apartment early the next afternoon during proper visiting hours. But when he arrived, he found only Fern and Noel, because Ann had neglected to tell him that she worked on Saturdays. He spent a pleasant two hours holding the baby while

Fern sewed baby clothes, until she put her materials down and pointed to Noel and the door. By that, he assumed she meant it was time for a feeding with the neighbor. He walked out the door with her because he wanted to see that the woman kept herself clean and looked respectable.

From the glance he could take at her through the door, she appeared to be a tidy woman. He could see an older child on the floor playing with a doll. The child looked healthy and content, so he nodded his thanks to Fern and left the building. He would return the next day. It didn't hurt to give Ann time to think about her situation.

Feeling at loose ends, he went to his club, thinking he would check the papers for potential houses for his expanded family. When he perused them, in a comfortable club chair, he found some promising rentals in Enfield that would do for now.

"Mr. Redcake?"

Gawain looked up to see a waiter. "Yes?"

"There is a Mr. Bliven here to see you."

Gawain could not imagine who that might be. The only Bliven he knew was hiding in Madras the last he'd heard. "I do not know any Bliven."

"A Theodore Bliven."

Gawain would have shot to his feet if his hip allowed. What was this? "About my age, with curly dark hair, nearly black?"

The waiter nodded.

His entire body tensed. Should he see the man or send him away? He glanced around the room. This was a club of younger men, so there weren't any old fellows slumbering next to the fire. A couple of engineers played chess, and a carriage manufacturer was reading in a corner. None of his usual allies was about. He made a quick decision. "Tell him he can call on me at the house on St. James's Square in an hour."

"Yes, sir."

Gawain watched the waiter leave the room. He rubbed his forehead where pain had begun to gather and stayed in silent meditation for a few minutes, giving Bliven time to vacate the club. Then, he remembered he'd had a telephone installed and he could call Hatbrook House and see if the marquess was in town. He'd want to know. He might even have some advice.

Gawain was home twenty minutes later. Unfortunately, no one

answered the telephone at Hatbrook House. He tried to reach the Farm but the family was out for the evening. He would have to deal with Bliven on his own.

Pounds, the Redcake family butler, was in residence, and he came to the library to announce Bliven's arrival. The butler's face was impassive as he made his announcement.

"What do you think, Pounds?" Gawain asked. "You see Matilda and Jacob far more than I do. What would the reaction be? Should I toss him out on his ear?"

"Mr. Jacob is only fourteen months old," Pounds said. "If his father wants to come up to snuff, he's young enough not to remember when his father was gone."

"So you think if he's willing to marry Matilda now, that would be for the best?"

"To give her his name, at least. I shouldn't like her to be hurt. She's been through enough already."

"I quite agree. She's all the better for her suffering, I think, but it has been enough. Very well. Send him in."

Pounds nodded and a few moments later Gawain saw Hatbrook's old school chum walk in. Theodore Bliven, his tanned face showing every one of the wrinkles he had earned in thirty years, walked in with a somber expression. He had left England two years ago, claiming to have a fiancée waiting in India. At that time, he had thought to one day inherit an earldom. Gawain had heard that he'd been pushed down the line though, due to the birth of an unexpected heir. His trader Khan had said Bliven remained unmarried. Had he come for Matilda now that his prospects were gone?

"Bliven," Gawain said, staying seated behind his father's oversized desk.

The man stepped forward tentatively, then, at Gawain's imperious gesture, sat in front of the desk on a waiting chair.

"What brings you by?"

"I went to India with a charge from you," Bliven said.

"That was a long time ago."

"The trip alone took close to half that time, as you well know." After he spoke, Bliven seemed to realize that cheekiness would not go over well and swallowed hard. "Listen, I did a bit of this and that while I was there, but I took your business seriously." He reached into his jacket and took out a carved box, then set it on the desk and pushed it to Gawain.

"What's this?"

"I have tea as well. It's in the main hall. Four different kinds of single estate Assams. Enough to offer for sale. I spent half your money on expenses and half on goods. I hope you think that is fair." He glanced down at his hands, spread across his legs.

"What happened to your fiancée?"

"She had already married another before I arrived," Bliven said with a vague frown. "I had a fever when I arrived. I was supposed to meet her at a prearranged time and didn't make the appointment so she went to another suitor."

"How inconstant of her," Gawain said acidly.

Bliven met his gaze for the first time since he'd walked in. "You do not care about any of that. But this you will care for." He pointed at the box. "I got it in Kerala."

"What is it?"

"Dhanvantari's Nectar."

Gawain knew that Dhanvantari was the Hindoo physician to the gods in their religious lore. But he'd never heard of an herb called Dhanvantari's Nectar. "An herb?"

"A preparation, created by a family who practice the traditional medicine there."

"What is it for?"

"I remember you as a singularly focused man, Redcake. How you have changed. Why, of course, it is the preparation that will cure your damaged eye."

Gawain couldn't speak for a moment. He stared at the simple rosewood box. "Cure my eye, you say?"

"Yes. I described your symptoms at the temple there and this is what they gave me. They guaranteed it would work. I wouldn't have returned without it." He seemed to run out of breath.

"You wouldn't have returned unless you needed money," Gawain said, pulling the box toward him.

Bliven's mouth tightened.

"How many pounds of tea, did you say?" Gawain asked, opening the box. He found a fine dark powder, coarsely ground. When he sniffed he didn't recognize the main notes of the compound.

"Four hundred pounds. One hundred of each."

Gawain stood and limped to a painting, then pulled it aside and opened the safe. He pulled out some money, relocked the safe and pushed the bills across the desk. "For the tea."

"You already paid for it."

Gawain sat down and picked up the box again. "Go, Bliven. I want to be alone with my nectar."

Bliven pulled a sheet of paper from his coat and pushed it over. "Do you read Hindustani? These are the directions for the medicine."

Gawain did not read Hindustani. He swore softly.

"Want me to translate for you? I know it well enough."

Gawain fixed his gaze on Bliven. "Tell me."

Bliven smirked with more than a hint of his old bravado and pulled out another sheet of paper, this one written in English. "Here you go. I was going to charge you for this, but you've already paid me well. See? I'm an honest man."

"Get out," Gawain said, turning away with the sheet of translation clutched in his fist. He closed his eyes until he heard footsteps moving away, then the door opening. When it closed, the only sound in the room was the fire's crackle.

Could Theodore Bliven really have found a cure for his damaged eye? What would his return mean for Matilda and Jacob?

Chapter Six

"Take this to my father in the bakery." Betsy Popham showed Ann a large white Redcake's box meant for holding two-tiered cakes. "Her ladyship will be in for it at any moment."

"A titled lady is going to pick up her own cake?" Ann asked, allowing Betsy to transfer the heavy box from her own plump arms to Ann's.

"I know, but Alys set the style for ladies to pick up their own cakes. I believe she is taking it to her daughter's luncheon party or some such. You should take the elevator. It is safer."

Ann knew Alys was the Marchioness of Hatbrook. Betsy invoked her name often. Though the marchioness owned Redcake's now, she had once worked in the Fancy with Betsy. Of course, Alys was also Noel's aunt and Gawain's sister.

She went to the elevator with the cake box, but it was full of carts and irritated bakers.

"Take the steps," Alfred Melville, her supervisor, ordered.

"Yes, sir." Ann maneuvered down the hall and found the door to the stairs propped open. Thankfully, that did not spell disaster, as she was the only person on the staircase. It took some maneuvering to open the door at the top, and she could feel sweat on her forehead by the time she managed to turn the knob while still keeping the cake steady.

She made her way down another hall, narrowly missing two cakies with empty trays as she turned the corner to the passage just behind the bakery proper. When she went through the bakery, her hip bumped a cakie's and the box slipped in her hands. Her palms began to sweat, but she kept the box upright.

The other girl apologized profusely. "Is that the luncheon cake? My goodness, but her ladyship is impatient. She's only been here two minutes."

"We didn't know she'd actually arrived."

"Get the cake in there."

Ann tried to hand it to her, but she demurred. "No, I've got cocoa on my hands. I must wash."

Ann knew she didn't look her best, with her hair all frizzed from the heat downstairs and the stress of her trip up the stairs, but she straightened her spine and marched behind the long, tiled counter, which was covered by glass cases containing first-rate baked goods.

Ralph Popham, Betsy's father, frowned when he saw her and straightened the long graying hair plastered across the top of his head. She suspected that was a hint to tidy her hair, but the cake was much too heavy to manage one-handed. After making it to the counter without incident, she carefully set the cake down, then looked around for a likely candidate for her ladyship. When she saw a woman hovering by the éclairs, dressed a long maroon dress with velvet cuffs and collar, over an underskirt of embroidered white silk, she guessed she had found her aristocrat.

"Your ladyship?" she called.

The woman didn't respond. Ann turned to Ralph Popham, who nodded encouragement.

"Your ladyship," he said, coming to stand next to Ann. "Your cake is ready."

The lady approached them and looked down her long skinny nose at the bakery manager. "You allowed a darkie to carry my cake in here?"

Ann felt her spine lock into place but didn't respond. She remembered similar scenes when Wells had first taken possession of the inn. People soon forgot the color of her skin and simply noticed her superior cooking.

"S-she works downstairs," Popham stammered. "No one else must have been available to bring the cake up."

"You're sure she didn't touch it?" her ladyship demanded.

"It was already boxed when she came in," Popham said.

"Of course I touched it," Ann said without thinking. "I made this beautiful cake, your ladyship. Then it was decorated by Betsy Popham."

"Take it away," the woman said, staring at Popham. "I won't have it."

"I make many of the cakes here. I've been cooking and baking for years. No one has ever become ill from my food," Ann said.

Finally the woman allowed her bug-eyed gaze to descend on Ann. She seemed to focus on her hands. "How can anyone tell if a darkie is clean?" Then she sniffed and turned away.

"I'm cleaner than you," Ann cried, outraged. "I can see a stain on your left glove." She slapped her hands on the counter. "Look, perfectly clean."

"Mr. Popham," the lady said over her shoulder. "I will never patronize your establishment again if this, er, person, continues to be employed. Do you understand me?"

"Yes, my lady," he said, giving her a brisk nod. "Ann, pack your things and go home."

"You aren't my supervisor," she said.

"I will tell Melville that you shouted at a customer. Now, that will do. We'll send on your wages."

He wouldn't even look at her. No surprise, given his exaggeration of what she'd done. She folded her lips between her teeth, snatched up the heavy box, and ran through the passages until she reached the elevator. No one stopped her and the Fancy was empty when she pushed the door open.

An hour later, she found herself at home, with a huge, heavy cake box, her coat and reticule, and no memory of anything that had transpired since Ralph Popham, that coward, had told her to go.

Fern took one look at her face before her lips started to tremble. She closed the front door and took the box to the kitchen table.

"They sacked me." Ann's eyes started to burn with humiliation, and they fell into each other's arms, crying, like they hadn't done since Wells died.

* * *

Ann had somehow found calm by the time the landlady knocked on their door shortly before five PM. She had been going over her accounts with Noel in her lap. Without a position, they were going to have to return to Leeds. The reality was that life was easier here in London. If she went back to the inn, she'd have to resume all the cooking and take up with her patients again. She didn't have the energy to work from before dawn to after dusk seven days a week as well as care for Noel. There would be no handy wet nurse at the inn either.

Redcake's, with its five-and-a-half-day work week and settled hours, not to mention the excellent pay, had been perfect for her. Fern could manage their small flat with ease after years of cleaning inn rooms. All she could do was scan the papers for another position, and this time, make sure she stayed hidden from paying customers.

"How can I help you?" she asked the landlady, settling Noel's head on her shoulder.

"There's a gentleman to see you. Same one as before."

Gawain. "Thank you. Please tell him to come up." She knew he'd come a couple of days ago when she'd been at work, but hadn't returned since.

"I don't like the idea of you having male callers."

"He's a patient," Ann said. "I'm a healer. Remember? I explained that."

The woman sniffed and walked away.

While Ann hovered at the door, listening for him on the stairs, she heard the bells of a local church. Five PM. Gawain had waited until she was home from work before calling. He obviously didn't know what had happened. At least he couldn't be blamed for her misadventures.

She saw a bowler hat at the top of the stairs, then he appeared, his strong warrior's face focused, that broad body so powerful, even with its determined, limping gait. Her breath caught in her chest as her very flesh remembered the elemental attraction they shared.

He nodded when he saw her and she inclined her head with a gracious ease that belied her fast pulse.

"To what do I owe the pleasure of this visit?" she asked.

"You know we have many things to discuss," he said soberly, but then his face broke into an amazing grin that she'd never seen before. It made him look almost a boy, if it weren't for the hawk's nose that made him look so wicked.

"What?" she said, with an answering smile. His grin was as contagious as it was unexpected.

"I had the, well, someone I never wanted to see again came to the square with this." He reached into his greatcoat pocket and pulled out a box. Then he dug under his coat and pulled out a sheet of paper, thrusting them both at her.

"You had better come in." She turned without taking either, since she had Noel. Fern came from the kitchen to take him. Gawain stopped her, and bent down to give the baby a kiss. Noel didn't wake. Fern took him with a nod and went back into the kitchen.

Gawain's gaze took in the room. She wondered if he noticed there were no signs of packing, but he didn't mention that. As soon as her arms were free he handed her his box and paper again.

"Take a look," he urged. "Have you heard of this?"

"This what?" She stared at the square wood box.

"Dhanvantari's Nectar."

Medicine. "No. What are the ingredients? This isn't a very large portion of whatever it is."

"I have twenty pounds of the stuff," he assured her. "Back at the house. All direct from India, courtesy of Theodore Bliven."

"I've never heard the name," she murmured, moving to the fireplace to peruse the paper.

"You will learn all about him soon enough. He is the father of my nephew Jacob."

"That is one of the babies, correct?"

"Yes, the oldest of Noel's generation. He's a year old, Matilda's son."

"So this Bliven went to India."

"Yes, he travelled to Kerala at one point and met a family of physicians. When he described my eye damage, they gave him this."

"There are certainly legitimate physicians in Kerala, who have a special affinity for Dhanvantari," she told him. "It appears that this is a raw compound. It needs to be boiled and strained, then used as an eyewash." She opened the container and sniffed.

"Do you recognize any of it?"

"I believe it is based on the ingredients of *maha triphala ghee*. It needs to be prepared with ghee and milk, then left to sit overnight in water. The eyewash I'm familiar with has thirteen herbs but I expect this mixture has twenty or so. It is a complex procedure. First honey in the eye, then this mixture, then ghee. An hour of your day will need to be devoted to it." She perused the sheet again. "I can finish the receipt for you, so you can complete the preparation. Do you have good honey and ghee, the clarified butter?"

"Yes, that will not be a problem."

"Then come back tomorrow. I will have it prepared and dried for you. You'll be able to start Wednesday morning."

He sat down in her single armchair as if suddenly deflating. "How long do you think it will take to have an effect?"

"Your eyes will probably burn the first few days," she warned.

"That isn't what I mean. How long before I know if it is helping?"

"A month or two. You should discontinue the program if you don't see any results after that."

His lips curved. "And how long should I continue my program with you?"

"What do you mean?" She put her back to the fire and faced him.

"How often should I ask you to marry me? How often should I demand you move to my family home? I have been looking for houses for us in Enfield."

"You haven't asked me today." She thought about the few pounds she had left, the need to eat good food so that she could feed Noel. Clothes for a growing baby. Coal for the fire. The censure she would face back in Leeds for having an illegitimate child.

His gaze left the box she was holding and moved to her face. "You are correct. I have not been following my own program. Ann, will you marry me?"

She shivered. Could she tolerate a loveless marriage? Or to phrase it better, could she bring a husband who didn't love her to love? Gawain had not yet had a chance to love her, but at least he had come looking for her. He had come twice, to Leeds and then to London. He loved Noel already. Thankfully, he had no doubts there. She was lucky the baby took after the Redcakes and not her family.

Going back to Leeds felt wrong. She had to move forward for Noel's sake. Clasping her hands around her upper arms, she whispered, "Yes."

"Yes?" he said doubtfully.

She swallowed hard and nodded. "Yes. It will be best for all of us. You caught me by surprise last week, but yes."

He moved his head back and forth as if beating time. "Would you like a civil or religious marriage? We can be married a bit sooner with a civil marriage."

The unromantic nature of the moment deflated her further. "Will you not kiss me to celebrate?" she asked. "And worry about details some other time?"

He let his cane drop to the ground next to the armchair. With a wolfish grin, he reached for her arm and pulled her down to him. He sighed and set his head against her shoulder. "I should not remember the feel of you, Ann, but I do."

"My body is completely different since Noel. And I don't even smell the same."

"You smell like cake and wind now," he said. "It's not a bad thing. But there is still a spicy under-layer that will never leave you."

She wriggled. "I am glad to hear it." He held her firm. "Don't do that, not with Fern here."

She allowed him to wrap his arms around her and kiss her neck. Closing her eyes, she wondered what he would think of her if he knew why she said yes.

Gawain arrived at Ann's flat the next evening, excited to pick up his Ayurvedic treatment. He'd done two of the three steps that morning, to practice using the ghee and honey in his eye. It had stung and been messy, no doubt about it. But, if he could reverse his sight loss it would be worth the trouble. Recently, his hip trouble had superseded his one-eye blindness, but no more. Ann had given him a massage the evening before with her infused sesame oil, and he already felt lighter on his feet. She had been the cool, assured woman of medicine with him, rather than the sensual lover, but he could see the idea of remarriage troubled her. As long as she married him, he would not question her moods.

Fern opened the door to him and offered a small smile before holding out her hands to receive his outerwear. He gave her his cane as well, and tucked his fingers into his bright yellow waistcoat. Yes, he was feeling sunny. He'd written his family to announce his engagement. His child he would introduce in person. It wouldn't take long for them to come rushing into London full of questions. One look at Noel would answer all of those.

"You look very pleased with yourself," Ann said, stepping across the room with Noel in her arms.

He plucked the child from her.

"He needs burping," she warned, smoothing a rag over his shoulder. "Here, let me show you what to do."

Gawain patted the baby's back until the desired effect was achieved. "No mess," he declared, pulling Noel away from his shoulder, his hand carefully guarding his neck.

Fern put on a little hat and pointed to the door.

"Wear your shawl, dear," Ann said. "It is cold in the hallway."

The girl made a face but bundled herself up properly.

"She has to have some fresh air," Ann said.

"It's not very fresh out there," Gawain said as Ann led him into the kitchen. "Tell me, she seems very intelligent. Has she always been mute?"

"No, not at all."

"When did it begin? Did a doctor see her?"

"No doctor necessary. I know the exact cause." She spoke over her shoulder from the stove.

"What is that?"

"Trauma."

He could not help taking a close look at Ann's loose housedress. It would be easy to remove, but how long would Fern be gone? "To her throat?"

"No." She set a steaming teapot down on the table. "Are you sure you want to know?"

"Why wouldn't I? She's going to be part of my household, if not exactly a relative of mine."

"I won't have her turned into a servant."

"Of course not," Gawain said. "I have plenty of money for servants."

"That does not always stop people from taking advantage of young girls. I will return," she said, moving swiftly out of the room.

She must be going to get his medicine. He stretched out his legs, relieving pressure on his hip. Noel snuffled and turned his head. Gawain kissed the bit of his forehead that was visible beneath his tiny knitted cap. "Do you need anything for the baby? Anything I can purchase?"

She walked back in, carrying a box. Not his rosewood box, but a larger one. When she set it on the table, she gave him a considering glance.

"You don't know about this, I suspect, or you'd have said something," she told him.

"I take it this isn't about my medicine," he agreed.

"Keep a firm grip on Noel. I don't want you to startle him."

He had no idea why she'd said that, but he wrapped his arms firmly around his warm little bundle. Ann unlocked the box with a key from around her neck, and rifled through a sheath of papers. Finally, she pulled one out and spread it open on the table in front of him.

His first impression was red. Lots of red paint. Then, he began to understand, as the horror of the painted scene hit him. It was childish work, but the man depicted was nonetheless undeniably dead. He was mature, with dark hair and staring blue eyes. Blood dripped from lips of almost the same color. He saw some kind of stick poked into the man's torso in a couple of places, bloody wounds in others. When he saw the man was wearing an old uniform jacket, he thought he understood. "Wells?"

She pursed her lips together and nodded. "Fern found him. She's never spoken a word since. She screamed continuously that morning until I got enough poppy syrup into her to put her to sleep. That was the end of her voice."

"She was ten?"

"Yes. I had given her a box of paints that year and she drew this about a week after the murder. She's never painted since." She folded the disturbing image back into her box.

Gawain wondered what else was in the box. "I did not know your husband had been murdered. At the inn?"

"Yes. I had hoped leaving there would help her."

He wondered why she had waited so long, given that she had the ability to support herself. "She seems happy enough now. Does she have nightmares?"

"If she does they are silent," Ann said. "I'm a heavy sleeper."

"I should ask if your husband's murder was solved."

"No." She glanced away. As if just noticing the teapot, she jumped up and started pouring fresh dark tea into teacups.

He had to say it. "Of course, you didn't kill him."

"No." She frowned and added sugar to the teacups.

She was being evasive, but not suspicious. "Do you know who did?"

She poured milk in next. "No idea. We suspected a horse thief, because Fern found Wells in the stable."

"Were any horses missing?"

She set a teacup in front of him. "No, but Wells could have surprised someone."

He smelled Indian spices wafting from the cup. "Did anyone suspect you?"

"Never, Gawain." She took a deep breath and he knew he was about to hear the rest of a bad story. He freed one hand and she grasped it. "I was with child. Visibly. And I lost the baby after. The baby stopped moving inside me and I went into labor a day later. I was out of my mind. I loved Wells so much. To lose the child too—"

"You must have been devastated." He wanted to reach for her, but he had the baby against his chest.

She squeezed his hand and stared at Noel. "I was lost. But Fern needed me, and I didn't have anywhere to go. I owned the inn, after all, as Wells's widow. But I never went in the stable again."

"Of course not," Gawain said. "How could you?"

"You don't think I'm a coward?"

"Not at all." He squeezed her hand and smiled at her. "I am amazed you stayed as long as you did, especially with the crime unsolved."

"His killer was long gone." She withdrew her hand and stirred the contents of her teacup. "I can't imagine he would ever return to The Old Hart for fear of discovery."

Noel snuffled and bleated. Ann immediately reached for him, and when the baby was calm, she insisted on massaging Gawain's hip again. Like the previous night, her touch was impersonal but effective. When he had dressed again, she handed him an oiled pouch containing his mixture.

"You have the instructions," she said.

"I do. I look forward to trying it."

"It will be painful."

He laughed. "You know I am used to pain." His hip felt ten degrees hotter than the rest of his body, thanks to her manipulations.

But he knew he would walk better tomorrow as a result. Would he see better too?

"Take a day to rest your hip, then come again on Thursday," she said.

"I'd like to see Noel every day."

"Very well. Come in the evenings." Her eyes narrowed for a moment, then her impassive expression took hold again.

He nodded. "Tomorrow we shall discuss our wedding plans."

She glanced at the ceiling for a moment before looking back at him. "Until tomorrow."

He put his hand on her shoulder, then kissed her cheek, hoping she would turn into the kiss. She didn't. As he left the flat, he wondered what it was about their engagement that she disliked so much. Was she upset that she hadn't received a betrothal gift? Or that he hadn't spoken to the head of her family? Did she consider Harry Haldene to be the head of her family?

He considered going to Leeds to talk to Harry, since Fern couldn't tell him anything. But for now, he found a cab and went home, clutching his precious pouch of herbs.

The next morning he was resolved to deal with a mound of correspondence and visit his warehouses, but the first post brought a letter from Hatbrook Farm.

This was nothing unusual. Too much of his family resided or visited there, but he rarely had a note from the marquess himself. He always opened these wondering if he was being notified that Lady Beth had returned home. It couldn't yet be a congratulatory note as there had not been time for a response, or indeed, time for his letter to have arrived in the south.

He glanced at it again and realized he'd been so distracted by the pain lingering in his eye from the treatment that he hadn't noticed it wasn't a letter but a telegram.

He slit it open and stared at the words.

FAMILY EMERGENCY COME AT ONCE

Chapter Seven

Late that afternoon, Gawain stepped down from the cab and went up the front steps at Hatbrook Farm. He wondered all the way south what had happened. Something with one of the babies? A health emergency for one of his parents? But that telegram would most likely have come from Redcake Manor.

Mindful of Ann's revelation about Noel's early birth, he wondered if Alys was expecting again and something had gone wrong.

Matthew, one of the footmen, opened the door. "Oh good," he exclaimed.

Gawain raised an eyebrow. "What is going on?"

"It's a right mess, Mr. Redcake. Everyone is at sixes and sevens."

"I assume your master is well. Your mistress?"

"Very angry, both of them."

Angry. Well, this was a clue. In fact, he even had a suspect. "Has Theodore Bliven made an appearance?" Why had he not thought of what Bliven would do next? The man must have returned to England looking for more than money.

Matthew nodded vigorously. "He has, and a dreadful racket it has been around here ever since he appeared last night, expecting a bed from the marquess as if they were still the best of friends."

"Did Hatbrook give him one?"

"Sent him to the inn and said they would talk in the morning.

But then who arrives today? Miss Matilda, here to celebrate Lady Redcake's birthday."

Gawain slapped his hand to his forehead. His mother's birthday. It had completely slipped his mind. At least he'd sent a card on Friday, just before he'd seen Ann again. But this reminded him that today was Valentine's Day and he should have sent something to Ann, even if she didn't want to see him today.

Why wouldn't she have wanted to see him on this lover's holiday? Perhaps it had slipped her mind. Neither of them had expected to be engaged, after all. Should he send a telegram? He couldn't get back to London tonight.

"Why didn't Matilda go to Redcake Manor?"

"Lady Mary Ellen has a cold and Lady Hatbrook didn't want her to leave the house, so everyone came here."

"Even me," he said with a sigh. "Is Bliven here now?"

"Everyone is here," Matthew said with emphasis. "In the winter parlor."

Gawain held out his hands as if they were manacled together. "Take me to the battle."

Matthew took his valise and Gawain stepped into the passage. He retained his cane, the travel having already diminished the effects of the previous night's massage, but he was pleased to see he didn't really need it for balance.

Matthew, ahead of him, threw open the double doors into the winter parlor. Alys had refreshed the room with ivory wallpaper flecked with ivy leaves. Fires burned in enormous fireplaces on each end of the long room. All traces of the trademark rose furnishings of Hatbrook's late mother had vanished in favor of tasseled green sofas and solid tables that no baby could push over. Vividly imagined paintings of rural landscapes decorated the walls. Gawain wondered who had chosen the paintings. They seemed far more Hatbrook than his sister, who would probably have decorated her home like she had decorated Redcake's, with photographs of cakes.

He hovered in the doorway, thinking he'd like Ann and Noel to be photographed. There were plenty of studios in London. The thought left his mind when he saw his father's florid face in an attitude of outraged anger as he rose from one of the sofas.

"How could you allow that man to descend on us again? And you gave him money?" Sir Bartley Redcake stalked toward him.

Gawain thumped the floor with his cane and moved forward to meet his father. "Bliven is gone again?"

"He is in the village as we speak."

"Better than being in the house. What has it to do with me?"

"He told us he saw you."

"Yes, he came to my club. I did meet with him at the house. You know I had hired him before I knew of his, er, inappropriateness with Matilda."

Matilda stood, white-faced, clutching her son Jacob a bit too tightly.

"What?" he asked his sister. "He came with goods that I had paid for. Why shouldn't I see him?"

She turned away. Sir Bartley tucked his fingers into his waist-coat pockets and glared at him. "Not well done, Gawain, and on your mother's birthday, too."

Gawain waved to his mother. "Happy birthday, Mother."

She smiled faintly, then bent her head to baby Lady Mary Ellen, who was snuggled in her arms.

"Did anyone receive the letter with my news?" he inquired.

"What news was that?" Hatbrook asked, setting a newspaper aside. He was tucked into the corner of a sofa next to Alys.

"My engagement?"

He heard Matilda squeak her outrage. She had the right to be annoyed, but he wanted the subject changed. Why hadn't he sent a cable to the Farm instead of hopping the next train? Still, he supposed he'd have to be the one to confront Bliven in the village.

"I haven't seen the mail today," Hatbrook said. His gaze met Gawain's.

He knew the marquess was thinking of their chat so long ago when he'd asked for Beth's hand in marriage. Hatbrook must think this was his way of moving on, giving up on Hatbrook's sister. The family would soon find out the truth, that there was a baby involved here as well.

"Her name is Ann Haldene. Her parents were a British officer and an Indian maharani. She is the widow of a Lieutenant Wells Haldene, who perished a couple of years ago."

"Where did you meet such a person?" Sir Bartley asked.

"In Leeds. She owns an inn there. Lord Judah and Cousin Lewis met her as well."

"Right when Beth disappeared?" Hatbrook said. "You've been courting her all this time?"

"No," Gawain said. "She's come to London now." He did not reveal she worked at Redcake's. Alys would figure that out soon enough.

"Absurd," Sir Bartley said. "Why on earth would you choose a half-Indian innkeeper to be your bride?"

"She has royal blood," Hatbrook said. "And no doubt some aristocratic connections here in England, given that she's the daughter of an officer."

"Not that I'm aware of," Gawain said blandly. "When you meet her, you will understand my commitment to her. We will marry soon."

"From the Manor?" his mother asked.

"No, in London. We will be making our home there. I have no connection to Sussex and neither does she."

"And I'm exiled to Bristol," Matilda said bitterly. "Aren't you going to ask what Mr. Bliven wanted?"

"Tell me," Gawain said, "if you are so inclined."

"He wanted to see his son," she said.

"Did you allow him?"

"No." Her mouth twisted. "After what he did I owe him nothing."

He glanced around the room, looking for the final member of the family party, his sister Rose. "Where is Rose?"

"She is at the Manor," Alys said. "With a fever. She didn't want to pass it to the babies."

"Do you want me to go to the inn and tell Bliven to get the next train out of here?" Gawain asked.

"I can do that," Sir Bartley growled.

"Then why send for me?" He turned back to Hatbrook. "I thought a serious illness or accident had taken place, rather than an emotional maelstrom."

"Your name was being impugned, given that Theodore said he'd seen you," Hatbrook said.

"Forgotten telephones exist?" Gawain asked. "You could have called the house. I had a telephone put in for business."

"A telephone is not a good mechanism for a family meeting," Hatbrook said.

"Matilda can make her own decisions. She is, what, twenty-three now, and a mother. What do you want to do, Matilda?"

Her lips trembled. Her skin had never looked more pale against her shocking orange hair. "I would have said a son should know his father, but such a father."

"I can learn his intentions if they were not clearly stated," Gawain said.

"Are you going to do more business with him?" Sir Bartley asked.

"That all depends on the quality of his offerings. The tea is good but it will be a month before I know if the herbs he found are efficacious."

"What kind of herbs?" Alys asked. "Culinary?"

"No, medicinal. I am testing them now."

"Did he explain himself?" Matilda asked.

He could tell she was close to shrieking. "His fiancée married someone else before he could get to her. I can't say more than that, like why he didn't write to propose to you when that marriage fell through."

"I expect he stayed in India until your money ran out, then came back with whatever dregs he could drag up to sell to you," Hatbrook said.

"None of it was dregs," Gawain said. "He made some effort. I did not have a long conversation with him."

"Why not?" Matilda demanded. "Do you not think it was your duty to do so?"

"Without knowing what you want, Matilda, what would I ask? Do you want him to marry you?"

"Of course not," she snapped.

"Why not? Isn't it the right thing for Jacob?"

"I can take care of him."

Because their father allowed her the money to do so. He shared doubts with his father about his sister's ability to manage the mills and factories, but his father was letting her try. Rather shocking, really. "Then that is an end to the matter. I'll rid ourselves of him."

"I can do that," his father said.

Gawain threw up one hand. "Then do so, and kindly leave me

out of it." He limped to his mother and kissed her cheek. "I am sorry I did not bring a gift."

"Just seeing you is gift enough," Ellen Redcake said. "Will you stay for dinner?"

"I shall have to, given the time of day." He gestured to a lingering maid to bring him a chair and resolved to spend the evening avoiding both Matilda and his father.

Out of sheer stubbornness he was successful, and after dinner excused himself to ride down to the inn. Upon entering Hatbrook's stable, he was reminded of Wells Haldene's death in a similar milieu. He didn't like the idea of leaving such a mystery unsolved. How could the family be so sure it was a random crime? What if the murderer eventually came after Ann, Fern or Noel? The only reason he could think of not to solve it would be that the person who did the killing was more important to Ann than the crime itself. He didn't suspect her for a moment, as she had clearly been besotted with her husband. Then there was Harry Haldene. How much prestige and money had he received by the happy accident of his brother's death?

He had the stableman find him a horse with a steady gait, since he was much too urban a fellow to ride often, and went into the village. Past the pub where he'd met Sergeant Bowler Martin the year before, he ran across an ancient inn, wreathed in Tudor charm. As it was the closest to the Farm he suspected he'd find Bliven inside.

In fact, Bliven was the first soul he ran across, seated on a low chair in front of the fireplace in the main room. The man didn't look at all surprised to see him, just lifted a thin, tanned finger to the serving woman. She came over as Gawain pulled off his muffler and unbuttoned his coat.

"A bottle of port," he said. "One glass."

Bliven chuckled. "Not going to share?"

"You are turning into a demander," Gawain said flatly.

"I am no blackmailer. I simply wanted to see my son."

"Did you not realize that my sister is his mother? A real, flesh and blood woman you ruined?" Gawain bared his teeth at the man when Bliven tried to speak. "I don't care what the particulars were. You knew you had no intention of marrying her if she got into trouble, and she fancied quite the opposite."

"I just wanted to see my son," Bliven repeated calmly.

"And then what?" The woman brought the port, an inferior bottle, he guessed from the looks of it, and set it down on a small table, then added a glass. He tossed her a coin.

"I don't know. Isn't it natural for me to want to see my own child?"

"He's as little your child as it is possible to be. Why don't you go away?" He poured himself a glass and took a sip. The port had a sour taste to it.

"I haven't decided what I want to do yet. Wasn't sure of the lay of the land, you understand. I had a letter that said Matilda had all but died with the boy's birth, you know, but she's blooming now. I never cared for freckles, but on her they are charming."

Bliven's mischievous smile made Gawain want to growl. He set his glass aside. "Why did you ever court her at all?"

Bliven shrugged and those damn curls of his fell over his brow. "I was meant to take a look at your twin, you know, Alys. I can't quite explain how things went the way they did with Matilda. I suppose I had an itch to scratch and she was all kinds of willing."

With a smirk, Bliven stood to stir the fire. When it was leaping to his satisfaction, he set the poker down. Gawain's blood boiled hotter by the second, fueled by sheer rage and family insult. When Bliven turned back again, grinning at him with those merry eyes, Gawain leapt to his feet and slammed his fist into the man's jaw. Bliven fell back into the armchair, a look of astonishment on his face.

Without another word, Gawain stormed out the door and into the stable yard, shaking his hand free of the pain. He found his horse and mounted, then headed back to the Farm. Why were some men so unwilling to deal with the consequences of their actions? Perhaps he shouldn't have hit Bliven, but no sane man would have been provoked to a different response.

The next day, he hung around all morning and into the early afternoon, gratified to see that Bliven had not made another appearance. He spent the time consulting with his father and twin about aspects of the Redcakes' businesses that touched upon each other's interests. Only Hatbrook noticed his swollen knuckles.

"Took care of him in a direct fashion?" he asked after luncheon.

"A momentary lapse of civility," Gawain said.

"But a reasonable one. Do you want me to take you to the train in the trap?"

"I wonder why you don't have one of Lewis's horseless carriage contraptions down here. The roads are good enough."

"No mechanic," Hatbrook said. "Judah says they are forever needing repairs."

Gawain felt himself smiling. If the carriage hadn't broken last year, he'd never have met Ann. Noel would never have been born. "Just a challenge for a mechanic."

"If I run across a good man, I'll have to commission a carriage from Lewis." Hatbrook rang for a footman to go to the stable and have the trap brought around.

An hour later, Gawain had said his goodbyes to his family and was on the way to the station with Hatbrook.

"It has not escaped your attention that no one is discussing your engagement," Hatbrook said.

"Out of sensitivity for Matilda, no doubt," Gawain said. "What with Bliven prowling around."

"Or out of distaste."

"If my family forgets its humble beginnings, I shall be pleased to remind them," Gawain growled. "Ten years ago, if I'd found myself an inn owner the family would have been thrilled, no matter the color of her skin."

"You've quite given up on Beth," Hatbrook said, snapping the reins.

Gawain saw a muscle twitch in his cheek. "We'll never give up on finding her, but marriage is certainly off the table. You'll understand when you meet Mrs. Haldene."

"When you marry you'll have no time to go to Scotland anymore." Hatbrook held his body rigidly, and didn't look at Gawain.

"Judah has continued to travel and so have I. Be glad that I have business interests there now. It's another reason to visit."

"I wonder if Beth is even in Scotland anymore."

Gawain stared at his hands. The left one was too swollen to fit in his usual gloves and it was now red with cold. "I have begun to doubt it myself. I must say, I have no faith in inquiry agents."

"All this reminds me of Judah in India, back when we thought he was dead. He wasn't though. It was all a misunderstanding. I just have to hope that in the end this resolves in the same way. The family reunited, everyone happy."

"And unsuitable marriages all around."

Hatbrook's hands clenched around the reins and then relaxed. "The good news is Alys and I are happy, and so are Judah and Magdalene. I wish the same for you and your Mrs. Haldene."

"The heart knows what society does not," Gawain said.

"Or intelligent people can make the best of things. Luckily, neither my brother nor I have a great deal of interest in the fashionable world. Of the four of us, only Magdalene does."

"Has that been a problem?" Lord Judah seemed happy enough.

"I'm sure there are compromises."

"I understand they only go out one night a week. That way Magdalene can see people and Lord Judah gets enough sleep."

"A good compromise."

He would be giving up some of his future dreams in exchange for a son. And for a woman he lusted after. Still, he hung some hope on the Queen's fascination with India, keeping the door from shutting entirely on his plans.

"At any rate, don't give up on Beth. This summer, I hope to go up to Scotland myself, and see if a marquess can rattle any gates."

"We won't give up until we find her," Gawain said as the trap pulled up to the station. He offered Hatbrook his hand.

"Thank you for coming down," Hatbrook said. "I'll keep tabs on Theodore."

"I'll let you know if he approaches me again."

"Please do. And I hope the new medicine works. You seem to be walking a bit better."

"Mrs. Haldene," Gawain said. "She's an accomplished healer."

"That is worth a great deal to you," Hatbrook said. "I look forward to hearing more details."

"I'm going to go to her home tonight and try to coax a wedding date out of her." Gawain clamped his hat to his head as the wind gusted. "I've got to go if I want to catch the train."

Hatbrook lifted his hand in goodbye, and turned the horses as Gawain moved into the station, already focusing his thoughts on London.

At five PM, he descended upon Catherine Street, carrying a receiving blanket and rattle he'd found in a shop, as well as a small cooked joint he'd bought. The warm package kept his hands toasty and it would make a good dinner too. He navigated the steps painfully after the landlady announced him.

Ann opened the door. "Well, hello. I thought we would see you yesterday."

"I apologize. I had to go down to my twin's home in Sussex for a couple of days."

She stepped aside so he could enter. He stooped to kiss her cheek, even though she hadn't exactly invited it. Still, she was his fiancée.

She smiled at him. "That was unexpected?"

Good. The kiss had been welcome. "Yes. But it resulted in me being even more certain that we must marry soon. We can get a license to marry in fifteen days, or have banns called, which will take closer to a month, I suppose."

"We can discuss it later." She turned in to the kitchen, where Fern sat at the table, scrubbing potatoes.

He set down his joint and other package. "No, Ann. I want to get our marriage plans under way. For Noel."

Fern glanced up at him and he spoke to her. "You agree, don't you, Fern? I want to give Ann and Noel my protection. You as well. I live in a beautiful house. You'll never want for anything."

Fern frowned at her potatoes.

"No more scrubbing," he said.

"Do not say that," Ann protested. "I still have the inn, after all."

"You'll never have to work a day. Not at The Old Hart, not at Redcake's. You can focus on Noel and our other, future children. Fern can have a dowry."

The girl began to slice the raw potatoes with great deliberation.

"I brought a joint for dinner," Gawain said. He pushed the warm package toward Fern. After a minute, she lifted a finger to it and stroked it.

"I can afford meat for my family," Ann snapped.

"I never said you couldn't."

Fern stared at Ann. She stomped to the table and picked up the package. "Get the potatoes in the water or the joint will be cold before they are done."

Fern grinned and jumped up from the table.

"What is in the other package?"

"A blanket and rattle for Noel. I know he hasn't discovered his hands yet, but he'll have fun with it when he does. And the blanket is very soft. My niece has one just like it."

"Is your family well?" she asked in a softer voice.

"Yes, just a little disruption thanks to our Mr. Bliven. It was also my mother's birthday. And I announced our engagement. I haven't told them about Noel yet. I want them to see him."

"Are they happy for you?"

"I'm sure they will be, but since it is known that I had asked for Beth's hand in marriage, and her fate is still unknown, my announcement is bittersweet."

"That poor girl. I wonder what became of her?"

Gawain shrugged. "Maybe she and Manfred went out to India or one of the other colonies. It will take a long time to find out. But Theodore Bliven has put in an appearance, so I'm sure we'll find them too, in the end."

"Did Mr. Bliven show up down south?"

"Yes, wanting to see his son."

She glanced away. "How are your eyes?"

"No change as of yet. The mixture still hurts my eye during the application."

She nodded. "It's too soon for anything else. Of course, your limp has returned fully with the traveling."

"Your ministrations will be welcome," he admitted.

"Then come, while Noel is asleep and the potatoes are cooking."

An hour later, she had given him an oil massage and they had eaten dinner. Noel was wrapped in his new blanket. Ann fed him by the fire and Gawain read an old magazine at the kitchen table while Fern darned a pair of her stockings.

He took surreptitious glances at her, wondering if her speech would ever return. When he and Ann were married, he would take Fern to a psychopathologist. There must be a cure for her muteness. He wondered if she could have seen the killer and not just her brother's body.

"Did you see who killed Wells?" he whispered.

Fern looked up from her darning, her forehead creasing.

"When you found him, did you see anyone else?"

She shook her head, not angrily, just confused. And why not? He had asked the question in a random fashion.

"Do you know who murdered him?"

She shook her head again, a short, nervous movement.

"Would you like to know?" he tried.

She stared at him, then looked down at her stocking, and nodded. Then shook her head no.

He pulled a notebook from his jacket and a pencil. "Do you know who did it?"

She took the paper and pencil from him and made a tiny notation in one corner before handing it back. He looked down and found she'd written "10."

"Ten pounds? Someone stole ten pounds?"

She shook her head and pointed to herself.

"Oh. You're saying you were only ten years old when Wells died."

She nodded.

"I suppose you are right. Ten is pretty young. But not too young to work, right? We are a lot alike, you and me. I had to work for my family at ten too. In a factory. We weren't wealthy then."

She reached out and clasped the lapel of his jacket between thumb and forefinger.

"Yes, it's good cloth. I have plenty of money now. Too much to ever find myself working in a factory again. And you'll be comfortable too. We'll find you a good husband and you'll have a home of your own in a few years."

Fern let go of his lapel and took up the pencil again. She drew quickly and he saw her first figure was Ann. Then she drew a man, but scratched a deep cross mark over him, cancelling him out. Then she drew tears coming from the Ann figure's eyes. So many tears they formed a pool at her feet.

"She lost a baby too. Not just her husband."

Fern drew a smaller figure with arms wrapped around Ann. The baby? No, it was herself, Gawain saw, as she drew long hair and a dress on the child.

"You love her a great deal," he observed. "I'll take good care of her."

She stared at him.

"I won't let myself be killed. How about that? I survived being a soldier, you know." He pointed to the scar running down his cheek. "That's how I got this. A bloodthirsty Pathan took a knife to me after I fell, thanks to a bullet in my hip. Lord Judah Shield, the manager where Ann works, rescued me. Have you met him? He's a solid fellow. We'll have to have him to dinner when we're settled in a new house."

She frowned. Probably didn't like her attention being drawn to his scar. No female did. That's why he wore the patch over his eye, to hide the worst of it. That part of his cheek displayed not much more than a thin white line these days, but it was puckered at the top. Still, if he got his vision back, he'd throw away the patch and damn the ladies.

"How about this? I'll go up to Leeds, talk to your brother and see what he says about Wells. Maybe uncover something for you and Ann. Would you like that?"

She nodded, then shook her head.

He decided to take it as a yes. "Very well. I'll do just that, as soon as we take care of matters at a church, for the wedding."

She stared unblinking.

"You'll have to have a new dress for the occasion. You and Ann both. What do you think? Shall I accompany you ladies to a dress-maker's shop after we organize the banns?"

She bit her lip and nodded.

"What is your favorite color?" he asked.

Before she could think of a way to tell him, Ann came into the kitchen. "Noel is back to sleep."

He could see a droop in her eyelids. "You look tired."

"He woke up hungry three times last night. Usually he's up only twice."

"He just wants to be with his mother. I completely understand."

She smiled faintly. "I think I'll have some hot chocolate and then retire."

Fern jumped up and Gawain was touched by how eager the girl was to care for Ann.

"I have an idea. Let's go to the local church on Monday and make arrangements to be married. After that, I promised Fern we'd buy you both new dresses for the wedding."

"You promised Fern?"

"Yes, we're starting to understand each other, I think." He pulled the sheet of paper from the table as casually as possible and folded it over, not wanting her to see the crossed out image of her late hus-band.

"Why don't we go tomorrow?" said Ann. "Then the first banns can be called on Sunday."

He put his hand over his heart and smiled. "Yes, I like that even better. Do you have a parish?"

She nodded, taking Fern's chair and pulling it over to him. "We go to the church just around the corner. I'm sure the vicar there will marry us."

He leaned over to her and cupped her cheeks with his palms. "That is just the plan. Thank you."

Her lips curved and he couldn't help swooping in for a kiss. Soft lips welcomed his, parting slightly. After a moment of shared breath, he pulled back, smiling at her. He resolved to spend the train journey to Leeds poring over the advertisements for an acceptable house to rent.

They needed their privacy.

Chapter Eight

Gawain was to marry Ann Haldene on March the sixth. The meeting at the church had gone well and the first banns had already been called. As planned, he had boarded the train for Leeds, but only after postponing the trip until Tuesday to have two additional massage treatments from Ann. He had also acquired a companion for his journey.

He turned his head to Lewis, who was perusing a newspaper. He'd run into his cousin at his club two nights before and over a celebratory glass of champagne had told him about the Leeds trip. Lewis had insisted he come along since he'd been planning to talk again with the blacksmith they'd met about some metalsmithing.

"I must say, I thought I was more the domestic type than you are," Lewis said. "Never thought I'd see you married first."

Neither did I. "May I tell you a secret? You can never admit you knew this before Alys."

Lewis lifted an eyebrow and set down his newspaper. "Before Alys, Cousin? My, you two have drifted apart."

"You must admit, our lives have gone in separate directions. I remember those days when we were factory children and you were our fancy London cousin."

"Until my mother died and I came to live with you."

"Yes. We thought you'd be a right pain, but you weren't swelled in the head as we suspected you to be."

"Long ago," Lewis said.

Gawain suspected the memories were painful, because that was when Lewis had fallen in love with Alys. She hadn't loved him back and even worse, Sir Bartley had rejected Lewis utterly as a son-in-law.

Still, Lewis had proved his image of himself to be truer than Sir Bartley's. He was now a sought-after inventor, with a machine shop and apprentices of his own, and doing very well financially.

"You just bought a house," Gawain said as the thought struck him. "I need to buy a house. Any properties suitable for a family near you?"

"Lots of building going on. Planning for children soon?"

"That is the secret," Gawain said, feeling his chest puff. "I am already a father."

Lewis lifted his hat and pushed a tousle of blond locks out of his eyes. "You don't say."

Gawain nodded. "It was at the inn after your steam carriage broke down."

Lewis put a finger to his lips. "You impregnated the innkeeper?"

"Yes, that is Ann. I never looked back until the holidays last year when I went back to Leeds, though I thought of her during the long months of searching for Lady Elizabeth. I had no idea until after the child was born. He has red hair, Lewis. Looks just like me."

"A boy?"

"Noel. Born Christmas Day."

Lewis laughed. "Congratulations. What a secret to keep."

"I wanted my family to know about the wedding before learning about the reason for it."

"I understand. Let Aunt Ellen focus on one idea at a time. Sure you want to wed her?"

"I can't let Matilda's disaster fall upon another woman," Gawain said. "Jacob cost her the London society life she wanted. And truly, Ann has much to recommend her."

"She's an excellent cook."

"And a genuine Indian healer as well. I can already see what a good mother she is, both with Fern and Noel." He went on to tell Lewis about her past.

"Who do you think murdered her husband?"

"I'd say his brother, Harry Haldene, unless he knew he was getting nothing when his brother died. What bothers me is that Ann inherited the inn."

"But Haldene got a position out of it. What was he before?"

"He worked in the inn."

Lewis tucked his chin into his hand while Gawain shifted in his seat. Pain shot from his hip with the movement.

"Need your pills?" Lewis asked.

"I need to get off this train."

Lewis leaned forward and looked out the window. "Less than an hour to go."

"Thank God. Distract me by solving the murder, if you will."

Lewis laughed. Eventually, they arrived at The Old Hart. Luncheon was still being served and they took a table in the dining room. The new cook remembered Gawain and brought them a hearty meal of meat, bread, pickles and cheese, then sent for Harry Haldene. He arrived as they finished their meal, and the gingerbread and cream dessert.

Gawain's eyes narrowed as he noticed how much less villainous Haldene looked this time. He wore a new suit and his dark hair looked shiny and clean. The stable hand had transformed into an accountant.

"Going courting?" he asked, when the man arrived at the table.

Creases formed around the man's eyes as he smiled. "Well, if it ain't Redcake again. Thanks to you, we 'ad a letter from our Ann."

Gawain leaned back in his chair, surprised by the man's cheerful welcome. "I'm glad she finally wrote."

"Indeed she did." Haldene pulled out a chair and sat down. "We were sore worried 'bout her, you know."

No, he didn't know that. As he recalled, there was little concern when he'd been here after Christmas. At least, in front of him. "I am glad she relieved your mind. Did she tell you we are to be married? The first banns were called on Sunday."

Haldene's lips split in a grin. "You don't say? Many happy returns." He clapped Gawain on the shoulder then waved at a corner of the room. "Jemmy, lad, come say 'ello to one who's about to become a new cousin!"

A long, stringy lad, with hair sticking out, hay-like, in every direction, about the age Lewis had been when he came to live with Gawain's family, detached himself from a stool along the wall and came forward. Gawain vaguely recalled meeting him the previous year.

He held out his hand and shook with Jeremy Haldene. "What do you do here at the inn?"

The lad shrugged and glanced at Harry.

"He's not one for talking. You can go, Jemmy." The boy slouched away as Haldene added, with a shake of his head, "Jemmy and Fern. What a pair, eh?"

Gawain took the opportunity presented to him. "Ann showed me the painting Fern made after she discovered your brother's body. In the stable here, right?"

Haldene's smile vanished. "Why would she do that? Ghastly thing. Told 'er she should've burned it."

"I asked why Fern didn't speak. She must have kept it as an explanation." Gawain watched Haldene carefully for signs of anger, but the man didn't so much as tighten his meaty hands into fists.

"It were the trauma, right?" Haldene shook his head. "She was a girl in love with horses back then. Had to bring 'em carrots, apples, sugar, whatever she could cadge from Ann. Stumbled over Wells when she went in. Came out screaming, her shoes dripping in blood."

"Who do you think killed him?" Lewis asked.

Haldene shrugged. "We never knew. The police suspected a thief. Someone 'ad broken in at Hammer's blacksmith shop the night before, and a window was smashed at a second-hand clothes shop the same night as well."

Gawain noted the new information. "Was he killed during the night? What was he doing in the stable then?"

"Naw, it were early the next mornin'. Lots of travelers leave early, have to get on the road at first light. But the police thought it were all connected, bein' the same night."

"What was he killed with?" Lewis asked.

"The police said he were beaten with a poker, stabbed too, and Hammer was missin' a few things."

"No one in the neighborhood acted guilty later?" Gawain asked as if astounded at the possibility.

"Can't say as I noticed. Ann's health failed utterly and it were touch and go 'round here for days. Between plannin' a funeral, taking care of Ann, and Fern's strange behavior, I wasn't keeping an eye on the neighbors. Had to run the inn too, and I wasn't used to it. I'd been doin' all the repairs, carpentry work, fixin' the roof. It's an old place and Wells 'adn't had it long."

"I suppose you would have expected a smoother transition?" Gawain said.

Haldene scratched his ear. "Transition? Hell man, it were a disaster. Wells worked like two men, and Ann and Fern couldn't do their bits for weeks."

"What about Jeremy? Did he help?"

"He'd just come here. Lost 'is dad. He's the oldest and his mother couldn't support him, so we took him in for odd jobs."

"Do you think it would ease Fern's mind to know who killed her brother?" Gawain watched Haldene carefully.

He sniffed. "I don't see why. It won't change her findin' his body. Horrible for anyone. I expect we should just leave it in the past. Ann has a new family and Fern is happy enough with 'er."

"And you get to run the inn," Gawain stated.

Haldene shrugged again. "Keeps it in the family. I expect I know the business now. Ann will get a regular payment. No worries there." His expression hardened suddenly. "Are you plannin' to return to Leeds to run it yourself?"

"Of course not, my good fellow," Lewis interjected. "Gawain has his own prosperous business to manage."

Haldene relaxed visibly. "That's right. Your teas and herbs are sellin' fast to the local blacks. They do miss Ann. She should come visit when the weather's better, bring the little one. We'd all like to see her."

"I'll mention that when we return," Gawain said. "For now, we shall speak to Mr. Hammer on a business matter. Can we have a pair of rooms for tonight?"

"Of course," Haldene said. He glanced at Lewis. "Bringin' some more work for Hammer?"

"Yes. I felt he'd be the man for the job, after he made my pipe last winter. Very precise."

"Aye, 'e's a good fellow," Haldene agreed.

Gawain gestured to his new suit. "You must have somewhere to be."

Haldene smoothed his hand down his tie. "I'm to be pallbearer at a funeral this afternoon. Bought new clothes."

"My condolences," Gawain and Lewis said at the same time.

"It were his time. We worked in the church garden together. Got a little committee who does it, and he were in charge for fifty year or more."

"Then we won't keep you any longer."

"I'll get the girl to take you to your rooms," Haldene said, and stood, then headed for the kitchen.

Gawain and Lewis glanced at each other.

"What do you think?" Lewis asked.

"I see points both in favor and against." Gawain rubbed his chin. "But he's the most likely person."

"He benefited the most," Lewis agreed. "But I think you are missing some key part of the story."

"Yes, but how to find out what that is?"

"Ask around, I suppose. I'll inquire at the blacksmith's about the break-in. You can speak to the servants here."

"I think they are all new, except the Haldene boy, Jeremy."

"Track him down," Lewis advised.

"I'll go to the Leeds police as well. They must have some information about the investigation. What they suspected, even if no one was arrested."

Gawain was disappointed by the lack of progress in his murder investigation as he sped south by train the next Monday. Everything had been as Ann had said. The police suspected a passerby thief. Harry Haldene had an alibi, as did Jeremy, and the police weren't willing to share enough information for Gawain to investigate more deeply. They were offended by his questions and couldn't seem to comprehend that Ann's fiancé might be concerned for her safety. After all, the murder had been nearly three years before, and she had never seemed to be in any danger since.

When his train arrived in London, he immediately hailed a cab to go to Ann's flat. It was six PM and she should be home. He was eager to see Noel after nearly a week's absence.

Fern opened the door, offering him a small smile for the first time. He patted her shoulder and offered her a peppermint stick he'd purchased at the train station for just this moment. She hesitated before snatching it from his hand with a soundless giggle, then reached for her cloak and hat and slithered past him into the hallway.

Almost too easy. He had Ann and Noel to himself. When he walked into the kitchen, he saw Ann at the stove, her back to him. He walked silently into the bedroom and found Noel in his cradle. The baby had a couple of tiny fingers in his mouth and was sucking vigorously on them.

"Hungry?" Gawain asked, picking him up.

Ann appeared around the corner. "He would cry if he's hungry. He just started sucking on his fingers a couple of days ago."

They stepped toward each other, meeting halfway. Gawain kissed her on the cheek and she touched his arm, then smiled at Noel.

"How long have you been back in London?" she inquired.

"I came straight from the station."

Her lovely dark eyes widened. "You are becoming attached to Noel."

"And you. I've spent the last few days banging my head against the past in Leeds, trying to discover if you are safe from it."

"Did you learn anything more?" She put her hand to her mouth. "About Wells?"

He shook his head. "Not really. I can understand why the police decided it had to have been a stranger passing through."

"You accept that now?"

"No. I still think Harry did it, but I can't quite tell you why. It's instinct. The way Wells was killed seems so intimate. The person who killed him was standing right in front of him. The killer damaged his face so badly. Why would your husband let a stranger get so close?"

"He struggled. The police said he did."

"He was a big man, with a wonderful wife, a child on the way. Why didn't he win the fight? What prevented him?"

"He fought," Ann said, then pressed her lips tightly together.

Gawain saw tears hovering on her underlashes but he couldn't help pushing. "He wouldn't have fought so hard if it was his brother attacking. They were close?"

Ann wiped her eyes with her apron. "Yes."

"Was Harry jealous of Wells?"

"It wasn't Harry," Ann said, putting one hand over her heart but not answering the question. "I won't believe it. We lived in that inn together for years. I never saw any evil in him. And where did the bloody clothes go if he did it?"

"I thought about that. Couldn't he have put them in a carriage leaving town, something like that? A cart that was passing through?" Noel's hand fell from his mouth and he yawned hugely. Gawain admired his toothless gums and lifted him closer for a kiss.

Ann took the baby and hugged him close for a moment before setting him back into the cradle. "He didn't have many clothes, Gawain, and I don't recall any missing."

Because she was out of her mind with grief for Wells and her dead baby. But she wasn't going to seriously consider Harry. "I'm sorry to upset you so. I know I'm missing something important."

She sniffed. "You have plenty to do without mixing yourself into my old affairs."

"You are going to be my wife, very soon now. I want to keep you safe. Make sure whatever happened is finished." He put his hands on her shoulders, then pulled her close when she relaxed. "Come sit by the fire. I'll put my head on your knee and we'll relax like an old married couple."

"Shouldn't I be sitting on the stool by you?" she teased.

"Ah, but you're the princess, and I'm a mere serf here to do your bidding."

She chuckled, a low, melodious sound that had a hint of the expanded musical scale of Indian music. He led her to the armchair near the fire and settled her in it, spreading her skirts around her feet. A hint of perfume, just kitchen smells, maybe, but with her scent underneath, caressed his nose, and he knew what he wanted to do with her.

He saw a low stool by the fire, a recent purchase that hadn't been there when he'd visited last. Had she really thought to sit with him in that way? The thought drained the last of the February cold from his bones and he smiled to himself as he pulled it close and sat facing her.

"Don't you mean to sit at my elbow?" she asked, her gaze dark under lazily lowered eyelids.

He wanted to nip at that fat lower lip, but no need to give the game away, when her other plump lips were his target. "At your feet," he murmured, seating himself.

Her feet were crossed daintily at the heel. Gently, he lifted one stocking-clad ankle and separated her legs, then pulled himself in between them.

Her eyes looked less sleepy. "I should massage your hip while Noel sleeps."

"I'm not in pain now." He wasn't, at least not at the hip. His cock was making itself known, a thick rod rubbing against his clothing. He slid his fingers up her legs, feeling for where the stockings ended and she began.

There, a ribbon marked the spot, then an expanse of warm flesh pointed the way to his goal above. She sat up a little, her legs spreading more. He thought it accident and not design, but then he knew she was a lusty woman, and it had been a long time. He'd been told by fellow sergeants who knew such things that it was best to ease a woman back into fleshy pleasures after having a child, to make love to her rather than go straight to intercourse.

His fingers danced higher. When she didn't protest, he let his thumb graze the inside of her thighs, as they continued their path north.

She didn't wear drawers, in the style of camp followers in hot climates. He had noticed they kept the flat warm, probably for the baby. Feeling the heat himself, he pulled off his jacket and tossed it to the floor before finding his place between her thighs again with one hand, and using the other to pull up skirt and petticoats. His head went under all that fabric and he heard the sound of her voice, but the flannel muffled it just enough that he couldn't quite tell what she said.

He felt her move in her chair, but it seemed she was simply settling herself. Her hand reached for him, a ghostly touch through the fabric, as it caressed his head. When he sighed with pleasure, she jerked. He realized he'd blown hot air against her inner thigh. Did she like it? He tried again, on the opposite side.

She didn't bat at him, and she knew where his head was. He blew again, making a trail of his own up her inner thigh. Underneath her skirts was claustrophobic and soothing all at once. Scents changed as her body heated with desire. When his breath met the juncture between her thighs he sensed not just heat but moisture.

He had pleased his princess. His tongue darted out to test her and found perfumed juices. He spread her legs further and soothed his tongue along her seam. Those perfect lips, every bit as plump as her mouth, opened at his touch. Distantly, he heard a little gasp, felt her hands rustle in her skirts. She adjusted, leaning back, giving him access.

His princess was willing to let him worship. *Good.* He used his mouth, his tongue, even his teeth, to tease. When she moved restlessly he made an assault on her pearl, licking and sucking the tiny nub until her moan was entirely audible even beneath the petticoats.

When she was writhing in earnest, he put his finger in her channel and moved it in and out. But this wasn't enough so he inserted another, and continued to make ingress on her pearl, until he had her hips bucking against his mouth and sliding along the armchair.

All of a sudden she gasped and her body stilled. Then, her back arched, lifting her off the seat. He added a third finger and she cried out, shaking. With all the skill he had, he gentled her down from her peak, then slid out of the scented bower to take a breath of cool air.

They stared at each other while he pulled his collar from his sweaty neck.

"You are a most noble knight," she whispered.

He bowed his head. "Ever at your service, my lady."

"Did you enjoy doing that?"

"It was as much a pleasure as a duty." He straightened her skirts, then found her ankles with his hands, with some thought of pulling her on top of him, when he heard a key at the door.

Ann bolted upright, her hands going to her hair.

"I didn't touch your hair," he said.

She swallowed hard and laughed a little. "Not that hair."

"To think I am so intimately acquainted below and yet have never seen if the color matches."

"Black as night on both ends," she said with an earthy smile, then put her hands to the armrests and pushed herself up from the chair.

She swayed a little and he leapt up to catch her, then swayed himself as his hip protested.

Fern made a face at them as she peeked into the room, but Gawain knew she could see no actual evidence of lovemaking. Still, he couldn't wait until he had them in a proper house, with doors. Tomorrow would be an excellent day to set property acquisition in motion.

* * *

Gawain spent the next day wandering Battersea. Lewis's home and machine shop were near Nine Elms, where the locomotive sheds were located. Many of the small businesses needed for inventors were nearby.

By the end of the day, he'd purchased a new brick row house on Kelmscott Road. Only a ten-minute walk to Clapham Junction railway station, it seemed perfect for his growing family's needs. The six miles it placed between him and the family home on St. James's Square seemed a perfect amount of distance between his old life and his new. He appreciated the cosmopolitan, bustling atmosphere of this newly developed area, which would still be fields if not for the railway.

After finishing his business, he found his way back to the family home and dressed for an evening at the club. He hoped he'd see Lewis there so he could share the news of his purchase.

His valet came in with a tray holding a card. "The comtesse is here to see you, Mr. Redcake."

Gawain straightened his bow tie in the mirror and turned to his valet with a frown. "She's never come here before."

"It has been some time since you've seen her."

"Nearly a year," Gawain agreed. He'd always gone to the comtesse's home for their assignations when she had been his mistress. Why was she visiting him? Surely she hadn't lost her looks and position as one of London's premiere courtesans in less than a year.

"Will you see her, sir?"

"Put her in the green parlor," Gawain said. "I'll be down shortly." He didn't want her in any of the family rooms, but the green parlor was small and rarely used. After finishing his toilette, he went downstairs.

"Marie," he said, walking into the room. It had given him a thrill to bed a titled lady when he'd first known her, even if her favors were for sale, but she was never formal in private.

Dressed in luxurious purple silk with gold accents, Marie's pale skin and dark hair gave her the appearance of a fairy tale princess. Gawain still found her beautiful, but not sexually appealing. No, his tastes might still be on the mysterious side, but give him his Indian princess any day. As Marie stalked toward him and rapped him on the arm with her ever-present fan, he thought he saw the start of wrinkles in the pinched look of her mouth.

"I thought you sacrificed me to *les loups* for a pink, aristocratic child, Gawain, not for some black girl!"

He took a small cigar from his case and toyed with it for a moment before responding. "So you've heard about my engagement."

"An Indian? How you insult me."

"In what way?" He took out his clip and removed the tip of his cigar, then held it to the fire.

Marie swiped it from his hand and put it to her lips. Yes, he could see the beginning of lines around her eyes now, when she squinted against the smoke. She was a few years older than he, perhaps thirty-two or thirty-three now? Ann, at twenty-five and not a smoker, had far better skin.

"Why on earth would you marry such a creature?" Marie demanded.

"First of all, I would have married my pink, aristocratic girl, as you call Lady Elizabeth, if I could have found her. But she has vanished. I met Mrs. Haldene during my travels and we suit very well."

"A widow," Marie sniffed, seating herself on an ornate chair.

"Yes," he affirmed, lowering himself to a spot on the sofa next to the chair. "Her first husband was murdered a few years ago. She inherited his inn up in Leeds. That's where we met."

"And she's black."

"Half-Indian. Her mother was a maharani."

"Oh?" Marie waved the cigar. "Are you sure that isn't just a story?"

"I didn't hear it from her," Gawain said. "Yes, I'm sure. Her parents were rather famous in their day."

"I suppose she is quite exotic in her saris and gems," Marie sneered.

"No, she is very English in most ways. Her mother taught her traditional medical practices of her people, but other than that, it is only her skin that gives away her foreign background."

"Does she have a title? No, I would imagine not," Marie sniffed. "I cannot imagine why you would give up your plans for such a creature. She does not sound at all *intéressant*."

"On the contrary. She is a sensual, appealing creature, just like you. Not so young as Lady Elizabeth, but younger than me."

"She has studied the Indian arts of lovemaking then," Marie said. "I can see you being fascinated by that."

He laughed and took the cigar from her fingers. "Is this why you pay me a visit? To berate me?"

"To warn you, darling. You will lose your place in Society if you marry such a creature. She can be your mistress, if necessary, but do not marry her." She placed one arm on the back of the chair, displaying her décolletage.

"I will do exactly that, and succeed despite her if necessary," Gawain said, finding himself immune to his former mistress's practiced wiles. "I will not abandon my private goals. And she will be my wife very soon."

Chapter Nine

Ann pushed Noel's pram through the door of the select Pim's Photography on Regent Street, followed by Gawain. He'd insisted their family be photographed with the intentions of offering *cartes de visite* to their wedding guests. She liked the idea of having Noel immortalized on paper so she had agreed. Fern trailed in the rear. Ann felt for her, sensing the girl did not know her place in this new family unit, despite Gawain's promises of a better life for her.

"Welcome, welcome!" said a thin man with an even slimmer moustache, emerging from behind a velvet curtain dripping with tassels. Ann smiled politely, but before she could respond to his greeting he walked forward and looked down at Noel. "What a lovely child. Just the baby today, or baby and father?"

She glanced back, confused. Had Gawain made this arrangement?

No, he was frowning as he came to her side. "What is the procedure here?"

"Four poses for five shillings, sir. We could do you and your baby, the baby alone, perhaps the baby with his ayah, people do like to see a hint of the exotic, and then," he gestured at Fern, "the baby and his sister?"

Ann's fingers tightened around the pram's handle. She wore her best dress, but it wasn't new, and could easily have been her mistress's cast off, were she indeed an ayah, an Indian baby nurse. How could she fault him for his misunderstanding when she wasn't dressed as the wife of a successful businessman, but as a provincial innkeeper in her Sunday best?

Gawain put his hand on her shoulder. "This is my child's mother, sir."

The man stroked his moustache with spidery fingers. Without a hint of embarrassment, he continued smoothly. "A family portrait then. Four poses of all four of you? Or some other combination? Or perhaps you want more than the standard package?"

Ann's fingers relaxed. There wouldn't be a problem.

"Let us take the photographs of us together first and then we will see. If you do a proper job, I will be purchasing one hundred copies," Gawain said.

He clapped his hands together. "I see, I see. Let us get to our work then, and perhaps you would like to step into the bookshop next door while I develop the photographs? It should only take an hour or so."

Gawain patted Ann's shoulder again. "No, I will come back tomorrow to see the results. We don't want the baby out that long."

"No, no, filthy air," the man agreed. "Please, come into the studio. We can take you right away." He held open the curtain.

Gawain tossed shillings on the counter, then gestured Ann and Fern to move ahead. Should she have asked Gawain to bring along a maid from his family mansion to make them look more respectable? She needed to start thinking of these things now, for Noel's sake. Whatever she had to do to prevent future misunderstandings must be done. She glanced down at her fingers. No wedding ring. Now that was an obvious error. For the first time, she wished a gold band rested there.

A mother's love could move mountains, but a father's position held the kernel of his son's future. She was right to marry Gawain. The sense of this sank into her bones.

She turned and whispered. "Should we return after I've had a new dress made? Something more suitable? My bustle is all wrong for this year, and my neckline too, I suspect."

"I forgot." Gawain reached into his pocket and pulled out a jewelry case. He opened it, displaying a pearl collar with an exquisite pagan cameo in the center, backed by onyx. "I thought this would look glorious against your skin."

Fern let out a sharp exhalation and looked at Gawain in wonder.

"It's gorgeous," Ann said, astounded by the beauty of the gift. The necklace was fit for a princess. Her mother might have worn something like this if she'd been raised in London rather than in Caliata.

"What do you think? For the portrait? And our wedding, if you like."

She nodded. He handed the box to Fern and turned Ann gently so he could close the clasp around her neck. Inside the studio was a small mirror, presumably so ladies could make final adjustments. She looked at herself with the collar, and for the first time, saw a prosperous tradesman's wife. Gawain must treasure her, to bestow a gift like this. The rumblings in her stomach, like so many bees buzzing, calmed instantly. She knew no one smiled in portraits, but she saw her teeth in the mirror now, her expression one of peace and happiness.

"I am ready," she told Gawain, her dress all but forgotten. "Thank you, my dear."

He nodded silently. She reached her hand up to his hat and removed it, then checked over his hair, sorting through the lightly pomaded blond locks, until his part was perfect. Then she confirmed that Fern and Noel looked their best.

"Do you know what kind of backdrop you would like?" asked the photographer as he turned on bright electric lights. "I have a number of choices."

Ann inspected the canvases. "I like the columns," she told Gawain, pulling back a couple of backcloths on poles, one of a simple dark fabric and another simulating ferns and statuary.

"I have some lovely tree stumps you can sit on," the photographer volunteered. "With ivy."

"Why would we be outside?" Gawain asked. "Why don't we sit on chairs?"

"The first one then?" Ann said.

"That is very popular," the photographer said. "But simulating the outdoors is a common fashion for portraiture."

"We'll take that sofa," Gawain said, pointing to a heavily tasseled and padded loveseat in a corner. "For us. Fern can sit on that stool there, next to Ann, who will hold Noel."

Ann let the cloths fall from her fingers. A sober grouping would be more refined than a more fanciful background, after all.

"Just the wall, then?" asked the photographer. "Any art? Ferns?"

Gawain went to the cloths and pulled them away to expose the painted wall. "Yes, it is fine."

Ann took Noel from his pram while the photographer fussed, then seated herself on the sofa. Fern perched next to her.

"Any other poses, sir?" the photographer asked Gawain.

"No, just take our picture four times. No doubt our expressions will change." He glanced at Ann. "Is this acceptable to you?"

She nodded. "It is a simple family portrait, after all."

"We can come back another time and do the columns if you like. Just the two of us."

She touched the pearl collar. "That would be nice."

"With a new dress."

She smiled at him. How could he read her so well? "Of course."

"I'm ready," the photographer said, glancing up from his camera and tripod. "Stay still, please."

"They say you can tell the difference between the living and the dead in photographs because the living are often slightly blurred," Gawain said.

Ann felt her eyebrows lift, just as the photographer took the first picture. That would not be an attractive pose. Quickly, she schooled her features to impassivity. She adjusted Noel subtly for each of the last two photographs, having no idea how he might best be displayed.

"We are done," the photographer said. "Thank you for your patience."

Gawain stood and held out his arms for Noel, cuddling him for a moment while Ann and Fern stood and straightened their clothing. "I will return tomorrow for the results."

"Could you take one more?" Ann asked impulsively. "Just like this? Of Mr. Redcake and Noel?"

Gawain looked quizzical as the man eagerly complied, but he sat back down with Noel in his arms. Ann smiled as the picture was taken. This would be the best of all. Gawain hadn't had time to erase the tenderness from his expression. She wondered if he ever would look that way when he saw her.

* * *

Gawain was far too busy with house arrangements to check on the results of their sitting until late the next day. He chose the third photograph for their wedding cards, because Noel's mouth was closed in an adorable little pout. Other than in the first photograph, where Ann looked startled, the three older subjects looked much the same in all the portraits. When he ordered his one hundred, he also ordered a larger portrait of the final option, the one with him and Noel alone. He could not be impressed by his appearance, but nonetheless, the sentimental pose, the way Noel's chubby arm had been captured, lifting toward his father's chin, made the photograph an instant keepsake. "I'll take two of those," he told the photographer, "mounted and framed."

"Very good, sir. Will you pick them up tomorrow?"

Gawain received his package the next day, and was on Ann's doorstep around 3:00 PM. He knew she wouldn't have returned from Redcake's yet, but thought he'd leave a copy of each portrait with Fern while having some quiet time with Noel, if he wasn't with the wet nurse. To think he had run the risk of never meeting his son.

He knocked at their door and was surprised to see Ann opening it, not Fern. "Home so soon? Did I have your schedule wrong?"

She bit her lip, looking both guilty and troubled. "Come in, Gawain. Was I expecting you?"

"I have the photographs."

"So soon? How lovely." She shut the door behind him.

He handed her the package and unraveled his muffler. Though it was the first day of March, the weather still felt decidedly wintry, though at least he was covered with rain, not snow. The smell of damp wool overpowered the scent of a spicy curry bubbling in the kitchen. "What are you doing home so early? Do I have your schedule wrong? I hope you are not ill."

"No." She walked in and set the package down on a small table next to her armchair. Then, she stood with her back to the fireplace, her hands behind her back as if she were a soldier about to receive discipline.

He pressed on. "Clearly I have some misunderstanding."

"I do not work at Redcake's anymore."

He blinked, his bad eye feeling gritty behind the eye patch.

Lately, it had seemed to feel better when he left it exposed, instead of hidden behind the black square. He took it off and wiped the corner of his eye.

"Do you feel a change in your eye?" she asked eagerly, reaching for his face.

He tilted away from her. "Ann, what is going on?"

"They terminated me weeks ago," she said calmly. "But your eye, Gawain. Are you having unusual sensations? Let me light a lamp so I can see it."

"The only thing that matters is whether or not I can see better," he said testily.

"Can you?" She lit a small lamp and held it up to his face.

"No, but it feels different."

"Close your left eye," she instructed.

His vision vanished as he complied.

"Can you see the lamp moving?"

"The flame, you mean?"

"Move your eye to what you see."

He concentrated, following a vague lightness, which did indeed move around. "I could see light and dark before."

"You couldn't follow it." The light stopped moving.

He heard the sound of her setting the lamp down.

"Can you see my fingers?"

He waited, but no aspect of his vision changed. He did, however, hear a rustling as Noel moved in the cradle behind them. "Noel is stirring."

"My fingers?" she repeated.

"No, Ann. Now stop this nonsense and tell me about your position."

She sighed, making it clear she cared more about her medical interests than her employment. "I had to go up to the bakery to deliver a cake and a customer objected to being served by a woman with dark skin. I was rude to her and was fired."

He hated the rote way she said the words. Where was her anger at being mistreated? "What happened exactly?"

"She claimed I wasn't clean and I said I was cleaner than she was, given that she had a stain on her glove. So Ralph Popham fired me."

He opened his good eye so he could see her. She appeared as calm as she sounded. "You worked for Alfred Melville, not Popham."

"He said Mr. Melville would do the same, once he told him that I'd shouted. Though I didn't, not really."

"Either way, it sounds like you had adequate provocation."

She blew air through her nose. "I was impolite to a duchess."

"Judah wouldn't have fired you," Gawain said, wanting some kind of emotion from her. Perhaps she had already made her peace with it, but she hadn't reacted to the photographer's assumption that she was a servant yesterday either.

She looked away.

"When exactly did this happen?"

She stared at the floor. "February eleventh."

"The same day you accepted my proposal," he said slowly. He found his patch in his pocket and tied it back on. "I see. I did wonder why you changed your mind."

He expected some word of comfort to him, or some hint of defiance, or words about protecting Noel, but there was nothing. How could he blame her for her actions? Yet, a sensation of lightheadedness crept over him, as if trying to focus his bad eye had sapped his strength. He cleared his throat. "I came to show you the photographs. I believe I will let you see them on your own time. Good evening, Ann."

She didn't stop him as he walked from the room, pulling his things from the hook by the door as he exited. He couldn't remember how he got there, but eventually found himself entering his club.

Drinking alone sounded like the best approach to the evening, but a waiter suggested a tea tray, given the early hour and he agreed, because they used Redcake's products thanks to Lord Judah's membership. He had just finished a delicious little lemon cake that nonetheless tasted like sawdust to him, when the man himself appeared.

Lord Judah's long body dropped into the chair opposite him. "You are here early."

"So are you." He blinked, wishing the unsteady feeling would leave his head.

"It's after five," the Redcake's manager said. "I didn't have any late meetings."

Gawain straightened and pulled the patch off his bad eye again.

The bloody thing itched like the devil. Lord Judah, an old soldier, didn't react to the scars.

"Eye bothering you?"

A note of honed anger crept into his voice. "Not as much as learning that Ann had lost her position at Redcake's. Did you know that?"

Lord Judah shook his head. "Magdalene had a bad cough and went to Cornwall for a couple of weeks with her cousin, Lady Bricker. They both needed fresh air. I must have been traveling when it occurred."

"You don't see employee reports?"

"Nothing so specific as who has been let go. I'll tell my secretary to modify my reports in future to give me more detail. What happened?"

Gawain repeated what he had been told.

His friend frowned. "I should have been told that a duchess had been shouted at, at the very least. That could destroy our business if she spoke against us to her friends."

Gawain clenched the handle of his teacup, tilting the cup until it dripped on his fingers. Who cared about the bloody duchess? "Has there been any trouble?"

"No, none whatever."

"I'd like to think her ladyship felt ashamed of herself."

"Do duchesses feel shame?" Lord Judah grinned. "I think not. But I'd be happy to give Ann her job back, if she's willing to never shout at a customer again. I cannot control the prejudices of customers, but with a little common sense, such scenes ought to be avoidable."

"Thank you." He wondered if Ann would refuse to marry him now that she had employment again, but she could always return to Leeds and work at the inn. Employment wasn't really the issue for her, nor was money, when he would give her anything she needed, marriage or not. No, she had decided marriage was a safer institution for her than Redcake's.

Lord Judah stood. "What are you waiting for, old man? We'll speak to her immediately, offer her job back."

He didn't think Ann would want Lord Judah showing up at the door of her humble flat, not when she was concerned about appearances. "Thank you for your enthusiasm, but I think a note would be best. I'll deliver it to her tomorrow."

His friend sat down. "If you're sure. I'll speak to Popham and Melville tomorrow, and I'll instruct Mrs. Haldene to be at work on Monday at her usual time." He called for a waiter to bring pen and paper.

Gawain took the note when he was done and thanked him. Then Lewis arrived, along with a few of his cronies who owned a wheel factory. He was glad to spend a few hours talking politics and industry, and when he returned home he felt clear-headed once again.

Late the next morning, he went to Ann's flat with Lord Judah's note.

Fern opened the door and gestured him toward the fireplace before he could even take off his coat. With more animation than he'd ever seen from her, she pointed to the photographs on the mantel, then tapped herself in the family picture.

"Did I pick a good one?" Gawain asked.

She nodded vehemently. He smiled at her. Had he gained an ally? "You should take one of the cards for your very own."

Her eyes widened.

"Yes, for your new room. Do you know that I've bought us a house? My cousin Lewis lives nearby. It's on quite a nice street, with shops within walking distance. A park too, I think. I have furniture coming. We should be able to move in on Thursday, right after the wedding."

She shook her head, but as if in wonderment, not denial.

"I know, it is all happening very quickly. Is Ann here? I need to show her a letter."

Fern pointed at the wall separating the room from the kitchen.

"Thank you, my dear," he said, the endearment thick on his tongue. He resolved to try harder to communicate with the girl. She was clearly intelligent. He unbuttoned his greatcoat and hung it on the hook with his hat on the way into the kitchen.

Ann had her back to him as she stirred something in a pot. Noel was in his pram, clutching a wooden spoon. After enjoying the domestic scene for a moment, Gawain bent and kissed his forehead. The baby smelled fresh and sweet.

"Had a bath?" he asked.

"Yes," Ann said. "I just threw out the water."

Already frustrated with her dull tone and lack of greeting, he kissed her on the cheek. "Fern is very excited with the photographs."

"She's never been photographed before."

"Have you?"

"Yes, my wedding portrait with Wells."

"I haven't seen it."

"It's put away in a trunk at the inn. It hurt me too much to look at it." Her voice caught.

She still loved her first husband. Wells was the only person who seemed to bring any emotion to her voice. He had to solve the man's murder so they could both move on. While Wells was present in her thoughts he had no way into her affections.

He pulled the envelope from his pocket. "I know you are busy, and with our wedding this week this is probably the last thing on your mind. But both my sister and Lady Judah have been terribly reluctant to let Redcake's slip through their fingers, despite their positions in society, so I thought you would want this."

She turned, wiping her hands on her apron and took the note from him. When she had read it, she handed it back, her expression serene. "You are right. Redcake's is the last thing on my mind. I won't return unless you insist I do so."

He tucked the note back into his pocket. "Why would I insist?"

"Perhaps you want an unwanted wife to be financially independent?"

"Unwanted? Are you mad?" His voice had raised but he quickly controlled himself, not wanting to upset Noel or Fern. "I assure you, madam, I eagerly look forward to our wedding this week. I wish you did the same."

"I am happy to marry you."

"Then I wish you would display this happiness. It is not evident to me."

She smiled, but he could see it didn't reach her eyes, which crinkled slightly when she smiled for real. When she touched his cheek he closed his eyes, hoping for some kind of tenderness, but she removed her hand far too quickly for that.

"How is your eye today?" she asked. "Shall I have a look? Or work with your hip?"

Was that all she could think of? "No, I shall have to tell Lord Judah you won't be returning after all," he said. "I'll ask Fern if she wants to walk with me. Has she been out today?"

Ann shook her head. "Is it raining?"

"Not when I came in."

"I'm sure she'd be happy to go."

He nodded. "When are you going to pack up the flat? Do you want me to send over assistance?"

"I will need it, with Noel," she admitted.

"Is the furniture yours?"

"Some of it, but none of the larger items, like the bed."

"I'll send over a couple of footmen on Wednesday morning, then. They can move everything during the wedding. Fern will sleep at the St. James's Square house on Wednesday night with my family while we stay at a hotel, then we'll all move to the new house in Battersea on Thursday."

"I'll write up a list of what needs to be moved," Ann said. "I've already spoken to the landlady."

"Excellent." He considered a variety of instructions, but discarded them all. Ann was a competent woman. "I am sorry about what happened at Redcake's, and the photographer's behavior the other day. But I think you'll find money will smooth over any prejudice."

She picked up her stirring spoon, holding it in front of her apron like a shield. "I hope so, for Noel's sake."

"Is there anything I can do?" he asked, feeling her pain. They could not know who Noel would favor as an adult.

"You have to reconcile yourself to the realities, Gawain." She looked directly into his eyes. "People are going to see me differently."

"Are you entitled to any special form of address from your mother?" he asked. "A title does wonders."

She smiled a little at that, for real this time. "If I am, I don't know about it. I have lived most of my life here. I have no contact with India. I love the medical aspect of my heritage but that is about all I have left."

"And the food. I wish your mother were still alive."

"Yes, you'd have liked her, even if she wasn't a maharani."

"I'm thinking about your own protection, not anything I would get out of your titles," he said, stung.

She nodded, but he could see she didn't believe him. And why not? She knew he'd been chasing a title when he met her. But she didn't know Beth, who was a sweet, lively girl. He shuddered to think of what had become of her. All he could do was look forward now. He'd given Beth enough time and must focus on new ways of obtaining his goals.

"Have a good evening," he said, his voice stiff. He kissed his soon-to-be-wife on the cheek and went to look for Fern.

Fern nodded when he asked if she wanted to go to the tea shop and followed him out of the door with a bounce in her step. He knew she was likely to be dependent on him for the rest of her life if her speech issues weren't cured. She would never marry or have a position in her current condition.

Somehow, she had associated the experience of finding her brother's murdered body with the physical process of speaking. He had been reading psychological texts in the evenings, trying to figure her out. What could it mean? Had someone threatened her at the murder site, thereby causing her fragile mind to shut off her voice?

"I am having some difficulties with Ann," he told her frankly, as they walked along the street, dodging men who were moving a heavy side table into a cart. Fog drifted through the streets, toying with their ankles.

Fern looked up at him. When her hat brim obscured her view she tilted it back.

"Yes. She is a sad lady at the moment, I think. The only passion she seems to feel is when we discuss your brother's death."

Fern's lips tightened.

"What don't I know, Fern?" He stopped at the corner, watching horses step by, carrying loads that looked top-heavy for a blustery March day. "Why was he killed?"

She put her hand shyly in his and tugged him forward. They walked in silence until they reached Regent Street. She walked him past the photography studio and a couple of stores, before stopping in front of a display window that fronted a jewelry store. Here, she stopped walking and pointed.

"Is this about Wells?" he asked.

She nodded and tapped the glass.

"This is a jewelry store."

She licked her lips and glanced up at him expectantly.

"He was killed over jewelry?"

She frowned and grabbed his hand again, pulling him into the store. Inside the air was hushed by fabric-covered walls and plush velvet furnishings. This was a shop that catered to the best families. A salesman frowned at Fern, but Gawain knew he was dressed as a gentleman.

"My young friend wishes to show me something," he said in his haughtiest voice.

The man bowed slightly and stepped back.

Fern walked around the cases, pulling him with her, until all of a sudden she stopped and tapped the glass. The salesman winced to see her ungloved finger touching the clean surface.

Gawain pulled a half-crown from his pocket and tapped it on the glass. He bent over the surface and stared down. "It's a sapphire necklace with pearls," he said.

She poked at the glass again, right over the sapphire.

"Wells's death was related to a sapphire?"

She nodded eagerly.

Gawain left the coin on the case and lifted a finger to the salesman, who trotted over.

"Sir?"

"What can you tell me about the central gem?"

"It is a cushion-cut sapphire of about twenty carats," the salesman said.

Fern nodded, but made a circle with her hands and expanded it.

"The stone in question was larger?" Gawain asked.

She nodded.

"How did your brother acquire such an item?"

She shook her head and pointed to her ring finger. Gawain didn't understand but now the salesman entered the game.

"It was a ring?" the man asked.

She shook her head again.

"Just the stone," Gawain clarified. "You are pointing to where he would have worn his wedding ring."

"Oh," the salesman exclaimed. "His wife?"

"The stone was Ann's?" Gawain asked, incredulous.

She smiled and nodded.

"Your brother was killed over Ann's large sapphire?" Gawain asked.

"Do you have it?" the salesman inquired.

"No," Gawain snapped. "Pay attention. Her brother was killed over the stone. Fern, did you do more than discover the body? Did you see Wells robbed and killed?"

Chapter Ten

Fern shook her head vehemently.

"Talk, girl," the salesman ordered.

"She doesn't speak," Gawain said. "She hasn't spoken since her brother died."

"I see." The man stared at her curiously.

"So, Fern, you didn't see your brother killed, but you know he was killed over Ann's sapphire. Why do you know that? Did the stone disappear the same day?"

She shook her head.

"It didn't disappear. You know where it went."

She nodded.

"Did Harry take it?"

She shook her head again.

"Ann will be happy to know that. She's a champion of your brother."

"Who has the stone then?" the salesman asked eagerly. "It's worth a great deal of money, little girl."

Fern's gaze wandered. Gawain suspected this interlude had exhausted her. He stared down at the necklace, which was a gold choker, with pearls between the choker and the suspended sapphires.

"What is the source of this necklace?"

"Caliata, India," the salesman said.

Fern's eyes widened and Gawain grinned at her. "It's a sign. I'll buy it for Ann's wedding gift."

The salesman smiled then. "I'll give you a good price, sir."

"Yes, you will. I have a friend who is a gem merchant, and if you serve me badly, I will know."

The man nodded nervously. "I will get the owner, sir. For a necklace of this quality he will want to speak to you." Quick as a hummingbird, he snatched the half-crown off the case and moved toward the back room.

Ann muttered to herself as she packed extra clothing and baby items Noel had already grown out of into a trunk on Monday morning. "Thought I should return to Redcake's this morning, did he? Two days before my wedding? Is the man mad?"

She still had the hem to finish on her new dress, the one she was wearing to be married in. Fern had spent hours embroidering scallops on the hem, and had worked gold thread into the bodice of the silk gown. The fabric had taken most of Ann's remaining money, but she wanted to look appropriate before Gawain's family. Meanwhile, he thought she should be a baker in the basement of his sister's business. The nerve of the man.

She had been so flattered and relieved by his solicitude at the photography studio, and then he had brought the letter. It left her wondering what her place in his life really would be. Was she to spend her days living in the basement of his home, an ignored, forgotten wife, as hidden as if she were in purdah? In comparison, when she thought of how proud Wells had been to make her his wife, she wanted to scream.

She heard a bang on the door, and Fern's light footprints as she scurried to answer. Gawain's knock had a more pleasant tone, so she continued her packing, moving onto clothes they wouldn't need in the next two or three days.

Fern walked in, followed by a large woman with a very red face. Ann recognized her as the wife of a cooper who lived a couple of doors down. She held her back with one hand and seemed to be having trouble breathing. *Back pain.*

Ann put down a handful of towels and stood to meet her guest. "Mrs. Bang, yes?"

The woman nodded. "My back did not like coming up your steps, Mrs. Haldene. I've 'eard people in the neighborhood say you're an 'ealer. Well, I've need o' one of them if you 'ave the time."

"Certainly. Your back, is it?"

She nodded. "Pain's been coming on ever since winter set in."

"Make me some garlic oil, please," Ann told Fern. The girl nodded and went into the kitchen.

"What's that for?"

"To rub on your back at home, followed by a hot compress." She pulled out a stool and had Mrs. Bang sit down, then took her through an inventory of her daily habits.

"You need to return to your summer habits," she told the woman when she finished. "Your current diet is far too fatty and heavy now, and it's affecting your back. Drink some lemon juice every day with a bit of salt for your digestion."

"I know my clothes are too tight."

"That does not help either," Ann agreed. She persuaded the woman to allow her to rub her lower back while they discussed in detail how to use the garlic oil, and a couple of movements she could do to relieve the pain.

After a simple series of stretches, Mrs. Bang was already moving a bit better. Fern brought in the warm oil in a bottle and Ann told her patient how to make more.

"I cannot thank you enough," Mrs. Bang said at the doorway on her way out. "We used to 'ave a queer old fellow on the street who had come from India as a servant to a military family. Made charms, I think. He was the healthiest old man I ever seen. People said 'e was about ninety-five when 'e died."

Ann smiled. "I cannot promise that, but your back pain will ease with these simple changes."

The woman smiled and left. Ann put her payment into the box on the kitchen shelf. Her sense of satisfaction reminded her how much she enjoyed continuing the work her mother had done in Leeds. Gawain may think she was only suited for basement kitchens, but she knew better. She had been trained in the medical arts of Indian royal families, after all, and had the blood of maharajas in her veins. She wouldn't be cast aside.

Somehow, she needed to find the way to his heart. If he loved her, life would be perfect, just as it had been with Wells. Of course, if she'd been an ordinary woman, instead of the daughter of Indian royalty, she wouldn't have inherited the gem that had probably gotten him killed. No one but she knew that one of the fabulous sapphires was still in her possession. She had given Wells the first one to sell so they could buy a second inn, since The Old Hart had been doing so well. They thought they had found their perfect employment. He'd told her to keep the gems a secret, but obviously someone found out and killed him for it. The question was, who? And what would happen if the killer discovered she still had another one?

Gawain needed to stop poking around in that business or the killer might get suspicious. She'd never really suspected a stranger had done it. Probably one of the locals who frequented their dining room had overheard them talking about Wells's plan to buy The Royal Arms a couple of miles away.

She went to the trunk and dug down, until she found a carved box with a lock. The key fit on a chain around her neck. She pulled it from under her dress and unlocked it. When she had the box open, there sat the gem, nestled in its bed of cotton and silk, the last physical remnant of her mother's royal life. In this case, not a loose stone, but a finely carved gem held onto a gold ring base with tiny prongs, jewelry fit for a queen. She resisted the urge to put it on her finger, but placed it back in the box and locked it, then hid it away again, just as she heard Fern at the door.

"She didn't want to return?" Lord Judah asked, passing Gawain a plate of almond pastries that a cakie had delivered to the upstairs office at Redcake's.

"Thank you. No. I think she was irritated." He took a bite, savoring the light, buttery flakes of the pastry.

"You are getting married mid-week."

Gawain laughed. "I might have overlooked that point, but it is a good one."

"The family will be here tomorrow?"

"Including hers," Gawain agreed. He opened the Gladstone bag at his feet and pulled out his new acquisition. "Take a look at this."

Lord Judah opened the slim wooden box and whistled at the necklace inside. "Wedding gift? Looks Indian."

"Caliatan, supposedly." Gawain named the price he had paid. "Fair, do you think? I threatened the jeweler with your expertise."

Lord Judah examined the necklace closely. "Within a hundred pounds. I think the central sapphire might have a small flaw, but in this light I can't say for sure."

"I can live with that. I actually wanted to talk to you about another gem." He took the case back from his friend and replaced it in the bag, then pulled out a sheet of paper. "This is a drawing I had Fern make after I bought her a new set of colored pencils. But you can also use the central sapphire in the necklace as a mental reference."

"For what?"

"Fern doesn't speak, of course, but I have the impression that her brother was killed over a larger version of that sapphire, which was attached to a simple gold chain. There may have been a pearl suspended between the chain and the sapphire, but she isn't sure."

Lord Judah's tiger eyes narrowed. "This is a new wrinkle."

"Yes. I haven't spoken to Ann. Not the sort of thing to discuss just before one's wedding, but I was wondering, with your connections to the trade, if you could find out if such a necklace, or a large sapphire alone, had changed hands in the past couple of years."

"Depends on how big it was. The setting isn't distinctive."

"I know," Gawain said. "It's a long shot. But the sapphire sounds unusually large."

Lord Judah nodded. "I'll ask for you. Think it will lead to the killer?"

"Yes," Gawain said, reaching for another pastry. "I expect it will."

"You seem irritated by these events."

"If Wells Haldene was murdered over something worth this much money, you'd think the killer would be in funds now."

"So?"

"Harry Haldene isn't living like a man who has the price of an inn under a pillow."

"Waiting to make his move?"

"What has he been waiting for? It's been three years." Gawain shook his head. "He may not be our killer."

"Did Lewis uncover any good gossip in the community when he was making arrangements with his blacksmith?"

"No. Nothing."

"Then the gem is your best lead. I'll let you know what I find. Right now you'd better make sure your house is ready for a family of four." He took Fern's drawing and tucked it away.

Gawain nodded. "I leave the matter in your capable hands."

The next day, family homes filled with guests. Gawain had arranged for his possessions to be sent to Battersea, and the house there had been put in order by Redcake family retainers. Pounds, the family butler, had done minimal hiring for the house, choosing a housekeeper, a footman, and a couple of maids. Gawain wanted to leave some of the staff concerns up to Ann, such as nursery maid. He would choose a carriage when he had time, and a mechanic if he purchased a horseless one from Lewis, or stable hands if he went the old-fashioned way.

Ann had asked him to meet Harry and Cousin Jeremy at the station since they had no familiarity with London, and to take them to an inn near the church where the wedding would take place the next day, followed by a meal at the Redcake mansion.

Before going to Ann, he'd begged a nursemaid from the housekeeper at Hatbrook House, managing to avoid family, who would have wondered why. When he arrived at Ann's flat, accompanied by the nursemaid his sister's housekeeper had spared from the nursery, he found the air of the place to be abandonment-in-process, with crates, trunks and boxes stacked along the inner wall.

"It's a good thing Noel isn't crawling yet," he said, kissing Ann on the cheek.

"Yes, I can't wait to settle in again," Ann said, cradling the baby against her shoulder. "All this activity is upsetting his digestion."

"Poor mite," the maid said, peering around Gawain to look at Noel.

"This is Jenna Wilson," Gawain told Ann. "She's an experienced nursery maid and I thought she could sit with Noel while you went to the station with me. You must need a break from all the packing."

"Fern is helping," she said absently.

"Why don't you come with me to greet our Haldene guests?"

She sighed and wiped her face. A streak of dust came away. She looked down. "Am I this dirty all over? It doesn't seem possible. We didn't live here very long."

Jenna reached for Noel. "Amazing what soot can do in a short time."

Ann smiled ruefully and handed Noel to the nursemaid. "It would be polite to collect Wells's family personally."

"I'll take good care of him," Jenna promised. "The marchioness has never had a complaint about my work with Lady Mary Ellen."

Ann attempted to stare down the maid, but Jenna met her gaze with calm competence. When Ann turned to Gawain, he knew she would depart with him.

"Fern, do you want to go with us to collect Harry and Jeremy?" Gawain called.

The girl poked her head out of the kitchen and shook her head, then mimed eating. Ann put her hand to her forehead.

"We forgot lunch, didn't we? Oh, I'm so sorry."

"At least the baby just ate," Gawain said, taking a milk-stained towel off Ann's shoulder. "Pull a coat over your dress and no one will see the dust."

"And my hair?"

"A big hat," Gawain said firmly.

"One that covers most of my hair," Ann agreed. She found a black felt toque banded with white ribbon and pinned it over her mass of frizz, leaving only a fringe of black curls in front. Then she pulled her heavy cloak from its peg. "Too heavy for the season?"

"Not in this muck. You'll have to brush the hem later, though. Mud is everywhere."

"At least it will cover my dress." She gave Jenna a last assessing glance, but apparently saw nothing that would concern her, because she then waved to Fern and opened the door.

Gawain followed her out, pleased for a few minutes alone with his fiancée. The station wasn't far, near the church, and they waited under an overhang near the tracks for the Haldenes to arrive on the next southbound train.

He spotted the telltale can of a hot potato seller and went to purchase some, since Ann had missed lunch. He'd only been away for a couple of minutes, but he saw a man next to her as he walked back, leaning much too close.

"Excuse me," he heard Ann saying.

"Just a little company," the man coaxed in a nasal whine. His hat brim covered his eyes, but he looked young and his clothing dissolute.

Gawain forced his bad hip into a fast trot and was soon taking Ann's arm. "Is he bothering you, my dear?"

Ann squeezed his forearm. "My fiancé has returned, sir. You may depart as quickly as you please."

The young man stared at Gawain's shoes then worked his way up insolently. When his eyes met Gawain's hard, one-eyed stare he blanched. He stammered his apologies and moved away.

"I shouldn't have left you alone for a second," Gawain said, holding back a pungent curse. He handed her a potato.

"It was worth it for this," she sighed, holding it between her gloves. "I had no idea I was so hungry."

"You are eating for two."

"Yes. Thankfully, I have a big, strong man to help me." She batted her eyes.

He wondered if this was a gentle reprimand, since he had not been around for either the pregnancy or early weeks of Noel's life, but the suggestive way she smiled at him made it seem otherwise. He never would understand the gentler sex. Hadn't she been utterly uninterested in him recently, mired in secret cares?

"The sapphire," he said, the thought of it suddenly come to mind.

She raised one finely arched eyebrow, her mouth full of potato.

"Fern mentioned it," he said. "Wells was killed over a sapphire."

She swallowed her mouthful, cold creeping back into a visage that had so recently been soft and loving. He cursed himself for a fool. Had he not told Lord Judah that this was not the topic to discuss just before their wedding? But he was in for a penny now. And a pound.

"Fern doesn't speak," she said.

"She drew me a picture. Of a necklace with a sapphire. Maybe a pearl too, I wasn't sure. I have a feeling that she did more than just discover Wells's body. I think she saw the murder, or at least part of it."

She sighed. "It wouldn't surprise me, given her reaction. Maybe she's trying to protect herself."

"So you think the murderer is someone she knows? Someone who might feel safer because she doesn't speak?"

"I have wondered about many things since that morning." She forced a smile. "But we are moving forward, you and I."

"Has Fern seemed any more relaxed since you moved to London?" Gawain persisted.

"I think her habit of not speaking is utterly ingrained by now. She's a child. Whatever happened is beyond her understanding."

"Was the necklace real?"

Ann nodded. "It was my mother's. She was literally saved from her husband's pyre by my father, and one of her servants smuggled out some of her possessions later. Most of it was sold to pay for expenses over the years, but the necklace came to me."

"Who knew about it?"

"I couldn't say. It was hers after all. She wore it for special occasions."

He heard the clitter-clack of the train coming into the station. "Why did Wells have it in the stable that morning?"

"He was taking it to an appraiser to prove it was as valuable as the inn we were about to buy."

"Who bought the inn when you didn't?"

She stamped her feet. "I don't think it changed hands for months after Wells died, and the new owner wasn't anyone I knew."

"Did anyone in your life come into money about then?"

She shook her head. "Don't you think I've thought about these things?"

"It's possible you haven't wanted to, considering how much loss you suffered and the busy life you led."

"I had plenty of time to think," she said bitterly. "My bed and my arms were both cold and empty."

The noise from the train increased and steam filled the air as the iron beast rocked alongside the platform, brakes compressing in a deafening roar. Ann took a savage bite of her potato, cutting off conversation even if the noise had not done it.

"I've been reading several articles about French psychopathology lately. Very interesting material."

Ann kept chewing.

"Have you heard of therapeutic suggestion? The idea is, you use it to counteract the self-suggestion that has created problems in a traumatized mind."

She frowned.

"Not you, but Fern. There is no doubt she is traumatized and you've told me doctors find nothing physically wrong with her, and that she spoke fine until just after the murder."

"What is your point?"

"Perhaps we can talk to her daily, and affirm that her dumbness is not incurable. That is therapeutic suggestion."

Ann sniffed. "And this will magically make her speak again?"

"I have no idea. Or any notion of how long it takes. We should take her to someone trained. But there can't be any harm in telling her she can speak again."

"No, I can't see any harm in that," Ann agreed. "I am glad you are concerned about her."

"She loves you and Noel very much. I want her to have a good life."

"Me too."

Gawain turned from her and watched the train as people began to exit. About five minutes passed. Ann ate another potato. Then, he spotted Harry Haldene with a carpetbag, walking toward them from one of the cars in the rear. He appeared to be alone.

Ann took his arm. "Just Harry? I wonder what happened to Jeremy. I hope he isn't ill."

Harry wore the same suit Gawain had spotted him wearing in Leeds, plus a new bowler. "He looks ready for the city."

She smiled. "I can see Wells in him just now and that is rare."

Harry did look rather dapper in his good clothes. "Welcome to London. I hope you'll enjoy your first visit here," Gawain said, stepping forward with his hand outstretched.

Harry took it and pumped it enthusiastically. "Many happy returns. But this isn't my first London-bound train, though I 'aven't been here since Wells died."

"That's right. You were here that day, weren't you?" Ann said with a significant glance in Gawain's direction.

Gawain sighed. No wonder she never suspected her brother-in-law. He'd known the man had an alibi, but of course Ann remembered the events clearly.

"That's right. Wells sent me 'ere to arrange with some new suppliers. We were going to 'ave a second inn, but of course all that fell apart when he died."

"Because the thief stole the money we were going to use," Ann said.

Harry looked at her in surprise. "I didn't know that."

She smiled wanly. "I don't remember anything much about that time."

"You wouldn't. You nearly died losing the baby," Harry said. "Come, give us a kiss, sister. I'm glad you've found happiness again."

The broad, muscular Harry hugged Ann as if she were delicate china. Her smile at him was genuine. Gawain's opinion of the man took a permanent turn for the better.

"And Jeremy?" he asked. "Is he on a later train?"

"His hands were like ice last night and 'e was coughin' to beat the band. I insisted he stay. Didn't want your baby to take sick."

"I'm sorry to hear that," Ann said.

"Ah, well, he doesn't clean up as nicely as me." Harry grinned. "Where's little Fern? With the wee one?"

"Yes," Ann said.

"Let's get you to your inn," Gawain suggested.

"I'd like to see the baby," Harry said. "Curious to know if he's got Ann's beauty or your ugly smiler."

"You'll see him tonight at the dinner," Gawain said. "My family doesn't know about Noel yet."

Harry let out a raspy chuckle. "That's goin' to lift some eyebrows."

Gawain nodded. "But I felt they ought to see him before tomorrow's ceremony."

"There's no reason Harry shouldn't see Noel earlier," Ann said. "Let's stop at the inn, then go back to the flat."

"You have a lot of work to do," Gawain said. "How are you going to make yourself ready for the party with so many people in the flat?"

Harry patted Ann's shoulder. "I'll see him tonight, Ann. Listen to your fiancé. I know how long washin' your hair takes."

She glared at him and he snorted at her.

In hindsight, given the obvious closeness of these two, Gawain wondered how Ann had left Leeds for London so easily. She really had been desperate to find him. He couldn't help but be flattered, especially since her desperation hadn't simply been that she wished to wed.

Chapter Eleven

Gawain stepped into the vast foyer of Hatbrook House, which glittered with gold-framed mirrors that threw sparking gaslight around the space, followed by Ann, Fern, and Harry. The nursemaid Jenna was with them as well, but Ann held Noel in a rather tight grip, her trust not being earned easily. Harry and Fern had both been wide-eyed as they'd been retrieved in the marquess's gleaming carriage and their wonder was renewed in this newly redecorated opulence.

Cousin Lewis was just ahead of them. "You would have arrived in better style, Cousin, if you'd come in a horseless carriage."

Gawain poked Lewis's arm with his cane. "I was wondering if you were going to sell me one for the Battersea house."

"Happy to," Lewis said with a wink. "Let's keep me in business in case I come across a lady as irresistible as your princess."

Ann seemed to handle the praise well, blushing as Lewis shook Harry's hand. Footmen and maids came forward to collect coats.

"How are the machine parts comin' along?" Harry asked Lewis. "Ye're mentioned frequently in our dinin' room these days."

"I'm glad to hear it. We can't keep all the work in Nine Elms."

Gawain took Noel while Ann was helped off with her coat. Underneath she wore a rich red dress he'd seen before, but that she had updated with lace cuffs, collar and gold Indian embroidery down the bodice. Her full breasts strained the white neckline, and a dizzying wave of lust came over him. Tomorrow night. Tomorrow night he would have her alone in a luxurious suite at Claridge's.

Almost alone, at any rate. Noel would be there. Thankfully babies slept most of the time. And once they moved to their new house, Noel would be in the nursery. They would have some actual private moments.

The party, along with Lewis, was directed into the grand drawing room by the marquess's butler. Family was arranged, standing and in seats, around one of the vast fireplaces. The room had been redecorated in olive green, which suited his sister's red hair much better than the former rose-hued scheme. But she was not the formidable one in this room, nor were his sisters, or even his mother. No, that was Sir Bartley Redcake, his father.

Gawain permitted himself a moment of self-congratulation that he'd given up on pleasing the man years ago in favor of his own interests. Still, a man wanted his choice of wife to be welcomed and approved of by his kin.

The butler cleared his throat and spoke. "Mrs. Ann Haldene, Gawain Redcake, Lewis Noble, Henry Haldene, Fern Haldene and Noel Redcake."

Gawain saw the frowns as the name of his son was pronounced. Grandmother Noble, his mother's mother, was getting a bit deaf and she said loudly, "Speak up, man!"

With a sigh, Gawain took Noel from Ann's arms. He'd hoped Ann could be petted before the baby was discussed, but that was a forlorn dream. He walked toward the armchair to the right of the fireplace, where Grandmother Noble sat in grand style with Uncle Jacob standing to one side.

"This is my son, Grandmother. Noel. He was born Christmas Day." As he looked defiantly around the room, he saw his mother pale and his father redden. He placed Noel in his great-grandmother's arms before she could speak a word of protest.

But instead of snarling, her face wrinkled into soft motherly appreciation. "You are a little love, my duckling. Two months old, you say?"

He turned to Ann and smirked. The oldest person in the room hadn't chastised them.

"I want to see the baby," Ellen Redcake, his mother, fluttered.

She rose from her seat next to his twin Alys, Lady Hatbrook, and rushed to her mother's side. Soon, all the ladies in the room took turns holding and cooing over Noel.

In the interim, Gawain took Ann's arm and led her to a sofa, then urged Fern to sit beside her. Jenna waited in the wings, ready to rescue the baby and take him to the nursery with the other babies of the household.

"I like your dress," Lord Judah said, coming to perch on the armrest of the sofa next to Ann. "Did you learn that embroidery from your mother? It reminds me of fancywork I saw in India."

She nodded. "I've taught Fern now, too. My wedding dress is decorated in the same style."

"I'm sure it will be lovely, and that present Gawain brought you will look very well with it."

Her face took on an expectant expression, and lost any hint of the nervousness that had been there before. "Present?"

Fern beamed as Gawain said, "Little Sister here helped me pick it out for you."

The girl plucked at her skirt. Ann glanced down. "Yes, my wedding dress is navy blue, just like Fern's dress tonight. Doesn't she look pretty?"

Gawain and Lord Judah both agreed. "Where is Lady Judah this evening?" Gawain asked.

"She's terribly ill, actually."

"I wonder if she has the same illness as my cousin Jeremy," Ann said. "He didn't come down."

"I'm sorry to hear that, but it is definitely not the same thing," Lord Judah said with a wink.

Gawain's hearing perked up. "Some news in the offing?"

"You didn't hear it from me," Lord Judah grinned.

Gawain looked up to see his father looming over the sofa. The older man cleared his throat. "That's a handsome lad you have there, son."

"Thank you."

"Wedding tomorrow."

"Couldn't come soon enough."

Sir Bartley nodded. Gawain was relieved that this was all he would say on the subject. After Matilda's misadventures, how much censure could his father have to offer? Still, this evening could not have gone more smoothly.

The group circulated for fifteen minutes, greeting Ann and discussing Noel. One person who didn't speak to them was Hatbrook himself. Gawain finally noticed this and looked around for his brother-in-law. He spotted him on the window-side of the room, standing next to an olive green velvet curtain, seeming lost in thought.

"I had better approach," Gawain said, with his chin lifted in the direction of the marquess. He kissed Ann on the cheek and stood, leaving her with Fern and his mother.

Hatbrook turned when he moved to the man's side, but said nothing.

"Missing your sister?" Gawain said after a moment's contemplation of Hatbrook's aloof air.

His cheek clenched. "Yes."

"I am somewhat astounded that she and I are now linked in your mind."

Hatbrook's mouth twisted. "You were my hope for her salvation, but that's lost now."

"If she's anywhere on this earth, we'll find her. Someday." Even if he had no further hope of her for himself, he could never forget the enthusiastic and charming girl.

"Will we find her on this earth or under?" Hatbrook's usually resonant voice was soft.

Gawain shook his head. "I wish I knew."

Hatbrook folded his arms across his chest and stared out at the rain-soaked stone beyond the windows. "We've had a cryptic note from Manfred Cross."

"You have?" Gawain could scarcely contain himself from shaking Hatbrook. Had the case broken at last? "When? What did he have to say?"

"Nothing useful regarding my sister. But one of them is alive, at least."

"They aren't together?"

"He didn't say. But Lady Judah insists that the handwriting is indeed her brother's."

"That is excellent news. I shall pursue it next week."

"No." Hatbrook put his hand on Gawain's arm. "Your part in this is done. We'll take it from here. Clearly you've delayed your happiness too long as it is."

"I didn't know about the baby until January," Gawain said. "We're marrying about as soon as it is possible."

Hatbrook's cheeks worked again. "At least I don't have to feel guilty about that."

"You wish you'd let me marry Beth now?" He couldn't help digging in the knife one last time.

"I can see you love your Mrs. Haldene, so I don't feel guilt on your account. But on Beth's? Yes. Something went very wrong for her, something you might have protected her from. Assuming she'd have agreed to marry you, something that is far from certain."

"Let us be done with insults," Gawain said, holding back his cruel rebuttal for his sister's sake. "You have released me from this situation."

Hatbrook nodded. "I wish you happiness."

"Will you come and meet my bride?"

Hatbrook forced a smile. "Of course."

Gawain didn't expect that he and Ann would be dining at Hatbrook House again. Hatbrook would hold a grudge against him, however subtle. Would she notice or mind? Glancing over at the sofa, he could see she appeared to be in perfect command of herself, gracious and smiling, her head held high, no sign of nerves. Her royal blood coming to her aid, or her experience in greeting many kinds of people at the inn? Either way, she was magnificent. He wished he'd given her the necklace tonight, to set off that slender throat and magnificent bosom.

But he couldn't think of her curves and valleys now. His father was approaching with Uncle Jacob.

Harry met Ann in the cloakroom at Hatbrook House as she was getting dressed to leave after the wedding meal the next day. The family was moving into the drawing room post-wedding celebration, but she and Gawain were going to Claridge's. Fern would spend the night here in the nursery with the babies and even Harry had been invited to stay on through dinner.

"Congratulations," Harry said, holding out his arms.

She smiled and gave him a one-armed hug.

"He really is precious," Harry said, looking down at Noel. "I wish you hadn't lost your first bairn."

She nodded, then kissed Noel's forehead. "It would have been lovely to have a part of Wells still around."

"Yes. Say, that's quite the necklace Redcake gave you. Interesting choice, given the one Wells died for."

"I think Fern picked it out," Ann said, touching the choker. "He didn't mean any harm by it and it is lovely."

"I agree. 'Tis. Proves the man has money, at any rate."

"He wants to display his success like any man would."

"You were more than an ornament to my brother."

"I hope you realize how much Gawain has done by marrying me. He did not have to."

"I suppose he's honorable enough."

Ann took a deep breath. "I didn't realize you were aware that Wells had my necklace when he died. I had always assumed it was stolen then, but until Fern revealed her knowledge of it to Gawain I wasn't sure."

"He told me about it, Ann. I had some interest in the subject after all, since takin' on another inn would give me more work."

"I see." Wells's loyalty to Harry had come between them at times, as Wells had never shown any inclination to keep anything private from his brother. "Who else knew about it?"

"I don't know. He told me in private. But I think it's too bad you had to sell your mother's things. What do you have left of her, after all?"

"Her knowledge," Ann said promptly, keeping the information about her mother's last gem to herself. "She never minded selling off her jewelry. I remember her pawning a turquoise ring to pay for doctor's bills one year when Father and I were both sick. It didn't seem to trouble her, so why should I mourn a necklace when it was buying my family prosperity?"

"I suppose she didn't have happy memories of the life that brought her the jewelry, given she almost died on her husband's funeral pyre."

"Childless widows in India had a miserable life. Mother told me that many women in those days were happy to die, rather than to spend their lives in labor to their angry husbands' families."

Harry made a face.

"Her husband was much older than she though, and she'd fallen in love with my father, so of course she was happy not to die. But she wouldn't have wanted to stay in the zenana either, in a meaningless existence. I'm glad this society allows remarriage of widows."

Harry shook his head without indicating agreement or disagreement, and pulled a fluffy package from his pocket. "This is for you. The ladies of the Gupta family made it for your wedding night."

Ann took the package, pleased to be remembered by her patients. She had delivered two children for Mrs. Gupta in her Leeds years. "How kind of them."

"And this is from all of us at The Old Hart." He pulled out another small package, smiling sheepishly. "It's a French eau de toilette. The ladies chose it."

As he set it on top of the Gupta package, she blinked back tears, touched by the remembrances. "I'm sure I will love it."

Gawain stepped into the room, a frown making his usual stern face even more forbidding. "Why are you crying? What's going on here?"

Ann sniffed. "Harry was just giving me gifts, Gawain. Wedding presents from one of the families I cared for, and from the inn staff."

"Ah. Let me take Noel so you can put your cloak on."

"Nice necklace, Redcake," Harry commented.

"Fern has a good eye. It suits my bride's wedding gown beautifully."

Ann knew she had not glowed so since before Wells had died. Gold embroidery went well with her skin, as did gold jewelry. And who didn't look beautiful wearing pearls and sapphires? Her new curves made fitting into her clothing more difficult, but she couldn't help noticing how Gawain's eyes strayed to the bodices of her dresses far more than Wells's gaze ever had. Some of her new curves were worth having, despite the cost to the rest of her figure, and the tightness of her stays.

"Ann and Fern did a beautiful job with their new gowns. All the ladies of my family said so, and my mother was a fiend for making the girls sew. Rose wants to learn your embroidery technique."

Ann couldn't help smiling at that. "I'll be happy to teach your sister." She'd been nervous to meet the Redcakes, but they seemed to have taken the revelation of Noel's birth in stride. They didn't hide Matilda's little son either, which made her think their kindness was genuine.

"Is Noel bundled properly?" Gawain asked. "It isn't raining, at least. Lewis is going to drive us over to Claridge's in his horseless buggy."

"Is it safe?"

"Perfectly," Gawain said. "We never would have met if I hadn't been in one all the way from here to Leeds last year."

"We only met because it broke down," Ann pointed out.

"He is always making improvements. Come, you don't want to spend the rest of your wedding day in a cloakroom, do you?"

Ann blushed. "Of course not. Enjoy the rest of your stay in London, Harry. Will you have time to see us in Battersea before you go?"

"I'm leaving tomorrow. Best to get back with Jeremy ill."

"Happy travels then, Haldene." Harry shook hands with Gawain, then they all filed out of the cloakroom.

Ann's stomach was in her throat for the entire ride to the hotel. She kept Noel tightly clutched to her body, but appreciated that Gawain kept his arms around them both too. Still, she didn't relax until they entered the lobby of the grand hotel.

They were greeted with suitable pomp and shown to a penthouse suite. Staff took their minimal luggage to a bedroom while Ann admired the barrel vaulted ceiling and white marble fireplace in the sitting room.

"Jenna is already here," Gawain reported, limping toward the fireplace. "She'll care for Noel tonight. Is he still on a regular feeding schedule?"

"Yes," she hesitated, "but I don't know how he'll do without me in the same room."

"It's time to make the adjustment," he said. "He'll sleep in the nursery from now on. Jenna has agreed to stay with us."

"I don't think I'm ready for that," Ann said.

"You told me he's already only eating once during the night. I think he's ready."

She stared into the fire. Of course this would be how it would go. She wasn't marrying a man who could only afford a two-room flat, after all. Besides, the grandeur of Hatbrook House should have made it clear the way she was expected to conduct herself from now on. As a lady of means, the kind of lady who had nursemaids and nannies, who spent her time sewing and doing good deeds. That is what her new husband expected of her, not to be mooning over a healthy infant of ten weeks.

She glanced at him, and found his gaze hovering over her bosom again. And then, he might only care about the making of siblings for Noel. Or the activity that led to the making of siblings. A flare of memory, at the thought of that time with him in Leeds, flushed her cheeks. When she'd thought of nothing but satisfying herself, and him. Those simple animal pleasures they had experienced had led to complications, it was true, but also to this moment, when they might be together again. No more waiting. No more dreary flat. She was Mrs. Gawain Redcake now, spending the night at Claridge's in London. Her parents would have been so proud of her new place in the world.

"Your eyes have gone distinctly feline," Gawain observed.

A waiter rolled in a tray containing an iced bucket with a bottle. "Would you like me to open it, sir?"

"No, thank you," Gawain said, and walked the man to the door. "Is everyone out of the suite?"

"Except your maid," he said.

Ann watched Gawain hand the man a coin before he stepped out, pulling the doors closed behind him, with a motherly pang of regret that had nothing to do with her new husband. She handed Noel to Jenna.

"We'll be very cozy in the second bedroom, Mrs. Redcake. I had a peek and the fire is lit."

"I'll see you at feeding time then." She watched the nursemaid leave the room, her child in tow.

Gawain returned from the foyer and stalked back to her. She noticed his limp had become less obvious now, his presence more commanding, demanding. A wounded leopard, and all the more dangerous for it.

"You fed Noel just before we left, correct?"

She nodded.

He smiled. The purely wicked intent behind those bared teeth made her fingers tingle.

"Then you are all mine for hours."

"I am." But she'd had a baby since they'd last been together. Was she still what he expected? Could she still lose herself in his embrace?

He reached for her.

She danced away. "I have a special gown and French perfume. I should bathe, powder, make myself ready for you."

"Did you do all those things before you came to my bed in the inn?"

Flustered, she put her hand to her hat. "I don't remember."

"I doubt it. You were quite business-like when you came in. It was wonderful, amazing, even without preparation."

"But it's our wedding night," she protested. "People gave me gifts."

He dropped his hands. "You are delaying, Ann. We only have so much time before Noel needs you. I thought you'd want to spend it with me."

She sensed the hurt he expressed, though his outer appearance and voice were calm. "I will need you to act as my maid at any rate, because I can't get out of this dress on my own."

His eyebrows rose. "Oh?"

"I expect, once you've seen me out of my clothes, I never would have made it into a new nightgown and perfume."

"Unlikely," he agreed. A hint of a smile carved a dimple into one harshly planed cheek.

She unpinned her hat. A moment ago she'd been drawn to the fire but now it seemed scorching hot. She set her hat down on a table and pulled off her gloves, then unbuttoned her cloak.

"You are quite stunningly perfect," Gawain said, when her dress was revealed.

"I'm pleased you think so." She admired her groom in turn. Gawain was as beautifully dressed as she was, in a tightly cut morning coat. His gray silk ascot had a large sapphire pin in the center, the stone matching her necklace. "I am glad you had a photographer there. I think I will like this portrait better than the other one."

"Women always like their wedding photograph best. I think I would like you painted as well. As an odalisque."

She swatted at his arm. "I know what an odalisque is, Gawain."

He laughed and held his ground. "You would be perfect."

"No one is going to paint me nude." She draped her cloak across a chair and sat down to remove her shoes.

"In the best paintings, all you see is curves, nothing too revealing. Have you seen *La Grand Odalisque* by Ingres? Nothing shows, it is almost proper, yet incredibly alluring."

"So now you are singing the praises of some other woman? On my wedding night?" She stretched her toes, remembering what her mother had told her about her first wedding, and all of the henna tattoos laboriously painted on feet and hands.

"No, she is not a real woman. We shall have to go to Paris so I can show the painting to you."

"I would like that. It is strange to be considered foreign when I have never left England since I arrived as a young child."

"You cannot deny some unusual facets of your character. Most women would not have left the security you did to chase after me to London. You've never really told me why you did it." He watched her stocking-clad toes scratch along the plush carpet.

Feeling exposed, she tucked her feet under her skirts. "I expect it was my pregnancy at work, but I felt suffocated, increasingly so as it progressed. For some reason I thought finding you would cure me."

"Many find marriage suffocating."

"But they aren't marrying you. You are a restless man, Gawain Redcake. Life with you will never be the same day after day. And you appreciate my knowledge. That is extremely rare among white men."

"You only find white men attractive."

She tiptoed to him, feeling the deep pile of the carpet now that her shoes were off, and unbuttoned his coat. "All that pasty skin? What's not to love?"

"Some of me is permanently darkened after all those years in the sun."

"Just the back of your neck and your hands."

"You've noticed." The dimple returned and she had a sudden urge to lick it.

"I've paid attention. I've seen most of you a few times."

"And all of me?"

"Just once. But I've longed to see it all again," she admitted, unpinning his cravat.

"So those Ayurvedic massages of my hip were merely a ploy on your part?"

"Not entirely. It is hard to relax when you're in pain and I'm so glad to see you walking without a cane again."

"Oh?"

"Yes. You're a true predator without it." She bit her lip and looked directly into his eyes. "If you needed it I wouldn't mind at all, of course, but once I worked with you the first time I realized much of your discomfort could be alleviated."

"You were right. Your knowledge makes my life better."

"I hope my presence will, too."

He put his hands into her hair then, and began pulling out all the pins. Tension released as each pin dropped to the table. He massaged her scalp every time he pulled. The tips of her breasts tingled, then she began to warm at the top of her thighs. When she tried to take a deep breath, she found she couldn't.

"Stop!"

His hands stilled. One lock of her hair had fallen completely.

"My hair is going to get caught in the necklace, and I can't breathe." She stepped away, pressing her hands to her chest. She could feel the necklace against the tendons of her neck as she tried to take a breath.

"Ann, stop. Relax."

She coughed. Black spots danced before her eyes. "It is so hot."

"You're going to swoon. Come now." He put an arm around her waist, another at her shoulder, and led her into the bedroom.

The fire there had not been stirred so high. As her pulse beat harshly in her temples, he placed her in a chair by a writing table and lifted her hair. "I'll take your necklace off. That will alleviate one problem."

In a moment, she felt the collar sag and he placed the necklace in her hands.

"Now, onto these buttons. But I suspect the real problem is your stays. You cut your dress very small."

"I didn't want to look like a woman who had just given birth." She took shallow breaths, forcing herself to slow her breathing.

"You are magnificent," he said, tugging at the back of her dress, then swore. "I tore a buttonhole in my haste."

"I can fix it." She blinked. The spots were gone. *Good heavens, I nearly fainted.*

"All done with the buttons," he said a minute later. "Now to unlace you."

"Thank you."

"Who put you into this cage? Fern?"

She put her hands to her flaming cheeks. "No, she isn't strong enough. The wet nurse helped me."

"She must have arms like a stevedore."

She felt the tension release around her torso. Her fingers shook as she undid the buttons at the front of her corset. It was new and stiff.

"I can do that too. However did you feed Noel?"

"Jenna had to help me adjust some things. I think this dress will have to go into the trunk until he's weaned. It's just too much trouble."

"We'll order loads of dresses for you next week, after we've settled into the house and unpacked. You'll need a different wardrobe now."

"Being a new mother does tend to destroy clothing. Everything I own has gotten stained." She had to admit the idea of new clothes was appealing. While she enjoyed embroidering, she could do without the toil of dressmaking. Also, she never wanted to embarrass her husband with the worry that his wife could be mistaken for a servant.

"Do you feel better now? Can I finish with your hair?"

She took a deep breath. Her heart was still pounding, but she'd recovered enough to glance around the room. "I think I'd like to finish removing my clothing alone."

He nodded. "I'll get you a glass of champagne. I think you had better do the donning of nightgowns and powdering after all."

She reached up her hand and he clasped it. "Thank you for understanding."

"I should have realized that dress and lovemaking were incompatible," he said, kissing her fingers. "Beautiful as it is, it is too snug to contain those lovely breasts of yours right now."

"You've noticed?" she teased.

He turned the chair around, then leaned over her, resting his forearms on the back of the chair. "I have hardly slept from thoughts of caressing your voluptuous curves. It's maddening to be so close to you and yet not be able to touch you intimately."

Instinctively, she tilted her face up to him and he took her lips in a crushing kiss, the weight of his head pressing into her. She opened in response, but against all expectation, he slowed, softened. This wasn't what she wanted, so she swept her tongue along his lips, inviting him to take possession.

He pushed away, and ran a finger along her temple. "I'll go pour our champagne. Open the door when you're ready for me."

He left her hot and wanting. It felt good and she wanted to dance into his arms, be taken furiously and completely. She made quick work of her clothing and unpinned the rest of her hair, then looked around for her packages. They weren't in the room. She put a hand to her forehead. How could she have left them in the sitting room?

Gawain opened the bottle, poured, then took a sip of the champagne. First rate, just like the rest of this hotel. He wished they could spend a few days here, but Fern needed collecting. If any of his sisters lived in London, he'd have introduced her sooner to fix this problem, but now she was among strangers. And unable to speak. They had to encourage her to find language again.

How long would Ann need before she came out? Surely she'd already recovered from the near faint, considering the passion with which she'd kissed him. But he had already decided to be patient.

He heard a squeak behind him and turned to see a small brown foot peek between the door and jamb. A slim ankle followed it, then a shapely calf. He set down his wineglass, though his mouth had gone dry.

Ann's head popped through, her mouth forming a shocked circle when she saw him staring. Her leg was hastily withdrawn.

"Come in. It's warm enough," he invited.

"I left my packages on the sofa. I was hoping you'd be turned around."

"Come and get them," he said, silk coating his voice.

"Gawain!"

He laughed. "I'll get them if you really want me to, but I'd rather get a look at you. What I can see already shows promise."

Chapter Twelve

"You aren't being very gentlemanly." The door muffled Ann's voice.

"I'm your husband first, a husband who wants to see his naked wife."

"Do you even see my packages?" Ann watched until his back was turned as he hunted for them, then slid into the room. Surely this was a more grandly erotic gesture for a man who wanted an odalisque wife than waiting timidly in their bed with the door open. She would give her husband what he wanted, and in return he would love her.

When he turned around, holding the packages, she curved herself into a pose, covering her stomach and mound but exposing her breasts. His eyes widened, his mouth opened, and the packages dropped to the floor.

She attempted a seductive smile. He shook his head, then stepped forward.

"You minx. And here I thought my lusty lady had gone missish on me."

She had been right. This was what he wanted. Her fingers caressed the fine linen he wore. He stared into the deep cleavage made by her uplifted arms while she removed his cravat and unbuttoned his shirt. Then he pushed her away and held her at arm's length for inspection.

"Your nipples have darkened."

"That isn't all that is changed."

"I found your curves alluring from the first. All that ripe flesh makes me want to sink my teeth in and take a bite."

Moisture gathered between the lips of her intimate flesh at his husky words. She lifted her hand and tucked it behind her head, before bending one knee to pose. "Where do you want to take the first bite?"

He reached for her hip and pulled her to him, roughly. "Don't tease me, woman."

"I wasn't teasing." Her breasts rose and fell against him with each fast breath. "Take me, Gawain. Whatever you want of me I cheerfully offer you."

He cupped her face in his hands. "Get me out of this damned shirt. It's so tight that I cannot move properly."

"But so fashionable," she teased, pulling the bright linen from his muscled shoulders and sinewy arms. "You still look like a soldier, my husband."

He snorted. "I was little more than a steward in the army, a butler at best. But now I have as good a seat as any cavalry officer. If I went back now I could tiger hunt with the best of them."

"I can see that," she purred. Ambitious, her husband. Marrying her had not done him any favors, even if his family didn't mind.

He put his hand to his trousers and she immediately went to her knees to help him take off his shoes. As the rest of his clothing came off, she kissed her way up his strong, hair-dusted legs, not forgetting each twisted scar on his bad hip. His erection had jutted before she'd ever touched him, but now she saw moisture had gathered at the tip.

She smoothed it over him and smiled. "You are ready for me."

He hauled her to her feet and crushed her against him. "But are you ready for me?"

"Hmmm," she murmured, hoping to tease him further, but then his lips came down on hers. She met his lips, press for press, and his tongue, caressing his mouth, tasting the champagne. He overbalanced and dropped to the arm of the sofa.

At his look of surprise, she decided to go in all the way and pushed him down so that he slid to the cushions, her on top of him. Coming up quickly, she displayed her breasts. With the groan of a dying man, he pulled her forward and took one into his mouth. The sensation sent electricity through her body. She wanted him inside her, and she wanted him now. The scent of his body reminded her of their lusty romp at the inn and all the pleasure it brought her. Her throat went dry at the memory.

The champagne bucket was just behind the sofa on a table. She pulled the open bottle out and sipped directly from it while Gawain caressed her breasts. When he pulled back, surprised by all her wriggling, she dripped the bubbly liquid on his chest, then handed him the bottle and bent over him to lap it up. Using that as an excuse, she slid her body down his chest, leaving a trail of her intimate moisture on his belly. She was stopped by pressure from a hard rod against her bottom.

Glancing up at him, she saw his waiting expression, his eyes half-lidded with desire. Her lips curved and her gaze met his as she found his erection and fit her tender flesh over it.

He swore and grabbed for her hips, pulling her down in an endless, luxurious stroke.

"Completion," she gasped. "Oh yes, Gawain."

He helped her rise, then pulled down again. And again, until she found the rhythm that pleased them both. But neither of them could last long. She judged him to be as desperate for release as she, and perhaps as out of practice. When he grabbed for her breasts again, and sucked furiously on a nipple, she came in long, pulsating bursts, her body clamping viselike around him. He cried out and shuddered, her orgasm prompting his. When it was over, she rested her head against his chest and listened to his strong heartbeats, still feeling the aftershocks in her womb.

He let out a deep breath. "More champagne?"

"Didn't the bottle fall over?"

"I was a soldier, madam. We don't waste good champagne."

She laughed and sighed. "Too content to move, thank you very much."

He stroked his hands down her back. "For the sake of interludes like this, I believe we can make this marriage a success."

She rubbed her cheek against the hair on his chest. Exactly what she wanted to hear. A man satisfied in the bedroom would not look too closely at the disadvantages the woman in question brought him.

"Why don't we move our celebration into the bedroom?" she suggested. "Surely there is more passion where that came from. I believe it is your turn to ride me."

Gawain made a snort reminiscent of a spirited horse. She poked him in the chest and sat up, reaching for the champagne bottle as she did.

"Why don't you take your packages now? I'm curious to see that gown you were so eager to slip into."

She smiled. "I can do that. I want to smell the perfume."

"I will stoke the fire while you do so, my pet."

She would have preferred "my love," but at least her new husband had used an endearment.

The next week passed in a flurry of movement. Boxes, trunks, and baggage moved from Ann's flat, from the Redcake home, even from Bristol, as the Gawain Redcake family members installed themselves in their new semi-detached home in Battersea.

Gawain lifted his eye patch as he looked out of the bow window in his new study one morning. He closed his right eye for a moment to see if he was right. Yes, he could discern the green of the well-watered lawn with his bad eye.

He jumped out of his chair and ran to the study door, calling for Ann. But instead of Ann, Lewis appeared.

"You've got your patch off."

"It's working, old man," Gawain shouted, leaping forward to pump his cousin's hand. "My vision is coming back. I can see color again. I can even see that you've regrown that scraggly beard of yours. Get rid of it. It's appalling. Looks like dead mouse bits fell on your chin."

"You should patch your good eye now and see if that strengthens the bad one."

"I'd be worthless," Gawain said.

"Just during a free hour now and then." Lewis shrugged. "Makes sense that it would help. An eye is a muscle. Needs exercise to be strong."

Gawain stroked his chin. "You have a point. I'm too pleased with myself to even argue with you."

Lewis grinned. "Then this would be an excellent time to sell you a horseless carriage. What do you say?"

"You're lucky I'm rich."

Lewis clasped his hands together. "I'm mostly known for my steam engines, but I've started to experiment with some of the German models that are using four-cylinder, four-stroke engines. Want to give that a whirl? Absolutely the latest thing."

"Who let you in the house?" Gawain retorted.

"That new butler of yours. Chase?"

"We must encourage him to be more discerning," Gawain muttered. "Very well, Lewis. I will be the patron for your German model. But please promise me that it will not blow up any of my family."

"So noted. I will advertise for a chauffeur for you and instruct him properly."

"You've come a long way from mechanical birds, the past couple of years."

"I was in a different frame of mind when I made my little creatures. Now I am all about business." Lewis clapped his bowler back on his head. "I'll be on my way. Just stopped by to check on the progress here."

"Right." He knew Lewis had come to ensure his commission.

"I advised your lovely wife on one or two improvements that could be made in the kitchen. She's put in an order for a new oven."

"Excellent," he sighed.

"Eddy will be pleased to work on that," Lewis said, referring to his apprentice. "We'll have it to you in a couple of weeks."

Chase appeared in the doorway, smoothing down his thick hair. Young for a butler, he was a nephew of Pounds, the Redcake family butler, and had been strongly recommended. "Sir, a Theodore Bliven to see you."

Gawain swore.

Lewis stroked his beard. "Chase looks strong enough to toss the rotter out on his ear."

"No, I'll hear him out. Always a good idea to keep an eye on blackguards," Gawain said.

"You're in an almost painfully good mood."

"I admit it," Gawain said, pounding Lewis's arm and giving him a cheery grin. "Everything is right in the world at the moment."

"Nothing like a new wife in your bed to improve your mood."

His grin sharpened. "Try it yourself and let me know how it works for you."

Lewis's eyes seemed to take on shadow. "No time, no time. I prefer engines. Make more sense to me."

"You have to get over Alys one of these days."

Lewis's lips turned down. "Never think of her."

Gawain shook his head and walked with Lewis as far as the front parlor. "I'd better see what Bliven wants."

"I'll get started on your carriage," Lewis replied, following Chase into the front hall.

It had been a little more than a month since Gawain had seen Bliven. How much had changed. He wondered who had given the man this new address.

When he pushed open the parlor door, he scarcely recognized the man from the back. He'd shorn his unruly curls into a skull-framing cut. When he turned, his merry eyes seemed larger than ever.

"Gawain!" he cried. "Just the man I wanted to see."

"This is my house," Gawain deadpanned as Bliven rushed to shake his hand.

"Yes, yes of course. You must help me. I've hardly slept for a month, you know."

"Been ill? I did wonder about the hair."

Bliven touched his head. "Did it myself in a fit of melancholy. Held the scissors to my throat. For a moment I thought I'd end the entire thing, you see."

Gawain unbuttoned his coat and put his hands on his hips. He didn't respond to the dramatics, knowing Bliven would get to his point.

"How about a drink, old man? Do the thing up civilized?"

"No drinks cart in here. We aren't entertaining yet."

"Oh. I did hear you just moved. And married."

Gawain waited for Bliven to force a smile.

"Felicitations!" he enthused on cue. "And just having entered the blessed state yourself, I know you are the man to help me."

Gawain bent his head.

"Your patch is off, eh? Seeing some improvement?" Bliven's dark gaze sharpened.

"Yes, I do have you to thank for that. And my wife, for knowing how to compound the medicine you acquired."

"Got your vision back?"

"I can see colors. That is all so far."

"I'm sure it will continue to improve."

Gawain raised his eyebrows. He didn't want the conversation to remain personal. "Are you ready to return to India? Given your success, I'm happy to pay for you to return. And some living expenses, of course." His family would object to the expense, yet be glad he had gotten Bliven out of England.

"No, no, you must help me with Matilda." Bliven put his hand on the mantelpiece. He did an exaggerated double take when he saw the family photograph there.

"That is my wife, our son and her former sister-in-law." He closed his good eye. He could still see the basic outlines of the individuals. *Astounding.*

"She's Indian," Bliven said in a near whisper.

"Half. Father was a subaltern."

"Must take after her mother," Bliven muttered. "Still, good in your line of work to have an Indian medical expert handy."

"Indeed." He injected as much frost as he could muster.

"And she was clearly your mistress before you married, since you have a child together. You of all people in the world should understand what I'm going through with Matilda."

Coldness was suddenly easy. "My sister wasn't your mistress. She thought she was your fiancée."

"That's what she said after," Bliven smiled.

"Mrs. Redcake was a widow, a woman of the world. My sister was an innocent, gently reared. You never had honorable intentions toward her, given this other woman you had waiting for you in India."

"But that's all over," Bliven said impatiently. "I'm ready to marry Matilda now. Give the boy my name. Just like you have just done with your, er, what's his name?"

"Noel."

"Noel, then."

"What is your son's name?" Gawain asked, wondering if Bliven even knew.

One side of Bliven's mouth lifted. "Jacob, for Matilda's uncle. It's a family name of mine as well, and Michael is the second name, for my old friend, the marquess."

Gawain nodded approval. "I would have sympathy for you if you hadn't been so cruel to my sister. But there you have it. If it's money you want, I will make my offer to you again. Passage, living expenses, and payment for the goods when they arrive at my warehouse."

"I want her. It's my right. She wanted me once. And a man should marry a decent girl if he takes her innocence. I know that now." Bliven's words stumbled. "I am s-s-sorry it took me all this time to recognize that."

"Why do you want her?"

"I love her, of course. Bad poetry and everything." He patted his waistcoat and pulled out a crumbled sheet of paper. "I wrote her a sonnet."

"How nauseating."

"Look." Bliven knotted his fingers. "I'm going to get her back, her and my son."

"How much?" Gawain asked.

"What do you mean?"

"How much money are you looking for?"

"It's not about money."

"Then what is it about?"

"I do not think I can father another child," Bliven said, his face contorting. "I had scarlet fever in India, and mumps. High fevers both times. I'm surprised I'm still alive, to be perfectly honest. But it does not matter what my reason is, I want my son."

"Not my sister," he observed.

"Of course I want her," Bliven roared. "I'm not likely to get anyone else. I have no income unless I return to India. My cousin's wife, damn her, just gave birth to a son three days ago."

The veil lifted. "You think you've lost your shot at the earldom, then?"

"Well, don't you think so?"

"Babies die." The mere thought hurt his stomach, to be truthful, yet was true. Thank God Noel was a healthy child with a doting mother.

"I should be so lucky," Bliven spat, saliva bubbling at one side of his mouth.

The sentiment sickened Gawain. "You need to go back to India."

"So I can die there? With yet another disease?"

"I never had a problem."

"No, you just got shot." Bliven smiled suddenly, and his face transformed back into its usual merriment. "Give her to me, Gawain, and give me my son. I know you are training her to run your father's businesses. She won't like that. I can take over. I've proven myself to you."

"Now you want to work?" Gawain couldn't hold back a chuckle. "Besides, Matilda has decided she likes business. She is more like Alys than she wanted to admit. The business mind must come with the red hair."

"So Rose isn't interested in business?"

"You aren't going to turn your attentions to Rose," Gawain snapped.

Bliven held up a hand. "No, no. Just making conversation."

"Why don't you return to India, prove you can manage to set up a business there, importing herbs of the quality you found for me. The teas as well. Give Matilda a couple of years. Who can say? She may very well be tired of working and be ready to settle into domesticity by then."

"You'll find her another husband."

"Me?" Gawain laughed. "I've settled here now. I have no reason to even see Matilda, much less marry her off."

"I see there is no reasoning with you. I'll have to approach your father. He'll see reason." Bliven pressed his shoes together and bowed his head with Germanic drama. "Good day to you, Gawain."

Gawain followed him out of the door, requesting his return. But Bliven pulled his hat from the stand by the door and walked out, ignoring him.

As the door shut, Gawain swore. He'd have to go down to Redcake Manor to help his family deal with this problem. So much for settling in here. He knew that Matilda, as usual, was consulting with her father in person, rather than staying in Bristol where she theoretically lived.

Chase stepped into the entryway, closing the open front door, then looked inquiringly at his master.

"Send Mrs. Redcake to me, would you? And have my bags packed for a short trip to Polegate."

Chase nodded and went up the stairs. Gawain stepped back into the parlor and fiddled with a cigar. Why did the idea of leaving Ann dig such a sour hole in his gut? He'd only be gone a couple of days.

The next day, the entire family descended from the platform at Polegate. Ann had insisted on accompanying him and he hadn't had the heart to disagree. She did not have his mother's decisiveness on decorating schemes, but her years at the inn had given her a shrewd judge of servant characters and he thought she'd managed the hiring admirably. The nursery was shaping up comfortably and their own quarters were an oasis of peace and sensuality, for at least a few hours a night.

Jenna Wilson had travelled with them. He knew he needed to offer to return her to Hatbrook Farm but he hoped to persuade her to stay with them. If she preferred city life, Ann might get her newly announced wish to keep the competent nursemaid in her employ.

Anything for Ann, who had proven herself accommodating to his every wish so far. He gazed at her fondly as she stood rocking Noel, Fern at her side. Sir Bartley's coach pulled forward. He recognized the driver and raised his hand for it to stop. One of the stablehands jumped down from the back and began to load the luggage with the help of a porter.

"Is there room for all of us?" Ann asked.

"Should be. Robbie," Gawain called to the driver, "can you take all of us?"

"Yes, Mr. Redcake," Robbie said. "Unless you want the servants to travel different."

"No, no," Gawain said quickly, not wanting to know who Robbie might think was a servant. They hadn't had time to order new clothing for Fern yet and Ann wasn't in one of her new dresses because of the train.

Ann nursed Noel during the drive to the Elizabethan-era house his father had purchased sight unseen a few years before. All but uninhabitable when Alys and Rose had tried to live there a couple of years ago, it was clean and repaired now. Even the grounds were looking manicured. Gawain tried to focus on the property updates, rather than watch his infant son caress his wife's breast as he fed, though the sight was such an endearing one. Ann wouldn't find the time to sit down at all if she wasn't nursing. Setting up a new household had proven a busy enterprise.

"Will that man 'ave made it 'ere before us?" Jenna asked.

Gossip travelled quickly in his new house. "If he caught a late train," Gawain said. "But I doubt he could have managed any kidnapping scheme by now."

Ann's arms tightened around Noel. "He wouldn't take Jacob."

"I don't know what he's capable of," Gawain admitted. "Those illnesses he had might have affected his brain. His moods were alarmingly changeable."

"I should have taken a look at him," Ann said. "If we do see him, I will examine him."

"Don't go near him," Gawain warned. "What if he tried to use you to get to Matilda?"

"He might need medical attention."

"Let him get it elsewhere." He was saved from further pronouncements by the sight of the three-hundred-year-old stone building coming into view.

"Have you been here before?" Ann asked Jenna.

The nursemaid shook her head. "I stay at the Farm. It's not far away. Mostly the family comes there for parties and such. It's cozier, I'm told."

"This house is enormous," Ann said.

Fern's eyes were wide too.

"There's supposed to be ghosts," he said. "Not that I've seen any. There's a ruined abbey nearby."

Fern shivered.

"Not going to explore?" Gawain teased. "I'm sure Rose would take you for a walk through the ruins. Muddy, of course, at this time of year, but we can find boots that will fit you."

Fern brightened at the suggestion of walking. The carriage stopped on the gravel drive.

"Who are the ghosts?" Ann asked, rearranging her clothing. Noel snuffled and fell asleep.

"Roman soldiers," said Robbie, opening the coach door. "Look behind the house. There's a mound with the remains of a shell keep on top."

"Not the monks then?"

Robbie shrugged. "I haven't walked the ruins at night, if you get my meaning."

Fern bounced on the squabs and grinned at Gawain.

"You won't be bored," he promised her, relaxing against the upholstery. "Between the walks, the babies and my mother demanding to fit you with a new wardrobe, there will be plenty to do."

"And Theodore Bliven," Ann said somberly. "Let's not forget about him."

Chapter Thirteen

When Gawain had his family settled at the Manor and verified that Bliven had not been seen there yet, he took a horse and rode north to Polegate to nose around the taverns and see if the man had been noticed in the town. He took his patch off as he travelled, enjoying the blur of colors in the fields. The hint of spring in the air tantalized his nose.

He'd sent a telegram to his old comrade, Sergeant Bowler Martin, late the previous afternoon, hoping the man could have his cronies keep an eye out in the area for a stranger fitting Bliven's description. The regiment had deep ties here and should know if anyone was out of place.

Gawain arrived on time to meet with Martin at an old pub on the outskirts of the railway town. He tied up his borrowed horse and bent his head to go through the low doorway of the ancient building. The air inside was thick with smoke and the scent of stew, probably cooked daily for centuries. He pulled his patch back down over his bad eye. The ability to see color wouldn't do him much good in the dim room.

"Redcake!"

Gawain blinked, then saw a hand waving to him from a stool at the bar. He moved forward, then clapped Martin's shoulder. "Thank you for meeting me."

The old soldier wiped his mouth on his sleeve. "Any time, old friend. I could use a fight to get the blood running. Was your Mr. Bliven at the house?"

"No. I've just come from there. I asked my sister to make up a sketch for you. She's a good artist."

"Seen him before, yourself?"

"Yes, a few times. This man, he was a friend of the marquess, and his father is a friend of my father's. I employed him."

Martin picked up his tankard. "Bad business."

"Yes, and my sister has her own share of the blame. Her wish to be married outshone her sense."

"It's hard for the girls," Martin said. "Silly young things. I think we expect too much of them and punish too hard."

"Do you think we should have forced Bliven to marry her?" Gawain pulled out a stool and sat.

Martin shrugged. "As long as she can live quietly I don't see that not being married has done her any harm. That's the beauty of money, eh?"

"True enough. I'll get you the sketch tomorrow."

"Plenty o' boys from the old regiment to keep an eye out around here."

Gawain pulled out a bag of shillings and pushed it down the bar to Martin. "For those who don't want to answer questions for free."

Martin nodded and tucked the bag away. "Last you were here, we were discussing a different matter."

"Ann Haldene's family."

"Right." Martin gave him a shrewd stare. "I heard you married. Her?"

Gawain nodded as the barman approached. He ordered a tankard of the local brew.

"I asked about her again, you know. After we met." Martin's bushy brows came together.

"Did you?"

"You said the husband had died. The first one, I mean."

Gawain took off his hat and set it on the bar. "Yes, murdered in his stable. I didn't know that part before."

"A bad business." Martin shook his head as Gawain's tankard appeared, along with a refill for Martin.

"Did you hear anything about the murder? I've been able to

clear his brother of the crime, but I'd like to solve it. His sister saw something, maybe everything. It made her dumb, from the shock. There was a theft involved, it seems."

"Really?" Martin asked.

"You seem surprised. Apparently, some royal gems had made their way back from India with Ann's mother."

He pulled out a handkerchief and blew into it. "That might fit in with what I heard."

"Oh?"

"Sure. Someone who knew the family, knew they might have property like that." He put the linen away.

"Who?"

Martin's gaze raked Gawain's face. "I wouldn't like to say, not with you newly married to the girl."

Now what? Gawain set down his tankard. "I don't like the sound of that."

"You can check with your wife," Martin said. "Ask her who she might have told about these royal gems."

Ann was no gossip. What was Martin implying? "Why would she have told anyone?"

Martin coughed again. "You know, pillow talk. The things a girl might say to imply she has a dowry."

Gawain's blood ran cold. He flattened his hand on the bar. "What are you saying?"

Martin sighed. "Given that you're a man with sisters, you know how the girls do make mistakes. Word is that your wife was a bit free with her favors back in the day."

"Are you saying she was a whore?" Gawain started to move off his seat, but a sharp pain bit into his hip. He stiffened.

"No, no." Martin put a hand on his elbow, anchoring him in place. "I'm just saying she took her time choosing a husband, didn't marry the first man in her life. Or so they say. The Indians, you know, don't see things the same way we English do."

"She is English." He twisted, trying to relieve pressure on his hip.

"Born in India. Her mother raised her. Not just Indian but royal too. Royals don't think like us any more than Indians do."

Gawain grabbed for the edge of the bar and hoisted himself more securely on his seat. If he hadn't covered his bad eye with the patch, he'd have blamed it for the flashing red dots around his vision. Surely none of this could be true, though Martin made a bold point. Ann's actions often surprised him.

"I see," he managed to say, after a long pause. "So you think Ann had a lover who killed Haldene for the gems."

"Perhaps."

"Two years after she married him?" That made no sense.

Martin shrugged and reached for his tankard. Gawain's gaze caught the missing fingers and remembered this man was a brother of the sword. He wouldn't lie, had no reason to. Gossip was one thing, but usually there was truth in gossip.

"Did the gossip say she'd kept a man on the side after her marriage?"

"Don't know about that. I'm just saying that there's tales of royal gems, so someone mentioned them over the years. Yet no one stole from the girl's mother."

"So the maharani is the one who passed around the stories. Or someone she told."

"Right-o. Except she died long ago, well before the murder." Martin drained his tankard. "I need to get back home. The wife will have tea waiting for me."

Gawain wanted to shake the man, but he'd gotten what he came for and more. "Thank you for coming all the way down here. Use that money for your expenses too."

Martin shook his head. "Always happy to help. You going to come back with that sketch tomorrow?"

"I'll have to send someone," Gawain said. "From the Manor."

Martin held out his hand. After a moment, Gawain shook it.

"Don't be too hard on your wife," Martin said. "Let bygones be bygones."

Gawain laughed harshly. "But what if she does it again?"

Martin rubbed his nose. "She's lucky to have you. A smart girl won't ruin what she has."

"I hope you are right," Gawain said. "I had better get back too. Send word to the Manor, or Hatbrook Farm, if Bliven is spotted."

"Will do."

They walked out together. Gawain mounted his horse and Martin gave him a salute, then set out on foot for the railway station.

Gawain made it back to the Manor in a red haze, not seeing any green fields or early wildflowers this time. The scent of spring might have been cold ashes in his nostrils. Ann may have been playing a model wife, but she'd been no modest woman. What they'd done had been nothing special or even unusual for her, apparently.

"It will be so much fun for the children to play together in a couple of years," Lady Hatbrook told Ann as she settled Noel into a fancy crib by the fire in the nursery. "The time passes so quickly. I can't believe Mary Ellen is almost a year old."

"She's a very pretty girl." Ann straightened and then smiled at the copper curls of the baby in her sister-in-law's arms.

Lady Hatbrook made a face. "I wish she hadn't inherited the red hair, but the color does seem softer than mine."

"It's beautiful," Ann assured her.

"She seems to have Michael's eyes," Lady Hatbrook continued. "And those quirky lips of his. I'm already seeing Beth in her expressions."

Ann had never had the opportunity to learn about Gawain's lost love. "Were you very close?"

"She was a sweet girl, but I don't think anyone knew her well. We had no idea she planned to run off."

"Secretive?"

"You'd never have guessed a thing." Lady Hatbrook's own eyes, the color of deep-brewed tea, stared into the fire. "But it seems some mysteries are not meant to be solved."

Ann nodded. Like her first husband's death.

"Did you have time to settle in your new house before coming down here?" Lady Hatbrook asked, changing the subject.

"Not really," Ann admitted. "But Gawain was very worried about Matilda and Jacob." She glanced down at the rug, where Jacob was chewing placidly on a wooden train engine. Jenna was keeping an eye on him from the corner, where she was mending a blanket.

"I don't understand it myself. Gawain has offered him money to start over in India. What could be better for him?"

"I think he's afraid to go back and die there, given the severe illnesses he had. I wish I had gotten a look at him. I might have been able to help."

"That's right, you are a healer. How is Gawain doing?" Lady Hatbrook asked calmly.

"His limp is much better. No cane needed anymore. And he has regained a little vision."

"I hope this progress has sweetened his disposition. He was such a charmer when we were young."

Ann smiled. "He still has charm."

Color rose in Lady Hatbrook's cheeks. "I meant in general. He had a sunny spirit once. Clearly he hasn't lost his charisma, to be so successful with his businesses. His astounding results haven't been because he loves numbers."

"He loves his products, all of the Indian goods."

"That I know. He persuaded me to stock some of them at the bakery. And he was right, they sell well."

"We are both fortunate to have husbands who can easily provide for our families."

"True."

"But we are both women who thrive outside the domestic sphere," Ann said carefully.

"That is also true. But I had my moments of battle with the marquess." Lady Hatbrook stared into the fire.

"I didn't know that."

Lady Hatbrook nodded. "It was early on in our marriage. The conflicts could have destroyed our happiness."

"Any advice for me?"

Mary Ellen stirred and rubbed her nose. Lady Hatbrook lifted her and tucked the girl's small face against her shoulder. "You need to show my brother the real you. Happiness isn't going to survive in an atmosphere of polite accommodation. If there is some work you must do to be happy, you need to do it. In this modern age, a woman's sphere can't be tied only to her home."

"There's a great deal to do in a home with children," Ann said doubtfully. "I was used to cooking and managing servants and using my Ayurvedic skills, but add a baby to that? I didn't have brothers or sisters or nieces or nephews. I had no idea of the work involved."

"You are in the fortunate position of having help to lighten the load," Lady Hatbrook said, with a nod in Jenna's direction. "And it will be much easier once you've weaned Noel."

"I'm not getting much sleep," Ann admitted.

"Why don't you take a nap now? He's sleeping."

"I should," Ann said with surprise. As a guest in someone's home, much of the burden of domesticity was gone. She really didn't have anything she must do.

Shouts came from the courtyard outside the house. Jenna set her mending aside and took Mary Ellen from Lady Hatbrook, who rushed to the window. Ann followed, hoping the noise wouldn't wake the babies.

"Bliven," her hostess muttered, pointing at the slight man holding his finger in front of a groom's nose. He stomped up the steps to the house and disappeared under the portico.

"His color is bad," Ann observed.

"He was angry." Lady Hatbrook's gaze went to Jacob. "I hope he doesn't have a weapon."

Ann realized the risk. She lifted her skirts and ran to the nursery door. "Is there a key?"

"I don't know. This isn't my house." Lady Hatbrook stood.

Ann took a chair and put it under the doorknob while Lady Hatbrook did the same with the door that connected into the servants' bedroom. Jenna dropped the blanket and picked up Jacob.

"Where is your sister?" Ann asked.

"In Father's study, I imagine. Going over accounts. They're sure to be able to lock themselves in."

"Is anyone in the house armed?"

"I don't know."

"It seems likely he would come with henchmen if he was going to storm the house by force."

Lady Hatbrook nodded. "I am certain you are correct. He must know no one in this household is going to give up a child to him."

In Jenna's arms, Jacob yawned.

"Time for his nap?" Lady Hatbrook asked.

"Yes. I'll tuck him in and stay close," Jenna said.

By the time Jacob was settled down, Noel was awake. Ann fed him, muscles tensed for the sounds of shouting or violence down below. But they were on the second floor of a large, well-constructed house and were unlikely to hear anything that went on at the ground floor level.

Lady Hatbrook sat in the window seat, watching the courtyard for signs of activity. After about an hour she gestured Ann to the window. Ann set Noel back in the crib and joined her sister-in-law.

"That's your father?" Ann thought so, but she had only met him once.

"Yes, with Theodore Bliven."

The large, portly figure with a messy shock of faded red hair walked beside the slighter Bliven. Sir Bartley gestured toward a groom. It looked as though every man on the property stood nearby, waiting for a sign. The man disappeared around the corner, presumably moving toward the stable block.

"Looks like he's leaving," Ann observed.

The second man turned and glanced up to the window. Lady Hatbrook frowned. "That isn't Bliven. It's one of the local medical men."

A sharp rap sounded on the nursery door. Both women turned.

"Do you want me to answer it, my lady?" Jenna asked.

"No." Lady Hatbrook stood and straightened her skirt, then marched to the door. "Not while Bliven is unaccounted for. Who is it?" she called.

"Pounds, my lady. Mrs. Redcake is required in the library."

"I wonder if Mr. Bliven has taken ill," Ann said. "But I don't have any supplies with me."

"There must be some advice you can offer, but don't take him back to your home with you," Lady Hatbrook said. "At the very most, have them put him up in some hotel. I'd hate to think of him stealing away with Noel."

"Right," Ann said. She bent over Noel and kissed his forehead, hesitating.

"I'll stay here," Lady Hatbrook assured her. "You have nothing to worry about."

"Thank you." Ann forced a smile then pulled the chair from the door and opened it to find the butler.

"This way, ma'am," he said.

She waited until she heard the scrape of the chair being moved against the inside of the door, then followed him down two flights of stairs, to a corridor that led to the east wing of the H-shaped house. "Is Mr. Bliven injured or ill?"

"Not that I'm aware of."

Ann frowned. "Then why was I summoned away from my child?"

Before Pounds could answer, a footman opened the library door and gestured. Ann stepped inside.

No one was in the book-lined, square-shaped room except her husband, at the fireplace in the center of one wall. He turned as the door closed behind her.

She had never seen such anger in his face. His brows were knit tightly together and the bridge of his nose was white with tension. She moved toward him, hand outstretched. "What did Mr. Bliven say?"

"I could care less about Bliven. It is your behavior that concerns me."

Her hand dropped to her chest. "Me? I've been waiting in the nursery, worried that your sister and I would have to defend the children to our deaths."

"Do you know what the rumor is about Wells's death?" he rasped.

Ann put her fingers to her forehead, where a dull headache had begun to thrum. "What does Wells have to do with Mr. Bliven?"

"I went to see an old comrade about Bliven. To have an eye kept out in the district for him. And he told me about you." A sneer she'd never seen before marred his face.

"Me?" She felt like she was swimming upstream against a fast current.

"You. Your lovers. Why Wells died."

"Lovers?" She put her hand against her stomach. What had he heard?

"Yes. Wells wasn't the only one."

She'd been married. He knew she hadn't been a virgin. "Wells was my husband. I was never with him before our wedding night. You are the only man I've been with since he died."

"And before?"

"Before what?" she queried, stalling. But he knew.

Gawain's smile glittered indecently. "Before that first wedding night."

Her knees weakened. She dropped into a gilt chair at one side of the fireplace. "What would that have to do with Wells?"

"You had a lover who you told about your mother's royal gems."

She shook her head. "I did not tell anyone about them. Until Wells."

"So the rumors are untrue?"

"About some lover of mine killing Wells? Yes, of course." She left the details unsaid.

"How many lovers, Ann?" His nostrils flared.

She lifted her chin. "One, Gawain. One man, who I thought loved me, thought would marry me. But he left to marry a white woman his family approved of, unlike me."

Gawain pressed the fingers of one hand against his forehead. "You didn't use the gems to entice him?"

"There was no point. He had money. At least his family did. They'd have cut off his allowance if he'd chosen me over their own choice." He'd broken her heart and it had taken Wells to restore her faith in men.

"A gem that is the price of an inn is a good dowry, especially when more might be forthcoming."

"An inn would not entice a man like him. His family owned a shipyard."

The tips of Gawain's fingers were white with pressure. "So you tried to marry up and found yourself shackled to a mere soldier like your father."

She could smell the stable on him, and ale, sweat. Soldier's smells. "I loved Wells." She blinked, feeling the dampness of tears. "How can you think for a moment that I didn't?"

"I don't know what to believe about you anymore. I should have known that a woman who was intimate with me would have done the same with other men."

Like he was so pure? He knew more than she did. He made her body sing. "Three men in seven years. Am I such a terrible person?"

"You aren't as English as you think," he growled.

Her head snapped back as if he'd slapped her. Not English? "How dare you! Your own sister made the same mistake as me!"

Gawain waved his free arm. "And see how she never stops paying for it? Why should you be any different?"

"Because you're my husband now. You are supposed to protect me, not be my accuser."

He folded his arms across his broad chest, effectively distancing her. "I am merely repeating what I've been told."

She raised her hands, shook them. "That I'm little more than a whore. Oh, excuse me. A whore with royal gems." What had she done with her life? "I thought you might learn to love me, but now I see that you are looking for any excuse to hate me."

His gazed bored into her, like a woodpecker destroying a tree. "I would not like to think I could ever hate the mother of my son."

"At least you don't doubt he's yours." Her lips trembled. "My foolish act brought us Noel. But I assure you, it was only one foolish act. I don't regret the passion we experienced. We must be meant to be together."

"And your first lover? You were meant to be with him too."

Ann knew his voice had gone dangerously soft. "I loved him at the time. I love with my entire heart and body, Gawain. I wouldn't have it any other way."

"When will you stop loving me and love another?"

"Not as long as we are wed." She met him, forcing defiance, then realized the impact of what she had said, the thought it might give him. He wouldn't consider divorce?

She might not have been chaste, but she had never been an adulteress.

"Take a tray in the nursery," he told her. "I don't want to see you again tonight. I will speak to you in the morning. I'm too angry to think."

"What about Theodore Bliven? Why was a doctor here? Is your sister safe?"

"That is not your concern."

How could he say that so calmly? "It is. Lady Hatbrook suggested that Mr. Bliven might kidnap Noel in order to get Jacob."

"Jacob without Matilda doesn't do him much good. He'll be on a boat to India in a couple of days, so you do not need to trouble yourself further."

As if her question had reminded him, he turned away slightly and pulled his patch back over his eye. She stepped toward him and put her hand on his shoulder, but he flinched. Her hand dropped.

"I will do as you ask," she said dully. "I'll tell Lady Hatbrook that being away from Noel makes me too nervous tonight."

Gawain didn't speak again as she left the room.

The next morning, Gawain ignored the tea a maid brought and went immediately to the writing table when her opening of the curtains woke him. He penned a note to Ann, instructing her to pack and be ready to depart early that afternoon. His family had welcomed her but he didn't want them forming any more ties, not when he was so uncertain of the wisdom of their involvement.

How could he, with his ambition, drive and accomplishments, have married someone so unsuitable? He felt as if he thought he was marrying a virgin and was deceived into taking a camp follower. How could he have thought her a chaste widow when she had jumped into bed with him so readily? It was not as if he, with his scars, was irresistible. Far from it.

The morning light stabbed at his bad eye. He folded up the note and replaced his patch before reaching for the bell pull so his instructions could be taken to the nursery.

He debated the wisdom of allowing a footman to travel with Ann, Noel, Fern and Jenna, but decided it was safer to escort them himself. But he'd have to be available to ensure that Bliven appeared at the London docks for the next India-bound ship.

The confrontation yesterday had been ugly. Matilda had refused to see Bliven, so Gawain and his father had attempted to take emotion out of the situation and make the man see reason. Gawain couldn't tell if repeated fevers had addled the man's wits or if he was simply desperate for a family now that his health had been ruined. Either way, Matilda no longer wanted him and his father wasn't about to force her, not when she was proving so useful in business matters.

Gawain could see Matilda didn't have his business sense, or even Alys's, but with a good set of advisors and their father's input, the businesses would be safe enough. She was a reasonable figurehead. On the matter of Theodore Bliven, however, she could not be rational.

Any more than he could be in the matter of Ann. It had not been terribly rational to marry her. He saw that now. Her background was too exotic to be ignored. With her mother's royal past, these gems and her husband's murder, her life had elements of the sensational. Of course, people would gossip about her. At least her story was unknown in London. She'd been smart to leave Leeds. She could live quietly in Battersea. He would continue to focus most of his energies on his businesses and they would rub along well enough together. But he didn't know how he could touch her again, and that meant no brothers or sisters for Noel, unless she was already increasing.

How could she expect him to believe she'd loved the first man, when she hadn't loved him, her supposed third?

Late that morning, their belongings were piled into the coach for their return to the station. Ann's expression was pinched, as if she had the same headache he did. The train ride back to London was dreadful. Wind rocked the train carriage, and Noel cried every time in piercing wails that made the other passengers in the compartment give them dirty looks.

Back in London, they were soaked to the bone while waiting in a queue for a hansom. By the time they arrived back at their front door, Gawain wondered if Noel had caught a cold.

"Let's get Noel up to the nursery and get him undressed," Ann said to Fern and Jenna, who huddled around her, ignoring Gawain as soon as he unlocked the front door and instructed Chase to have the luggage retrieved.

"Is there any luggage you need immediately?" he asked.

Ann looked at him. "No, we have everything we need."

"Do you want me to carry Noel upstairs for you?" A foolish question as she was more able-bodied than he.

"We'll be fine. Go warm yourself in your study. I'm sure you have business to attend to." Ann spoke like a queen, then swept up the stairs, her handmaidens following behind her.

When Gawain arrived in the library, where a fire was just being lit, he reflected that the greatest hurt was that Fern wouldn't even look at him, when they had formed a certain rapport.

No, that was not the greatest hurt at all, and silly of him to think that. When the tweeny was done with the fire, he asked her to send to the kitchen for hot coffee and sandwiches, and to send someone to the nursery for instructions there. He sat stiffly in the chair closest to the fireplace and contemplated his soaked shoes and pants. What he needed now was warmed sheets and a willing woman.

And he might have had it, if he hadn't learned about Ann's past. Damn Bowler Martin for telling him. Then again, how had he thought he could investigate a murder without uncovering uncomfortable truths about his wife and the Haldenes?

Chapter Fourteen

On Saturday, Gawain woke in a bed that had been empty of his wife for three nights now. He had banished her at Redcake Manor, and it was no surprise that she hadn't reappeared in their rooms for the two nights they'd been home in Battersea.

The maid came in. After she pulled back the curtains she put his tray by the bedside. His appointment diary was on his writing table, and he took the tray to the table so he could open it to double-check when he was supposed to meet Bliven and his father at the train, and then escort Bliven to the docks.

His eye caught the notation for evening plans. He swore when he realized he and Ann were meant to go to Lord Judah's home this evening for dinner with his friend and his wife. This was not a time to socialize. Should he cancel? Did he really want the cracks in his marriage showing? He couldn't explain why ice existed between them. But social niceties should hide their problems. Ann would converse with Magdalene, Lady Judah, and he would talk to his friend. They could play cards, something that would take all their attention. It might help his anger defrost. Magdalene had been a relatively unsuitable bride for Lord Judah. Though she was an earl's niece, her scandalous family had not endeared her to her prospective in-laws. Maybe Lord Judah could give him advice as to how to deal with the situation he found himself in now.

But unlike his, Lord Judah's marriage was a happy one. Gawain's problems had started before the wedding, not after.

He glanced at his schedule again and noted that one of his secretaries was supposed to be here in an hour with a couple of lascars, Indian sailors who'd somehow lost their passage back to India. Gawain would pay one or more of them to go along with Bliven as servants, since he was still unclear as to how ill the man actually was. He didn't wish to send Bliven to his death, yet he needed the man to be as far away from Matilda and Jacob as possible.

This was one of those mornings when Gawain wished his coffee had a good dollop of whiskey in it. He drank it down and rang the bell to order his bath.

His plate of eggs, tomato and sausage was still half full when Chase came in to announce his secretary. Ann had not made an appearance in the dining room.

"Would you make Mrs. Redcake aware of our engagement at Lord Judah's this evening?" he said to Chase. "I should return early enough to travel with her."

"Yes, sir. The men are in the study."

Gawain snatched one last bite of sausage, then wiped his mouth and set down his napkin. "We need to leave in about twenty minutes for the West India Docks. Order a carriage?"

Chase nodded. Gawain followed him out of the room and into the parlor, where one of his reliable hands, Frederick Skill, a former soldier who spoke three Indian tongues, waited with a trio of skinny brown men dressed in little more than rags.

Skill stood when Gawain entered. "I know you said two, but each of them speaks a different set of languages and I thought that might be useful."

"Any in common?"

"They all have a smattering of English and are competent in Hindustani."

Gawain used that language as he inquired of each of them as to how they had found themselves stranded in London. He heard tales of incompetent or bankrupt shippers, and one marriage to a white woman that had caused the third man to jump ship during a long wait in London between voyages.

"What happened to your wife?" he asked.

Dead of tuberculosis before the year was out. Their son died soon after.

Gawain nodded. "Skill, take all three down to the docks and make arrangements. I'll expect them to be waiting for Mr. Bliven when he boards this afternoon."

"Yes, Mr. Redcake."

The men offered cheery smiles as they realized they were finally going home. At least Matilda's misfortune had made someone happy.

Gawain went back to finish his breakfast, knowing it would be a long day.

After a trip to the docks, watching the ship with his father and some employees to make sure Bliven stayed aboard until it left its berth, then an inventory review at his warehouse, he returned home to dress for dinner. He then went to the nursery, where, not surprisingly, he found Ann rocking Noel in the company of Fern and Jenna.

"Are you ready to leave?"

She looked up at him, unsmiling, then handed the sleepy baby to Fern before following him out the door.

"You should have given Noel to Jenna. She's the nursemaid, not Fern."

"I cannot do anything right in your eyes, can I?" Ann observed in a low voice.

Gawain grasped the handrail as he walked down the stairs. Going down was hardest on his hip, and after standing all day he was not at his best. He hoped Lord Judah had his best port available.

"You need a treatment," Ann said.

"We don't have time. The carriage should be waiting." He glanced at her low-cut dinner dress and tried to ignore a wave of lust. "Dress warmly now, it's a cold night."

She left the staircase for the rooms, while he continued down, wincing at each down step. When they were in the hired carriage, Gawain put his cane on the floor and leaned back.

Ann narrowed her eyes. "You are obviously in pain. Are you certain we should not cancel?"

"I will be fine," he rasped.

She clutched her coat lapels around her throat. "Your pain has put you into a gruff mood."

"It is not only the pain."

"Did you have difficulties with Mr. Bliven?"

"Not especially. Matilda stated her position quite succinctly."

"She wasn't willing to give him the chance to prove himself?"

"He wreaked havoc on her life. She expected marriage and ended up ruined with a bastard child. Why would she give him another chance? He has only returned because he's lost his chance for a title, lost another wealthy woman he thought he would marry."

"She must have loved him once. He might flower in a stable household."

"He might spend the Redcake money and destroy the Redcake businesses. Hatbrook wouldn't let him marry Beth when he offered for her before she debuted."

"He wouldn't let you marry her either," Ann observed.

"Well there you go. We are both of us a bad bargain." He thumped his cane and wished for Antifebrin.

"I gave you a second chance."

"I am hardly a Bliven."

"You had money to smooth your business path."

"He had a first-rate education and friends to smooth his way," he snarled. "Do you have any idea of what I come from? I worked in factories from the age of nine. Was in the army from the age of seventeen. No proper education, just apprentice work at Redcake's, learning accounting."

"My point is that a woman's heart must be forgiving."

"A forgiving heart can lead a woman to ruin." What is this rot that his wife was speaking? Could she truly not see the difference between him and Bliven?

Ann played with the buttons on her coat.

"Is it too tight?" he asked, observing it was a bit shabby.

"I had it before Noel."

"We need to get a new wardrobe ordered for you. Your dress is all but indecent and the coat is a disgrace."

"I know." She bent her head. "But I've been busy with the move."

"Make your clothing your next priority," he ordered.

He caught her irritated look as the lantern swung above her head, and said, "A forgiving heart but not a placid mind."

"What do you mean?"

"You do not like to be told what to do. You prefer to give the orders. Perhaps in marrying me you thought to put me under your thumb. I assure you, madam, that the opposite is true."

"I do not think your family gave Mr. Bliven a chance when he returned. All you wanted to do was ship him back to get more herbs, when what he needed was a soft bed and time to recover his health."

He wanted to roar at her, yet this was the woman who had done the opposite of Matilda and had taken her lover to wed. Could she be right? "Do you think we sent him to his death?"

"Not everyone thrives in the Indian climate."

"I sent him with three lascars to tend him."

She made a noise in the back of her throat. "Did any of them have medical knowledge?"

He didn't know the answer to that. "You think I should have applied to you for counsel."

"You know I have the skills to examine him. I could have prepared medicine for him. It might have helped."

"You have other duties. And he came directly from Polegate from my father to the ship. There was no time for an examination."

She stared at the lantern in the corner. "Of course there was. He didn't need to take a ship today. There is always another ship."

Gawain admired her profile like some besotted husband. "There is no point to continuing this line of discussion. He is gone and his fate will not be determined by you."

"Now what?"

"We will continue to settle into the new house. The weather will improve soon. I'm certain the coming of spring will lighten everyone's mood."

"And you'll focus on your business, not Wells's murder from now on? Not Lady Elizabeth's disappearance?"

"I have never had much spare time for either, as you well know. Do you want me to pursue the murder? Dig up this old lover of yours and speak to him?"

She turned back to him, and he could see the outrage in the way the skin around her eyes tightened. "Of course not. He had nothing to do with it."

"How do you know?"

"He never knew about the gems for one thing. Certainly he'd have had no interest in me marrying a man who was buying an inn."

"What was his name? Is he from a Leeds family?"

"No, we didn't live there until we inherited the inn. Truly, there is no connection."

He wanted to believe her. "I see. As to Lady Elizabeth, that is out of my hands. When I married you, it was understood in the family."

"Lord Judah is her brother. Won't you be discussing her tonight?"

"Not in your hearing, certainly. Tonight the plan is for you and Lady Judah to become acquainted. You both worked in the Fancy."

"Her brother is the one who ran off with Lady Elizabeth," she observed.

"That is in dispute. If you don't mention the situation, I am certain she will not either. Talk about Redcake's, or Noel or fashion. She adores fashion."

She dismissed him with a wave of her glove. "I've never had any interest in it."

"Now you can indulge yourself. She has two nephews she's very fond of, off at school now. You can talk about raising boy children."

"I feel like it is a mistake to have an engagement tonight, when you and I are at such odds." She set her hand on his leg and caressed him.

He moved his leg away. *Temptress.* "Lord Judah is my good friend. You need to know these people."

"With a wife like me you still plan to move in circles with aristocrats?"

He thumped his cane again. He was turning into his late Grandfather Noble. "Why not? You are a maharajah's legal granddaughter after all. Your father was a gentleman. You have nothing to be ashamed of."

"Other than my actions, my profession and my skin color." She gave him a cold smirk.

He growled. "If you hold your head high and ignore what is said in whispers, no one can upset you. Do you think everyone is perfect?"

"You expect me to be."

He had never heard snappishness in her tone before. Well, he supposed he deserved it. How could he be surprised that the woman who had bedded him in her inn would have not fallen into bed with someone she loved and wanted to marry? Especially at eighteen. Matilda had done it at twenty-one. She was a lusty woman and he had to accept that.

"I do not expect perfection, but I do not manage well with unpleasant surprises. I have a great deal on my mind."

"I am sorry you had to hear about my past from a friend. I should have laid out all my faults to you. If I think of any others I will be sure to tell you immediately."

He laughed. "Thank you." When she put her hand on his thigh again, he didn't move away.

The carriage pulled onto the genteel street where Lord Judah had purchased a large row house for his bride. It was a far cry from the modest bachelor establishment he had rented when first returning from India, but his gem import investment had paid off handsomely. He worked as well, managing Redcake's. Gawain knew he wanted to buy the establishment but his sister had refused to sell it. She'd always had an attachment to the place that he did not. At least Ann hadn't fallen in love with Redcake's the way Judah's wife had. She still worked there on a limited basis. He was glad Ann had refused to return.

Lady Judah had refused to hire a butler, but they did have an adequate complement of staff. A parlor maid opened the front door and helped them with their coats before leading them into a stylish room with an oriental appeal.

"I see you've continued the tea theme, with all of these teapots," Gawain observed.

"The toile on the walls has people drinking tea," Lady Judah said, as she and her husband appeared in the doorway. His friend wore proper evening attire, but his lady's gown was almost as low-cut as Ann's.

Gawain chuckled and went to examine the walls. "I need something like this myself. Wrong country though. I'd want Indian scenes."

"I'm sure your mother can come up with something. She's very artistic."

"Did she help you with your decorating, Magdalene?"

"She did. Gave me all her best names and sources in London. I did all the choosing myself though. I do love spending money."

Gawain shared a glance with his friend. He wondered if Ann would soon be the same. So far she'd shown little interest in the house beyond making sure the nursery was hygienic. But they had been very busy and could not be said to have settled in, whereas the Shields had been married for a year.

"I would love to see more of the house if you are willing to show me," Ann suggested.

Magdalene seemed shocked by the suggestion and didn't respond, just stood there in the doorway. Of course, public areas of a home were just that, and private the same, but surely she could show Ann the rooms on the main floor.

Lord Judah cleared his throat and walked deeper into the room.

Gawain winced as Ann seemed to notice her gaffe.

"Or just the nursery," she said in a low voice. "I would love to see what a modern nursery looks like."

"Nursery?" Judah said. "Oh, we haven't one of those yet."

Ann frowned. "But you have a baby on the way. With everything that can happen during this special time, I always think it is best to make over a nursery early."

Lord Judah's gold-flecked eyes seemed to darken. Magdalene went pale and put a hand to her mouth, then turned quickly and dashed out of the room.

"See?" Ann smiled at Gawain. He shook his head and she glanced at Lord Judah. "Well, good heavens, he must know. She's visibly lost weight since we saw her last. She must be losing every morsel of food she puts into her mouth. How could her husband not know?"

"I thought she had an illness," Lord Judah said.

"A nine-month one," Ann chuckled. "She should be in bed, Lord Judah. I can send you over a tea that I've found very helpful in these cases. Make certain she drinks a lot of water, even if she can't keep food down for a short while. It's very important."

"Thank you," Lord Judah said, making a helpless gesture with his hands.

"You want to cancel our dinner?" Gawain asked. "Maybe Magdalene needs you."

"Could you go to her?" Lord Judah asked Ann. "There must be something our cook can make, or one of the servants can be sent for, if you made a list."

"Of course. I can make a list for someone to give to Fern, who lives with us. She can send what you need back from our house while I stay with your wife."

Lord Judah smiled slightly. "Yes, please. Unless it makes Magdalene more upset. I should have known."

"Why?" Gawain asked. "When have you ever been around an increasing woman?" He went to a set of decanters and poured his friend a stiff drink, then rang for the maid.

When Penny, a long-term employee, appeared, Lord Judah collected himself long enough to say, "Could you take Mrs. Redcake to Lady Judah, please? Follow any of her orders as if they were my own."

Ann followed the maid out without looking back.

"She's in her element," Gawain said, saluting Lord Judah with his own glass.

His friend collapsed onto a chair. "She's been ill, or so I thought, for some time now."

"Matilda was sick for about two months. Alys was only queasy. She had an easy time of it."

"Then this won't last forever?"

"Eventually she'll have the child."

Lord Judah laughed half-heartedly. "How far along do you think she is?"

Gawain drained his glass. "You're asking me? I honestly don't know, but based on my sister's experiences, anywhere between one and five months."

Lord Judah's stomach rumbled. He and Gawain shared a rueful glance.

"Think Magdalene will have my head if we dine?"

"What else are we supposed to do?"

"Should we send a tray for your lady?"

"It will probably make yours sicker. I expect Ann is used to doing without in these situations."

Judah sighed. "Would you let your wife move in for the next several months?"

"No." Even if he wasn't amused by her social awkwardness, what did he expect? She wasn't used to a fashionable society lady like Magdalene, but he suspected the woman would soon learn to appreciate Ann's competence in medical matters.

As he and Lord Judah went into the hall, they saw Penny dashing down the corridor.

"Why the haste?" Lord Judah asked, stopping her.

His servant waved a piece of paper at him. "I'm to take the carriage to Battersea for this medicine for Lady Judah, sir."

"Is she any better?"

"She's pretty rough," the maid answered frankly. "But Mrs. Redcake says if she can be set to rights, this medicine will do it. But doesn't she have a little baby that needs feeding?"

Gawain swore under his breath. "My wife is used to having a wet nurse across the hall, but of course we don't have that now."

Lord Judah said nothing, but Gawain knew what his old brother in arms was thinking. "I'll go to Battersea and bring back the medicine, as well as Noel, if you can spare a room. That way Magdalene doesn't lose Ann's care."

"Shouldn't I see how serious things are?"

"Pretty serious," Penny interjected. "I can bring back the baby and his nurse, sir."

"It's better if I go," Gawain said, "but thank you."

"I'll have Cook keep dinner warm for you," Lord Judah said. "I'll order my carriage."

A moment later, Gawain and Penny were alone in the hall. Penny sighed. "It's a nice carriage, sir, and fast."

"You can come with me," Gawain offered.

She smiled. "No, my place is with my mistress. But thank you. Do you want me to ask around for a wet nurse, for when your lady is called out?"

"We won't be needing one, but thank you."

Of course, he was wrong about that. When he arrived home on Monday from a long day at his warehouse followed by an hour discussing carriage design with Lewis at his machine shop, he could hear Noel crying upstairs, yet Ann was in the parlor with a roughly dressed woman he'd never seen before.

"Ashwaganda is excellent for rebuilding female strength," she was saying.

Ignoring the conversation and what it might mean for now,

Gawain stomped upstairs to see what the fuss was. His son was squealing in his cradle, while Fern sat by the fire, sewing a pinafore. A ragged doll rested at her side, next to a neat pile of clothing and a pile of scraps.

Noel screamed louder. Seeing red, Gawain reached down and brandished the pile of clothing. "First, I see she's turned my parlor into a consulting room, and now she's got you making doll clothes for sale?" He threw the clothing into the fire, scarcely noting Fern's horrified expression, and snatched up Noel.

The baby stopped crying as soon as he was picked up, and let out a loud burp.

The door to the nursemaid's room opened and Jenna rushed in. "Oh, he's spit on your lovely coat." She rubbed at his shoulder with a nappy.

"Why weren't you here?" he growled.

"Sick, sir," Jenna said, clasping her stomach. "We've all a touch of it. I set Fern to making clothes for her old dolly so she'd stay still. Moving seems to make it worse. I've been bent over the chamber pot these past ten minutes."

She reached for Noel but Gawain clutched the baby to his breast. "Go and lie down, Jenna. We don't want him catching it."

"He's already sick, isn't he? Spoiled his nappy four times today."

"Go lie down," he repeated. "Is my wife sick as well?" He coughed as the scent of burning fabric filled the room.

"No, sir, but she had a patient come in. An *ayah* who works at the house on the corner. Turned up at the back door asking for Mrs. Redcake. The *ayah* doesn't want to lose her job, but can hardly get up in the morning. Mrs. Redcake didn't want to send her off since she knew she could help."

He held back his growl. "Thank you for that information. Now, go."

Jenna flashed him a grateful smile, then puffed out her cheeks and, suddenly pale, ran for the door. Gawain turned to Fern. Tears were sliding down her cheeks. With a sigh, he put Noel back in his cradle and crouched down beside the girl, ignoring the pain in his hip.

"I'm so terribly sorry, Fern. I shouldn't have acted without thinking."

She sobbed audibly, the sound harsh yet lovely to his ears. She was making noise!

He patted her shoulder. "There, now." He pulled a half-crown from his pocket. "Here, you can buy all the new fabric you want for your dolly's clothing. I wasn't thinking and I'm so very sorry I threw her dress in the fire."

She drew a deep, vibrating breath. "C-c-c."

"And coat," he agreed. "Oh dear, what else did I ruin?"

"S-s-s."

"Stockings?"

She nodded. "P-p-p."

"Petticoat?" He put a hand to his mouth. "Oh dear, her unmentionables. How dreadful of me."

She giggled, silently this time.

"I am so proud of you for speaking to me, and I'm only sorry that I had to put you in a much deserved rage for you to speak."

She shook her head.

"No, no, I understood you very clearly. I knew you could speak, and you'll do better next time."

She pulled a handkerchief from her sleeve and wiped her nose. For a moment, all was quiet, Noel in his crib and Fern by the fire. Then, Gawain heard an unholy noise from the region of the crib and a terrible smell offended his nose.

"Maybe Lady Judah really had a stomach illness after all," Gawain muttered, as he got painfully to his feet.

Fern stood too, and together they changed Noel and resettled him. After, Fern held him while Gawain rang for additional assistance from his household, then he took the baby while Fern ran from the room, green as Jenna had been pale.

Most men would flee to their club about now, Gawain knew. But he couldn't leave his poor son. He kissed the baby's forehead. It felt warm, but not dangerously so. Didn't Ann have a treatment for her own child? He pushed a rocking chair away from the fire before he sat down, just in case.

A few minutes later, the housekeeper entered the room, followed by Ann.

"As you can tell by the smell, things have not been going terribly well up here," he observed.

Ann took the baby while the housekeeper removed Noel's mess. "Can you take these?" she asked, putting a couple of small coins into Gawain's hand.

"You took money from that woman?" he asked, incredulous. "You should not be taking payment."

Ann shrugged. "She insisted. My skills are worth compensation."

He frowned but kept his voice modulated for Noel's sake. "Have I not provided you with an adequate home? I understand why you would help a desperate woman who showed up at our door, one time, but if you take money the word will get out and they will keep coming."

"They will only keep coming if what I offer helps," Ann said, shifting into a comfortable pose. "Now, I need to feed Noel. He needs to feed a great deal while his tummy is upset."

"Won't he just keep getting ill?"

"It doesn't matter. He needs the milk flowing through his body."

"I will tell the servants to turn off anyone else who comes. You are needed here to care for your own child and family."

"I thought you wanted Jenna to care for him," she said.

"There are things only a mother can do," Gawain growled. "You are not to develop a reputation as doctor to the local servants."

Ann didn't respond, just focused on Noel and his feeding. Gawain watched them for a little while, then the housekeeper came back to the door and he left to ascertain the health of the other servants. How dare she twist his ability to hire household help into a way to turn his home into a hospital for local servants? He would not accept her choosing her medical interests over her wifely duties. She was no longer married to a provincial innkeeper and she had no need to earn a living.

What would the neighbors think of him if he allowed his wife to work? They would probably think he needed the money and that wouldn't do. He'd come so far from those factory days, from those army days, from those employed-by-his-father days. He'd earned the right to have a decorous wife.

Chapter Fifteen

Fern squealed as Ann pulled her toward a hired carriage late on Wednesday morning. While she couldn't take one more minute of this constrained, loveless existence, Fern seemed content to endure Gawain's moodiness.

"Come along," Ann said, already having a difficult time balancing Noel in one arm. "We need to be on the next train." They had to be gone well before luncheon-time in case Gawain returned.

Fern pulled her arm away, then stopped on the sidewalk.

"Come along," Ann repeated impatiently. "I'm not going to stay here another minute and be told what to do. We're going back to Leeds." Pretty dresses and less hard work were no compensation for a zenana-like existence.

Fern stamped her foot.

"He burned your dolly clothes Monday night, Fern! He has been utterly cross with me. He told the servants to turn away my patients. And he didn't say a word when his friends were rude to me on Saturday." Why did she even have to explain? Fern should trust her without question.

Fern pointed to Ann's hand.

"Yes, I know we are married. But I cannot take another breath in this house. I need to go. He doesn't love me. That became perfectly clear when we were at Redcake Manor. I think he regrets marrying me. I need to go home."

Fern set her jaw. The carriage driver called impatiently.

"You are my family, Fern, not his. Now come along," she ordered, in a tone she never used.

Fern complied, but very slowly.

When they reached the station, they discovered they had missed the next train, but found seats on the one after that. Ann was grateful that Noel was so young. He didn't provide complications, other than the need to carry him.

"If my skin were white, none of this would ever have happened," she told Fern. "He doesn't mind the things his sister Matilda did. I've heard the entire family is pretty fast. And that precious Magdalene Shield is from a scandalous family. Her aunt was mistress to the Prince of Wales, can you imagine? But me he has no forgiveness for. He's a hard man."

Fern turned away, pretending to ignore her. After a few more outbursts, Ann gave up speaking. It wasn't as if Fern would have a conversation with her. She knew what Fern would say if she could. That she had married Gawain and she needed to remain with him. Two weeks ago she'd married him with hope in her heart. They'd had a perfect wedding night but since then nothing had gone right. None of the love she'd imagined had been evident, at least for her. No, he'd focused his attention on Matilda's problems. For her, he offered only irritation or outright anger. Wells had petted and supported her, and she would accept nothing less from Gawain.

Still, she wanted him to follow her to Leeds. It might be the only way to regain his attention. If only she didn't want it.

Gawain walked into the Redcake's manager's office, holding the letter Lord Judah had sent. His friend's secretary set a tasting plate of biscuits on the table by the fire and closed the office door behind him. Lord Judah was already seated in one of the two cozy armchairs and pouring from a large brown pot.

"You didn't ask me to come in order to taste test," Gawain said.

Lord Judah handed him a steaming cup of Darjeeling. "Tea biscuits. Changed the blend of spices. See what you think."

Gawain sighed and sat down. He could use a restorative. While Noel and Fern had seemed to recover from their illness by the time he returned from the warehouse yesterday, Ann had continued to hover in the nursery, fussing over them. And without her in their shared bed he hadn't slept well. He was already used to her.

He sipped at his tea, then took a biscuit. "Delicious."

"You have the look of a man who might as well be tasting cardboard," Lord Judah said.

"You do not look so lively yourself. How is Magdalene?"

"Your wife's tea is helping, but she isn't sleeping well. Too queasy."

Gawain yawned. "We had a stomach ailment blast through the nursery over the past few days. I did wonder if Magdalene really had that instead."

Lord Judah set down his teacup. "No, I'm sure she is expecting. Hopefully our household will stay healthy."

Gawain was glad Ann had been right. It would be embarrassing for a healer to misdiagnose an illness for a pregnancy. "That would be best."

"I called you here because I've had word about that Caliatan royal necklace."

Gawain sat up. "It has surfaced?"

"About six months after the murder. A London collector has it now. It took me a few attempts to get him to tell me who had sold it to him. I have the fence's name. Do you want to interrogate him with me?"

"Yes," Gawain said, dropping his cup into its saucer with a clatter. "Do you have time now? The seller is likely the killer."

"For this, I'll make time." Lord Judah went to his safe and unlocked it, then pulled out his pistol and tucked it into the pocket of his greatcoat. "We're going to Seven Dials."

"I'm glad it's full daylight," Gawain commented. "Do you have one of those for me?"

"You've got your walking stick. I happen to know it has a steel interior." The two men grinned at one another, then Gawain followed Lord Judah downstairs and out back into the alley, where a nondescript carriage awaited them.

The carriage drove out of the fashionable area of London and into the eastern part. The air seemed to thicken into murk. Even though it was day, Gawain found it hard to see by the time they reached the mouths of the seven passages that made up the Seven Dials.

"The fence is on the second floor of a building on Earlham Street," Lord Judah said.

The back of Gawain's neck prickled, as if they were being watched. The carriage pulled into a narrow cobbled street lined with multi-story brick buildings. When the men descended, the driver called to the horses and set off at a quick clip.

"Doesn't want to stay around to meet the Ripper," Lord Judah joked.

"He's long gone. Hasn't murdered in months," Gawain said, glancing up the building.

Lord Judah pointed through the gloom. Sunlight scarcely touched the ground floors of the buildings. "I think that is a door."

"Lead on." Gawain tapped his cane on a stone and stepped over a fetid stream of rainwater at the edge of the street.

Lord Judah opened the door and disappeared inside. Gawain, senses alert, caught the door and followed behind. They went up a staircase, the air darkening with every step. The corridor beyond was deserted, though he could hear noises behind the doors, a couple arguing, a baby crying, an old man's voice calling out in fear, then the babble of multiple male voices in a foreign tongue behind one door at the end of the hall. Smoke curled under the door and hung in the corridor, adding to the sense of fog even inside the building.

"I find it hard to believe that the kind of person who could afford to buy such a necklace would come here," Gawain said.

Lord Judah rapped on the door. "Met them in a pub, I would imagine."

The sound of voices didn't cease. Smoke curled over Lord Judah's half-boots, as if enticing him in. A couple of minutes later, the door opened a crack. Gawain saw a flare of light behind the door, though more smoke dribbled out. A man's shape was mostly shielded by the wood.

Lord Judah pulled a paper from his pocket, a sketch of the stolen necklace from Fern, and thrust it at the man at the door. The man took it, and coughed, phlegm rattling in his chest.

"Never get enuf o' this kind o' merchandise," he rasped. "You got it wif ya?"

"We aren't selling it," Lord Judah said. "We want to know who you bought it from."

The man shook his head. "Ain't got it now."

"I know. You sold it to Lord Mews eighteen months ago. Who did you buy it from?" Lord Judah demanded.

The man rubbed his nose and coughed again. With a sigh, Lord Judah pulled a banknote from his pocket and passed it over. The man snatched it and slammed the door shut. Gawain leaned against the wall, then stood when he felt the damp plaster denting from his body weight.

Inside, he could hear voices crescendoing, followed by a wave of coughs. He was about to ask his friend if he thought the door would reopen, but just then it did. This time, the man at the door was a wizened specimen with a long beard and a black skullcap covering his bald pate.

"Gentlemen," he said, in a surprisingly cultured tone. "Why are you asking for such confidential information? I'm sure I can find you a similar piece."

"Taken off a dead man, just like the first necklace?" Gawain asked.

The man put up his hands, palm-first. The gesture only took his arms up to the height of Gawain's thighs.

"Taken off a dead man?" the fence asked.

"He was murdered for that necklace."

The man scratched his nose. "I don't know anything about that. I bought it from a receiver who works out of Leeds."

"A receiver?" Lord Judah asked. "So he wasn't the original thief then."

"No, my lord, no." The man smiled, showing spikey, yellowed teeth. "I wouldn't do business with a thief."

Gawain snorted. "What is the receiver's name?"

The man sniffed and called over his shoulder. "Bartholomew? Come here." He turned back to them. "You are in luck, gentlemen. My friend happens to be visiting London."

A minute later, another ancient man, a couple inches taller than the first, joined his friend at the crack in the door, still holding his pipe. "What ye want?"

"These gentlemen want to know who sold you that royal necklace. You know the one. Royal House of Caliata?"

Gawain hadn't realized the necklace was part of the crown jewels of a royal house. He wondered if Ann had realized what she was sacrificing to her late husband's desire to own two inns.

The man puffed on his pipe, sending more smoke to paint the already yellowed walls. "Only saw him the one time."

"Memorable piece," Lord Judah commented. "I'm in gems myself."

"Were," the first man giggled. "I know who you are, Lord Judah Shield. None of your Indian merchandise has come my way yet, but it will. Always does."

"Makes me glad I deal in comestibles," Gawain muttered.

The second man puffed his pipe for a couple of minutes more, his crêpey wattle jiggling with each inhalation. "What if this man has more merchandise to bring me?"

"He doesn't," Gawain said boldly. "He's a murderer. One crime, one necklace. If he hasn't brought you anything since, he's unlikely to now."

The man coughed, then spat. Lord Judah held his ground, even though the yellow mucus nearly hit his half-boot.

"Don't know his name, never did," the man finally said.

Gawain took out a small notebook, wishing he could have brought Fern along. "Then describe him. Tall, short, thin, fat? Young or old?"

"Tall, thin, young. Arrogant."

Gawain drew a male shape, though his skills didn't lend to much past stick figures. "Clothing?"

"Eh, don't remember."

"I mean, was he dressed like a laborer, a gentleman?"

"Oh, somewhere in between, I suppose."

"Eyes? Anything unusual about them? How did he smell?"

The man chuckled. "The only thing I really remember was his hair." He patted his head. "Since I don't have much left of my own."

"Yes?"

"*Goyische* hair. Yellow, straight. Looked like a haystack on top of a grasshopper."

Gawain tucked his notebook back into his coat. Lord Judah glanced at him, and he nodded. He knew who killed Wells Haldene. The rotten little bastard.

Lord Judah took another bill from his pocket and passed it to the fence. The man took it, shrugging.

"I'm sorry your friend was murdered."

Lord Judah thrust his hand back into his coat. "He wasn't my friend."

The man's gaze moved to Gawain, who stared back, unwilling to offer any information that these men might sell. "Some lovely merchandise in the front room, if you're interested. Some loose stones too, if you want to get back into the trade, Lord Judah."

Lord Judah shook his head. "No. I'm done with gems."

The two men stepped back and shut the door without further conversation. Of one mind, Gawain and Lord Judah moved rapidly down the corridor and down the stairs.

"I'm somewhat surprised they gave us the information," Gawain said when they reached the front door.

"I don't imagine they would have if they had any hope of repeat business. I don't suppose the murderer appeared to be the sort to offer any more goods."

"And he hasn't been back since. I wonder if he's looked for more jewelry, if Ann realizes how vulnerable she has been. Also, I wonder what he did with the money? He's still where he was at the time of the murder, doing the same thing. How could it have benefited him?"

When they reached the street, Lord Judah asked, "Who was the killer?"

"His cousin," Gawain spat. "The family charity case."

"The one who didn't come to London for the wedding?"

"Exactly. Probably wanted the time to search the inn for more gems while Harry was here."

Lord Judah swore under his breath. "We're probably in for a walk. No hansoms at Seven Dials."

"Keep your eyes peeled," Gawain said, though they could only see a couple of inches ahead of them through the ever-moving yellow fog. He could sense men huddled in front of nearby buildings.

"Yes. What are you going to do now?"

"Go home, tell Ann. See what she wants me to do."

"Sadly, I don't see how this will help the police. You aren't going to get a fence to finger the cousin."

"Maybe they can get him to confess, now that we know the truth."

"Must be a desperate lad, to do it. I'm thinking he must have had gambling debts, or some such, if he's never left the inn."

"Or he's waiting for another opportunity before leaving. More jewelry?"

"No, not for all this time. We're talking what, three years now? The money is long gone, and presumably he hasn't had a reason to need more since."

"Or he simply killed Wells in a fight, then took the necklace when he spotted it by chance, and sold it, but feels too guilty to spend the money."

Lord Judah pointed down a murky street. "Does it matter? Let's go this way. We aren't too far from Covent Garden and we can find a hansom there."

They chatted over possibilities until they found cabs, then separated so Gawain could return to Battersea. When he reached home, he found the place oddly deserted. Chase didn't answer the door and he had to use his key. He took off his coat and went upstairs to the nursery.

Inside, Jenna was sitting in the rocker, her eyes red, a handkerchief crushed between her hands.

"What's wrong?" he asked. "Did Noel get sick again?" Where was his son? Why wasn't the fire lit?

She shook her head. "I've been sacked."

His frantic glance around the room returned to the nursery maid. "I'm the master here. You haven't lost your position."

"Mrs. Redcake said I wasn't to go with them."

The chill invaded his bones. "With them? What do you mean?"

"She went to Leeds. She took Fern. I offered to go, but she said no, that I could go back to Lady Hatbrook if she'd have me. She was in too much of a hurry to write me a reference. What will Lady Hatbrook think of me?" the girl sniffed.

"Why did Mrs. Redcake go to Leeds?" Gawain growled.

"I don't know. She didn't tell me, but they left about four hours ago."

Gawain left the room, calling for Chase, who also acted as his valet when one was needed. He was digging through his dressing room when the man appeared. "You need to pack for me. I must leave immediately."

"You'll be following Mrs. Redcake, sir?"

"Exactly. When you're finished here, please have someone tell

Jenna she isn't sacked. I'll write from Leeds when I have a clue as to what's going on."

"Yes, sir. Do you want me to come with you?"

"No, but send word around to Lewis. Have him let me know if any Haldenes are seen in the area. He'd recognize both of them."

"We've had Mr. Harry Haldene here, sir. Am I to understand he is *persona non grata*?"

"No, he's fine. It's the other one. Jeremy. Yellow hair like straw. You see him, call the police."

"Yes, sir."

Gawain stared at the shirt in his hand. "Did anyone come to see my wife?"

"Just that *ayah* again, but we turned her away as you instructed."

Gawain felt a pang of guilt at that. He had been guilty of rash behavior in relation to both his wife and Fern recently. Why had he expected a wife would fold herself neatly into his life and chosen lifestyle, instead of bringing her own occupations, interests and relatives into his household? He'd been a fool. He hadn't married a child. They needed to have a frank discussion about their life.

"Thank you, Chase. I'll be in my study consulting the train timetable. Please bring down my bag . . . oh, and check with Jenna to make sure my wife packed sufficiently for Noel."

"Yes, sir."

Gawain was not lucky with the trains and it was morning before he pulled into Leeds. He told himself not to worry, that Jeremy and Ann both had no idea that he knew the truth about Wells's death. Still, his palms were clammy beneath his gloves all night long and he scarcely slept. His hip nearly folded beneath his weight when he stepped onto the platform and he had to rely on his cane to get him into a hansom. His journey was no improvement over that night in the horseless carriage nearly a year before.

Fifteen minutes later he was stumbling out of the hansom in the muddy yard at The Old Hart. It looked much the same as ever when he walked inside. The pub room was full, but the air smelled of English breakfast, not a spicy Indian one. He was glad Ann hadn't capped off fleeing their marriage by immediately returning to her position here as cook.

As he glanced around the front hall, he realized he didn't know where the family rooms were. All of the inn's rooms were up the stairs on the first floor and to the side of the staircase was a blank wall. Were the family quarters on the other side? He glanced around until he found a door behind the staircase and tried to open it, but it was locked. He pounded on the door and waited.

After a couple of minutes, he had just about decided to go up the stairs and see if his family had moved into a rented room, when the door opened. Harry stood in the doorway, his black hair hanging over his forehead.

"Redcake," he said in a flat tone that matched the dark circles under his eyes.

"You look like you've been up all night."

"It's your fault." Harry yawned hugely. "Ann has been hysterical, Fern has been hysterical. The baby kept wakin' up every couple of hours. You couldn't pay me to marry and have a passel of brats of me own."

"And here I decided you had a heart. I guess I was wrong." Just when Gawain had decided he'd best not trust Harry Haldene, the man gave him a sympathetic grin.

He glanced at the cane. "Hip botherin' you again?"

"I was up all night on the train. Too much time to think, and not about anything pleasant," Gawain admitted.

Harry snorted. "Could have sent a letter. It might have done you as much good."

"Meaning what?"

"Meaning nothing. You took a girl with the biggest heart in the world and snapped it between your fingers." Harry pointed his finger at Gawain. "What did you have to do that for? Don't you know she just has to help people? You can't lock her in your house and refuse to let her talk to anyone. That's sick. I thought you knew better, bein' interested in the same kind of Indian business she is."

"I made mistakes, Harry. I know that. I need to see her." At least he now knew heartbreak had sent Ann fleeing, not mortal danger.

Harry's heavy fist knocked the lintel above his head. "No, you don't. She just got here last night. Everyone is exhausted. She said Fern and Noel had just been sick. Go away for a week or two."

"I can't," Gawain said. "Listen to me carefully, man. She isn't safe here."

Harry's eyes closed into squints. "What d'you mean?"

Gawain glanced behind him. The front hall remained empty. He lowered his voice. "I know who killed Wells."

Harry's thick black brows rose. "You do?"

He leaned in so close that he could smell coffee on Harry's breath. "A friend of mine traced the necklace. Found who bought it, who sold it, and who originally brought it to a fence here in Leeds."

Harry's mouth dropped open. "It weren't no stranger? Why else would you say she's in danger?"

"Exactly." Gawain stepped even closer and put his hand on Harry's shoulder. "I'm sorry, Harry, but your cousin Jeremy sold the necklace."

"No," Harry said. "You're wrong."

"I'll go through it all again, but we need to get Ann away from here, bring in the authorities. It's their job to straighten it out. All I care about is my wife. You can see she can't stay at the inn, don't you?" Gawain released Harry and stepped back, stumbling until he caught himself with his cane. He had to make Harry understand he wasn't simply engaged in a power struggle with Ann, but was worried about her very life.

Ann crept closer, straining to hear. She'd recognized Gawain's voice at the door, felt a momentary thrill that he'd come right after her. But instead of offering protests of love and devotion to Harry, he'd started right into talk about Wells. She stepped through the room, silent on bare feet, still in her nightdress and wrapper. But Gawain lowered his voice when he revealed the murderer and she had no idea what he'd said.

She stepped closer, just as Harry's vocal chords expelled one loud word.

"Jeremy?"

She jumped and fled back a few steps. Jeremy? The orphaned cousin they'd taken in at fourteen had killed her husband? That couldn't be possible. While he hadn't shown any emotion during those terrible first couple of months after Wells's death, he never showed emotion anyway. And he never spent money. She'd had no reason to think he had any beyond the small salary they paid him in addition to room and board.

But Gawain kept speaking, talking about the chain of people

who'd sold her mother's necklace and how he'd identified Jeremy. She had to admit it sounded damning. How could he? Jeremy had been like a younger brother to her. She'd nurtured him, even tried to teach him how to read. She put her hand to her forehead. Too many late nights, recently. She couldn't think straight.

No, this was some gross error. Gawain was wrong. She'd never even seen Jeremy kill a spider, much less behave violently toward another human being.

After thrusting her feet into an old pair of boots, she ran out the back door and went to the storage building where they kept supplies. Jeremy was often out there, taking inventory or feeding the chickens that were kept in a nearby coop.

She folded her arms around her chest as the misty rain hit her in the yard. Her boots squelched in mud puddles and she nearly lost one because they were too large without thick stockings. Jeremy didn't appear to be around the chickens so she went into the storage building.

Inside, sun filtered in through chunks in the rough walls. Wells had meant to pull the old building down and rebuild, but Harry hadn't made it a priority. Ann blinked until her eyes adjusted to the light.

"Jeremy?" she called. She would resolve this. He must have some explanation for this damning evidence against him.

She heard footsteps in the loft and a couple of moments later she saw his head peep out above the ladder. He didn't smile or offer a word of greeting. No one would describe him as friendly, but he was family and she'd never had a reason to fear him.

"Would you come down here for a moment?"

He disappeared. The next thing she saw was his boots, and then his legs and backside as he descended the ladder. She'd always thought him ready to please, even if he didn't say much, and here he was, doing what she'd asked, despite her taking him away from his work.

When he reached the lower rungs he jumped off, landing in a crouch in front of her. As he stood, she both realized how slender he was and how much taller than she, with a body all muscle, unlike her curves, rounded even more by new motherhood.

She stared into his face, noting his dark eyes that were so similar to Harry's, though every other part of him was narrow where his cousin was broad. Had this been the last face her husband had seen? She shivered, losing her sense of certainty.

"What's wrong? Why are you dressed like that?" he asked.

She looked down at herself, just then noticing what she wore. "We came in last night. I just woke up."

"I know you came home. Harry told me this mornin' 'afore he sent me out to restock the kitchen."

"We keep kitchen supplies in the loft now?"

Jeremy glanced away instead of answering.

"What's up there?" she asked in a friendly tone.

He shrugged. "I was just takin' a minute. I like lookin' out at the town."

"That's fine. You work hard." She forced herself to touch his arm but the truth was, he didn't work that hard. He had a tendency to moon around, glowering, as if he didn't want to be there. But then why hadn't he left? It made no sense to her, especially if he had the price of an inn squirreled away all these years.

He stared at her. "What do you want, Ann?"

She thought about walking away, going back to the safety of Harry, or even Gawain, but she owned this inn, still, and she had always made her own decisions, fought her own battles since Wells had died. It was her property that had disappeared, her husband who had died, her business alone. "I want to know about my necklace."

"What?" He seemed to have no idea what she meant.

"My necklace from India. People are saying you had it in your possession once. Is that true?" She looked into his eyes and suddenly she just knew. He shifted, uneasily, as if caught in a lie.

He shrugged. "I maybe held it for a minute."

"Where did you get it?" She held a last hope that he had stolen the necklace, but hadn't killed Wells himself, that he had found it on the body. Couldn't that be what Fern had seen?

"What?" he repeated, glancing over her head, as if he weren't really paying attention.

But this was important, too important for his carelessness. Her hands twitched as if she was losing control of them. "I know you sold my necklace. The one Wells had with him the night he . . . died. He was taking it to sell, so we could buy another inn."

His gaze refocused on her. "You know?"

No lies, no pretended confusion, just those two words. His face expressionless as usual. Her finger pointed almost outside of her control. Fury clouded her vision. She poked him in the chest.

"Where did you find it?"

He took a step back. "Find it? You goin' to be that stupid? God, women are stupid."

She pressed her lips together until they ground painfully against her teeth. Had she been wrong about him? Was this his repayment for her kindness toward him all these years? She had to know. "Did you kill Wells? Why would you do that?"

He sneered, the first sign of emotion she'd seen from him, but said nothing.

She could feel her heart beating, her pulse pounding in her throat, her wrists, her belly. Her voice rose in fury. "You did, didn't you? Your own cousin, who took you in, loved you, taught you his business."

He sniffed and crossed his arms.

"How dare you stand there and say nothing. I lost our baby after that. I lost my husband and my baby," she shouted. "Over that blasted necklace? Over the price of an inn?"

"You don't get as much money when you take stuff to a fence," he said conversationally. "It wasn't the price of an inn."

She stared, incredulous. Who was this monster? How could she have nurtured him? "Why didn't you leave? How could you stay?"

He shrugged and thrust his hands deep into his trouser pockets. "Not enough money to break free. I was comfortable here."

"No one has ever expected very much of you," she spat.

He sniffed again. "Harry said that was all you had left from your mother. I don't think that's true. I bet you have more, and it's enough to get me out of here. Out of working for people. What about it, Ann? Where's the rest of the family jewelry?"

She stepped back, but before she could do more than lift one boot, he had a knife in his hand.

"Come, Ann, tell me where the jewelry is. I won't hurt you. I just want enough money to go. I can't stay now."

She set one boot down, then moved the other back, but her muddy heel slid and she started to fall. How could she have put herself in so much danger? Why hadn't she believed Gawain? She called out. "Harry! Gawain! I'm in here!"

Jeremy reached out and grabbed her by the arm, his corded fingers digging into her flesh. He lifted the knife and flashed the blade in front of her eyes, so triumphant with his power that he didn't stop her when she twisted her arm away from his grip and stepped back, shouting again, but knowing she was too far away from any possible salvation.

"I've searched time and again. Found nothin'. Where are they?" he demanded.

Chapter Sixteen

"I don't believe you," Harry said, the skin tightening around his eyes. He looked much more awake now.

"I am sorry," Gawain said, "but you can see why I need to remove Ann from here."

"She does not want to see you," the man said stubbornly, as if this point was the important one.

Gawain clenched his jaw until his teeth ached. "That may be true, but I am still her husband. I'm a reasonable man. I will return to my father's house in London and she can stay in Battersea, if that is what it takes to remove her from Leeds."

Harry pushed the hair out of his eyes. "You would do that?"

"Of course." He sighed. Time was wasting when he should have been calling in the authorities, but he had no access to Ann except through Harry. "Did she tell you why she is angry with me?"

"She said you were making life unbearable."

He gripped his cane, ashamed of what he had to admit. "I was mean to Fern. It was inexcusable. I was in a rage. That is what I am sorriest about."

"I'd like to punch you," Harry muttered. "Fern is a defenseless little girl."

"Later. For now we have a common enemy," Gawain said. "Listen. I didn't want Ann hanging out her shingle as a healer, as if I couldn't pay the bills for my own household."

"I thought all the women in your family worked."

Gawain would have laughed if he weren't under such strain. "Not all of them, no, but I seem to be related by birth or marriage to a few such women."

"It surprises me that you'd worry what people thought about your financial status. You've always had money."

Was that the impression he made? He wouldn't have credited himself with so much polish. "Not me. I was a factory brat from the age of nine, then the army. I wasn't the heir until after I'd left for India and my older brother died. In some ways, Ann married beneath her. Her people were Indian royalty and English country gentry."

"I don't think she thinks that."

Gawain put his hand out to Harry. "Let me see her. Let me protect her."

Harry scratched his ear. "It would be best to have the family out of the way when I confront Jeremy."

"I'd have the police nearby when you do that," Gawain said. "He's killed once."

"You don't know that. He might have stolen the necklace during the madness after Wells died and Ann lost her baby."

"So he's either a killer or a man willing to steal from a new widow. Either way, no conscience," Gawain growled.

Harry dropped his hand from the lintel to his stomach and turned so Gawain could squeeze by.

Thank God. He'd won. "Where are they?"

Harry pointed to the left. "Second door."

They were in an ancient part of the inn, and the floor sloped downward. Gawain had to use his cane for support. When he reached the door he rapped twice then opened it. Inside was a close-smelling room with a fire burning in an old fieldstone fireplace directly across from the door. Fern sat on a blanket in front of the fire, rocking a low cradle.

Gawain stepped in and glanced around, but Ann wasn't there.

"Where's Ann?" Harry asked from behind him.

Fern glanced up, frowning when she saw Gawain.

"Sweetheart, we need to find Ann," he said in his gentlest voice. "She might be in danger."

Fern used the cradle to pull herself up, then went to the window and pointed. Gawain stepped closer to her and looked outside.

"What is that building?"

"Storage," Harry said, following him in. "Then the chicken coop. Then food storage to the right."

"Which one did Ann go into?" Gawain asked.

Fern pointed to the storage building on the left.

"What is in there?"

Harry started to answer, but Fern's eyes grew wide and she turned to Gawain. When her lips parted Gawain put up his hand to silence Harry.

"J-J-J," Fern stuttered.

Harry looked as upset as his sister. "What did you say?"

"Jeremy," Gawain said grimly. "I expect she's telling us that Jeremy is out there. Right, Fern?"

She nodded.

"Did you see him take Ann's necklace from Wells's body in the stable?" Gawain asked.

"J-J-J," she stuttered again, then nodded hard.

"Sweet Baby Jesus," Harry swore, as Fern gave up trying to speak and nodded again.

"Did you see Jeremy kill Wells?" Gawain asked.

Fern held up her hand, tightly balled into a fist, then slammed it to her chest repeatedly.

The two men glanced at each other.

"I'm going after my wife," Gawain said. "Watch over Fern and my son, please."

"Should we go for the police?" Harry asked.

"No time," Gawain shouted, rigid with the urge to act. "Why would she have gone out there?"

"I can't think of a reason," Harry admitted. "Except that is Jeremy's hidey-hole. Ann never goes near that building."

Fern went back to the cradle and knelt protectively over Noel.

"Could she have heard us talking at the door?" Gawain pulled his Enfield service revolver from the pocket of his coat. He hoped the barrel wasn't rusted. He couldn't remember the last time he'd cleaned the gun, but he'd inserted six fresh cartridges just today.

He glanced down at Fern and saw silent tears rolling down her face. "Don't worry, I'll bring her back safe."

Fern glanced up and sniffed. He knew he wouldn't be able to restore the relationship between them unless he did exactly that. "I promise. I'm going to make everything right again."

"I have a shotgun," Harry said, swaying from side to side. "She's a spirited girl, used to making her own decisions. If she heard us talking she might have gone to confront Jeremy."

"Stay here," Gawain ordered. "Protect my son in case I can't."

Harry started to protest, but Gawain said, "It's your cousin out there, man. You don't want to do this."

"I'll load the shotgun and stand at the window," Harry said, his face settling into hard lines that aged him five years in a moment. "Won't take me but a minute."

Gawain clapped him on the shoulder. "Good man."

"I'll show you the back door."

He scarcely felt his old pains as Harry led him into the small pantry in the family quarters and pointed out their hidden exit. They shook hands and Gawain turned the doorknob, noting the door was unlocked. What had Ann been thinking when she went outside?

"If I don't make it, tell Ann I'm truly sorry." He just hoped he wasn't too late to protect her, whatever he found out there.

Harry frowned. "I won't need to tell her anything. Jeremy isn't going to hurt you."

"Lock it," he told Harry, then shut the door behind him, wishing he had Lord Judah or even Bowler Martin at his back. He had tested true under fire, but he hadn't been this kind of soldier except in the most unusual circumstances. Never had he taken a battle to an enemy.

The old habit of being aware of one's surroundings returned. He might have been back in a Northwestern village in India. When he scanned the yard, he saw nothing amiss. The only movement was chickens pecking at the dirt behind their fence. He had to turn his head to catch the full spectrum and swore. In India he'd had both eyes. He lifted his patch, hoping his eye had continued recovering, but no, he could only see color. Wait. No, that was wrong, he caught a flicker of movement in the corner of his bad eye. He turned to the left and saw a mouser slinking around the side of the inn. Good, the eye had some value after all. He could smell the stables even though they were out of sight, back where the cat had come from.

Fingering the revolver in his pocket, he stared hard at the storage building. Three windows provided light to the ground floor, but they were covered by dark brown shutters. A second story had open windows but he didn't see Ann or Jeremy through them. They had to be on the ground floor, behind a closed door.

He assessed the risks awaiting him. Lit lanterns, most likely. Pantry items that could be thrown, even if there weren't farm implements and the like. An unfamiliar landscape. His wife, whom he couldn't possibly risk hurting.

On the plus side? He'd have no problem hurting Jeremy Haldene, who was at best a heartless thief and at worst a cold-blooded killer, and had continued to live under the roof of the blameless woman who had lost her child in the grief over the events in that stable.

He walked forward slowly, his shoes burping in the mud, watching for any sight of shadows behind the shutters, but the building did not give up any secrets. He debated breaking through one of the shutters and going through that way, but didn't know if there were glass panes. A deep puddle sucked his shoe down, rotating his hip unpleasantly. He swore soundlessly and pulled out his foot. His cuff dripped with muddy water but his sodden shoe remained on his foot. His limp returned as he moved toward another side of the rectangular building, gripping the walnut handle of his revolver.

The door, on the shorter side, had a latch hook and lock, but they weren't open. He slid his fingers around the crack between the door and the lintel and opened it, hoping it wouldn't squeak. Nonetheless, the light would give him away unless Jeremy was distracted.

Inch by inch, he pulled it open with one hand, using the door as cover. When he had it just wide enough, he debated going in gun first, but he didn't know if Ann had really gone in to confront Jeremy. A small chance existed that he could just walk them out of there and deal with Jeremy without the added risk of Ann's presence. He prayed for that scenario.

When he slipped in, he noted three lanterns illuminating a central aisle. Tall oak shelves forked out from the walls, creating dark recesses. The pungent scent of onions filled the space. On the south side was a long loft. He couldn't see the access point.

Down the main aisle, past where he could see, he heard a man's voice. He stepped forward, trying to hear.

Then the voice rose to an angry shout. "Where are they?"

Gawain's pulse began to pound in his temples. *Jeremy.* He pulled the gun from his pocket and cocked the hammer. Ann was in danger. *His wife.*

He crept down the aisle, his wet shoes and trousers leaving dark dots on the rough wooden planks of the floor. When he brushed past a wreath of garlic, it swung gently in the air. Bundles of dry herbs fluttered from where they hung along clotheslines strung across the shelves. How long until the movement gave him away?

Ann's voice floated down the aisle to him. "There isn't any more jewelry, Jeremy. The money you have now is all there is. You need to take it and go."

Jeremy laughed harshly. "I don't believe you. You were always a deceitful bitch."

The gun's handle warmed under Gawain's grip as he crept forward. He heard staccato footsteps. Was Jeremy moving toward Ann? Did he have a weapon?

As he came to the end of the building, he saw Ann, surrounded by a nimbus of light that must be coming from an open window on the south side of the building. An arm, holding a sharp knife, came out of the shadows of a shelf. Gawain saw a ladder just to the right, leading to the loft. Could he take Jeremy down before he had Ann under the control of his knife?

"What lies have I ever told you?" Ann cried. "I have never—"

"You used to lie to Wells all the time," Jeremy snarled.

The boards creaked as Ann moved a step down the aisle. "Never."

Good girl. Stay in the center, don't let him trap you between the shelves.

"You lied all the time," he countered. "Promisin' you'd stop seeing sick people because of the baby, when you let 'em in every day. That's why your baby died. You caught somethin' from one of them filthy niggers."

Ann took another step. "Not true."

Gawain saw her more clearly then, as she stepped under a lantern. She only wore a gray wool robe. The white hem of a nightdress peeked out underneath, though she had stout, unlaced boots on her feet. He watched closely as she reached behind herself, fumbling for something on a shelf. She must be trying to find a weapon.

Thankful that he hadn't yet been noticed, he hovered in the shelves' shadows as he took tiny steps forward.

"It's all your fault," Jeremy sneered. "One of these days you're goin' to kill the entire family with some nasty Indian disease."

"I don't even live here now. I live in London." Ann's hand disappeared into a shelf and Gawain saw it reappear behind her with a glass jar containing some kind of powdered substance. She pushed it against the edge of the shelf and unscrewed it slowly, rotating the jar.

Was she planning to fling it into Jeremy's eyes? He hoped she did it well out of reach of the knife. Gripping the revolver tightly, he moved again, attempting to close the gap between himself and Jeremy.

A muscle in his thigh suddenly contracted. He bumped into a shelf on the south side of the aisle. A basket of apples swayed. He slid into the aisle, as Jeremy said, "Who's there?"

"No one," Ann said soothingly. "We're only talking, Jemmy. Just us."

Gawain peered out and saw Jeremy's face contort.

Jeremy swore at Ann again and rushed her. Ann brought up her glass of powder and flung it in Jeremy's eyes but he kept coming. He screamed as his knife arm lifted. Reddish powder dusted his face. *Cayenne.* An image of Fern thrusting her fist into her chest flashed through Gawain's mind.

He stepped into the aisle, took aim at Jeremy's left side, as far away from Ann as he could manage, and fired. Jeremy's shoulder hitched. Ann screamed and sneezed at the same time, then stumbled back, but the knife kept coming. Gawain cocked the hammer back, going down hard on one knee as he fired again.

Jeremy's knife hand went to his chest. His eyes widened, dripping powdery red tears. The knife dropped to the planks. He swayed, his tortured gaze catching sight of Gawain.

As Gawain staggered to his feet, preparing his revolver for another shot, Jeremy seemed to melt, his legs going rubbery. He sank down, then fell face first, his forehead landing on Ann's boot. A fresh gust of red particles dusted into the air. Gawain felt the first sensation of cayenne on his tongue. He closed his mouth and uncocked his revolver, then grabbed for Ann's arm.

She still held the glass jar and her eyes were red, tears and snot dripping down her face. He found her hand, tugging her down the aisle and out of the building, then stumbled for the barn.

"Horse trough?" he cried, mud making their running steps difficult.

Ann fell, one foot coming out of her boot. Gawain thrust his gun into his pocket and picked her up, running in a shambling gait through the yard. Men stopped moving, their hands stilled on valises and pipes as he ran. Through his streaming eyes, he saw a rain barrel under a drainpipe and angled toward it, then set Ann down next to it and pushed her in.

Men shouted as her head went down, her long braid flying into the air in reaction to her head dipping. He pulled her out and she came up gasping, clawing for her face.

Grabbing both hands, he dunked them too.

"Stop that," someone yelled, and Gawain felt rough hands on the back of his coat, pulling him away from her.

"Pepper," he gasped. "Got to get the pepper off her." He sneezed.

"Crikey," an old man muttered. "Look at his face."

A second later, he was being pushed face-first into the rain barrel. His mouth was still closed but he felt icy water fill his nose. He came up spluttering.

Next to him, slim brown hands reached in. Ann cupped water and splashed her face.

"Let me look at you," said a voice with a strong northern accent. More water splashed. "There, Mrs. Haldene, the powder's all gone but your eyes are going to be red."

Gawain and Ann sneezed simultaneously.

"Call for the police," Gawain gasped. "Jeremy Haldene tried to kill my wife and I shot him. Think he's dead."

"Your wife?" the northern voice said.

"I married Mrs. Haldene," Gawain said, grabbing the edge of the barrel for support.

"Did you now?"

Gawain realized his eyes were still closed from his trip into the water barrel. He opened them and recognized one of the blacksmith's cronies. "A couple of weeks ago. Look, Jeremy killed Wells Haldene."

"Did he now?" the man said patiently.

"He's not lying," Ann said. She shivered hard.

Gawain remembered it was still March, much too cold to be outside while soaked to the bone. He unbuttoned his coat, which wasn't entirely wet, folded down the damp part, and laid it over Ann's shoulders. She turned to him and he put his arm around her.

"Mind the gun," he said in a low voice. "In the right pocket."

"Where's the body?" the man asked.

"Around back. In the storage building."

"Go inside," the man said, then stepped away. "Mrs. Haldene, do you have a telephone?"

"No," she said, teeth chattering.

The man clicked his teeth.

"They've got one at the butcher shop," another man said.

The first man raised his hand in acknowledgment and kept walking. Three men escorted Gawain and Ann back into the inn. They started to steer them toward the dining room and its huge fireplace, but Ann protested.

"I need to put on some dry clothes."

"She didn't kill anyone, I did," Gawain said.

The men separated and two took him into the dining room as the third escorted Ann back to the family quarters.

Gawain felt like he was walking onboard a ship as he climbed the steps toward the room Harry had assigned him late that night, after hours of questioning by police. He hadn't seen anyone except Harry, but had been promised that Ann was fine and had corroborated everything he'd told the police. Harry had received assurances that no charges would be filed.

Gawain pushed open the door of the room, his thoughts flashing to the moment when he entered the storage building. Since he'd never had any emotional trauma over the battles with the Pathans in India, even the battle where he'd been wounded, he was surprised to find himself already troubled by the events of the morning. Just one more way to be wounded.

He shut the door with a groan and sagged against it, desperate to finally remove the shoes and stockings that had never fully dried.

"Let me help you," said a soft voice. A hand led him to a cane-backed chair next to a small table.

He heard a flutter of skirts as she knelt on the floor and began to work on his shoelaces. "Ann?"

"Of course."

"Where is Noel? Is Fern okay? I promised her I'd come back but then the police kept me with them all day."

"It's fine," she said. "Fern knows you saved my life. You can see her tomorrow. Noel just ate and he's asleep."

"You must be exhausted," he said, his own weariness seeming to coat his voice with molasses.

"I'm not so bad. Your shoelaces are a disaster. I don't know if I can undo the knots."

Gawain squinted down at his shoes. This was one area where his bad eye definitely didn't help. He pulled one foot up to the chair and began to pull at the sodden mess. "I'm surprised you came up here."

"You're my husband."

"You left me." He felt a little give in one lace and concentrated on pulling there.

"My actions may have been ill-considered."

"I'm amazed you would take Noel here."

"He was perfectly well again." She said something low in an Indian tongue he didn't recognize.

He had never realized she spoke anything other than English, since she'd left India so young. Perhaps just curse words. "In future, I would hope you realize it is easier to bar me from our home, rather than remove my son from comfortable surroundings when I am beastly."

He heard a hint of a smile in her voice when she answered. "I will remember that." He felt a tug. "There. I think I can get this one undone."

He focused on his shoe until the knot had given up its secrets and a minute later pushed it off his foot with a sigh of relief. Someday his toes might be warm again. He pulled off his black silk sock and tossed it on the floor, then wriggled his toes. "Heaven."

"I am almost done." A moment later, Gawain felt the other shoe give way and soon that foot joined its partner in nudity. "Your trousers are a disaster."

"I agree." He stood and shed the offending wool, then reseated himself.

"Did you bring any fresh clothing?"

"One set of clothes, yes. But I'm not sure where they are."

"Where are your pajamas?"

"You cannot expect me to remember everything."

"Take off the rest of those damp things then, and get into bed. I'll stir up the fire and run a warming pan over the sheets."

"Why are you taking such good care of me?" he asked, complying as she fussed around the room.

"I don't want you to take sick."

No, then he would remain here at the inn. With that mordant thought, he climbed into the soft bed and tucked two pillows behind his head. Ann handed him a teacup. His fingers closed around it and he let his eyelids close as he drank the spicy, milky concoction. It warmed him as well as the fire did, and he was half asleep by the time he felt the left side of the bed dip. He set his teacup on the side table and turned. A curvy body smelling of jasmine and cloves curled against him.

He hadn't been expecting this. His hand curled around her naked shoulder. He ran his fingers along her arm, then dropped to her flank. No clothing anywhere. Despite the events of the day, his manhood stirred with interest. He pressed himself along her back.

"If you intended to warm me up, you're succeeding."

She didn't answer, just put her hand behind her back and wrapped her fingers around him. He hardened completely in a moment and slid down deeper into the sheets. When his head was resting just above hers, he found one breast with his hand and tested the weight. He touched the nipple and it hardened as quickly as he had for her. She gave a little gasp, moved a fraction of an inch away, then settled again.

Feeling confident now, he let his fingers dance down her abdomen, nearly as flat now as it had been when they met. When he quested into her curls, her grip tightened on him. He rotated his hips, thrusting against her palm, then found her lips and parted them with his fingers.

She was as hot as a cauldron and dampened enthusiastically as he moved his fingers through her sweet heat. He dipped into her opening then traced the moisture up again, circling her pearl. Her bottom pressed against her hand and his erection.

He drifted his fingers through again, then pressed the hood above her pearl. She gasped and turned over, pulling him down over her body.

"This will warm your toes."

He pulled her thighs apart, his knees finding cool places on the sheets. Any thought of cold vanished a moment later when he slid into her hot, welcoming sheath. Her own warm feet found his thighs, then she locked her legs around his waist as he moved in for another long thrust.

The stoked fire cast firelight and shadows in turn across her lovely, exotic face. He pushed tendrils of hair away from her temples and kissed her on each side as he moved inside her.

"Why do we ever fight when we have this?"

She tossed her head and ran her fingers along his back, gently abrading him with her nails. "In bed we have a shared goal."

"Passion," he agreed. Now he felt very warm. He tugged down the blankets, exposing his torso to the fire, and lifted himself on his elbows so he could see her amazing breasts. Her throat needed a kiss so he touched her tenderly there, then buried his face between her globes and reached for her thighs.

She gave him everything, but it only worked here at the inn. An hour or two later, Ann rebraided her hair, which had come undone when they made love a second time, with her on top. She smiled at the soreness of her inner thighs as she slid out of the sheets, recalling how she'd ridden him like a jockey at a race, urging him on. How could he be so adventurous in the bedroom and so old-fashioned out of it?

He was her hero, and her lover, but she didn't know if she could keep him as her husband. Leaving her shoes wherever they'd fallen, she quietly opened the door and tiptoed into the corridor and down the stairs, until she reached the family quarters. She checked on Noel, breathing quietly in his cradle, and then went to her belongings. A few minutes later she sat by the fire and opened the small rosewood box containing her mother's ring, the last jewel she possessed. How could something so small have such power? Jeremy hadn't even known it existed, yet he'd died in hopes of obtaining it. For her, it had been her last remaining bit of security once the necklace and chance of a second inn had evaporated along with her husband and dream of a child.

Now, she had a husband again, and Noel, and the cache of money Harry had found hidden in the loft of the storage building that afternoon. Not the price of an inn, but enough money for a house of her own. Jeremy should have taken it and gone. She picked up the ring and let the thin, worn gold band slide down her finger. If she wanted she could have a house and a maid-of-all-work and practice her medicine for expenses. What she didn't want was this ring. Her mother's jewelry had brought her nothing but pain, and her mother had never intended that.

But if she sold it for a house and servant pay, choosing that life, she wouldn't have the fire and passion she'd experienced upstairs in Gawain's bed. She stood up and went to the small desk where she and Harry did accounts and wrote Gawain a note. She'd let him decide. What would his response be?

Chapter Seventeen

Gawain woke the next morning when the door shut. He struggled to an upright position and noted a small, steaming teapot on the bedside table. The curtains had been drawn and he saw his trousers and shoes had been dried and brushed. He might be family but was being treated like a guest. Ann had still been there when he'd fallen asleep but she was long gone, tending to Noel, most likely. Had their lovemaking mended their problems enough for her to pack for the return trip to Battersea?

His manhood stirred, but he'd already woken with an erection. Remembering the use to which it had been put the night before, he experienced a moment of disappointment, especially because he could still smell the lingering scent of jasmine in the room.

For now, he should restore his energies with a cup of tea and think about breakfast. When his fingers quested for the teapot, they brushed against a piece of paper. A note? He picked it up and limped to the window so he could see clearly.

The inside of the pane was fogged with cold. He rubbed at the glass and was rewarded with little more than a view of rain and dirt. At least the light was good enough for the note. He opened it and read, "Dear Gawain, Jeremy was correct. I did have one more gem of my mother's. It is in the box on the tray. Please dispose of it as you will. The royal jewelry needs to be out of my life. I want the rumors about it to end in my lifetime so Noel isn't plagued by it as I have been. If my mother had not left it to me, perhaps Wells and Jeremy would still be alive."

Gawain rubbed his chin. Why was she blaming the jewelry when Jeremy's greed was the culprit here? He walked back to the tea tray and picked up the finely carved Indian box that was also there. Inside, he saw a gold filigree ring with a large sapphire. He picked it up, noting someone had worn it for many years since the band was much thinner on the back then along the sides. Lord Judah would know what it was worth. Would Ann like it if he reset the gem in another setting, one that appeared more English? Then she would still have something of her mother's, but it wouldn't resemble a "royal" treasure. He'd give her the price of it too, so she knew he didn't covet her material possessions as Jeremy had. Nor did he need to spend her money like Wells had. He could afford to keep her in style.

While he drank his tea he dressed, hoping Ann would reappear. Eventually, he went to the dining room and ate eggs and sausages. No Indian breakfast was on offer, which he took as a good sign that Ann hadn't settled back in. When he was done, he knocked on the door of the family quarters.

Ann answered the door, looking harried. "You are still here?"

"Of course," he said. "Are you packing to return?"

"Fern's sick," Ann said.

"Is Noel all right?"

She pushed frizzy curls off her forehead. "For now, but Fern is too ill to travel."

He checked her clothing for signs of feeding gone wrong. "Is Noel at risk?"

"I've tucked Fern into her little room, away from him."

"I don't suppose you will come home with Noel and leave Fern here."

"Who would take care of her?" Ann asked sharply.

She sounded like an irritated doctor now, rather than the sensually pleasing wife of the night before.

Harry, but he couldn't suggest that, not with the trouble of Jeremy's burial still to come. "I understand. Can I get you anything? Medicine, or could I purchase Fern a little gift? A book or something?"

"You should go," Ann said. "Before you take ill yourself. And if you stay here, the police may come looking for you again."

He reached for her hand. With a reluctant look, she allowed him to take it. "Don't worry about the police, Ann. I have nothing to fear in a clear case of self-defense."

"You are probably correct."

"Well?" He squeezed her hand. "What can I get you?"

She pulled her hand away. "Nothing. We'll be fine. I know you have business to take care of in London."

If he hadn't noticed her lips trembling slightly, he'd have thought he meant nothing to her. "How is Harry doing?"

"He's trying to find out if he can bury Jeremy. Penning the letters to the rest of the family was difficult too."

"This must be hard for you as well. I am suddenly taken by the realization that you didn't know what he'd done until just yesterday. Only Fern knew."

A tear welled in Ann's right eye and dripped down her cheek.

"Let me help you, sweetheart."

She wiped her eye. "I'm still suffering side effects from the cayenne yesterday. You can help me by going. I need to be here right now."

Her words stung, but he knew he was fighting a losing battle. "I did come here without making arrangements. I'll go back for now, but I'll return soon, and when I do, I'll expect you to come home with me."

"Harry might need me."

That irritated him, made him sharp. "You can't do Jeremy's work, whatever it was. He'll have to hire a boy."

"I'm very upset." The words required comfort, but her tone held a hint of accusation.

"I understand that, but I thought we comforted each other rather well last night. We have some spark that brings us together."

"I know," she whispered. "But I can't think about that right now."

He sighed. "Take care of Fern. Her illness may be as much emotional as physical, after yesterday's events."

"I thought so, too."

"Tell her goodbye for me and that I'll see her soon."

"I will."

Slowly but firmly, Ann shut the door in his face. He had a sudden urge to kick it down and hoist his wife on his shoulder, drag her out of here like a caveman or a medieval Scot. But that would achieve nothing.

All he could do was keep his business afloat, and figure out how to win Ann back. She wanted to communicate by letter? He could do the same. And bring her money, and a remade ring. Maybe displaying a hint of sentiment would melt her heart. He had all but forgotten, after yesterday's events, that she had fled their home.

The inn's maid disappeared shortly after Gawain left in a hired cab for the station. Ann had to tend the two children and clean most of the rooms. That night, Ann and Harry sat in their sitting room. He looked as tired as she felt.

Harry rested his head on the back of his favorite old armchair. "I suspected she were dallyin' wi' Jeremy."

"She must have been frightened when he died."

"Maybe she thought Gawain was going to the authorities about her when he left so abruptly."

Ann stared at the tiny shirt she was sewing for Noel. She crumpled it into her lap. "He didn't leave abruptly. I sent him away."

"Upset that he killed the boy?" Harry closed his eyes.

"No, not that. I would have done it myself if I'd had a weapon. He wanted to kill me." She touched the corner of one eye, remembering the pain of the cayenne. Under some circumstances it was actually used as medicine in the eye, but not like that.

"I forget you already left Gawain. I don't understand why. Seems a decent enough fellow." Harry sat forward in his chair, as if hearing some noise, then sat back. "I thought I heard Fern."

"She hasn't made a noise since she took to her bed."

"Has she ever?"

"Yes, now and then. Gawain suggested a program of encouragement, since her problem was inside her head. I guess I thought she'd start speaking again, now that Jeremy is dead. Her terrible secret is in the open now."

"She don't need to be afraid anymore." Harry made a fist. "I can't believe I failed me own sister this way, bringin' Jeremy here, not realizin' what he was."

"He was kin. Wells—"

"I persuaded Wells. Jeremy's mother was mad and he didn't want him in the inn with you. But I said we couldn't leave him to the rest of the family. There aren't many of us, and we were best suited to find him work."

"He killed over my mother's necklace," Ann said. "Without that, there would have been no temptation."

"He murdered his own cousin, Ann. You can't blame yourself for any part of that."

Ann turned away, fighting back the tears that had been ever present for a day and a half. "But I do."

Harry lifted his hand then dropped it to his knee. "I need a dram o' gin. I'm goin' to the common room."

"No singing," Ann warned. "Let Noel sleep."

Harry grinned. "I'll go visit Thomas. He'll let me sleep on a pallet by the forge if I'm too drunk to wander home." He stood up and strode away.

Ann noted that Gawain's boots needed resoling. But he wasn't her responsibility anymore. She'd left him. Still, she wasn't taking her responsibility toward Harry any more seriously. Where did she belong? If Gawain came back, she guessed she'd know. Meanwhile, she should think about finding Harry a wife.

She curled up in the chair, hoping to sleep for a bit before Noel woke for his midnight feeding. Fern needed to feel better tomorrow, so she could watch the baby while Ann cleaned the rooms.

She drifted to sleep as she composed the advertisement for a new maid.

By the next evening she was exhausted, since she hadn't had to clean a floor full of rented rooms since the first month of her pregnancy with Noel. She tossed her buckets and rags in the little room set aside for storage, and put the dirty sheets in a bin, grateful they'd hired out the washing over a year ago.

Back in the family quarters, she pushed open Fern's door to check on her and Noel. The girl was seated on the rug in front of the fire, playing patty-cake with the baby. While she didn't sing, precisely, she was mouthing the words and an occasional sound came out. *Progress.* As Fern finished the game, Ann saw Noel smile.

"Oh!" Her hand flew to her chest. "His first real smile, Fern!"

The girl smiled and picked up Noel, kissing him. The baby snuggled against her.

Ann sank awkwardly to the floor, unsure if she'd be able to get up later. Fern handed Noel to her.

"Is it time for a feeding?"

"No."

Ann's gaze flew up from her baby. "Fern? You spoke?" She watched the girl swallow hard.

Fern nodded.

Ann reached for her hand. "Please, speak again."

Fern smiled tentatively. "Ann."

Again, Ann felt the tingle of tears at the base of her eyes. "Thank you," she whispered. "I have missed hearing your voice."

"G-g'wain?" Fern had trouble with the pronunciation.

"He's gone back to London. I sent him away," she confessed.

Fern frowned.

"He wasn't very nice to either of us," Ann reminded her. "With the doll clothes, and sending away my patient."

Fern pointed at Noel.

"I know I have Noel to care for, but he hired Jenna. What does he expect me to do all day? It's silly to form societies for good works like ladies do when I have skills that can help people directly. I don't even need to take money."

Fern just looked at her.

"Of course, I don't want to bring disease into our house," Ann said. "I am not certain how best to manage the situation, but certainly I could be a midwife to poor local women, just by word of mouth."

"G-g'wain," Fern said again.

"I need to speak to him," Ann said. "We didn't talk about my plans, not that I had clear plans. Maybe he didn't either, and that was the problem. He found the house, moved us in, and then went back to his work."

Fern gestured around the room.

"Yes, the house needs to be furnished," Ann agreed. "But that takes time. And I don't really know how much money there is to spend. Gawain didn't give me an allowance or a household budget."

"M-money?"

"We have the money back from the necklace," Ann said. "And I gave Gawain my mother's ring to sell. So that's a dowry, certainly. I'm sure Gawain has plenty, but even if he didn't, we have money for furnishings now."

Fern looked at her, bemused.

"Well, he was an enlisted man. He's only been in business for a couple of years. I don't know how much money his father has given him, but even he's been rich for only a few years."

Fern rolled her eyes.

"I'm reaching for excuses, I know. Gawain and I, we need to talk about our marriage, not assume. We only have one thing in common—Noel."

"Herbs," Fern said, and coughed.

"That too," Ann said. "You're right. Which makes it all the more inexplicable that he'd ban me from working with them."

Fern parted her lips, then shook her head.

"What?"

Fern waved her arms, as if the thoughts in her head were too big to speak. Ann decided to spare her and change the subject.

"Harry needs a wife," she said.

Fern said, "Leeds," and made a face.

"Not in Leeds?"

"Batt'sea."

"You think I should sell the inn and persuade Harry to move to Battersea?"

Fern nodded vigorously.

"I hadn't thought of that," she mused. "But with what happened here, it might be hard to sell anytime soon. Still, we could look for a nice girl for Harry in London, instead of here."

Noel woke and yawned, then began rooting for his next meal. Fern came to her knees and helped Ann into a chair so she could nurse more comfortably.

A week passed, bringing a couple of genuine smiles from Noel and more scattered words from Fern. Ann kept her supplied with hot tea and honey, as speaking seemed to give her a sore throat after such a long time of not using her powers of speech.

Ann found a new maid for the rooms late in the week that Gawain had left, and she began on Monday, the first day of April. The sky over the inn had lost its continually leaden look and green sprouted in the flower boxes on the upper floors after a couple of weeks of steady tending.

They spent the afternoon upstairs together, Ann training the new girl in her duties. She was carefully mopping the hallway under Ann's supervision when Fern came running up the steps.

"What is it?"

Fern smiled. "G'wain!"

Ann was pleased to hear Fern had lost her stutter, but her stomach lurched at the thought of facing Gawain. Had he come to fetch them home? Or serve divorce papers for adultery, though she hadn't committed it?

"Where is Noel?"

"G'wain," Fern said again.

Ann nodded. "Keep mopping," she instructed the new maid, then lifted her skirts and went down the narrow stairs, careful to keep a stately pace.

Her husband was cooing over Noel in the hallway. She admired his broad shoulders, covered in a light overcoat. His hair looked overlong, partially covering his ears. The front door was still open and wind brushed at Ann's hair, freeing a few damp tendrils. It felt nice, but she didn't want Noel chilled, so she dashed past Gawain and shut the door.

"Come into the family quarters, where it is warmer," she said.

"No kiss, no greeting?"

Ann felt that lurching feeling again. "I didn't know if you wanted a kiss."

"I always do." His patch was off, and his gray eyes looked at her with a business-like seriousness.

She walked in front of him deliberately, watching to see if both of his eyes followed her. When they did, she clapped her hands together. "Your vision is better!"

"Indeed," he agreed in his gravelly rasp. "But I would rather a kiss than an inspection."

Harry strode out of the common room. "Redcake!" he boomed. "Did you get my letter 'bout the tea order?"

"My office did. They sent a box for you along with me."

Harry rubbed his hands together. "Excellent. D'you know, the owner o' that bakery up the street likes it so much he wanted to get five pounds off me?"

"I'll be happy to sell it to him," Gawain said.

Ann put her hands on Noel, ready to remove her baby if the men were going to stand there and talk business.

"I thought I could sell it to him, since it's just a small amount," Harry said.

"You want to become a wholesale supplier?"

"Why not? We have the storage space, and I already sell the herbs."

"I was thinking of selling the inn," Ann blurted.

Both men's gaze swiveled to her. She snatched Noel out of Gawain's arms.

"You were going to buy me out?" Harry asked.

"I have the money," Ann said. "Remember?"

"I'd rather buy you out," Harry muttered. "This is my livelihood."

"I'm sure we can work something out," Gawain said. "A payment plan."

"It's my inn," Ann said. "Maybe I don't want to sell it to Harry."

"Why not?" Harry's eyes took on a hurt expression.

Ann suddenly realized she couldn't talk about moving to London, since she didn't even know if that was where she was welcome. What had Gawain come to say? She wanted to scream in frustration. This conversation had gone in the completely wrong direction.

"I'd like a private reunion with my husband," she said. "I didn't mean to hurt your feelings, Harry. I will consult with you later."

Fern jumped off the bottom stair and went to Harry, patting his arm. "Wife," she said very clearly.

Harry took a step back. "Wife?"

"She wants to find you one," Ann explained.

Fern turned to her with a look of outrage.

"It was my idea," Ann admitted.

"Because you're so happily married?" Harry snapped.

Gawain held up his hands before Ann could say anything. "I would like that private reunion, if you don't mind." He put his arm around Ann's shoulders and towed her off to the door below the stairs.

She transferred Noel to his arms, feeling self-conscious as she pulled her ring of keys from her belt and unlocked the door. "I look a fright. I've been teaching the new maid her duties and playing in the flower boxes whenever I had a minute."

"I like it when your hair gets all curly," Gawain said.

"It does that when I'm warm."

For the first time, her husband grinned at her, and she recognized he took her remark in a more intimate way than she'd meant it. Forcing herself to keep her hands away from her hair, she tossed her key ring onto the table.

She walked over to the fireplace in the sitting room and lit the fire. "So you came to bring some tea to Harry?"

"And to see you. I have something for you."

"Oh?"

"Where are you keeping Noel?"

"His cradle is in Fern's room. Come and sit down. I'll get it." She stepped out of the room and retrieved it, then came back.

Gawain gave Noel a tender kiss on his forehead and placed him on his small mattress, then tucked in the blanket.

"He's smiling," Ann said. "I'm sorry you missed it. I've seen him smile three times over the past week."

"I'm sorry, too."

"How is your hip? I know it hurts when you travel."

"I'm not limping too badly."

"I'll give you a treatment tonight. If you're staying."

The fine line of his cheek scar seemed to pale. "Do you want me to stay?"

She was scared to take a breath. How could she answer so soon? "I don't want you further injuring yourself with another long train ride."

"That isn't what I meant, Ann." He reached into his pocket. "Here, I brought two things for you."

She took a small book and box from his hands. With a sense of trepidation, she noted the box was familiar—her mother's ring box. The book did not appear familiar, though.

"What is it?"

"A pass book. I opened a bank account for you."

"Why?"

"I had your ring appraised and placed the price of it in the account. You can draw on it as you wish. You may also want to deposit the necklace money as well, so that you don't have so much tempting cash around, unless Harry dealt with it already."

"No, I would be obliged if you would take care of it."

"One of us can go to the bank when we are back in London."

"So you were able to sell the ring very quickly."

He patted the box in her hand with one finger. "Not exactly. Take a look."

She opened the box and was dismayed to see the stone she had wished gone from her life returned to her. Why was Gawain giving her all this money if he still wanted her to live with him? Was this his way of suggesting to her that she remain in Leeds to lead a separate life?

"Why?" she whispered.

"Take it out," Gawain said, clearly pleased with himself.

Though she had never wanted to touch it again, she reluctantly picked it up. "The band is different."

"It doesn't look Indian anymore. I had it reset on a plain gold band. You are the wife of a prosperous man, so no one would think you couldn't afford such a ring. You can wear it now without anyone thinking you are hiding the royal jewels of Caliata."

"It's still bad luck," she said. She let the ring drop into the box.

"You don't want it?"

"I asked you to dispose of it. Don't you see that I can't look at it without thinking about Jeremy, without worrying about someone coming after Noel someday like Jeremy did with Wells? With me?"

"But it was your mother's." He sounded like a child surprised to have displeased his parent.

"I have her mortar and pestle, all the knowledge she gave me. I don't need this ring." Agitated, Ann stood and began to pace the room.

He reclaimed the box with a wounded air. "Very well. I will sell it. I'll give you the money."

"You already gave me the money. I don't need any more."

"You shouldn't be angry with me. I tried to do as you asked."

"I asked you to dispose of it," Ann repeated. "If you want me to have expensive jewelry, then buy me something that isn't Indian."

"So now you want me to buy you jewelry?"

"No. You were the one who mentioned what your wife could have. Do you know, I wasn't even sure you could afford furnishings for the house? I have no idea. You didn't make any suggestions. You just hired Jenna to care for Noel and left me to my own devices."

"We were moving," Gawain said. "And we didn't hire a wet

nurse. Clearly you are still providing a great deal of Noel's care. You can't even sleep through the night yet."

She stared at the fire. "I have no idea what you expect from a wife."

"I thought you would warm my bed."

"Because you married a whore?" Ann asked. "Is that my only value? Or have you decided I was a mistake?"

Gawain's lips tightened into a thin line. "I did not think you a whore when we married."

"But you did later."

"What do you expect? Apparently it is common knowledge that you took a lover before marrying. This news shocked me."

"I suppose I should be pleased that you were shocked," she said sourly.

"I want you to come home," Gawain said. "To London. You and Fern and Noel. I want us to sort everything out—and be a family."

"Why?" Ann stopped behind an old, high-back chair and folded her arms on top of it.

"Because we are married."

Not because he loved her. "Can we be happy?"

"Why not? We enjoy each other's company, we already have a nice family unit of four."

We enjoy each other's company in bed. "What about my medical practice?"

"I would think you would be too busy with Noel." He held up an index finger. "I will release Jenna if that is what you wish, or keep her, or another maid. It is up to you. Plus, as you say, there is the house to furnish."

"I don't want my mother's knowledge to go to waste."

"Then write a book," Gawain rasped. "Write the package information for my books. But don't bring sick people around my child. And I don't want vagrants thinking our house is the one to come to. It isn't safe."

"A neighborhood maid isn't a vagrant," Ann countered.

"She was only the first."

"Who did you have turned away at the door? Do you even know?"

"Some acquaintance of that sick maid, no doubt."

"You are entirely opposed to me practicing? What if I had a small office?"

"Absolutely not. Noel needs you. Are you going to abandon him?"

"Of course not."

They stared at each other, at an impasse.

"I want us on the train back to London tomorrow," Gawain said. "Sell the inn to Harry, so you are done with Leeds."

"Fern wants him to move to London, so he is near us."

"Hasn't your husband's family caused you enough pain?"

"Harry has done nothing wrong. Nor has Fern."

"Fern is a child. I can see why she would live with you instead of Harry, her natural relative."

"You want to strip me bare of all my former connections," she accused.

"That is not true, my dear. You are the one who wants to dispose of your mother's ring." Gawain stood. "Is the room at the top of the stairs available tonight?"

"We are fully booked. Lots of tradesmen in town, now that the weather has changed," Ann said dully.

"Then I shall try that inn up the street. I will return first thing in the morning, and I expect you and Noel, Fern too if she is willing, to be packed and ready to depart." He bent over and smoothed Noel's blanket, then limped from the room.

Ann clutched the worn upholstery under her fingers. She would have to return to London, but then what?

Chapter Eighteen

While The Old Hart had by no means the standards of the finer London establishments, its beds were a far cry from the hostelry where Gawain had spent the previous night. He had to use his cane to hobble back to Ann's inn the next morning and his head hurt from whatever strange position he'd lain in during the night. The discomfort had him in a foul mood but he was resolved not to take it out on his wife or the Haldenes. They had been through enough.

He had taken the ring with him when he left since Ann so clearly disliked it, but had no idea what to do with it now. He thought that changing the setting would remove the stigma, but Ann's dislike of it ran deeper than simple appearance. Would she feel better about the ring if he had it blessed? It might be best just to lock it away and not bring it up for a time, when they had put Jeremy's death behind them, along with conversations about money. He couldn't help thinking their children might want it.

It had not rained overnight, and the yard in front of the inn was of a good consistency. The mud had dried up and there was no dust of yet. Muck didn't drag at his steps like it had the week before. The inn was busy with travelers, as Ann had said. Since he had not wanted to brave the other inn's breakfast after experiencing their beds, he went into the dining room to order breakfast.

"English or Indian?" asked the woman who'd served him before, not recognizing him.

"Indian?" Gawain said. "I didn't think you served it anymore."

"The owner prepared some of her old specialties this morning."

"I'll take the Indian, then."

As the woman walked away, he wondered if Ann cooked as a last goodbye, or if she was digging in her heels. If the latter was the case, he hoped she recognized that he could only divorce her for adultery and she'd have little hope of finding another husband if he was forced to that extreme. Not that he could imagine taking such a step.

A few minutes later, a platter arrived with some of the fine tastes of Caliata, crispy *paratha* flatbread stuffed with potato, yoghurt and scrambled eggs. But he could hardly eat, even though his stomach had made hopeful noises when he smelled the food. What was his wife planning?

A few moments later he had managed a bit of the bread and a few sips of tea, when his answer glided through the kitchen door, head held regally as she wiped her hands on an apron. He drank in the sight of her curvaceous body and creamy, glowing skin. Tight curls danced around her forehead and temples from the heat of the kitchen. Her full lips pursed when she saw him.

"I thought the smells of Caliata would pull you into the dining room."

His stomach gurgled in eagerness as his tension diminished. "I was very distracted when I came in, but when I heard the Indian breakfast was being offered I had to order it. My compliments."

She inclined her head, still an Indian princess. "Is this what you'd like served at home in the mornings? We never discussed any of these household details."

"No, I didn't want to make any demands on you while you were settling Noel in. I know how much time a baby requires."

"I appreciate that, but if you want me to run the household I have to know these things."

Hope settled his stomach. "So you are returning with me today?"

"You gave me a direct order."

"I'm not your commanding officer," Gawain snapped. His grip on his teacup tightened and the pressure made him realize he was giving in to nervous irritation. "I apologize. I simply mean to say I know I was being overbearing yesterday and I'd like to know your plans, Mrs. Redcake."

"I am packed. All three of us are. But I did enjoy cooking this morning. It won't be something I do much from now on."

"You can give your recipes to our cook, and provide as much direction as you desire. London needs more cooks used to delicious Indian food."

"I agree. But then, the kind of servants willing to cook in the Indian style are also likely to want me to treat them with my medicine," she warned.

"Do you really want to have this conversation now?" Even as he spoke, he saw the servant gesturing from the kitchen door.

"Of course not. I will finish up while you're eating and then meet you in the family quarters."

"Very good."

She looked down at him for a moment. He felt himself melting into the liquid chocolate of her eyes, then blinked as she moved away. Really, how did he manage to spend so many nights away from the electric connection he found with her?

When he went back to the family quarters, after polishing off his plate and enjoying his own Redcake-brand tea that had been supplied with it, he found the door open. Harry sat in the front room, cradling Noel as Fern, seated on a stool next to his knee, picked at a sampler.

"Why are your eyes red, little Fern?" Gawain asked. "I promise to never be such an ogre again, though I hope you will forgive me the occasional idiosyncrasy."

She sniffed and stared down at her sampler for a moment, then looked him directly in the eye. The bold movement gave him a hint of the woman she could become, now that she was no longer scared for her life.

"What?" he asked gently.

"H-harry," she said.

Gawain glanced at the man, who shrugged at him.

"Sorry, Gawain, but I think she doesn't want to leave her old brother behind."

"How old are you, anyway?"

"Same age as you, twenty-eight. Wells was a bit older, and me mother lost three or four babies between me and Fern. None lived long enough to be remembered."

"That's too bad. Like you, I lost my older brother, but I don't think I had other siblings who didn't survive." He looked at Fern. He hoped she wouldn't decide to stay here, but couldn't blame her if she did, given his actions with the doll clothes. Still, he thought she'd be better off away from The Old Hart.

"I was thinkin' 'bout the conversation yesterday. Lots to consider. Buyin' the inn from Ann, startin' over in Battersea."

"What were you doing four or five years ago?"

Harry smoothed the blanket more securely over Noel, who was kicking his legs. "I was workin' for a greengrocer's. Went into the business when I became engaged to the owner's daughter, plannin' to run it someday when she inherited. But she died and Wells made me an offer." He shrugged.

"It made sense at the time."

"That it did." Harry stared down at Noel.

"I am sorry for your loss. In any case, I can always use a man who understands inventory," Gawain said. "If you were looking to start over yet again, I'd give you work to tide you over, until you found a new place to buy, for instance. There are lots of fine hotels being developed in London now."

"Takes big money to make a place like that," Harry said.

"You and Ann have the money for two inns of this type between you. I can find at least four or five investors in my family alone."

Harry nodded. "I expect Fern'd be happy to see me make the change."

"So, you are coming with Ann and me?" Gawain asked the girl. She leaned over and kissed Noel's fluffy red hair.

"Doesn't look like the great-grandson of a maharajah, does he?" Harry said. "I expect that is best for him."

"I wish I could say it didn't matter, but after what happened to Ann at Redcake's, I would probably be wrong."

"I expect anyone would lose their position if they was sharp with an aristocrat," Harry said. "I'd fire someone who was rude to a rich customer."

"But she didn't start it."

"No, but the servin' class has to accept whatever the payin' customer has to offer, no matter how foul the brew."

"I had a few issues with officers myself, in my mess hall days," Gawain said. "I know what you're saying."

Harry grinned. "She can say just about anythin' she wants now, as your wife. She may have years of saucy comments to make, after havin' worked in this place."

"My tongue is as sharp as hers. We'll rattle the roof off my new house."

"I believe it. I've matched wits with her more than once."

"Who won?"

Harry lifted his eyebrows, but declined to admit to his defeats. Behind them, the door opened and closed again, and Ann came into the sitting room, the scents of the kitchen trailing behind her.

"Any o' that bread left?" Harry asked. "I love the way you make it."

"I left a plate under a towel for you."

Harry rubbed his hands together and handed Noel to Gawain. "Anythin' I can do to help get you to the station?"

"We'll need a cab," Gawain said. "How soon, Ann?"

"I need to change and pack a few last minute things. Half an hour."

Gawain checked his pocket watch. "That should work perfectly with the train schedule. Fern, do you need to gather your things?"

She shook her head. "All done."

"Two words," Gawain exclaimed. "You have been making excellent progress."

Harry rustled Fern's hair between his fingers and strode out.

The next day, Ann felt travel weary, but at the same time, the forced lack of movement on yesterday's train made her want to move around. After she settled Noel down for a late morning nap with the pacified Jenna, she and Fern went for a walk in the sunny spring air. They found their way to the shops in Northcote Road and were attracted to a large furniture store, which had an excellent display of chairs in their cheerful, white-painted bow window.

"This is our home now. We need to get to know the shops and the goods."

Fern nodded.

"Also, the house is practically empty," Ann continued. "I must admit, I do not know what style of furniture would please Gawain. But presumably, given his injuries, nothing overstuffed as it would be hard to rise from." Her husband had been racked with pain by the time they arrived and hadn't allowed her to touch him. He'd called for a bath and his pills, leaving her to settle in. She felt guilty for being the reason for his train travel and wondered if he could hire Harry to do his sales travel calls.

Fern took her arm and pulled her into the shop. Ann glanced around, overwhelmed. The Old Hart had come furnished. She'd had to choose new linens over time and the occasional piece was moved into the family quarters and replaced when it was too worn for paying guests, but she had never decorated a new home. She wondered if she should hire someone for the work. But that seemed silly. She was used to being industrious and had seen Lord Judah's home and Redcake Manor, both furnished recently. Redcake Manor had the Arts and Crafts style. Lady Judah preferred more monumental pieces in dark woods. Which did she prefer? Neither, really.

"Welcome to our store," said a young man, fingering his moustache as he approached them. "What can I help you find, ladies?"

"I am Mrs. Gawain Redcake. My husband purchased a home nearby recently and I have a great deal of furnishing to do."

The young man smiled broadly. "I would be happy to open an account for you. If you do not see what you need we do have catalogues from manufacturers that may be of benefit. Do you have a certain style in mind?"

"I am not well versed in them," Ann confessed. "This is only my second home and I didn't furnish the first."

"Any leanings?" The man put a finger to his lips.

"I know Arts and Crafts is too modern for me, but heavy woods are depressing."

"Do you have any other hints to offer me?"

"My husband was a military man and spent time in India. I was born there myself."

"Are you pleased with the present wall and floor treatments?"

"Everything appears to be in good order. Red damask wallpaper in the drawing room, a green chintz in the dining room. Rich amber paint in the library." She paused. "Oh dear. Fern, do you remember the walls in the morning parlor?"

"B-blue m-marble."

"Oh yes, that is correct. Blue paint treated with some sort of marbling effect."

"And you do not want to change any of it."

"No, just furniture."

"Then we have four rooms to work on." He took out a small notepad and pencil. "First priority?"

Ann stared at Fern. "I have no idea."

"P-parlor," Fern said.

Ann sighed. "Yes, that makes sense, as we are likely to spend hours there each day, but we really need it all done."

The sales clerk led them on a tour of his showroom. Ann felt her brain being dulled by all of the many choices. Medicine, she understood. Bodies in discomfort. But how was she to know how to make a comfortable home, a comfortable life?

Loving Wells had been so easy. They had lived with his parents and then stayed in the house when they died until inheriting the inn only six months later. She never had to think of these things. Really, her first marriage had love as easy as her love for Noel. She had seen Wells when he brought his mother to consult with her over health problems, and thought, "mine."

Her love for Gawain was nothing so simple as falling in love with a kind man in a soldier's uniform. Her attraction to him had been physical—prideful, even, that she could distract him from his pain with her body. The baby had cemented her connection with him forever and she had gone to London in search for him, understanding only that she wanted to know what man made up half her child.

But now, she'd fallen into this marriage, this new life, and she was adrift. Should she cut ties with Leeds? Sell the inn to Harry or a stranger? Should she encourage Harry to move close to them and keep what remained of the Haldene family unit, or commit completely to a new life with Gawain?

She found it fascinating that he had no interest in keeping his own family close, other than his cousin Lewis. They seemed to be men who only looked to the future. Their old pain had made the past forgettable, but she held on to her own past.

She chose the things her mother would have. Simply carved, dark wood furniture upholstered in brocades decorated in gold thread. Any cushion the shop had with embroidery. Low tables. Military style camp chairs and stools that could be moved from room to room. And a birdcage, made of wicker, suited for a conservatory, which the house didn't have.

"Do you have a bird, Mrs. Redcake?"

"My husband told me his cousin used to make talking metal birds. Maybe he can be persuaded to design one for us."

The man nodded. "A lovely idea. I'd be interested in seeing his work myself. We might be able to sell his birds."

"I will tell my husband. Do you think any of the things we've chosen will look good together in our rooms?"

"The bookcases, desk and chairs will do well in a gentleman's study. You've chosen a good dining table. Your morning parlor and drawing room are tending a bit Indian, but that makes sense given your background. I think you've made a good start and of course you can send back what doesn't work."

"Then please have it all delivered as soon as possible," she said. "And we'll sort it out at the house."

"Excellent. May I have an address for the bill, please?"

"Just send it to the house." Ann glanced at Fern. They had spent so long there that she needed rather desperately to get back to Noel. "Anything else?"

Fern pointed to a painting on the wall behind the clerk's desk. As he wrote up the order, Ann walked over. She didn't recognize the signature of the artist, but of course she wouldn't. The painting depicted a picnic near a grassy green stream. Three girls sat on a quilt, quite underdressed. One combed her hair, one ate a turkey leg and the third stared at the stream.

"Do you want it for your room?" she asked Fern.

The girl nodded vigorously.

"Oh, that isn't for sale," the clerk said, noticing where Ann was. "No?"

"I painted it," he said with a blush. "My father-in-law owns the store so I work for him, but I paint whenever I can."

"Was your wife one of the models?"

He smiled impishly. "The one eating the turkey leg. To be honest, she'd be happy if I sold it so she didn't have to see that image of herself."

"Why don't you let me buy it? That way you have an excuse to paint another."

"Please?" Fern said, clasping her hands together.

He looked her over, then nodded. "Very well, but you shall have to name a price."

Ann pulled out some banknotes she had put in her reticule. Part of Jeremy's secret stash, she thought it might as well be converted into art.

"Oh, I couldn't take that much," he protested. "I'm an amateur."

"Not anymore," she said firmly. "My sister-in-law has excellent taste."

As they left, Fern all but skipped down the street. "Why did you like that painting so much?"

"Real art," Fern said happily.

"Not much of that in Leeds?"

Fern shook her head.

"I can see I have many museum exhibits in my future," Ann observed.

Fern tucked her hand into Ann's and they walked briskly through the busy streets. At least one of them had found a reason to be happy with their new home.

The sun believed spring had come, and the next day was bright as furniture poured into the ground floor of the house. Gawain watched with amusement as Ann directed the proceedings with the élan of a commanding officer, almost forgetting he had business at his warehouse.

He had been in an excellent mood all day and it wasn't until evening, when he stared into his shaving mirror, that he realized why. He was amazed by how clearly he could see his stubble. Whatever Theodore Bliven had done to his sister, Matilda, he had most certainly done Gawain a favor when he returned with his Indian boxes and bags. Ann as well had served him in brilliant fashion, in mixing up the herbal remedy so competently. His vision had cleared almost to miracle level. From seeing just color, to vague shapes, he now had nearly distinct images of his surroundings and the working vision complemented his good eye so well that he'd be a fool to wear his eye patch anymore.

He smiled into the mirror and saw his face crease into unfamiliar lines. When had he begun to wrinkle around the eyes? Despite these signs of aging, he felt nothing but happiness. Getting involved with Ann had been the best thing to ever happen to him. She had given him improved sight, a better gait, much less pain, less fear of how his appearance bothered others, and a beautiful son.

She had told him the night before that furniture would be coming soon and that he could decide if it suited him or not. She was more insecure than he'd ever seen her, which made him tense and snappish. This morning, he'd been full of trepidation as it arrived. Would the furniture suit the position in life he wanted, or would it be the choices of a provincial innkeeper who knew nothing about entertaining the fashionable world? He'd had to leave before catching the full effect of her efforts and hadn't been able to return until after dark.

But what did he have to be angry about? Nothing. His wretched time in the factory was long over. His military experience had brought him a good friend in Lord Judah Shield, and his injuries had a much diminished hold on him. His business, with its roots in India, was flourishing beyond his wildest dreams. A beautiful wife, son, and home.

"It's time to be happy," he told the mirror.

"Oh, I'm sorry." Ann appeared in the open doorway, dressed in a nightgown and wrapper.

"Did you need the sink, my dear?" he asked in a positively jaunty tone. He smirked at himself.

She crossed her arms, still looking defensive. "I can go downstairs. You don't usually shave in the evenings."

"Couldn't see well enough," he said. "But I can now." He walked to her and set his hands at her waist, then picked her up and twirled her around.

"You can?" she asked. "That is excellent news."

"Yes, the herb is working. I'm never going to wear that blasted eye patch again." He gave her a smacking kiss on the cheek and set her down. "Poor Matilda. I'm not going to be able to let her eviscerate Bliven in conversation anymore. I owe him too much."

"I would have had the same results with you eventually. No one herb is ever a salvation. There are numerous approaches to any bodily problem."

He chucked her under the chin. "So you say, but I can see today. And besides, I give you a great deal of credit. You have brought me nothing but good things, and I am heartily grateful we were forced to marry."

"Forced?"

He shrugged. "Noel, of course. I may appreciate what Bliven had to offer me, but I would never have walked in his footsteps. And you, my dear, are far too sensible to have turned me down for long."

"No?" Her hands went to her hips.

"We are both intelligent, sensible people. Marriage was the right answer," he said.

"We are," Ann said, in a very definite tone. "And since you are so sensible, and so pleased with your progress, surely you see the sense in me continuing to practice medicine? We do not wish for my skills to become stale."

He responded instantly. "I don't want disease brought into this house. Surely you can see the sense in that."

She licked her upper lip. He wanted to pull her to him and kiss that plump mouth, but knew the conversation had gone from light to dangerous in only a few words.

"I don't want disease brought in either, Gawain. But my mother's knowledge is so valuable, and I have served it well, I think. We must come to some sort of compromise. Midwifery, perhaps?"

"Must we discuss this now? I do not wish to waste time being angry or grim or—"

"Petulant?" Ann suggested with an arch raise of her eyebrows.

"As you wish," he said. "I am happy we have made a family. I hope it will be a larger one. Noel should have siblings."

She blushed.

"Will you not be busy enough with children?" he said.

"A select midwifery practice?" she suggested.

"We will discuss it, after the house is set to rights. Do you feel the furnishings are adequate?"

She walked out of the lavatory, and sped through the dressing room, nearly empty, and their bedroom, which held only a couple of chests and a bed he'd taken from his rooms on St. James's Square. "I have not even thought about the first or second floors yet. What did you think of the ground floor?"

"I haven't looked yet," he admitted. "Dark when I came home, you know, and my vision isn't the best in gaslight. Need to get the house converted over to electricity now that it might not bother my eyes."

"Can we afford to furnish all three floors at once?" Ann asked.

"Without touching a penny of your money," he said grandly.

"Do tea and herbs really pay so well?"

"I ran my father's factories for a couple of years. He had to bribe me heavily as I did not want to come into the business at all. I suppose I have to be grateful to Sir Bartley for forcing me to structure my days after coming home wounded—yes, better that than to be angry for a few years of doing work I didn't like."

"How was it so different from running your own business?"

"I hated the factories after my time working in them as a child. Also, I was first thrust into accounting, and that is not the part of any business that I appreciate. Still, must be grateful for the knowledge I gained. Invaluable."

She walked to a bedpost and twined her arms around it, leaning her head against the mahogany in a dreamy pose. "You really are trying. I am happy for you."

He slid his arms around her, cupping her abdomen, where he hoped another child would grow soon. "Let's be happy together, shall we?"

"You were angry in the past, but I wasn't. I was happy, and now I'm trying to find my way to being happy again."

"You were happy when we met?"

"I was content, but I mean before. My childhood was a good one, and my first marriage. So much has passed since then. None of my moods has anything to do with you."

"What happened to Wells and Fern was hard. And then Jeremy, so recently—a blow."

"Yes." She closed her eyes. "And everything else. I've lost my independence."

"Isn't what you've gained so much more valuable?"

She opened her eyes, large dark pools that shone even in the gaslight. "That is the question, isn't it?"

"Let me remind you how we were joined into marriage in the first place," he murmured. "Beautiful girl."

Chapter Nineteen

"Beautiful girl?" Had Gawain just called her that? She was amazed her husband thought her beautiful. Surely her looks had faded, given the birth of a child, a near-death experience, three different moves, and lack of sleep caused by caring for an infant.

"Yes, you are so beautiful," Gawain rasped.

She turned fully, resting her back against the bedpost. "Do you ever see the color of my skin?"

"It is lovely skin," he said, putting a finger to her cheek and letting it drift down to her collarbone.

"I'll never fit into aristocratic circles," she said. "I know you have dreams and our marriage hurts them. The mistakes we made—"

"Not mistakes. Let me be the optimist now. I'm happy, Ann. Don't you think I'd rather have a healthy son, a home, our good health, than entry into the highest circles of society?"

"I don't know," she countered. "Do you?"

He nuzzled her cheek with that arrogant, commanding nose. "Yes, my darling." His single, delicately caressing finger moved down the slope of one breast, circling the nipple.

Her breath caught in her throat as he cupped her, testing the weight.

"I love your curves," he rasped. "I can't wait to see how you look large with another child."

His fingers left her breast and she sighed with the loss, but his hands went to the belt of her wrapper and soon he was tugging the fabric down her shoulders, then pulling her gown over her head. She stood naked before him in the flickering gaslight.

"It dances on your skin like sunlight," he said. "Over each contour of your lovely, soft skin."

"Will you become a poet now?"

"Who can say?" A naughty glint lit his scarred pirate's face as he took her hand and tugged her to the bed. She adored this view of him in pleasure.

Before he pushed her back, she found the ties of his smoking jacket and pushed it off him, then removed his shirt and pajama pants. His erection sprang out. Without thinking, she wrapped one hand around it. He gasped and she knew how to reward him for his good humor.

He was the one who went down on the mattress. She fell to her knees in the position of worshipper, taking him in her mouth and hands, tasting the musky saltiness of his body. His hands pushed into her hair, massaging away the small hurts of the day, and he undid her braid. Her hair fell over his thighs as she relaxed her throat and breathed in, taking him deep.

He begged her to stop, then not to stop, but her ministrations were relentless. She could feel him shudder, but he scooted back, popped from her mouth, then was next to her in a flash, more quickly than she thought possible. He moved her from her knees to her hands and pressed behind her, grasping her breasts with his hands and nudging her legs apart.

She hadn't realized how wet tasting him, pleasuring him, had made her, until his erection found her opening. He slid easily inside her channel. Her hair covered her ears and most of her face, creating sensory deprivation scented with his shaving cream.

When she pushed off her hands, to sit up, he plucked at her nipples until she gasped, then pushed one hand between her thighs to finger her pearl. Her head fell back against his shoulder and she moved her hips against him. Harsh breathing from both of them filled the air. He blew her hair away from his face. She laughed and tried to gather it together.

"Don't cover your breasts," he ordered, gathering it with his free hand.

She reached up and locked her arms around the back of his head, tugging him close so they could kiss. Their tongues slid together, and they drifted apart from the kiss, both breathing hard.

He grabbed her around the waist and pushed violently into her. She could take that and more, rotating her hips, feeling her completion coming fast.

"So beautiful," he whispered. "I love touching you."

She fell apart as his seed spurted into her, shuddering her pleasure. Maybe he hadn't exactly said he loved her, but he had said many things, all of them good. Loving words, loving actions, she could soak up those and try to be content too.

Gawain woke with the sense of happy clarity the next morning and his cheerful mood continued as he dressed and breakfasted at the new dining table. Ann had yet to find serving pieces for the room, but at least they didn't have to discomfort the cook by eating at the scrubbed, wooden kitchen table any more. Instead of heading straight to his warehouse office, he felt the need to see his wife, so he went up the nursery.

Ann's limited furnishings had been dotted around the top floor. Her bed had gone to Fern's room, and her armchair and kitchen furniture was in use in the nursery. While Gawain intended to upgrade his son's cradle, the simple one Ann had provided fit his small body well.

Ann smiled brilliantly when he entered and even Fern gave him a shy word of greeting. He settled in for a domestic interlude, taking Noel in his arms.

"I just fed him," Ann said. "He'll be ready for a nap soon."

"He sleeps a great deal."

"Babies and children do. It's the only way a mother can accomplish any of her other duties. If they were awake we'd wear the same clothing for months and dine on dry bread."

He kissed the top of her head. "Thank goodness for naps, then."

A knock came at the nursery door. Fern scrambled up and went to open it.

Gawain heard Jenna announce that the Marquess of Hatbrook, his brother-in-law, was paying a call unannounced.

"What time is it?" Ann asked.

"Much too early for a social call. I hope nothing is wrong with my family."

"Do you want me to come downstairs with you?"

"I'll send for you if I have to leave quickly." He kissed Ann on the forehead and left the nursery. His thoughts churned as he took the steps as quickly as he could. Stairs were the hardest thing for him to navigate. His father's once robust health had seemed to fade a bit over the past couple of years, with frequent colds.

Could it be him? Or had Bliven somehow managed to jump ship and circle back to Sussex? Or his youngest sister Rose, with her delicate health. The thought made his breath lurch, but he soothed himself with the thought that Hatbrook could be announcing that his wife was increasing again. Why couldn't the untimely visit be to share happy news? All these thoughts distracted him until he stumbled. Thankfully, he had done it on the bottom stair. His shoes clicked on the tiles of the entryway as he crossed it.

"Hatbrook!" he called, pulling open the door of the drawing room. For the first time, he saw the furnishings Ann had purchased and how harmonious they were with his taste. His gaze went to a decorative detail on one table. The white wicker birdcage reminded him of happy days with Lewis, but the comfortable, low sofas with their luxurious Indian fabrics in one seating arrangement, then the contrasting seating arrangement of French Empire bergère armchairs in another part of the long, narrow room, offered a mix of bright, happy colors. Anyone who visited would find their mood uplifted and would be pleased to spend time in the room, and he appreciated the smattering of easy-to-move tables that made the room flexible.

Hatbrook couldn't give bad news in a room like this. Gawain straightened his shoulders and marched in.

"You are settling in, I see," Hatbrook said, his arm outstretched to encompass the space. He had been at the fireplace, examining the photographs that Gawain had placed there a couple of days after their move. The wedding photograph was the latest, but he had images of his parents and siblings as well, even one stiff shot of Hatbrook and Alys shortly after their marriage.

"I didn't expect to see you in London until after Easter, or we would have invited you to dine with us."

"It's only me. I've come on urgent royal business."

Gawain gestured Hatbrook to one of the bright blue and gold

armchairs and seated himself. "Royal business? I expected family news."

"Yes, I would imagine so, given my early arrival, but nothing new with the family. Had a phone call from Windsor. New telephone at the Farm."

"I knew you had one put in. I need to have one installed here."

"Handy devices, though the calls never come at an opportune time. But—to my news. You see, it's been put about that the Queen is on her annual progress to the South of France, but she's actually been holed up in the palace for over a week, suffering headaches."

"And they contacted you? I thought she had dozens of medical staff."

"Quite a lot of them, certainly. But I'm friendly with some of the younger royalties and they contacted me because I'd been through the medical maelstrom with my mother and they thought I might have some suggestions."

"Did you? Is Her Majesty better?"

"No, I've just come into town. I thought of you and your wife, you see."

"Oh?"

Hatbrook leaned forward. "Yes, you see, the Queen is quite enamored of Indian things. Takes Hindustani language lessons, has Indian staff. I thought Indian medicine might help her headaches. Would you allow me to bring your wife and her medicine box to see her? It's the only thing I can think to offer, beyond what she already has available."

Gawain took, then released a deep breath. How hypocritical would he be to say he didn't want Ann treating the local servants, yet was fine with her treating the Queen? Yet, headaches were unlikely to be contagious diseases. "You put me in a difficult situation."

"I do?"

"I had thought to prevent my wife from practicing. We have a child now and a large house for her to direct."

"Women have their passions, same as we do," Hatbrook observed. "Alys would have been miserable without Redcake's Tea Shop and Emporium in her life. Can she work there as she used to? Certainly not, but some level of engagement with it keeps her happy."

"You are suggesting my wife will not be happy without medicine."

Hatbrook picked up the wedding photograph. "Perhaps doctoring you and your children, and the household, will be enough for her."

"She doesn't seem to think so."

A smile played over the corners of his brother-in-law's lips, but the man said nothing. He didn't need to. Gawain stood and went to the bell pull. When the butler came in, he said, "Would you send for Mrs. Redcake?"

The butler inclined his head and disappeared.

"Need anything while we wait? Tea, brandy?"

Hatbrook shook his head. "Don't want to get comfortable. I hope to leave for Windsor right away. My carriage is outside."

"I haven't ordered a standard one. Lewis is building me one of his modern contraptions." Gawain drummed his thumb against one arm of the chair, then forced himself to ask after his sister and niece.

Hatbrook replied that all was well.

"And what news of Manfred Cross? It's been nearly a month since you received the letter from him. Any word about your sister?"

"They aren't together anymore. I have been in touch with the private inquiry agent and hope to find her soon," Hatbrook said tersely.

"But she's alive?"

"I have no reason to think otherwise."

"I am most glad to hear that. Are you certain I cannot be of use to you?"

Hatbrook shook his head.

"I will instruct my household to pray for a speedy resolution," Gawain said after a moment.

Ann appeared in the doorway, looking quite lovely despite being dressed in mourning for Jeremy. She had insisted on observing six weeks for him, though Gawain couldn't be quite sure why. Perhaps Fern had wanted it that way. She was in mourning as well. At least the Queen appreciated a good mourning gown.

They both stood when she entered, looking concerned yet gracious. "Ann, you remember the marquess."

"Of course."

Hatbrook stepped forward and kissed her cheek. "My condolences."

She smiled demurely. "My husband's cousin."

"Of course," Hatbrook murmured softly, without any hint of betraying that he knew the entire story.

"Is the family in town?"

"No, I am here on urgent business. I hoped you would come with me to Windsor Palace."

Ann's head tilted, and she glanced at Gawain. "Whatever for, my lord?"

"The Queen has been suffering dreadful headaches for more than a week. She is all but bed-bound and the family and medical staff do not know what to do. I thought you might be able to help."

Ann's graceful fingers went to her temples. "The poor lady. She has suffered so many losses recently."

Hatbrook nodded. "It could be an affliction of the mind causing her pain."

"That would not make the pain any less. But I would defer to my husband on this. You are asking me to leave my home." She gave him a solemn glance.

Gawain cleared his throat. He could tell she ached to go, and Hatbrook did not need to be thwarted when he had so many troubles on his mind. "As it does not appear there is a risk of contagion, I expect the risks are few."

Ann regarded him solemnly. He had the feeling that their entire future happiness might depend on this moment.

"This is what you were trained for. The royal healing arts of your mother, and now an English queen requires your aid," he said.

She nodded. "My mother would wish me to do what I could for the poor Queen."

Gawain crossed his arms over his chest, then uncrossed them. He had not thought to have a wife with a profession, but Hatbrook rubbed on well enough with Alys, and she never let Redcake's take precedence over family matters. Perhaps he had been wrong to forbid Ann to continue her healing work. He went to her and took her in his arms. "I have no problem with you attending her."

He watched her gaze sharpen as she spoke. "I'll have to take Noel. We have no idea how long the Queen will need tending."

"Take Jenna, too," Gawain said. He had not expected to see the sun-bright smile that lit Ann's lovely face at the suggestion. How could he have thought to prevent her from practicing the medicine that brought her so much joy? Hatbrook, that old married man, had the right of it. They had married women too modern to be happy solely in the domestic sphere.

After giving him a kiss on the cheek, Ann asked Hatbrook a few questions. Gawain released her from his encircling arms as she attempted to glean as much information as he had to provide, then went to order Noel and Jenna for the trip and pack the necessary medical equipment.

When they arrived at the palace with entourage in tow, they didn't have any trouble entering, but much confusion was evident when they tried to gain access to the Queen. The marquess relayed information about the phone call he received and told the staff about her qualifications, emphasizing that she'd been trained by the late Maharani of Caliata.

Eventually, the Queen's Indian secretary was summoned, as well as a junior member of the royal family. After these worthies met with them, Ann was brought to an ornate but chilly bedchamber. Queen Victoria rested in an armchair, her plump legs up on a cushion.

"You are Mai Singh's daughter?" the Queen said, in a voice much younger than her seventy years.

Ann curtseyed. "Yes, your majesty."

"I knew your grandfather. Did you know he was educated here in England?"

"No, ma'am. I know next to nothing about my Indian roots."

"Your father was an officer in my army, I believe?"

Ann inclined her head.

"So unfortunate that your mother married into an old-fashioned family," the Queen said. "I'm glad she survived to marry again."

"As am I, ma'am. I am here because of your headaches?"

"You should not be living the life of a commoner," the Queen opined. "Dreadful for one of royal blood to have fallen into such obscurity."

"I am happily married, your majesty," Ann ventured. "My husband's sister is married to the marquess."

The Queen tilted her head and winced. "I believe we knighted your father-in-law not too long ago."

"Sir Bartley Redcake, yes, ma'am."

"Excellent Scotch trifle," the Queen said with a little smile. Then she winced and moaned. "Oh, my head. I do so wish dear Albert were here to soothe me. He knew the way."

Ann glanced at a lady-in-waiting, who rolled her eyes the tiniest bit. Dear Albert had passed to his reward about the time Ann was born. "I am sorry for your troubles, ma'am. May I examine you?"

"What can you do that my doctors cannot?"

"I would like to massage your head and shoulders. Sandalwood paste on your forehead would be very soothing. If we can talk a little, I can suggest some herbal teas or pills that might be helpful to you."

"Indian massage?" the elderly Queen asked.

"A specific technique my mother taught me. Used in royal zenanas. I massage with oil from India. If some of your problem is muscular, it will work wonders." The Queen sighed and looked at her Indian secretary, who nodded. "If this technique was used on such a distinguished royal family for years, it is safe to be used on our person."

Ann inclined her head. "Then if the gentlemen will be permitted to leave, I will begin, ma'am."

Two hours later she had accomplished everything an oil massage, sandalwood paste and a soothing tea blend could manage. She discussed her choice of herbal pills with one of the royal physicians, and he approved it. The attempt to gently suggest some alterations to diet, wardrobe and jewelry was rejected, however. She hoped the Queen would be able to endure her voyage to France now, especially since she'd instructed one of her serving women on the massage technique, and left oil and sandalwood.

Ann received a letter from the Queen's Indian secretary the next Monday, thanking her for her service and noting that the Queen had been well enough to make her journey. Shortly thereafter, Ann saw an article in the paper about the Queen's travels in Spain to see relatives. She was pleased to have been a small part of the Queen's success.

"What do you have there?" Gawain asked, coming into the morning parlor carrying Noel.

Ann admired the sight of her fierce husband cradling their small baby. "Did Noel need to escape the nursery?"

"I did. Did you really have to wallpaper the room with those self-satisfied milkmaids?"

Ann laughed. "They are a bit overwhelming. I could add a border of something different at the ceiling level."

"Or paint over them," Gawain said.

She ignored him. "Did you like the new rocking chair?"

"I did."

"I will appreciate it very much when teething begins in the summer." Ann yawned.

"You've done a great deal of work in a short time. I have no complaints about any of the furnishings."

"Wait until you see the accounts," Ann said. "Then we'll hear a yell out of you."

Gawain kissed the top of Noel's head and sat in a comfortable armchair. "It is worth it."

"How is your face feeling?" She had begun treating his scars with both pills and a paste, hoping to soften the tissue and alter the color to be closer to the rest of his skin.

"It itches a little."

"I'll add some more oil," she said. "We'll see if that helps."

"Have you tended any other patients?" he asked casually.

"You know I have not," Ann said. "You forbade me to."

"I thought Hatbrook might pop up here again with another royal patient, since you were such a success. And what of Lady Judah?"

"Oh, I have seen her. She paid a call last week. In fact, I need to return it. But she is feeling very well."

"Now that the house is finished, you must be getting bored."

"The house isn't finished, Gawain. I have only found half of the storage pieces we need, and if you are going to entertain grandly, I need to choose china."

"There is a wardrobe in our bedroom and in the nursery, and you purchased that monstrosity for the dining room."

"Yes, I've found a few things."

"It looks complete to me."

"Are you telling me to stop spending money?" She smiled sweetly.

"No. As long as I can make it as quickly as you can spend, we'll be fine. Did I tell you London's newest fine hotel will be serving my tea?"

"How wonderful."

"Yes." Gawain smiled in self-satisfaction.

His smiles had been so much more evident recently. "I'm proud of you, and if you want a home to reflect your success, I am afraid to tell you there is more to be done. Artwork, for instance. Fern has more in her bedroom than we have in the rest of the house."

"Did Lewis agree to make you one of his birds?"

"No. When he called, he said he was done with the birds, even though I told him I had a shop interested in selling them. But he did say your horseless carriage would arrive next week."

"I'll believe that when it appears in our carriage house. Are any of the local ladies paying calls here?"

"The vicar and his wife. She suggested I join one of the ladies' societies when I was settled."

"Good. No doubt you will find ladies to tend there."

"You're lifting your ban?"

He transferred Noel to his shoulder. "As long as you don't bring disease into the house, or neglect your responsibilities here, I will have no cause for complaint."

She knew what a concession that was. "What has brought this change of mind?"

"I realized today that you've done everything I've asked. Yet you've asked very little of me. Your one request has been to continue practicing what your mother taught you. And who can say when the Queen will call again? We must keep your knowledge of female complaints current."

The butler knocked at the open door. When Gawain waved his hand, the butler brought in the post and placed it on a table between the two armchairs, then soundlessly exited.

Ann rifled through the pile. "Looks like an invitation from Lady Judah. Maybe they are having a dinner party. And . . . oh dear, the first charges from the furniture shop."

Gawain chuckled. "What is that one?"

Ann pulled out a creamy envelope made from the finest paper. "It looks hand-delivered."

She took the letter opener that the butler had placed on a tray and cut open the top. When she saw the large signature scrawled across the top, she nearly gasped.

"What is it?"

"I think it is from the Queen." Her fingers felt all but nerveless.

Gawain stood and perched beside her. Ann drank in the smell of clean infant and handsome husband as they leaned close. "Don't let Noel drool on this. It will probably be a family keepsake for years to come."

"Of course. Is it a thank you note?" Ann read it. "My goodness. She wants to knight you." Was Gawain's fondest wish to come true so soon?

"What?" Gawain stretched out his hand as if to snatch it, but then cradled Noel instead. "Why would she want to knight me?"

"What will be next for you after you've achieved such a dream?" Ann asked. "Why, you aren't even thirty yet."

He shook his head. "I am astonished. But I am more content to be happy than ambitious now."

"You'll always be ambitious," Ann said. "It's part of your nature. But I am glad you've found serenity."

"I shall have to start dreaming big for Noel," Gawain said, with a wicked grin.

"That is a good idea."

"Now, what exactly does the letter say?"

Ann perused it. "She thanks me for my service. Says she would have written this letter in Hindustani but wasn't sure I would know the language. Her headaches are all but gone and she would have me consult with her chief physician for a supply of pills."

"All good."

"Yes. Then she says, in honor of my grandfather, and in thanks for my service, she will have you placed on the next investiture list and to await further instructions from her staff." She put a hand to her chest. How could this be? Had a simple medical treatment led to the fulfillment of her husband's dreams?

He stiffened. "You should be knighted, not me."

Ann smiled. A title had not been her dream. "I shall be Lady Redcake. That is good enough for me."

"What does she know of your grandfather?"

"He was educated in England and her majesty knew him when she was young. I had no idea, of course. I know nothing about my mother's family."

"Who would have thought it?" Gawain said.

"Exactly. I thought your marriage to me would put an end to some of your dreams, but that appears not to have been the case."

He leaned forward, taking her hand with the one not cradling Noel. "Ann, you've given me everything. I love you."

Ann gasped when she heard the words, saw the sincerity in his eyes. Her entire body swelled with joy. "Oh, Gawain, I love you too. You've made me so happy."

"I hope you know how sincerely happy you've made me," he rasped. "I could not ask for anything else but this wife, this child, this house."

She tapped the creamy paper in her lap. "And this letter."

He grinned. "And that letter."

Chapter Twenty

After he had given Noel to Ann for a feeding and she'd gone up to the nursery, Gawain went to his study to compose a letter to his father. He couldn't resist the urge to gloat a little. A man who had come out of his father's shadow was the happiest of men. Now there would be two "sirs" in the family, and two Lady Redcakes. No one would ever question his choice of bride again. Once her service to the Queen became known, she would need to take only the choicest of clients. Noble mothers-to-be, perhaps. He fantasized about being named godfather of a royal baby.

Being a practical man, his thoughts soon turned to business. He wrote to his trader, Zahir Khan, in Lahore, authorizing a larger purchase order for certain herbs they already stocked. Then he wrote to Theodore Bliven in care of General Delivery in Bombay, authorizing him to continue searching for the best herbs in every province. He drafted letters of credit for them both, to be mailed to his bank. Someone would report on the treatments that had healed the Queen, though officially she had been in Biarritz at the time the healing occurred, and there would be a demand for Ann's infused oil and sandalwood paste. Turnaround to India was slow, but eventually he would have the goods, and be first to market at that. He set down his pen and rubbed at the itchy scar under his eye. Ann must write up a case study of her treatment of the Queen, and he could make it available to his salesmen. He wondered if the Queen would offer his company a royal warrant. She likely drank his teas, since they had been a part of the deliveries Redcake's Tea Shop and Emporium had sent to Windsor and Osborne House for a year. He had been content to fly under his father's banner—but no more.

Three weeks later, on a beautiful, flower-scented day in May, Queen Victoria made one of her rare trips to Buckingham Palace. A dais had been raised in the famous ballroom, known as the largest room in London. The elderly Queen, looking not quite as stern as usual, stood there with her equally age-challenged Yeomen of the Guard. Other staff and Gurkha officers also filled the room, along with the families of those being invested.

Gawain noted that the gathering was smaller than when his father had received his knighthood in 1886, a more select group. Along with Alys's family, Lord Judah and his wife, his sister Rose, cousin Lewis, Ann, Fern, and even Harry, who had come in from Leeds for the occasion, his father beamed and puffed out his chest. As soon as the inn was sold, Harry would be moving to London to work for Gawain while he looked into the hotel trade locally. Ann decided it was better to let the place where Wells and Jeremy had died go out of the family. Harry liked the idea of a new challenge.

A number of old men in old-fashioned suits glowered around the edges of the room.

"The Queen's physicians," Ann whispered.

His wife, dressed resplendently in half-mourning, a white and black striped silk gown, had drawn the attention of every man in the room. Her looks might be exotic, but she carried herself like an Englishwoman, the equal of anyone in the world. She put her hand on his arm, and when he looked down, he saw with surprise that she wore her mother's sapphire ring with the new setting. He hadn't noticed it missing from the safe in their bedroom.

Seeing his surprise, her sensually full lips parted into a smile. "We might not be here but for the late Maharani of Caliata, correct?"

"Correct," he agreed. "I am happy to see the ring being given a better association than it held previously."

"As am I." She squeezed his arm. "Don't Harry and Fern look fine together?"

Harry had a new morning suit, and Fern wore a dress made from the same fabric as Ann's, cut to her diminutive size. With her hair pulled into a loose bun, black curls waving around her face, Gawain realized with foreboding that within three years or so, Fern would blossom into a beauty. And he would be responsible for her. Perhaps Harry should move to Battersea after all, to share the burden.

A small orchestra sounded the opening notes of "God Save the Queen." When the anthem was finished, the Lord Chamberlain mounted the dais and announced the first recipient of a knighthood or honor. The fifth and last to be called, Gawain felt a moment of lightheadedness and his hip wanted to buckle as he stepped forward in his stiff, new clothes.

He glanced around, and saw the rapturous gaze of his mother, the toothy grin of his father, the stern approval in Hatbrook's eyes, and the glee in Lewis's gaze. Most of all, he saw the love in his wife's face. He blew her a kiss then mounted the steps to the dais.

His hip supported him as he knelt on the investiture stool. His ears buzzed too much to quite hear what the Lord Chamberlain said about him, but then the diminutive Queen stood before him, holding an enormous sword. At least she looked nothing like the Pathan mountain warrior who had sliced him open, though she had a similar look of concentration as she lowered the sword to his shoulder.

It was done. The ceremony ended and the families shuffled out of the ballroom and into the Inner Quadrangle to socialize. Gawain was clapped on the back and shook hands with everyone in the room. Ann received her very first hugs from his mother and sisters. They knew she was responsible and the close-knit family would henceforth claim her as their own. Only Matilda had stayed away, busy in Bristol, for once, with factory business, thanks to striking workers.

But he never would have known Sir Bartley had any concern about his businesses, from the way he worked the room. Gawain tilted an ear in his father's direction, wondering what the man was selling. What he heard was rapturous praise of Redcake tea and herbs, not praise of Redcake bakeries. His father was promoting his son's businesses instead of his own. Would wonders never cease?

Ann came to him and wrapped her slim fingers around his forearm.

"It is undeniable that I finally have my father's blessing," he said, watching his father laugh and shake the hand of a middle-aged manufacturer with a luxuriant handlebar moustache.

"You've worked hard for it," she said. "But steered your own course. In the end, any father has to respect that."

"How about you, Lady Redcake? Resolved to steer your own course?"

She nodded. "I never would have thought to live the life I have now, but I feel my parents would be proud of me, both for embracing this English life and keeping my mother's teaching alive. I wish she could have met Noel."

He nodded and would have responded, but a footman approached him with a note. When he opened it, he found an invitation to a more exclusive gathering in a sitting room upstairs. He looked up and saw Hatbrook, that intimate of the royal family, had received a note as well. A footman hovered at the marquess's elbow and when he turned his head, he discovered the footman who delivered the note still standing next to him.

"Would you and Lady Redcake follow me, if you please?"

Gawain lifted his chin to his father, who nodded, then he and Ann left the room, with Hatbrook and Alys close behind them, led by their own footman.

A few minutes later, double doors were opened along a long, painting-filled corridor, and they were ushered into a somewhat dusty room that looked to have been decorated mid-century, with red velvet drapes and furnishings, and a tartan rug. Scottish landscapes hung from floor to ceiling, giving a windswept, craggy feel to the drafty space.

Queen Victoria presided over the gathering in a tartan armchair, her feet propped on a footstool. Her thick fingers, covered in rings, petted a small dog in her lap.

One of her royal grandchildren, a prince whose name Gawain didn't remember, stepped forward with a wide grin when he saw Hatbrook. "Sensed the Scotch trifle all the way from the ballroom, did you, Hatbrook?"

His brother-in-law stepped forward to shake hands with the prince. Gawain didn't hear what they said, too confused by the mention of Scotch trifle in May.

Alys tilted her titian head and spoke into his ear. "The palace begged us to make an exception, and since this was your investiture, I relented."

"Now I understand."

She squeezed his arm. "So proud of you, twin."

"And I'm proud of you, too. The tea shop and emporium are thriving."

"More thanks to Lord Judah than me," she said ruefully. "But the Fancy, where the wedding cakes are made, is finally staffed properly. I brought some girls in from Bristol. I think they'll be so grateful to escape the factories that they'll stay for a while."

He nodded, and unspoken agreement flashed between them. He, Sir Gawain, and she, Lady Hatbrook, had come a long way from their grimy beginnings on the factory line. "I wonder what Arthur would have thought of this."

"He had the best smile of any of us," Alys reminisced. "His cheeks puffed out to twice their size, and his eyes crinkled."

"But you could only see about four of his teeth." Gawain chuckled. "Yes, I remember his smile, and he's grinning down at us. I can see it now."

Together, they looked up, and saw a frieze of chubby cherubs staring down at them from the ceiling, arrows nocked in tiny, gold bows. Gawain couldn't hold back a louder guffaw and even Alys, more reserved as was her husband, had to squeeze her eyes shut in merriment.

"Would Lady Redcake approach?" asked a functionary, dressed like a crow all in black, who appeared from some corner.

Ann caught Gawain's gaze and he nodded, separating from his sister to get as close to his wife as possible. She walked to the Queen and curtseyed, as graceful as a Native dancer.

"Sit down," the Queen said. "We do not wish to crane our neck."

A footman brought a low chair and Ann sat, smoothing her silk skirts around her. The Queen and the maharajah's granddaughter bent their heads to each other. After a couple of minutes, Ann looked up and finding Gawain's gaze on her, gestured him over.

He bowed to the Queen.

"Pleased with your new title, Sir Gawain?"

"Yes, your majesty. I never expected such an honor."

"You are an ambitious young devil. We can see it in your eyes. A royal warrant should please you, eh?"

"Yes, ma'am." Gawain nearly stuttered in his excitement, but attempted to match his wife's serenity.

"You will not object to your wife being posted to our medical staff?" The Queen scratched behind the ears of her lapdog, a fluffy, tan Pomeranian.

"Ma'am?" He glanced at Ann, but her expression remained calm.

"She will not have to live with us, just be available for consultation if our headaches come back, or if we have any other issues within our family."

He wished he and Ann could communicate silently and decided to try. Kneeling down, he took her hand and squeezed it. She squeezed back and smiled at him fondly. He took that to mean she wasn't unwilling to do what the Queen desired. "I would be honored for my wife to have the post, and she is eminently qualified for it," Gawain said.

The Queen glanced at their clasped hands with a fond smile. "Very good. Have someone bring us a piece of the Scotch trifle, would you be so kind?"

With that, he was dismissed. Gawain let go of his wife's hand and stood. He turned away, bemused, as the Queen actually patted Ann's arm.

Hatbrook's pupils seemed to dilate as bowls of fragrant Scotch trifle were brought into the room on silver trays. His wife accepted cups of tea for them both, eschewing the trifle, though the rest of the family partook, even Lord Judah, whose position as manager of Redcake's must have had him heartily sick of the concoction by then.

After Ann left the Queen's side, Lady Judah approached her and they bent their heads together, blond hair against black. The lady seemed to be softening toward his wife. Her initial reception had been cold, but pregnancies had a way of softening women. Women other than Ann, of course. He wondered how long it would be before his bad dreams stopped, of her facing her first husband's killer in that storage room? The angelic light that had haloed her, the knife that had flashed. His desperate run to protect her as he pulled the gun from his pocket.

Seeing her laugh and touch Lady Judah's arm made him realize that all was right in the world. All the danger was gone. All rewards were theirs. Now they could enjoy life and each other.

* * *

A week later, Lewis delivered the Redcake family's first gas-powered conveyance.

"You'll need a chauffeur," Lewis said. "Because, although you can steer just fine, you have no patience for the fine, mechanical details."

"I'll hire someone. Don't suppose your apprentice Eddy wants to change fields."

Lewis made a face. "And give him the opportunity to stop trying to blow me up? I don't think so." He began to go over the details of the car.

An hour later, Gawain said, "You're certainly the next member of the family to be knighted. One of these days you're going to come up with a contraption that will come to the Queen's attention. I still think you could win her over with one of those birds you refuse to make anymore, but a superlative version of this horseless carriage might do it too."

"I covet much of what you have, but I'd be happy to have the successful business, the house, and the wife."

"Not the child?"

"I already have an apprentice wreaking havoc in my life." Lewis made a face.

"I think your priorities are out of order."

"Really?"

"You have to put the woman as the top priority. It's hard to be happy without a woman and it's impossible to be happy if she isn't happy."

Lewis looked thoughtful. "Can I afford a wife?"

Gawain shrugged. "There are all kinds of women. Choose wisely and it won't be a problem."

"I'd say you chose wisely."

Gawain glanced up from the carriage's engine to see his wife gliding across the yard to the carriage house. He smiled. "Beautiful, isn't she?"

"I thought so the first time I saw her, in Leeds. She's definitely for you, cousin."

"I quite agree."

Ann reached them, pushing black curls out of her eyes and laughing as the warm spring wind tossed her hair. Gawain wrapped his arm around her and kissed the top of her head.

"So, wife. Ready to go on a new adventure?"

"As long as you are by my side, always." She squeezed his shoulder and kissed his cheek. "What do you have for us, Lewis?"

Lewis smiled, but the expression didn't quite reach his eyes. Gawain didn't notice, because his gaze rested solely on his wife.

Keep reading for a special preview of Lady Elizabeth Shield's story in *His Kidnapped Bride*, a Redcakes novella, coming in September!

And don't miss *The Marquess of Cake* and *One Taste of Scandal*, available now wherever eBooks are sold . . .

Chapter One

April 5, 1889

"I'll take you to Lord Judah's office right away, Mr. . . . ." The young man who had escorted him into the back passages of Redcake's Tea Shop and Emporium paused and frowned at the telegram he held.

"Alexander. Dougal Alexander." Dougal put his hand out for the telegram he'd received, requesting him to travel from Edinburgh to London today and meet with Lord Judah Shield, his employer for the Cross case. As he needed to come to London for the case regardless, he had no problem agreeing to the journey.

"Quite a shocker that Manfred Cross has finally been found. Lady Judah must be so happy to know her brother's whereabouts."

"I doubt it," Dougal said, following the man up a steep flight of steps. "Given his circumstances."

The man turned back, startled, his hair gleaming in the light of an electrified sconce. "Oh, dear. I didn't realize there was trouble."

Dougal said nothing. As a private inquiry agent, he found it best to let others do most of the talking.

"Lady Judah is employed here too, you know, though we haven't seen much of her of late. Unusual women in the Shield family. The marchioness owns this establishment. Then there's Lady Elizabeth, who disappeared almost a year ago and has never been heard from again."

"Quite."

"Have you found her?" the man asked. "We'd all assumed she was with Mr. Cross."

"Are you a member of the family?" Dougal asked coldly.

"No, of course not. I'm Ewan Hales, Lord Judah's secretary."

"Then I will leave that discussion to the family," Dougal said, as they crossed the landing and went up another flight of steps. In truth, he had not found Lady Elizabeth, though locating a vanished lady of nearly twenty years, the Marquess of Hatbrook's sister, was a higher priority than recovering a jewel thief. But a police case and this private case had collided. The lady, after all, had run off with or run after Manfred Cross. Accounts varied.

When they reached the third floor, Hales opened the door and led him down a passage, then went through another door into a spacious anteroom. Steam curled from an iron teapot hung on a hook inside the fireplace. The warm, almost humid room offered a pleasant contrast to the rainy spring morning outside.

Hales opened another door, this one leading to the inner sanctum of the manager's office. Two men were seated in armchairs to the left, on either side of a small fireplace. Between them rested a tray with a teapot, cups, and soup bowls recently emptied. Crumbs decorated a plate in the center.

Dougal's stomach growled. He had not yet eaten that day, since he'd managed to empty his hamper on the train the previous day. But that did not trouble him. No, the faces of the two men in front of him, clearly brothers, was the issue. While the men had different hair and eye coloring, as well as slightly different physical forms, their facial features, noses, cheekbones, and eye shape were identical. He had seen those characteristics before, and recently. Where?

Both men stood.

"Hello, Alexander," said the taller of the men.

Dougal had met him before. Lord Judah Shield, brother of Lady Elizabeth. The man had hired him in person in Edinburgh the previous year, after weeks of fruitless searching on his own. He shook hands with his employer.

"This is my brother, Michael Shield, Marquess of Hatbrook," Lord Judah told him.

Dougal shifted his gaze and shook hands with the other man. While Lord Judah had been a soldier, evident in his penetrating gaze and fast reflexes, Hatbrook surprised him. No pampered aristocrat, he had the callused hands of a laborer and his clothes molded to a powerful, muscular form. These Shield men were unusual specimens for the aristocracy.

Lord Judah's striated amber and brown eyes were unforgettable, but he knew he'd seen Hatbrook's sea-blue eyes somewhere recently.

As he shook hands with Hatbrook, the marquess commented, "I'm not used to being stared at so frankly."

"I apologize. I'm cataloguing you," Dougal admitted.

"As if I'm a collection of parts?" The marquess quirked a brow.

"It's not that. You look very familiar."

"I've never met you."

Dougal crossed his arms over his chest. "I know that. You aren't the person I'm thinking of."

Lord Judah interrupted, gesturing to Ewan Hales. "Bring a fresh pot of tea and another round of soup and bread, will you, Hales?"

"Yes, Captain." Hales shut the door behind him as he went out.

"You look as though you could use it," Lord Judah said. "Long night on the train?"

"Yes. No sleepers available. I had to sit up. But still, far more comfortable than what Manfred Cross is facing about now."

"Please tell us the full story," Hatbrook urged. "We had a letter from him a month ago. I've been desperate for a substantive update ever since."

Dougal sighed and put his hands on his hips. "He must have posted it just after I spotted him. Perhaps he thought about returning to London, but it was already too late to escape the police. His capture was due to a routine canvas, really. I take cases from the police, you understand, not just private clients, and they had me going door-to-door in some of the *lands* on a wynd near the castle."

"The *lands*?" Hatbrook asked. "I am not very familiar with Edinburgh."

"Buildings with flats," Dougal explained. "The old town is built up very densely with tall buildings. I was looking for a jewel thief. An informant of mine indicated he lived on this particular street." As he spoke, he remembered coming to Manfred Cross's door. A maid-of-all-work had opened the door. A young woman with a pretty, angular face, black hair, and, yes, piercing, sea-blue eyes.

He put his hand to his forehead and swore an old Scots curse. Surely the maid couldn't have been the missing Lady Elizabeth? A marquess's sister with the reddened, sore-looking fingers of a scullery maid? And yet, the facial features matched, though not the hair.

She'd had an Edinburgh accent as well, though now that he thought about it, something seemed off to him. The vowels were right, but she didn't use enough cant for a poor servant. Had she been faking it? Dying her hair? Lord Judah had said she was blond.

"Your informant was obviously correct," Lord Judah said, interrupting Dougal's frantic interior catalogue.

"Yes. His maid refused to let me inside to see her master, which seemed suspicious to me. She didn't indicate he was ill or anything of the sort. So, I watched the building from a shop across the street. You can imagine how surprised I was to see Manfred Cross coming out of the door the next morning."

"I believe we had been concentrating our efforts on New Town?" his employer said.

"Of course. People don't live in *lands* by choice. Frankly, even a jewel thief could afford better than a flat in a crumbling building. But, he was hiding for more reasons than one."

"My sister," Hatbrook said. "Do you think she was inside? Had the maid been told never to let anyone in?"

"I went back with the police." Dougal's cheek twitched. "I had the complete dossier on Cross, of course, and you, my lord, had particularly remarked on his connection to Lady Mews, a lover of fine jewelry. I made the connection that Cross might have been a procurator."

"My sister wasn't there when you entered."

"No. Just Cross and his maid."

"There's something you aren't saying," Lord Judah said.

Dougal took a deep breath. "It occurs to me now, gentlemen, seeing you together and the similarities of your appearances, that Lady Elizabeth may have been the maid."

"What?" Lord Judah exploded. His hand slapped down on the mantelpiece, rattling a collection of tea tins.

"Preposterous," Hatbrook spluttered.

"Play-acting?" Lord Judah asked, visibly calming himself by breathing deeply. He turned to Hatbrook. "Would she do that?"

"I am afraid not," Dougal interjected. "You cannot fake the damage done to hands by housework. This young woman, this black-haired, Scottish-accented young woman, was clearly a maid. And yet . . ."

"And yet . . ." Hatbrook prodded.

Dougal shook his head. "I have a very good memory for faces. I am afraid she looked like both of you."

Lord Judah swore pungently. "So Manfred had her all along."

"Where is she now?" Hatbrook demanded.

"Still in the flat, if the rent is paid up. She'll be tossed out."

Hatbrook shifted restlessly. "Where is Manfred now? In a prison in Edinburgh somewhere?"

"No, he's here in London. I thought you would know that, since Lord Judah is married to Cross's sister."

"London?" Hatbrook said, confused. "I thought all these thefts were in Scotland."

Dougal grinned. "Unlikely. But he's in Newgate prison, because when he was interrogated, he said he knew things that could bring down the government."

Lord Judah's eyelids drooped. He sat down. "I liked him, you know. I really did. But I don't even recognize the person you are describing."

"I saw another side of him," Hatbrook said, following suit and gesturing for Dougal to take the third armchair. "He had a very twisted relationship with Lord and Lady Mews."

"The Scandalous Cross Legend will live another generation, I'm afraid. Are we going to be able to see him?"

Dougal sat. "We'll have to, if we want to get to the bottom of this business about your sister."

"Did she seem to be frightened, as if she were being held against her will?" Hatbrook asked.

"No, she was quite saucy and sure of herself. Maybe even that should have been suspect. Instead of yelling at me or threatening me, she wielded humor as a weapon."

"Was she wearing a wedding ring?" Hatbrook asked after a short pause.

Dougal flashed back to the girl's reddened hands. "No. If it is any consolation to you, she was very slender. No babes underfoot that I saw or heard."

Lord Judah made a fist as if he wanted to slam it into something. "I will make some calls," Hatbrook said. "Get us into Newgate."

The door opened and Ewan Hales entered with a tray. Dougal's stomach rumbled again.

Hatbrook rose. "I'll be in the outer office on the telephone."

Lord Judah sighed. "Eat up, Alexander, while you can. I'm going to dash off a note to my wife."

About the Author

Heather Hiestand was born in Illinois but her family migrated west before she started school. Since then she has claimed Washington State as home, except for a few years in California. She wrote her first story at age seven and went on to major in creative writing at the University of Washington. Her first published fiction was a mystery short story, but since then it has been all about the many flavors of romance. Heather's first published romance short story was set in the Victorian period and she continues to return, fascinated by the rapid developments of the nineteenth century. The author of many novels, novellas and short stories, she has achieved bestseller status on Amazon's Romance Anthologies and Historical Romance lists. She is also a Barnes and Noble Top 100 Bestseller. With her husband and son, she makes her home in a small town and supposedly works out of her tiny office, though she mostly writes in her easy chair in the living room.

For more information, visit Heather's website at **www.heatherhiestand.com.** Heather loves to hear from readers! Her email is heather@heatherhiestand.com.

*Some cravings
must be indulged...*

The Marquess of Cake

THE REDCAKES

HEATHER HIESTAND

His craving could be her undoing...

One Taste of Scandal

THE REDCAKES

HEATHER HIESTAND